MAGIC, MIDNIGHT & STARLIGHT

STRINGS OF FATE: **BOOK TWO**

MELISSA J. KINCAID

LOTS OF LOVE CREATIONS

Also by Melissa J Kincaid

The Strings of Fate series:
Love, Blood & Fury
Magic, Midnight & Starlight
Fire, Fury & Chaos
After The Fury

Content Warning:
Contains some scenes that may not suitable for younger audiences.
Includes stylised violence, course language, sexual themes, murder and
loss/death of a parent.

MAGIC, MIDNIGHT & STARLIGHT

STRINGS OF FATE: BOOK TWO

MELISSA J. KINCAID

Magic, Midnight and Starlight
A Strings of Fate Novel: Book Two
By Melissa J. Kincaid

Copyright © 2023 Melissa J. Kincaid

ISBN (Paperback): 9780645054835
ISBN (Hardback): 9780645054859
ISBN (eBook): 9780645054842
ISBN (Special Edition Paperback): 9781764048637

Published by Lots of Love Creations.

Edited by Carolyn Gilpin.

Commissioned art by @kalynne_art (Kalynne Pratt) consisting of characters Ariiaya, Elijah, Lorch, Krepth and Nemesis.

Cover design, map and illustrations by Melissa J Kincaid.

To my son, Elijah Gregory.
May you one day realise the boundless potential
that I know lives within you.

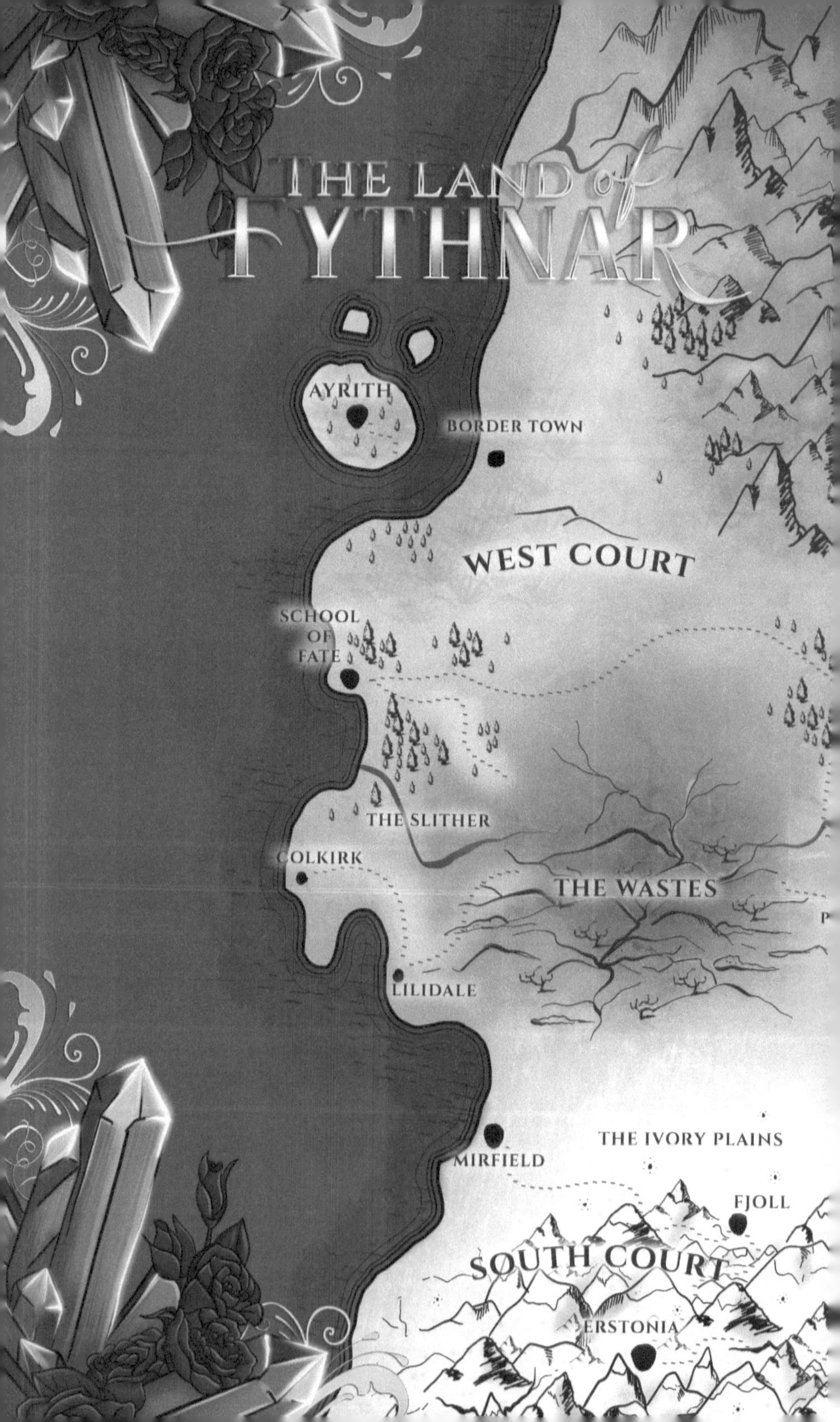

THE LAND of YTHNAR
AYRITH
BORDER TOWN
WEST COURT
SCHOOL OF FATE
THE SLITHER
COLKIRK
THE WASTES
LILIDALE
MIRFIELD
THE IVORY PLAINS
FJOLL
SOUTH COURT
ERSTONIA

THE DRAGON'S TEETH
NORTH COURT
BONEMIRE
VIRIDYA
THE
HIRE DEPTHS
AMBERBOURNE
TRADER'S BAY
EAST COURT
EVERGRAVE
THE COVE
SKAALD

Pronunciation Guide

Main Characters

Ariiaya Trillia:	Arr – ee – aya	Trill – ee – ah
Elijah Wolfe:	Ee – lie – jah	Wolf
Lorch Kruel:	Lor – k	Crew – el
Krepth Hallier:	Kre – p – th	Hal – ee – er
Nemesis Rion:	Ne – meh – sis	Ree – on
Tikkani Alinar:	Tik – an – i	
Emerson Alinar:	Em – er – son	
Quinn:	K – win	
Valdis:	Val – dis	
Lynnera:	Lin – era	
Sybell:	Si – bell	
Klotho:	Clo – tho	
Etropos:	E – tro – poss	
Lakhesis:	La – kes – is	
Devina:	Deh – veen – ah	
Iniq:	Ee – neek	
Lucada (Luc):	Luck	
Celadine Clover:	Cell – a – deen	Clo – ver
Valerie Gray:	Va – ler – ee	Gr – ay
Lyda Wild:	Lid – ah	Wi – ld
Roarke Serling:	Row – ark	Ser – ling
Cressa Serling:	Cress – a	Ser – ling

Court Families, Creatures and Towns

Freya:	Frey – ah	
Jero:	Jer – row	
Thogan:	Tho – gan	
Kadec Brolikian:	Kad – ek	Bro – li – kee – ann
Tyverus:	Tie – ver – us	
Hannera:	Han – eera	
Ghila:	Gill – ah	
Brohem:	Bro – hem	
Eliverus:	Ee – lie – ver – us	
Kryvern:	Cry – vern	
Fythnar:	Fi – th – nar	
Viridya:	Vir – id – ee – ya	
Ayrith:	Air – ith	

CHAPTER ONE

ELIJAH

"You may not know, but I do…"

Her eyes were like purple fire, bearing deep into his soul as emotions barraged against his thundering heart. He knew her words to be true as they left her lips.

"I know who you are... Eliverus Herington."

Through the haze and through the pain, Elijah knew that he was in the centre of a cataclysm of his own making. Electricity whipped around him, silver eyes open but unseeing. The doors to his memory flew wide – an unrecognisable past cascading across his mind's eye like the waters crashing beneath the golden castle of Viridya, so swiftly that he could hardly register them.

Pain was a vengeful beast inside Elijah's chest as memories of iron claws, sorrowful screams and rivers of crimson assaulted his mind, accompanied by the faint smell of copper and salt. Then there was the sickly-sweet taste of magic on his tongue.

It was all too much.

Power, there was so much *power*.

It ripped through him like a violent tornado, shocking its way through his limbs as his body jerked against his will.

Faces flashed before his eyes, his parents, his siblings, dancing through the mist. His mother – her hair like curtains of silk the colour of raven's wings, her eyes wide and gentle in a heart shaped face. His father – sharp jaw shadowed by beard and his dark brown hair flecked with grey, eyes the colour of moss, a face so similar to his own but touched by time. His brother, Brohem – an unruly mop of dark hair over expressive green eyes and a wide and wicked grin. His sister, Ghila – long black tresses like their mother, large eyes the colour of storm clouds and a face that – once she came of age – would cause men to weep at her beauty.

Ghosts of his past, brought back to life from one uttered sentence.

Memories assaulted him, that of the screams of his parents and those around him as he fled the golden castle halls – the crashing of an enraged animal behind him. Clutching his blanket and sprinting as quickly as his little legs would carry him, Elijah's bare feet slapped the stones as he ran across the bridge towards Amberbourne. He had not a clue where he was going, all he knew was that he needed to get away, as terror caused his mind to fog. Gravel tore at the soles of his feet, but he did not care. He had to escape the thundering beast behind him, the drone of alarm bells rising in his wake.

As he hit the trees and clambered over logs, he remembered his blanket being torn from his grip, and then there was pain.

Incredible, horrendous pain.

It cleaved along his back as something immense slammed him to the dirt – white hot agony tearing through whatever thought was left in his young mind. Water-filled eyes darted to his attacker, and he was met with a jaw full of glittering, serrated iron teeth and hot breath that smelled of carrion. He screamed as the agony tore through his little body, his vision darkening at the edges as his fingers scrabbled at the dirt.

Then there was white noise – and something snapped within him.

All he knew, all he was – was no more.

Eliverus Herington, the last remaining heir to the throne of Fythnar, was lost to the world that night, and now, just over twenty years later, he was returning.

How he had survived the Kryvern attack, he did not know. He was just a boy with no hope of surviving a mauling, and yet here he was. Fear, pain, denial, agony – all the feelings he had been shielded from for so long erupted within him now, the caged beast within him roaring and tearing through a moonlit strip of light as it cleaved forth

– its bellow of fury mirroring his own as Elijah dropped to his knees upon the dais of the throne room.

He returned in a flurry of magic so violent that it imploded before shooting out with such force that it shattered the glass above and around him, toppling heavy furniture and bodies alike. Pain sheared through him, and Elijah was not sure how much time had passed between his magic awakening and the moment Ariiaya appeared before him. She clutched his face between her palms, her eyes wide and burning violet. Her lips moved, and as his hearing returned, he heard her yell, "We have to go – now!"

He remained numb, distracted, mind barely registering the golden walls of the castle hallways as Arii fought their way to escape. She was relentless, taking no prisoners as she took the burden of his weight while carving a path to freedom.

As they plummeted towards the raging waters of The Sapphire Depths below, Elijah felt the haze begin to lift from his mind. He heard a swift intake of breath beside him, and he followed suit before the water slammed into them, vision blurring as they sank beneath the surface.

ARIIAYA

Arii's lungs were beginning to burn.

Water compressed her chest as she gripped Elijah's muscled arm. Bubbles burst from her nose as she moved her head, eyes squinting at the dark form beside her. Slowly, her head tilted up to the white mist above, thousands of tiny bubbles formed a thundering shield above them as she tugged at his weight, pulling Elijah closer in the dark water. They had to resurface – but she was certain the Red Guards on the castle landing above would be waiting.

Sure enough, her eyes darted to a flash of silver to her left, then her right, as arrows pierced the water, spearing past as if in slow motion. Pulling on Elijah's arm, she began to swim, legs beating with as much strength as she could muster, slowly propelling their two forms through the liquid world.

Beside her, Elijah finally moved, and she saw bubbles erupt from his mouth as he twisted, black hair floating around his face as his eyes met hers. Arii motioned with her hand, pointing above and then ahead as another arrow broke the surface, narrowly missing her shoulder.

They swam, spearing through the darkness blindly. She prayed to the Gods that they would not encounter any hungry lake creatures. Unexpectedly, a recollection from her early years sparked in her mind. Legends claim that a dragon was felled over this lake, its body so massive and its bones so solid that it plummeted to the bottom. The remains had never been discovered. Her chest tightened at the prospect of what might lie below, so she turned her focus upward and forwards. Neither of them had the strength to fight off an attack now. She knew that when Elijah's magic awoke, the entire North Court – and perhaps all the other courts in Fythnar – would have felt the disturbance, no matter how little attuned to magic they were.

He was far more powerful than she could have imagined, and she knew that what she had witnessed in the throne room was just a flutter on the surface of his true strength.

Frowning, Arii let go of Elijah and placed all her power into propelling forward, determined to see any sign of shallow waters. So far, all she could see was murky darkness.

Arii felt that the lake was much like her life up until this point. For as long as she could remember, darkness had clutched her in an embrace that she could not escape. Beaten down, belittled, silenced. Her voice trapped within by years of being told how to think, how to act and how to feel.

Until the last month – when Ariiaya had begun to question everything she knew and everything she believed. Too long had she been shaped to be what others wanted. Too long had she been forced to suppress all that she felt inside, a tide crashing against the banks of her heart.

No longer would she allow others to shape her.

Now, the only hands to weave her fate would be her own.

Scales flashed suddenly across her sight, and before them floated a figure. Arii's arms pinwheeled around her as she fought to come to a stop. Fins drifted around the woman, silver hair fanning out around her as her dark eyes regarded them with hardly a flicker of emotion.

A Water Nymph.

Arii's hand reached for her dagger on her hip – but a gentle touch from Elijah halted her.

Her eyes flicked to him as he motioned to the woman before them. The nymph lifted her hand, her long fingers curling in a beckoning gesture, fins drifting around her like lengths of tulle.

Arii realised then that this was the same woman they had allowed to escape during the attack on the castle during the night of the full moon.

Gods, that night felt so long ago, and now they had little choice but to trust that she was not leading them into a trap.

After brief glances at one another, they began to swim after the nymph as the creature speared through the depths – pausing every now and then to watch as they moved slowly after her, as if making sure they continued to follow. That decision Elijah had made to spare the creature's life now seemed to be working in their favour.

Finally, Arii felt she could no longer hold her breath. Her lungs felt close to exploding, bubbles rippled from her lips as she clenched her eyes shut. She could not go any further. The dark depths around her pressed in, squeezing her like she was within a liquid vice.

Hands clutched at her arms, and suddenly she was being lifted through the water. Her arm brushed scales, but her mind was so preoccupied with desperation for air that she hardly flinched as the sea creature propelled her towards the surface.

Their heads broke through and Arii's hair flew back as she breathed in a sharp, ragged gasp. Air, cool and precious, rocketed down her throat and into her lungs as she inhaled deeply. Beside her, Elijah did the same, his head bobbing as he turned to the silver haired woman across from them.

Onyx eyes regarded them coolly, her lips curling into a smile. "A life for a life, partly paid," she whispered, before adding, "Within the depths is where you shall find me – when your hour of need grows dire. Then my debt shall be repaid in full."

With that, the creature dropped below the surface with hardly a ripple in her wake.

Arii blinked water from her eyes, mulling over the woman's speech as they waded towards the bank. The creature had brought them to the far east lakeside, just beyond the view of the castle above. Under the cover of trees, Arii and Elijah emerged from the water, drenched and spent.

Elijah was first to drop to the dirt, rolling to his back with teeth clenched in a pained grimace. Arii cleared her wet mass of hair from her eyes and panted, hands braced against her knees as she spat lake water. Her eyes drifted to him and then she realised.

He was hurt.

She dropped to her knees beside him as he pressed a hand to his side. His leathers were drenched, black to the eye – but she could smell the tang of copper on the air. She whipped out her dagger and pinched his clothing where a tear was evident, cutting open the leather and cloth to reveal a large shard of glass embedded in the flesh of his stomach.

Elijah's breath was a swift snap.

"Hold still," Arii said, her voice gentle as she surveyed the glass, glimmering in the moonlight with hues of blue and red, mixing with a steady flow of his blood. A shard from the windows above the royal dais. His skin was pale, and she guessed he had lost a good deal of blood in the water.

She had to be swift, as by now guards would be breaking from the castle with orders to search for them.

Her hands moved to grip the glass shard, and Elijah's hand clutched her wrist. Her eyes snapped up to his, and her breath almost left her lungs as if she were once again under the surface of the Sapphire Depths.

His eyes were glassy, pained and confused. His black hair was a wet mass, pushed from his face to reveal his pointed ears and strong jawline. Never had she seen him look so… exposed.

Vulnerable.

Fae. He was a Fae, just like her.

Arii willed strength into her expression as she spoke. "This is going to hurt, but trust me… alright?"

He could not face on his own what was to come– not just this injury but what she did not doubt was on the horizon for them all. What was brewing in Bonemire was the first of their worries – and whether he liked it or not, Elijah was the only hope she could see now.

Years ago, Arii would have leaned back on the stone wall of The School of Fate, overlooking the burning land beyond with a shrug of contempt.

Let them all burn, she would have sneered.

But that was before a handful of faces weaved their way into her stone-cold heart. Now, looking down at one of those faces, Arii willed magic to lace through her fingers as she stared with determination into eyes that were desperate for guidance in a world foreign to him.

A world of magic.

With hesitation and a small nod, his grip eased and Arii braced herself for the shadow of sympathy pain. She had to make this quick.

Then she yanked.

Elijah's eyes snapped shut and a bark of pain broke from his lips as she dropped the shard to press her hands to the gushing wound. Starlight rose from within her and glittered through to her fingers as she willed the magic forth, a pale light emanating from her hands as she narrowed her eyes in concentration. She could feel the flesh slowly knitting together beneath her palms, the flow of blood gradually staunching as the wound healed. As the magic worked, she felt her own energy slowly draining.

Magic invoked such fear in those who did not understand it. It could be devastating and destructive just like Elijah's explosion in the throne room. But it could also be beautiful, weaving miracles from nothingness.

Magic was a blessing, and a curse.

After what felt like many minutes, Arii's hands slowly broke away from Elijah's skin – leaving just a pink scar beneath. She felt like her muscles were slowly being replaced with jelly as she leaned back on her haunches and surveyed her work. "Almost as good as new. Add that to your story of scars, I guess."

Her voice held a flicker of her usual bravado, albeit forced due to their strange situation. Elijah huffed, and her eyes met his, wide and staring.

Despite everything they had been through, Arii once again felt self-conscious under his heavy gaze. She had to remember that this man had been raised to fear magic, just like the humans in the court where he had grown up.

Arii's stare did not falter from his as Elijah propped himself up on his hand, leaning towards her.

"You can heal wounds?"

When Arii's brow quirked, Elijah's breath whispered between his teeth. "You continue to surprise me, Ariiaya…" He paused, brows narrowing as his words trailed into the night air. They were close now, so close she could see beads of lake water dripping from his hair. One bead dripped onto his temple, and she found herself tracking the droplet as it rolled down his stubbled, strong jawline.

Sweet goddess of darkness, she needed to get a hold of herself. And fast. Now was not the time to ogle his rugged, drenched beauty. The air was heavy between them as they stared at one another, before Arii moved to sheath her dagger.

"There is much for you to learn about magic, Eliverus."

Elijah's expression warped from awe back to stoicism.

"Don't call me that."

"It is your true name, is it not?"

With a sound of frustration, Elijah stood slowly to stand before wringing water from his clothing in silence. Well, it seemed not all had changed. Despite the reveal of his true identity, he was still the brooding, grumpy, stoic Elijah Wolfe she had come to know.

"We must head east to Evergrave. No doubt Valdis has ordered for search parties to find us, and my gold is on groups of guards heading to each town in the immediate area, and along the water's edge."

She straightened, twisting her hair to wring out the water before weaving it into a swift braid. "Freya Bloom will give us guidance on what to do first."

When she turned to look at him, Elijah's face was harsh. "Freya Bloom will hand deliver me right back to Viridya," he growled, mistrust lacing his words.

"Do you have a better idea? I trust Freya," she snapped as she tipped lake water from her boots.

Elijah was silent, and she took that to mean he did not have a better idea.

She could see it on his face… he was lost. She guessed for the first time in his life, he was without clear direction and true purpose. She wanted to tell him that she had chosen by herself to follow him back to Viridya and confide the truth about him. For once, no one had made that choice for her. She was not about to lead him from one cage to another.

"The Shifters can help teach you about the magic in your veins, and how to control it," Arii continued, pulling on her boots and straightening, hands resting on her hips.

"I do not *need* help. I do not *need* anyone."

"Gods, are you going to continue to be difficult? *We* need help, Elijah. We cannot hope to stop Valdis on our own. You saw with your own eyes what is happening in Bonemire."

Elijah ran a hand through his hair in frustration, turning to gaze across the rippling water towards Viridya. Arii watched as the moonlight tinged his strong profile, highlighting his dark hair. As before, she felt the pull towards him, her fingertips tingling at the thought of the night they buried in his hair when they'd kissed. She could still remember his scent… his taste. She did not blame him for his sour disposition now. In fact, he reminded her much of herself.

It was now, as she studied him, that she found herself imagining what kind of ruler Elijah would make.

Her thoughts faded as he turned to her, his expression softening ever so slightly.

"You came back to Viridya, despite the risk that Valdis and his army could have taken over the castle." He paused, features hardening before he added, "Why?"

Arii's brows lifted at the odd question, before she answered carefully. "I placed the pieces together about your identity. That small hope was enough reason for me to risk returning."

"What makes you think I can defeat an army of undead?"

Arii motioned at his form, hand fluttering from his head to his toes. "You were deadly enough before I knew you were Fae. Now, with powerful magic and some training, you could be our last hope in having a slither of a chance against Valdis." She motioned a hand, "It won't be just you in this fight alone, Elijah. You can be the beginning of a beacon of hope – the spark that will start an entire revolution. This land needs hope, no matter how small."

Elijah pinched the bridge of his nose as she approached him, her expression softening. "Just one string of hope is worth fighting for. What other choice do we have?" she whispered, pausing at his side.

His eyes slid to hers. "For an unfeeling killing machine, you sure do care a lot about the fate of this land, Arii."

Hearing her nickname on his lips caused birds to take flight in her stomach. Her mouth twitched in a half-hearted smile. "Sometimes all it takes is one person to make a difference. This land, with all its problems, is my *home*." Her head tilted to better look at his face, and he angled his own to survey her, his expression unchanged. His eyes paused on her lips before skipping to her eyes once more.

"Fine, Evergrave it is then. Best we stay off the roads," he said, but reluctantly. Despite everything, Elijah was still deadly and incredibly strong, even without magic. If he felt threatened in Evergrave, she knew they could not keep him contained there against his will.

If he wanted to leave, he would.

She hoped he would not make that choice.

"To Evergrave," she confirmed, and they turned from the water's edge and began heading east up the banks, leaving Viridya behind.

CHAPTER TWO

LORCH

Never had he felt so powerless.

Lorch gazed upon the people bustling about the throne room as they repaired the damage to the glass windows or righted and cleaned the furniture of the stained shards.

Powerless. He had been powerless against the wildness of Elijah's magic.

He would not feel that way for much longer.

Nexus Crystals, and a lot of them, were on their way to the castle from Bonemire and if what his father said was true, the stones allowed humans to use the magic just like the Fae.

Lorch had a feeling that what he had witnessed in this room was but a flicker of the power that Elijah had simmering in deep inside.

No… not Elijah… Eliverus.

His best friend was Eliverus Herington, true heir to the throne of Fythnar.

For years, Elijah had watched over him as he occupied the very space that was by right – his. Lorch now knew that Elijah's memory of his past was nothing but haze – if that was indeed true of course. What if he had known all along? Why wait twenty years to expose his true self and take back what was his? If claiming the throne was Elijah's intention after all.

Lorch chewed his lip as he watched the people hurrying to restore the room back to its former glory. His arms crossed over his chest, oceanic eyes remaining as hard as diamonds.

On the outside he retained a look of boredom.

But on the inside, his emotions were a riot.

His father sidled up beside him, his expression dour like he had just consumed a lemon. "Search parties have been organised," the man said as he tilted his head to survey his son. "Every town in the north will be searched, as well as the banks of the lake. If they are alive, we will find them."

"And if the fall killed them?" Lorch asked.

"The fall would not have killed them, son. They are Fae. Their kind is not so easily squashed." The man's voice dripped with the acid of hate.

It was strange, if the Fae were not so easily killed, then how had humans culled them so near to extinction over the last two hundred years? Lorch's mind was suddenly distracted as the throne room doors were thrown back on their hinges and Commander Hawke entered the room.

His eyes swept what was left of the chaos, before resting on the King.

"Did you find anything?" called Valdis as he turned to the Commander. The man bowed at the waist, before straightening under their gazes.

"No, no sign of them yet. Once day breaks, I believe our search parties will have better luck looking for tracks on the riverbanks," said Hawke, his eyes never leaving Lorch, their depths shadowed with sympathy.

It infuriated Lorch.

"Tell the men that those who deliver Eliverus Herington alive will be awarded five hundred gold crowns as a small incentive." Lorch saw a smirk spread across his father's face at his words. "And whoever brings me the Fury – Ariiaya Trillia – will be brought to the rank of second to the Commander."

Hawke's mouth opened to protest, but Lorch continued. "Emphasis on the *alive* part of those instructions, Commander, because I plan to kill them myself."

The Commander's expression was unreadable before he bowed

slowly. "Noted, Your Highness."

"Come, son, I have much to show you," said Valdis, motioning for them to exit the throne room.

Lorch nodded, before following his father down the golden halls towards the courtyard. Just before he had discovered Arii and Elijah in the throne room, his father had returned from Bonemire with a procession of covered caravans under heavy guard. It seemed that now he was to discover the secrets held within them.

Valdis approached one of the caravans, the canvas lit in the moonlight as he paused, twisting to look at his son. His hand grasped the material, before throwing back the cover to reveal the contents hidden beneath.

Within the cart was an iron cage.

And within that cage were two men.

Lorch's brows narrowed, and he stepped forward – but not before Commander Hawke's hand halted him in his tracks. He had not even realised the older man had followed them.

The men in the cage began to twitch, their movements jerky and strange. Their jostling rattled the carriage beneath, sounds of metal scraping wood. Suddenly they slammed into the bars, their lips curled back as angry cries of rage split from their mouths, causing Lorch to step back. Their chests glowed faintly with a blue light beneath their thin, dirty cotton tunics. Beside him, Hawke tensed, reaching for his sword.

Were these men like the creature Arii had faced in the castle caverns?

Before anguish could pierce his heart, he erected his walls once more against the memory of her. He wanted to forget her, forget all that had transpired between them, but his stupid weak heart still clenched at the mere thought of her name.

Did he truly wish her dead?

Yes. No. Perhaps.

Part of him wished to hear her side of what happened, part of him wished not to know at all. He could not deny that part of the reason he had ordered their capture was that he did not want them killed before he had a chance to alter his mind.

Lorch had little doubt that if it were left with his father, the man would have them slaughtered before even considering his son's feelings, though he couldn't quite get a handle on those feelings at the moment, his emotions a muddled mess.

Valdis stepped forward and lifted his hand, a glowing amulet clutched in his palm. The men in the cage struggled and snarled against the bars, frenzied in their pursuit to get at the people just beyond their reach. Their faces – although somewhat human – were pale, gaping mouthed and frenzied, looking like rabid animals rather than people. Slowly Valdis turned, lifting the amulet towards the creatures before uttering one word.

"Stop."

Suddenly the men ceased their struggling, their flailing limbs returning to the depths of the cage, heads bowing as if they had lost the will to fight. Motionless they stood, only their chests rising and falling quickly and shallowly.

Valdis was in complete control of them.

"How? What are they?" murmured Lorch, eyes wide as he surveyed them. Creatures who were human, but also not.

As his father turned from the cage, Commander Hawke stepped forward, hand hovering over the hilt of his sword. Lorch turned to see his rugged features twisted into an angry snarl. "You! You are the cause of the affliction on the Princess' handmaid, Ingrid Polaris!"

When Valdis' expression remained unchanged, Hawke took another step, before drawing his sword from its scabbard.

The guards around them drew their own swords in a chorus of singing steel.

Valdis' lips quirked. "Now now, Commander, lay down your sword. I would not wish for you to excite our *guests*." As if to emphasise his point, the cage behind him shook with a sharp rattle.

The Commander's stance did not change as he pointed the sword at Valdis's chest. "This is unnatural, what you have done to these people

– it is wrong!"

Lorch remained silent as the Commander turned to him, his dark eyes roving over the King before sliding across his men.

They all had their swords trained on him.

"What you see here is just the beginning, a new age for humanity," drawled Valdis as Hawke turned back to him. His face slowly morphed into a wide, deranged smile – a hint of madness shining forth. From behind him, one of the animated corpses groaned as if in agreeance.

Valdis turned, motioning to the small sea of carts behind him. "I have thousands more on the way from Bonemire. Soon, we will have a near unstoppable army – the likes of which Fythnar has never seen. Too long have we lived in fear, too long have we been at the mercy of magic wielders–"

"There are no magic wielders left that pose a threat, Valdis!" snapped Hawke, cutting Valdis off. "You raise an army out of fear of something which our forefathers wiped out many of years ago!"

"Eliverus Herington hid among us for over twenty years. Who knows how many more of his kind are doing the same thing – lying in wait, preparing to strike!"

"You are mad!"

"Mad? No… No I am not mad, Commander. I have foresight – foresight that will ensure the survival of the human race." Valdis strode up to the Commander, their faces inches apart as they stared at one another, the air tense around them. "One Fae, all it takes is one Fae to plant a tiny seed of rebellion in their minds. I have no doubt that word of Eliverus' existence has reached the other courts already." His voice began to rise, laced with a hint of paranoia. "It is what they have been waiting for – and when they come, demanding my son be removed from the throne, we will be ready."

The Commander spun to look at Lorch. "You aren't buying into this madness, are you?"

Lorch's expression was unsure and Hawke latched on – his hand motioning towards the carts. "Innocent people have been turned into mindless… things! Taken from their families and *slaughtered,* for fear of a long-gone threat!"

"Commander, perhaps we should not disregard what my father is showing us without more information–"

"More information? What more is there to know? This is insanity!" Hawke exclaimed.

His gut told him that Hawke was right, but Lorch's heart was broken, and in that moment it drove him to sway in favour of his father.

Lorch looked down at Hawke's boots, before bringing his attention back up, expression hinting resolve. "If what we witnessed in the throne room was a hint of the kind of power a male Fae can possess, then maybe we *should* prepare ourselves. What if my father is right? What if with his discovery, more Fae emerge in support of him – and this land is once again swallowed in a tornado of untamed, destructive magic?"

Hawke's eyes were wide as he took a step back. "He has gotten to you. Your Highness, think about this – think about what he is doing here. If he loses control, who is to say these creatures will not become a bigger threat than the one you hope to shield us from?"

"It is a risk we must take, Commander."

"Is it a risk you are *ready* to take, Lorch?"

Lorch's brows narrowed, his expression becoming dark. "It is."

Commander Hawke's sword began to rise as his face twisted with pain. "Well, I cannot allow it."

The Commander spun, sword singing through the air – aimed directly at Valdis.

Blue light erupted, and the sword halted in mid-air, a hair's breadth from Valdis' face. Raised in the air beside him was the Nexus Crystal amulet, the stone within pulsating with power. Valdis' lips curled, scar stark against his face as he bared his teeth.

Hawke's eyes widened, shooting to the sword as it shuddered in mid-air – as if gripped in the hands of an invisible enemy. His arms trembled, sweat glittering upon his brow as the blue light caused his eyes to squint. Suddenly, magic flared, and Hawke was sent flying across the courtyard, hitting the stones a few feet way.

Valdis held the amulet higher and it flared anew, then Hawke began to cry out in pain.

"You dare raise your sword against me? Against your king's wishes?"

Magic pulsed, causing the man to writhe in agony. Magic thrummed in the air, and Lorch noticed the guards around him had begun to twitch – their eyes darting to one another. Uneasiness, as well as fear mixed with the cool night air.

Nearby, a woman screamed.

Lorch turned to see his mother as she pushed through the crowd that had begun to gather, making her way to the Commander. He watched in shock as she dropped to the man's side, clutching him desperately.

"Hawke!" she called, her hands fluttering to his face.

Lorch's expression turned to confusion. What was she doing?

Valdis snarled from behind him. "Lynnera, move away from him – *now*." His voice was a hiss as he stalked towards them.

Golden hair twirling, Lynnera stared at her husband, her eyes wide. "Valdis, please, stop!" She moved her body to shield Hawke.

Behind her, Hawke's voice was a whispered cry. "No, Lynn."

Valdis swiped his hand through the air once more. "Move!" he snarled again.

When Lynnera's jaw clenched and she shook her head, her eyes never leaving his, Valdis raised the amulet again.

"What is this? Mother?" said Lorch, confusion wavering his voice.

"Now, son, you can see what has been happening behind our backs! We cannot trust them," he announced as the amulet flickered with light.

Lorch swiftly stepped forward. "Take the Commander to the dungeons, and my mother to her rooms," he said before further damage could be done. In his peripheral, the guards shifted. "This war is not between them and us, father. Save your energy for what is to come."

With reluctance, his father's hand dropped as he slid the amulet into his pocket. The guards around them seized Hawke, before following with his mother. Lynnera struggled, her hand twined with the Commander's as the soldiers pulled them apart.

Lorch's eyes were fixed on their backs as they were taken away, his face a mask of shadow.

NEMESIS

Nemesis raised her eyebrows and watched Valdis warily as his voice boomed around the room.

"When were you going to reveal that the true fucking heir to the throne of Fythnar was directly under my nose?" bellowed Valdis, his voice ricocheting off the stone walls of The School of Fate.

Etropos winced, glancing at Lakhesis as the silver-haired sister tilted her head towards the Tapestry of Life hanging on the wall behind them. Klotho descended the dais, her brows narrowed and hands on hips as she faced the man.

Valdis had arrived at the school at first light, his fury palpable as he stormed through the gates to the crumbling castle with a small procession hot on his heels. The Sisters of Fate had felt the waves of power rolling from him as soon as he entered the grounds, as did all of the women in the castle.

Nemesis had watched his procession enter through the front gates from her vantage point across the courtyard, holding back a shiver as fat droplets of rain pelted down, soaking her cloak and boots. It was not just the snap of cold that had her feeling jittery, it was also the strange feeling that followed Valdis' arrival, like the foreboding of a storm. She knew it, as did her sisters as they stood sentry, hackles raising and bodies shifting with the uncomfortable feeling upon the wind.

Valdis was in possession of magic.

Now, as he paced below the shimmering tapestry like a restless wolf, the sisters watched with an air of caution. To the sides of the room stood leather-clad women, armed to the teeth and with hair and eyes ranging in many colours and hues.

Furies.

Nem leaned against a cold stone wall, glittering aqua eyes tracking the man with an expression of cold anger. She had been summoned by the sisters with a small spark of magic, and that small spark had told her all she needed to know.

Be on guard.

How dare he speak that way to the Sisters of Fate, in their own home.

The man spun, finger spearing at Klotho as she paused before him. "You knew – you all *knew*, and you did not tell me!"

Klotho's lips curled yet her composure remained calm. "We did not know."

"Bullshit!" he spat.

"You are angry, and rightfully so. All you have worked for is under threat, all because of the existence of one Fae male." Klotho's voice was calm and cool. "But we assure you, Valdis, we had no knowledge of his survival. When you discovered him is when we felt his awakening also."

Valdis stared, his chest rising and falling in anger.

He was silent for a moment. "You speak the truth?" he asked, voice low.

Klotho nodded; her eyes unblinking as the man speared a hand through his hair. Every woman in the castle had felt the moment Eliverus Herington's magic crackled across the land. It was like a thunderclap – snapping across their senses and causing their hairs to stand on end.

Such immense power. Nem had felt it to the core of her being, and she had no doubt every being attuned to magic in the land had felt it too. It did not take long for news of the situation to spread. Nem wondered how long Arii had known of the man's true identity. When they next spoke, Nem had a handful of serious questions for her friend.

That was if she could get to her fellow Fury before Valdis did.

"If it were not for your assassin seedling, Eliverus would not have escaped," continued Valdis, towering over Klotho. The woman did not flinch under his anger. "She is a traitor to the crown, and I will have her head. Tell me, where would your little Violet Assassin go if she wanted to hide from me?"

Nem supressed a visible flinch at the quiet venom in his words. When Klotho remained silent, Nem saw a shadow move in her peripheral vision. Her eyes flicked to Devina as the red-haired assassin's lips curled in a smirk. Before Nem could stop her, the woman was striding forward, hips swaying.

"I would try where she grew up – in Evergrave," purred the woman, hands hitching on her hips. "It is where I would look first."

Anger bubbled in Nem's blood. How could she sell out a sister? Gods, Devina was truly conniving. Did her petty hate run so deep that she would hand over a fellow assassin to her death, without first hearing her side of the story?

Valdis turned his head, expression guarded. "The East Court?" He paused, eyeing the Fury before his expression registered with mild surprise. "Ah, Devina Divine," he said, his mouth curling in a sly smile.

Devina waved a hand in a theatrical display, before dipping into a low bow. "My Lord, I am a big fan of Viridya, and I think this is obvious with how frequently I visit your lovely home."

Valdis' brow rose as Devina stepped forward, her expression changing from bold to eager. "Send me. I will bring her back to you – besides, I have a score to settle with our little Violet Assassin."

Fucking traitorous bitch. Nem's thoughts were livid, flames of rage flickering into an inferno, but on the outside she was as cold as stone, features giving nothing away. Her poker face was perhaps better than Arii's.

Valdis considered for a moment, his eyes sliding thoughtfully across the women lining the walls before turning back to the Fates. "Ariiaya and Eliverus will not be easy targets. Perhaps sending a small legion of Furies will save me losing a few tens of men." He turned to face Klotho again. "Send your best assassins to Evergrave – bring the traitors back to me alive. Do this, and you can consider yourself spared."

Spared? Spared from what?

Klotho's throat bobbed, before she nodded swiftly.

Nem could not hold back any longer.

"Since when do we take orders from *him*?" she snapped, taking one step forward.

"Our alliance is simple. I bring you whatever Fae that my forces find, instead of killing them, and in return you lend your aid when needed. If not for me, your school would be half the size it is today." A tiny quiver moved in Valdis' brow, his eyes darkening in a way that told Nem that he would much prefer to slay those Fae as soon as they were found rather than sparing them. But this was a man made of cunning, a man who did not do anything without gain. Words hissed from between his teeth like slithering snakes. "Small favours in exchange for small mercies."

So, the sisters had help finding their recruits. This was news to Nem, and by the small shifts and coasting eyes around the room, it was news to some of her sisters too.

The room stood silent for a tense moment, before Etropos' fair voice drifted across the space between them all. "Nemesis, stand down. Our alliance still stands, Valdis. We will send word when we find them."

The man bowed swiftly, before twisting and heading to the doors. Every eye was fixed on him as he exited the room, the air becoming lighter in his wake. His guards quickly followed, tossing the women sour glances in their retreat.

"You don't really expect us to turn on one of our own, do you?" said Nem as the room began to bustle into activity around her. "Ariiaya must have good reason to have done what she did, we must hear her side of the story before handing her to him."

Etropos finally moved from her position, her face drawn with sadness. "Your sister has acted against the crown, Nemesis. She defied the orders given to her from the Gods."

"Those orders proved to be false, her target untrue."

"Be that as it may, we must comply with Valdis' wishes. If not, we lose a very powerful ally."

"But you sent Ariiaya to kill his son!"

Etropos paused with lips parted as Lakhesis spoke from the dais.

"Nemesis Rion, hold your tongue!"

Nem bowed her head. Anger rippled through her body in waves, boiling her blood.

A Fury must not think, a Fury must not feel…

A Fury must always obey.

No matter how Nem felt about Arii, the woman had gone against her orders. Nem knew that. Arii had chosen her heart over her duty. She had chosen feelings over fate.

Klotho's eyes slid to Nem, then to Devina. "Devina, Nemesis – prepare to travel to Evergrave. You have your orders." The woman's eyes fixed back on Devina. "Remember, they must be brought back to Viridya *alive*." The woman emphasised the word as she eyed Devina. Devina had the gall to snort.

"Anyone else aiding them," Klotho paused before a slow smirk cracked her beautiful features.

"Kill them."

ARIIAYA

CHAPTER THREE

ARIIAYA

Birds chimed in song as early morning light pierced the clouds above, painting the tall trees and thick underbrush in saturated gold. Arii lifted a hand, hovering her open palm before her as they walked through the dense forest. A little sphere of magic formed, shimmering on her palm like a crystal ball. She turned and trotted backwards, holding the glowing sphere out to the man who trailed silently behind her. He hadn't spoken much over the hour or so since they began their path to Evergrave, and the silence had Arii feeling edgy.

When Arii was edgy, she tended to use her hands.

Elijah slowed, eyes lifting to her offering, before he paused mid step, brows drawn in a look of mild agitation and wariness.

"What are you doing?" he murmured, uneasy.

"You could do this too – all you need to do is *will* the ball to form. Watch," she added a second palm to the first, another sphere rippling into existence beside the first as she cupped her palms together.

Elijah's voice was a low snap. "No."

"Just try! You have to learn to control your magic, Elijah."

"I said *no*."

Her eyes lifted to see the man stopped dead, arms folded across his chest and his lips drawn in a deep frown.

Stubborn bloody brute.

"Look, magic is like a muscle. The more you use it, the easier and stronger it gets."

When his expression did not change, she lifted her palm, willing the two spheres to meld as one before bouncing the ball upon her palm. Her eyes slid from the magic to Elijah's face again.

Elijah huffed and she saw a tick of frustration forming on his jaw. "I… What if I…" He paused, glancing away, his silver eyes fixed on anything but her. "I cannot risk causing another explosion – a repeat of the destruction I caused in Viridya."

Arii bit her lip, fighting back a very inappropriate giggle as his eyes slid slowly back to her, his face turning incredulous. "Did you just… laugh at me?"

Her brow quirked as she placed a hand on her hip, continuing to bounce the ball of magic upon her palm. "I understand you have been raised for the majority of your life to fear magic, Elijah, but it isn't as scary as you think." Arii inhaled loudly before she suddenly grabbed the ball and threw it hard and fast, right at Elijah's head.

The man ducked as the sphere whizzed overhead, slamming into a nearby tree with a light *crack*.

As he slowly recovered, gazing at the smoking black mark left on the tree, Elijah's head turned back to her. Arii bit her lip, sucking in another giggle as it bubbled up from within – taking in the look on his face.

His expression was livid.

Gods, perhaps lake water had leaked into her brain. Rarely did she *giggle*. Actually, she was not sure she had ever giggled in her entire life. She raised her hands – palms up – as Elijah stormed the small space between them like an enraged bear.

Suddenly, magic rippled in the air, and the taste of syrup doused the back of her tongue – causing the hairs on her nape to stand on end. Elijah's dark hair danced as a breeze picked up, and Arii swore she felt the ground beneath their feet shudder. The trees swayed above them with a little more vigour than what she would deem as natural, branches creaking as they rubbed together.

His anger was a weight on the air around them and the feeling was now all too familiar.

If he would not willingly explore his magic, perhaps she would annoy him until he had no choice but to use it. The hope of the land lay on his shoulders now, whether he liked it or not. There was a possibility he could kill her in the process, but that was a risk she had to take.

Magic crackled between her fingers, blue sparks igniting as her lips curled into a slow, sardonic smirk.

"Don't you fucking dare," he hissed, raising a warning finger – but too late.

Another small ball of magic flew past his head.

Then another.

"Arii!"

Crack.

"Hah ha!" Arii chuckled.

He ducked another sphere, which narrowly missed his head again. "By the gods–"

Crack.

Arii whipped up a large ball, before snapping out a hand like lightning, aiming for his chest. The ball speared through the air, and she was sure she was about to land a hit.

The sphere suddenly halted in mid-air, an arm length away from Elijah's chest.

His hand was outstretched, fingers splayed as if to catch the sphere. His arm shook, little ripples vibrating down his broad shoulder – teeth clenched with a hissed breath as his chest rose and fell with anger, and possibly a smidge of fear.

Her eyes lifted, and she was met with a look of pure silver rage.

Uh oh.

The sphere fell and disintegrated on the forest floor, and suddenly within a blink he was before her. His hands gripped her upper arms, and before she could protest, he slammed her back against a nearby tree.

"Ow, what the fu–"

"Shh." Elijah hissed suddenly.

"Don't tell me to–"

"Arii, listen!"

His tone had her halting. She heard the leaves around them rustling, birds chattering in the distance, and then she heard the heavy thump of his heart. He was so close, his fingers tight on her biceps, his face inches from her own. She felt sparks ignite in her stomach as she gazed up slowly, eyes tracking up from the rip in his fighting leathers, up his lightly bearded neck, then to his strong chin – finally resting on his eyes. They were narrowed and dark, like rolling storm clouds over the sea. The anger in their depths had dissipated as quickly as it had appeared, his fingers loosening around her arms yet he still remained close. His palms pressed against the tree either side of her, and she swallowed harshly as his scent drifted over her. Salt, lake water, pine and musk.

Her eyes fluttered closed, and she pressed the back of her head to the bark. She thought back to the night they had kissed at the School of Fate after he had rescued her from Bonemire – and he had revealed his scars. He had shown a side to himself that she was sure he had never revealed to anyone else – a vulnerability she knew he hid like she did herself. The moment was raw, and she remembered the look in his eyes as he had turned to her after she finished placing kisses upon his scarred back. She wondered if he felt a flicker of the same warring emotions she had been battling with since that night. In many ways, they were much the same – both brought up being told how to feel, how to think.

Being manipulated into lying to themselves.

He shifted, causing her eyes to snap open and she saw him tilt his head, his voice low as he said, "We have company."

She felt her spine stiffen as he glanced around the tree.

Footsteps, more than one pair in the distance, stomped through the foliage without a thought of being stealthy. She felt Elijah's glare on her, not needing to meet his eyes to know it was accusatory.

"Red Guard soldiers, at least six of them. No doubt they heard your little show of magic. What were you thinking?"

Arii rolled her eyes. "Or perhaps it was the mini earth tremor that *you* caused!"

"I didn't cause any tremors!" he hissed defensively as the footsteps grew closer.

Arii leaned back against the tree, eyes narrowed as she slid a dagger from her belt, twirling the metal through her fingers.

"*Bullshit.* It's your untamed magic, Elijah – it happens when you grow angry. Haven't you noticed the strange weather anomalies that suddenly appear around you? Thunderclaps, earth shakes?"

He was staring now, lips downturned as usual, but he remained silent.

"Your magic is so powerful, it could hurt innocent people! Another reason why you need to learn to control it," she muttered, chancing a swift peek at the oncoming soldiers before unsheathing her second dagger and offering it to him. Countless times when she was around him in the castle had she noticed sudden booms of thunder when there were no signs of a storm in the sky. A hint, she now knew, of the colossal power hidden inside him. He had admitted to her in the library when she had first gazed upon his face that he had trouble sleeping during thunderstorms. Perhaps it was his suppressed magic keeping him up at night, the storms a reflection of his inner turmoil.

"Stay here," he said as his fingers curled around the hilt of the offered dagger, brushing her own and causing warmth to slither up her arm. How could such a tiny touch incite such strong reactions from her body? Never had anyone coaxed so many conflicting emotions, so many feelings from within her. It was confusing. Naught a few months ago, the only feeling within her was cool indifference – hardly a ripple fluttering against her walls of stone as she watched the world through a haze of grey.

Not even Lorch had brought forth such a storm of feeling from within. It was as if Lorch had begun to thaw her defences – like a candle to ice. Elijah was a heavy silver mace – poised to shatter her wall completely. The question was, was she ready to allow that to happen? She wondered if he had any inkling of her own thunderstorm raging beneath the surface when she was in his proximity.

She pushed those thoughts aside. After a few drawn-out seconds, their gazes locked until he moved away and his expression became emotionless as the footsteps approached closer. They were being hunted after all. Now was not the time to fixate over how she felt or guess how he felt about her, like some sort of chaotic, hormonal teenager. As far as she was concerned – he probably hated her for what she had done. She had shattered all he had known, opened the door to the flood of his memories he had spent years supressing.

What she should be fixated over was why he had not slit her throat yet, and not the trained, languid grace of his body as he silently moved away, taking on all the signs of a trained warrior.

Arii estimated they were just on the outskirts of Amberbourne now, a short stroll to the gates of the town. Their clothing was still damp from the lake water, and they were in need of weapons – Elijah having been unarmed somewhere during their escape from the castle.

All they had were her daggers.

It was all they needed.

The soldiers stopped to survey the clearing, and one of the men halted by the base of the tree where Arii's orb of magic had singed the shadow of a perfect circle in the smoking bark. The man moved his hand towards his sword – just as steel pressed against his throat.

"Lower your weapons, back away and return with your men to Viridya. Do this without a fight – and we will let you live," whispered Elijah, his voice low and dangerous, his form materialising from the shadows of the tree that the soldier had been surveying seconds ago. The man's eyes widened in surprise, and then narrowed in anger as his hand hovered over the pommel of his sword.

"Wolfe! You traitor," hissed the soldier, swallowing thickly as the steel pressed deeper into his windpipe. The other soldiers were all tense, swords drawn, eyes fixed on the hulking, dark presence behind the leader of their small search party. The man, despite the threat, continued to speak, "There is a pretty hefty price on your head, Elijah, one that will set us up for years. The King wants you alive – and your little Fury *bitch* too."

"You keep talking, Sykes, that is unwise."

"We no longer take orders from you, Fae scum."

Elijah's shoulders tensed. His lips curled back from his teeth, unbeknownst to him showing his fangs, as his silver eyes skipped over the five soldiers staring back at him. All men he had once worked with, all men he had spoken with over maps and strategized with in the council chambers. Some he had trained himself as recruits.

Five soldiers, not six…

Weapon raised, the sixth soldier dashed from behind a nearby pine tree, letting his poised arrow fly.

Several things happened in that moment. Silver flashed across the archer's neck – larynx opening to the air – red spraying in a bloody arch over the nearby ferns.

Then she was upon them like death riding the wind. Silver speared through the air, dagger embedding in the fifth soldier as Arii streaked across the clearing – her body a blur as she threw out a hand…

And halted the arrow in mid-air with a ripple of magic – inches from Elijah's face.

The arrow dropped to the forest floor as she dashed at the fourth soldier, hand snapping to swipe the dagger from the previous soldier's chest – before lodging it in the next man's throat.

She was like a blur, golden tipped tresses a fan around her as men died before they could scream.

Then she was before the second last soldier.

Her hands grasped the man's skull, her eyes like purple fire as her lips pulled back over her teeth in a feral snarl – a look of rage causing her features to twist as she moved to snap the soldier's neck.

"Stop."

It was Elijah's voice – the only voice that could snap through her blood rage in that moment. Arii paused, her nails lightly indenting the man's cheeks as he froze in terror, legs quaking and causing his metal armour to rattle.

Her head tilted, a lock of hair sliding behind one delicately pointed ear as she stared at Elijah, breath hissing through her clenched teeth. Her eyes flashed as they met his, challenge glimmering in their depths.

Perhaps the humans were not wrong in fearing a force such as her.

"I told you to wait."

"And miss the fun? Unlikely…" Arii purred against the soldier's neck, earning her an audible swallow of fear which stoked her inner beast.

"It didn't have to be like this, Sykes. Agree to leave now and you can save this man's life, as well as your own. All you have to do is deliver a message to the King."

Sykes' eyes were fixated on the Fae female before them, their depths watery with fear. When he did not respond, Elijah removed the blade and jerked the man around, before shoving him back towards his companion.

"Tell Lorch that we can talk about this and come to an understanding without any more bloodshed."

"Is it true, what they say about you? Are you truly a Herington?" Sykes croaked, rubbing at his neck.

Elijah bristled, his shoulders lifting. "What or who I am does not matter, my long service to the King should count for something. Tell him that I am willing to speak – peacefully."

Arii's head turned back to the soldier in her grip, offering him a slow, full-toothed smile – showing her fangs. The man whimpered as her fingers slipped from his face and she took a step back.

"I do not want his throne. Tell him that." Elijah added.

Arii felt her spine straighten, her brows narrowing as she stared at Elijah once more. He may not *want* the throne – but that did not change the fact that he was the one who was *supposed* to be upon it.

She was sure it was his fate.

Perhaps Freya Bloom could convince him to pursue his birthright. They could not allow Valdis to reign any longer – using his son as a political shield. The Courts had been divided for too long, the land and its people in chaos. Her head hurt at the thought of the massive task ahead of her. Not only did she have to try to convince him to believe he was good enough, and that it was his destiny to sit upon the throne and rule – but she was sure the other courts would need convincing too. The land of Fythnar needed balance – needed a strong leader upon the northern throne.

They could not face Valdis and his army of undead alone.

"Go," snapped Elijah, his words causing Sykes to flinch before he turned to the last remaining soldier and the two men fled from the clearing.

And then his heavy gaze was upon her once more.

"What in the world is wrong with you?"

"A thank you for saving your life would be more fitting to this situation, would it not?"

Elijah sheathed the dagger in his belt before growling, "They would have retreated had you not set yourself upon them like a crazed animal!"

"Hah! Crazed animal? Elijah, they were going to kill us – despite the reward on offer. Those men *live* to kill our kind."

"No wonder that is so – when you are upon them like a shadow and slitting open their throats!"

Her shoulders lifted in a shrug. "Old habits die hard, I'm afraid."

"Gods, you're truly unbelievable!" Elijah hissed as he shouldered past her, stomping in the direction they were headed before the interruption.

"I know," she grinned, dipping to remove two swords from the fallen soldiers before skipping after him. At least they now had some weapons, she supposed.

She held her palm out to his back, asking, "I'd like my dagger back now, please."

"You'll get it back when we reach Evergrave. Or perhaps when you show that you can be somewhat reasonable."

Jerk.

She cocked a middle finger at his back, bottom lip slipping forward in a mock pout as she followed in Elijah's heavy, anger-laced footsteps. "I tried being reasonable once… I didn't like it."

"Fates help me," the man muttered as they began picking their way through the shrubs.

HAWKE

Shackles clinked against one another as Hawke sat up, his back propped against the stone wall of his cell. He winced, aches blooming all over his body as he blew out a breath. He felt as if he had fallen and been trampled by a stampede of horses, and the slightest shift had his body flaring with pain.

Valdis was mad, truly and twistedly so. Hawke had always had a feeling that the man was off – but he had never thought he would stoop so low as to practice necromancy, using the very magic they all feared so much. It boggled Hawke's mind, causing nausea to roll. He had already been sick once and knowing the mess would not be cleaned up halted the bile halfway up.

Across the cell, he heard a light moan, causing his eyes to snap open.

Lynnera.

Shock jarred his body. He thought she had been taken to her rooms, not dragged to the dungeons with him.

As quickly as his howling body would allow, Hawke stood, moving to the bars to gaze across the small space between cells to where Lynnera sat. She was in the middle of the cell, her eyes squeezed closed and her hands pressed against her temples.

"Lynn," Hawke whispered, shackles clinking against the bars as he strained to see her in the dim light. "Lynn, are you alright? What are you doing down here?"

"I fought them, Hawke, as best I could. Rather than deal with me, Valdis had me sent down here to 'reflect on what I have done'." the woman whispered, her voice light… broken.

"My son, how could he…" she groaned, and Hawke felt his heart squeeze. He should have gotten her out long ago, along with Sybell and Lorch – before Valdis had the chance to sink his claws into them.

Now, he feared he was too late for Lorch.

Sybell, on the other hand, perhaps there was still hope for her.

"Lynn, listen to me. We need to find a way out of here. If what we saw in the courtyard is any indication – something is about to happen and I fear we may not survive it." He swallowed, cheek pressing against the bars. Gods, he felt twice his age in that moment, but he would rather die than let what had happened to Ingrid happen to Lynnera and his daughter. Suddenly his thoughts drifted over Arii and Elijah, and he did not blame them for fleeing the castle. It was still registering in his mind that the man who had stood by the King for so long was a Fae – and the rightful heir to the throne.

Despite the recent discovery of Eliverus' existence, Hawke knew that the darkness in Valdis had been manifesting far longer than anyone realised.

And now, that darkness was reaching out to Lorch with his father's influence.

"We can't leave without Lorch." Lynnera wailed, causing Hawke's chest to constrict once more in sympathy.

"Valdis has a hold over him now, Lynn."

Her blue eyes lifted, and he saw them swimming with anguish. He longed to hold her, dash the tears from her eyes and promise her a better world. Far too long had he watched the women he loved battle with pain.

"I will try to convince him, my love – but we must first get out of here and try to find somewhere safe. We need a plan. We cannot contend with Valdis' magic. He will not hesitate to kill us next time."

A sound caught his attention as someone approached the cells. Hawke felt his muscles tense in preparation for a fight – although he was not sure where he would find the strength. When it came to Lynnera, he would find the energy to fight, even if it meant drawing his last breath.

When dark chocolate eyes met his own just beyond the bars, he felt his insides begin to melt.

Sybell.

"Father," she whispered, her voice low and hoarse as she reached through the bars and cupped his cheeks. "I heard the commotion in the courtyard. My Gods, what did they do to you?" Sybell's head whipped to the sound of her mother's cry, and she dashed to clutch the woman through the bars.

"Mother?! What is happening here?"

"Sybell, you cannot be here – if they catch you…"

Sybell straightened quickly, her spine rigid and face twisted with anger. "Keys, where are the keys?"

"Sybell, wait."

"That conniving, two faced snake! How could Lorch lock up his own mother, and his long serving Commander?" she hissed. "I'll get you out, father. Where do they keep the keys?"

A clink of metal followed her words, and Sybell twirled, their collective attention dashing to see a figure a few paces down the hall.

It was Lorch – and lifted in his hand were the keys to the cell.

His expression was lost in shadow, but his voice was as clear as day. "*Father?*" he breathed, disbelief and anger simmering in the simple word.

Sybell straightened, her chin lifting as she stared her brother down. Hawke would have felt admiration had he not seen the flash of pain in Lorch's eyes.

"Give me the keys, Lorch – let us leave. We won't tell Valdis."

"Why did you call him father?" Lorch snapped, nodding in Hawke's direction. Hawke knew the young man was not a simpleton – Lorch knew what was happening here. He just wanted Sybell to admit it.

"Lorch, please," whispered Lynnera from her cell, her voice laced with pain. "Son, you cannot listen to your father – it's the magic, it is twisting his mind."

Lorch's eyes slid to his mother, and there was a flash of anguish in their depths. He hadn't known she was here, too.

As quickly as the look appeared, it was gone.

His lips curled back over his teeth in a look of rage none of them had ever seen on him before. Hawke was suddenly reminded of Valdis.

"Answer me!" Lorch bellowed, causing them all to wince in unison.

His mother slowly stood, pressing into the bars and attempting to meet her son's eyes. "My darling, we wanted to tell you – we truly did."

"Commander Hawke is Sybell's father?" he hissed, head turning to his mother, eyes narrowed to slits. "Is he my father too?"

"No, Valdis is your father, Lorch. Sybell… well, it was a surprise to us too." Lynnera's eyes met Hawke's across the space. There was no use lying or hiding it now. "I love him, son – have loved him for many years."

Deep down, Lorch had to know that his father was not a kind man, had never been kind to his mother. He was not a product of love – he was a product of an arranged marriage. Lorch's face did not show anger – as Hawke had thought he might. No, all he showed was cold calm as the truth hung in the air between them all. Hawke could see the subtle shift in the King's eyes, something beyond anger as it roiled within him, sure and true.

Resolve.

"Seize my sister and put her in her own cell," he whispered as two guards appeared behind Sybell. The girl screeched as the men grabbed her, throwing open the barred doors to a nearby cell and pushing her in roughly. Lorch strode to the door, sliding the key into the lock and clicking the latch.

Sybell threw herself against the bars, her hand shooting out to claw at her brother's face. He stepped back, just out of reach.

"You fucking weasel!" she screamed as she slammed against the bars.

Lorch's expression was coolly amused, bordering on bored – a look he often adopted at court. "Calm yourself sister, I'll let you out when you simmer down… or perhaps when I feel you can be civil. Don't hold your breath, though." He angled his head at Hawke and his mother as he added, "Same goes for you two. This news will take some time to process."

Dread settled in Hawke's stomach as the dungeon doors slammed shut with a thundering *boom* of finality.

TIKKANI & QUINN

CHAPTER FOUR

TIKKANI

"You're serious?" breathed Tikkani as the girl stared at her brother, his face fixed in a look so resolute that she did not have to read his thoughts to know that his mind was made up. It was not a secret by now that just about every guard in the castle knew what had transpired in the throne room, and what was now filling the castle storerooms and free spaces.

Nexus Crystal. Carts and carts of the stuff had begun to pass the gates of Viridya, along with people in cages, their eyes dark and haunted – skin the pallor of milk and their faces drawn in looks of agony. Not to mention the cages of iron clawed fucking *Kryverns*.

Something serious was about to go down, and as Tikkani, Emerson and Quinn huddled on their cots in the training barracks, discussing what they had seen as the others around them readied for bed – Tikkani felt a flutter of something in her stomach at her brother's hushed words.

"I'm serious, we need to get out of here and find Arii," Emerson repeated, his brows narrowing over his golden eyes. "Those crystals and those *things* that the King is bringing into the castle – it's all unnatural."

"Bloody hell, I agree with Emer – I don't fancy becoming one of those walking nightmares. Why keep regular breathing soldiers when they can have unthinking, unfeeling undead super soldiers! We could be next!" whispered Quinn beside them.

Tikkani checked that the other recruits were not listening in before she spoke. "Alright, how do you suppose we escape?"

"I might know a few… ways out," whispered Quinn, causing two sets of golden eyes to slide his way. He lifted a hand nervously to rub his nape. "Alright, so I found a few tunnels while looking for quiet places to tangle with a serving maid or two."

"Argh, gross." Tikkani wrinkled her nose. As much as she tried to press down the bitter jealousy, some of it still leaked through as Tikkani chewed her lip, unable to meet Quinn's gaze.

"I say we try the tunnels tonight, before this place is overrun," continued Quinn obliviously.

"We need to be careful. If we are caught – we may just end up as one of those creatures." Emerson pointed out. Tikkani sighed, straightening.

"Better we try than not at all," she agreed, a look of resolute steel flashing in her eyes before the trio turned to slide into their beds.

As the room began to fill with the light snores of the other recruits, three shadows shifted in the darkness. Quinn, Tikkani and Emerson dressed quickly and slipped from the barracks. Quinn beckoned the twins to follow, sliding through the darkness, hiding in the shadows of neighbouring buildings as they made their way downwards. Tikkani kept her fingers crossed as the trio slipped towards the storage rooms, nerves causing her palms to grow slick.

Guards paced the area, their eyes twitching at every sound as they marched their posts.

Nyx's arse, of course the storage rooms were guarded.

Emerson lifted a finger to his lips as they paused, hiding in a nearby shadowed enclave. The boy dipped a hand into his pocket to retrieve a handful of stones.

"Cliché, but whatever works," said Quinn as he accepted a stone. Emerson offered a tiny smile, before standing and throwing one of the stones across the space, so it landed with a rattle away from them.

The guards halted, eyes and ears drawn to the sound.

The recruits moved.

As they slipped along the walls behind the guards, Quinn lobbed his stone, causing the men's eyes to change course. Just as the soldiers' attention returned to their charge, the recruits slipped into the storage room.

Tikkani sucked in a breath, eyes widening as they were met with crates upon crates of glowing stones. Emerson was first to recover, grabbing Tikkani and Quinn's sleeves to pull them past the glowing stacks of crystals. The room hummed with energy – the air thick with a power that was foreign to them.

"This way," said Quinn as he unlatched the heavy door at the back of the storage area, motioning them to follow into the dank catacombs beyond.

Emerson passed first, before Tikkani paused by Quinn. "Again, this is gross. You bring girls down *here*? I'll bet that really impressed them."

Quinn's hand shot out, slapping Tikkani's bottom as she passed, causing her to squeak. "You'll thank me later!" he grinned, as she shot him a murderous look over her shoulder.

"Hey!" a voice called, and Quinn's head snapped to the storage room where the two guards now stood.

"Oh shit – go, go!" yelled Quinn, pulling the heavy door shut as the recruits broke into a run. The door would only slow the men for a moment.

The trio sprinted through the catacombs, feet sloshing through shallow water.

"Quinn, I can't see!" called Tikkani as she stumbled in the darkness. A hand caught hers, callused palms grazing hers, and she felt him pull her forward, guiding her as they ran.

"Don't let go," Quinn huffed, and Tikkani felt the consciousness of her brother just a few strides ahead. Quinn's hand clutched Emerson's sleeve, and soon the lanky young man was leading them both through the pitch black. Water filled her boots – foul, dank air speared down her throat as she inhaled the mouldy smells of the tunnel. They had to be in the castle's drainage system.

Behind them, she could hear the sloshing footsteps of the soldiers in pursuit.

Her hand gripped Quinn's tightly, and she wondered how he could see in the darkness. She chalked it up to familiarity and blanched at the thought.

Suddenly, Quinn's fingers ripped from her own – and Tikkani felt the ground beneath her feet disappear.

"Tikkani!" bellowed Quinn and Emerson in unison as she was thrown to the side, her back hitting the wet stone wall. The air left her lungs in a rush as a soldier grasped her tunic and threw her to the floor. Water doused her face and her clothing, and she spluttered as she tried to recover and take in a breath. She could hear sounds of struggle, the sounds of Quinn and her brother battling with another guard. How had they caught up so quickly?

Then there was an inhuman scream.

Tikkani's blood turned cold, for the soldier above her was not a man at all.

The smell of death hit her then, acrid and terrible, and she swiped water from her eyes to see blue light emanating from the thing.

Oh Gods, it was one of them. The undead.

She screamed as the creature's face was revealed with a flash of blue light, fingers twisting in her tunic as she struggled for her sword. Fear assaulted her mind, her own mixed with that of her brother's nearby as she felt Emerson's panic. She saw the outlines of Quinn and her brother against blue light radiating from two twitching figures.

Two undead monstrosities now.

A face coalesced from the darkness above her, its features highlighted in eerie blue. Two black eyes, like bottomless pits, stared back at her. What was once a man was now but a shell, a rotting, twitching shell. Fear clawed through her body, reaching every nerve ending. Where the man should have had a bottom jaw was an open, gaping space, as if the bottom half of his face had been torn away. Skin hung in flaps, his cheeks sunken, black blood coated his neck like a sick macabre painting.

Tikkani shrieked as the thing lifted her by her clothing and threw her across the tunnel as if she weighed nothing. She rolled, before planting her palms in the water and pushing herself up, boots slipping on the slick stones as she righted herself. Her head snapped up to see the shadows of Quinn and Emerson, silver swords flashing in the dim light as her brother speared his sword through the second creature's chest. The undead woman shrieked as the blade buried deep – but hardly flinched as she threw herself back into attack.

Tikkani moved, adrenaline shooting through her limbs as she clutched her sword and drew it from its scabbard. She thought of Arii, of the woman's fearless face and bared teeth as she faced down the Kryvern in Amberbourne. She imagined the woman's swift, fluid motions as she danced in the training ring with Elijah – all smooth movements and practiced grace. She remembered what Arii had said about the afflicted woman she had faced in the caverns below the castle, and how Elijah had killed the thing by removing its head.

Without further thought Tikkani moved, swiping her sword through the darkness – just as the man launched himself at her with a terrifying scream. Her sword bit into flesh, severing head from shoulders. She ducked and spun as the body flew by, then twisted to help the others. Quinn had embedded his sword in the woman's side and was attempting to jerk the weapon from her flesh – but all it did was enrage the thing further. The woman wailed and spun, clutching Quinn's head in her hands as the boy struggled.

"The head, you have to remove the head!"

Quinn's eyes met Tikkani's, his features washed in blue as he brought up his leg and booted the woman in the stomach, pushing her back.

Giving Tikkani the chance to strike.

Her sword was swift – and the woman's head splashed into a pool of water at their feet.

"Fuck me dead!" cried Tikkani.

"Strange choice of words given our current predicament," panted Emerson, snapping his sword back into its scabbard.

"Can't say I put a lot of thought into it, to be honest." She punched the air, dirty water spraying as she shook her sword – water mixed with blood on the steel. "Did you see that?!"

"If we weren't covered in blood and quite possibly *shit* – I'd kiss you, Tikkani! That was brilliant," said Quinn, wringing water from his pants, screwing up his nose.

Tikkani ducked her head against a blush, although the motion was pointless in the dark.

They did not have time to rest.

More sounds began to echo from behind them, and Tikkani grabbed at Quinn's tunic before clutching Emerson's arm. "We need to go, now!"

The light from the bodies of the creatures began to dissipate as the recruits ran, Quinn taking the twins' hands in his and leading them through the darkness.

When the light of the moon hit their faces, Tikkani almost wept with relief. They emerged below the waterfall, just to the east of the cliff where the castle was perched.

They did not stop, clambering down from the drainpipe and fleeing into the forest.

ARIIAYA

The moon was high above when Elijah finally convinced her to stop for the night. They were Fae, but that did not mean that they were invincible – and after the events of the last day, he was sure if they continued on and faced any more obstacles, they would not be at their best to defend themselves.

Arii was reluctant at first, anxious to keep going as long as possible despite the fatigue in her bones, but after some firm words and more than a few glares of Elijah's stony, mercury eyes – she finally relented. They had nothing but the clothing on their backs, nothing to set up camp. The night air was cool, but not freezing. For that she was grateful.

Elijah gathered wood and flint for a fire in a small clearing. Arii crouched down in front of him and cleared her throat to get his attention as he prepared to light it. Their supper, a rabbit, hung limp in her hand.

"You could just... you know... use your magic to start a fire?"

He stiffened at her condescending tone. "I'll do it without using *magic*, thank you."

"Gods damn, you're so stubborn," she groaned.

"I thought you would be used to my disposition by now – yet you have been complaining since we passed Amberbourne," he pointed out in a flat tone.

"I have not been complaining, I'm just incredibly disappointed."

"Disappointed?" Elijah said, brows narrowing.

"You have such strong magic, Elijah. It's been hanging around you like a dense fog since we killed those soldiers in the clearing, itching to be released."

"I killed no-one... *You* killed those men."

"Eh, a minor detail."

"I'm not using magic," he repeated; his tone stern and final as he continued his task.

Arii's head tilted, like a cat watching a mouse, surveying his long fingers as they worked. Soon, the kindling was smoking, and Elijah leaned down to blow a breath over the little embers beginning to flare. The amber sparks leaped from dry leaves to the bundle of dried tinder, and before long the small campfire was crackling with flames.

Elijah leaned back, his expression one she had not seen before.

It was smug.

Her brows climbed as Elijah's lips curled ever so slightly in the beginnings of a smirk.

"See, no need to use magic," he said, snatching the rabbit from her fingers and getting to work, preparing it for roasting.

"I can skin a rabbit, you know," she yelped incredulously.

"Oh, don't you just want to click your fingers and make the skin and fur disappear with *magic*?"

"I could!" Arii said matter-of-factly, pursing her lips.

"I do not doubt it, but I feel you'd be more satisfied digging your nails into its flesh and eating the thing raw."

"Hey! I'm not a rabid animal!"

Thick lashes swept his cheeks in dark arcs as he gazed up at her, silver eyes glimmering in the flickering orange light. His expression was… amused.

Was he trying to joke with her right now? How un-Elijah-like.

She watched as the golden light warmed his rugged features. The small smirk changed him entirely, and she swore she saw a tiny twinkle in his eyes.

Or perhaps it was a trick of the camp light.

Her lips pursed as their gaze severed, and he continued to skin the rabbit in quick, sure movements, using *her* dagger. Soon after, the rabbit was roasting above the fire on a makeshift spit of green sticks. She found herself wondering how often he had camped like this, surrounded by battalions of other men and women. She wanted to ask about his past – the past that was still fresh in his mind, but she drew herself short, in fear of overstepping the fragile boundaries they had put in place. So, she let the thought drift away on a cooling forest breeze.

The crackling of the fire was the only sound as they sat side by side in silence, both seemingly mesmerised by the dancing flames as the dark blanket of night sky twinkled above. The smell of roasting rabbit coiled in the air, and Arii suddenly realised that she was ravenous. When had she eaten last? It had to have been at least two days ago, if not more.

Elijah turned the skewer to roast the other side.

"So, are we going to talk about what happened the other night?" His voice was smooth like silk, deep and melodious, casual as if he were asking about something as simple as the weather.

It also had the hairs on the back of her neck rising.

"What is there to talk about?" she hedged, watching as the meat turned from pink to brown. Elijah's head tilted, and she could feel his gaze sliding over her face. There were a number of nights he could be referring to – and she was not sure she fancied talking about any of them.

"Arii."

Her eyes slowly lifted, meeting silver. The fire threw flickers of light over his strong jaw, tinging his thick black hair with embers of golden light. It was almost painful how incredibly rugged and beautiful he was – in a dark, masculine way. The silence between them seemed to stretch forever.

"I'm starving," she whispered, eyes drifting to the sky.

She was reminded of her view from the cell in Bonemire, the glittering orbs in the sky the only light she could see as she recovered on the stone floor after Valdis' torture. Something had changed within her that night, sealing what had already begun to manifest within her heart. She had felt fear, and anger – and the overwhelming need to *live*. Live to see the faces of her friends, the faces of the people that stirred so many foreign emotions in her cold heart.

One of those faces was watching her now with eyes of liquid mercury, questions swirling in their depths that she wanted so very much to avoid. Phantom pain bloomed across her chest as memories drifted across her mind's eye.

A dagger tipped with a glowing crystal.

Blood pouring over her breasts, hot and thick.

Unbearable pain exploding forth like she was re-living her magic's awakening.

Then, Elijah's lips on her own, his scent taking over her senses – his touch setting her ablaze like a lightning bolt.

Her mind flew back to the present as Elijah's fingers brushed her chin, and she felt sparks ignite on her skin as he tilted her head and forced her eyes back to his own, snapping her mind into focus with his words. "How did you figure out that I was a Herington?"

Oh, *that*.

Not the incredible, earth-shattering kisses they had shared after he had rescued her from Bonemire. Not that they had been a hair's breadth away from tearing each other's clothing off.

"It was not hard to figure out," she said, a hand rubbing the centre of her chest absentmindedly as her eyes fixed on his right cheek. His attention did not waver from her face as she continued, "Your scars gave it away… not to mention the inhuman speed and strength that you tried so hard to hide. You aren't the only one who is observant."

He huffed a laugh, a hint of teeth as he smiled slightly. "So it would seem."

"You must hate me," she whispered, and immediately wished she could swallow the words back. It shouldn't worry her so, but it did. His opinion of her weighed surprisingly heavy on the back of her mind. Once the words were in the air, she expected his features to change into anger once more. When they did not, she wished they would. She would prefer anger to the way he was looking at her right now. The softening look in his granite eyes had unexplained regret simmering in her gut. Despite his long-standing position working for a rising tyrant, it seemed he had a forgiving heart.

Instead, Elijah leaned forward slightly, skimming a thumb over her bottom lip.

"I don't hate you."

He should. And she wished he would. She had turned his life on its head – shattering all he thought he knew about himself. He should hate her, or at least feel revulsion when he touched her. She was a Fae, something he had been raised to treat with distain, as did everyone else. It would make things just a little simpler between them. Anger and hate were emotions she felt she would have better control over.

And Gods, she wanted to hate the hot fire shooting to her centre at his touch. But she did not hate it. She had been craving the feeling since he had left her at the School of Fate. It still floored her how this man made her *feel* with such intensity. He created a maelstrom of emotions within her, all from one look… one small touch. Never had she been so confused in her life.

Her eyes drifted closed as his warm breath tickled her lips, the deep and intense scent of him curling around her senses. He was close, so close that she could feel the warmth radiating from his skin as he leaned in slowly… oh so slowly.

"Nyx's heaving bosoms, I knew it!"

Their eyes snapped open at once, and Elijah was on his feet in a flash as a dark figure materialised from the darkness just beyond their campfire.

Krepth's face coalesced into a slow smirk as he moved into the light. A mocking curl of the lips that Arii had seen countless times before. But his eyes – his eyes were dark with anger.

Oh yes, she forgot they were destined to be interrupted.

"Who the hell are you?" growled Elijah, and Arii noticed the dagger was in his hand. She had not even seen him pull the weapon free. He was insanely fast.

"Oh, just a friend of the little Fury you were about to lock lips with, Your Highness."

"Argh gods…" Arii groaned, burying her head in her hands. News travelled fast – then again, Krepth seemed to know what was happening everywhere. He was not called a spymaster for nothing.

Arii stood as Krepth approached, his dark attire causing him to seem like a walking shadow. He and Elijah were the same height – albeit Krepth was slimmer in build. In that moment though, the Shifter's expression spoke for his stance.

"Huh, so you're the infamous Eliverus Herington." Krepth's green eyes slid over the man as if he were surveying something that had just slid free from under his boot.

Elijah's eyes narrowed, his usual glare returning in full force, the softness she had witnessed moments ago thrown to oblivion. Arii stepped between the two, the air crackling as they stared at one another.

"How did you find us, Krepth?" she said, hoping to sever the tension.

It worked.

Krepth's eyes lowered from Elijah to Arii as he tapped his nose. "I could smell you all the way from Amberbourne. Not to mention the towns are all crawling with Red Guard soldiers. You reek, Violet

Assassin."

"You know what happened in Viridya?"

"Little Fury, *everyone* in Fythnar knows what happened in Viridya."

"I still don't know who you are," interrupted Elijah, which drew Krepth's glare once more.

Arii noted the dark storm of dislike in his eyes. Great – this was going to be *oh so* fun.

"Elijah, this is Krepth Hallier. Krepth this is… well you know who he is, obviously," she finished, turning to snatch the roasting rabbit from the fire. Arii took a seat, hoping the two men would follow her example. She drew her dagger and began slicing meat from the creature, her eyes lifting to them before hissing, "Fuck's sake you two, sit down!"

Slowly, the men moved to sit. Krepth sat by Arii – Elijah moving a few paces to the opposite side.

"Now you two need to play nice, or I'll kick both of your arses."

Krepth chuckled, while Elijah huffed.

They knew she was not bluffing.

Slowly, Arii offered the rabbit to Elijah – who took it with a nod of thanks. Her attention moved back to Krepth. "What are you doing here?"

"I thought you might need a guide," Krepth said with a flourish of his hands that was not at all needed.

"I know the way to Evergrave," she sniped, popping a chunk of rabbit in her mouth. She suppressed a moan at the sweet taste of the roasted meat and shovelled more into her mouth without a thought of how unlady-like it was.

"I may have wanted to make sure you were still alive – and not in the back of a wagon headed to Viridya."

She paused; another slither of meat headed to her mouth as her eyes danced to Krepth. "You doubted me?"

"I doubted *him*," Krepth said, inclining his chin at Elijah, whose stoic features flickered in the firelight. "I thought he'd scurry back to the King, begging to kiss his arse until all was forgiven."

"Krepth…" Arii warned, as the campfire danced with a sudden breeze. Gods, on top of everything else she had to worry about, she didn't need to hold apart two testosterone-laden men like toddlers having tantrums. She watched Elijah, seeing his storm cloud eyes narrowed and jaw set like he was contemplating just how angry it would make her if he was to murder her friend. He could kill Krepth with just a snap of his wrist using magic – if he just learned how.

But Elijah did not need magic to run Krepth through with a weapon, she knew that too.

"Just because he is *meant* to be a king, it does not mean he has the balls to be one," added Krepth.

"What is your problem?" hissed Elijah after a beat of silence.

"Oh, I don't know, perhaps the fact that you stood by a fucking juvenile king who allowed the north to be run into the ground instead of taking your rightful place upon the throne?"

"I had no idea who I was!"

"Hah, lies no doubt. You've spent far too much time with the Kruel family."

"Krepth, shut your mouth!" hissed Arii, pointing a rabbit leg bone at him and glaring. "That's enough. Gods, you two are giving me a headache. I'm almost choking on testosterone here."

Elijah placed down the remains of his rabbit and stood suddenly. The air was dense, and she felt heat rising under her collar. Without a word, he turned and disappeared into the night.

"Whelp, there he goes again. Running from the truth."

Arii turned to her friend, anger rising and clawing at her insides. What *was* his problem?

"Krepth! You have no idea what he has been through!"

Her friend's face was incredulous. "Am I sensing sympathy, Arii? How unlike you."

"Fuck off!"

The man's lips curled in an infuriating smirk. She threw the remnants of her meal at his face, before standing and marching after Elijah.

He had not gone far, just beyond the firelight.

She approached him, eyeing his broad shoulders – the gentle point of one ear revealed as a breeze rustled his hair. She was surprised that he had walked away, fully expecting him to have snapped and leaped across the campfire to strangle the Shifter. Well, that's what *she* would have done. Elijah was proving to have far more patience.

His head was tilted back, as he stared up at the night sky.

"Elijah," she whispered, pausing by his side, and examining his strong profile. "Don't listen to Krepth, he's a bastard."

"He's right."

Her heart squeezed in her chest at his low whisper, and she felt the overwhelming need to defend Elijah's honour. "No, he isn't."

"Arii, I spent twenty years denying that I was different. Twenty years I could have spent trying to learn who and what I was. Perhaps if I had done that, I could have prevented what we saw in Bonemire."

She moved to stand before him, her features set in a determined glare. "Don't you dare blame yourself for Bonemire, Elijah. The darkness manifesting there is a product of years of unjustified, uneducated fear."

His eyes lowered to hers, and she could see a familiar haze clouding their depths, a look of haunting that she had seen a handful of times before. He blinked, and she suppressed the overwhelming urge to hold his face in her hands. Instead, her features softened, and her voice fluttered gently between them.

"Now you have the chance to make a difference."

He swallowed, his gaze never faltering from her own. Perhaps she could do this, perhaps she could convince him to lead the charge against the coming darkness.

"If you two are done fluttering your eyelashes at each other, I'll keep first watch while you both get some rest," came Krepth's voice from a small way over Elijah's shoulder.

Arii rolled her eyes, before sliding past Elijah and returning to the campfire. "Behave, you mutt…" she hissed, causing Krepth's hands to lift in surrender.

"Fine, no more comments. I promise."

"Good, you're getting on my nerves."

"Grumpy little Fury. Get some sleep," Krepth said as Arii found a spot beside the fire.

"Would it have killed you to bring some supplies, some bedding perhaps?" she groaned as she rested her head on the crook of her arm. "A snack or two wouldn't go wrong either."

"You have slept in worse places, and eaten even less."

"This is true."

Elijah joined them, sitting with his back against a nearby tree. He folded his arms across his chest, silver eyes resting on Arii, before flicking back up to Krepth and narrowing. "I don't trust you," he hissed.

"Makes two of us, Prince. Don't worry, as long as you don't snore – I won't touch a hair on your handsome head while you sleep."

Arii huffed, before staring up at the stars. Those glittering orbs twinkled in the sea of black, watching over them. She had not realised how tired she was until her body began to relax, a bone deep fatigue pulling against her consciousness. She was reluctant to sleep, fearful that when she awoke, Krepth may be a red smear against the trees.

She had to trust the two men would not tear each other apart while she slept.

Slowly, reluctantly, Arii succumbed, the sounds of crickets chirping and the fire crackling sending her into a fitful slumber.

⸸

Arii awoke to a gentle hand on her shoulder. Elijah leaned over her, his hair haloed in the mild light of dawn. She slowly sat up as he moved to kick dirt over their campfire. Krepth waited, leaning against a nearby pine tree, a slither of grass pinched between his teeth and his expression mildly impatient.

"Good morning sunshine," Krepth drawled.

For a second, she had hoped the last two months had been a dream.

A twisted, outlandish dream. When the smell of stale lake water and her own unwashed body found her nose, reality quickly replaced the fog of sleep. A sigh escaped her as she rose, rolling her neck until her spine cracked. "Gods, I miss the beds in the castle. They were like sleeping on clouds."

The trio began to move, Krepth in the lead as they headed through the thick forest.

It seemed the two males had not made up while she slept, unfortunately. The air about them was thick with tension, so dense that she could almost taste it. As soon as they left their camp, the two were again shooting insults and bickering like a married couple. For hours they argued, and the entire time she felt the crackle of Elijah's untamed magic on the air, dancing with the tension. Time and time again she glanced his way, subtly making sure he wasn't at threat of combustion. So far, he seemed to have a hold on the roiling power, but Arii was sure his insides were on fire from the strain.

"Valdis was the King's Hand before Lorch sat upon the throne. Do you not think Lorch would have recognised Elijah sooner?" Arii said, suddenly struck with the thought.

Krepth's head bobbed beneath a low hanging branch, "I wondered the same, at first. Valdis' family lived in the upper half of town and were brought to the castle soon after the King's death. Valdis may seem like a man whom would have a wealth of knowledge about the family he kept, but he is ultimately cursed with tunnel vision where power is concerned – according to a few of my sources. He had no interest in Tyverus' children, certainly not enough to commit their little faces to memory."

Elijah paced ahead as Krepth slid to her side, a grin plastering his infuriatingly handsome face. "So, care to enlighten me on what is going on between you and the King's lapdog?"

Arii did not meet her friend's eyes as she continued to walk in silence, skipping over a fallen branch before his gaze on her became too much. "Strange choice of words considering you are the *literal* dog here."

"Don't try to change the subject, Arii. Out with it."

She shot him a violet glare. "None of your *godsdamned* business!"

"Everything to do with you is my business."

"Since when?" she said, incredulous as she ducked a low hanging branch, letting the limb fly back in an attempt to hit her nosey pursuer.

Krepth ducked too and continued to speak as if she had not just tried to assault his face. "Oh, since forever. Arii, you are like a sister to me. I don't want to see you get hurt."

This had her slowing her pace, head tilting at her friend with a look of mild disbelief. Krepth was her oldest friend, and sure – she also thought of him as the sibling she never had – but to have him admit the same was strange to her ears.

"I can take care of myself," was her reply.

Krepth gave her a look that had her clenching her jaw in response.

"You and I know that emotion isn't something you are familiar with, those witches at the School of Fate made sure of that."

She did not argue. He was right. The intention was to ensure their assassins had no distractions and no temptations. But could you truly just *turn off* emotion and feeling completely? No matter how much training and time it took to smash it out of someone, she was believing it wasn't quite true. Perhaps she was proof that it was impossible. Or perhaps she was just broken. Instead of dwelling on the thought, she said, "Nothing is happening, Krepth, so you can untwist your knickers."

He clicked his tongue but wisely let the conversation drop. She knew she had not heard the last of it though, he would surely try again later – perhaps when Elijah was not around. It wasn't long before Krepth began talking again, and Arii had to fight the urge to roll her eyes back into her skull.

"So what is your plan, Arii? Take him to Evergrave and hope Freya accepts him with open arms? You know things are tense right now."

Arii chewed her bottom lip, knowing full well the situation. "We need her guidance, and perhaps she can persuade him to work with us rather than against us. His past is his past, and we need him *now* –

whether you like him or not," she added, shooting him a glare.

The Shifter shrugged, but she could see that for once he did not have a smart response.

They trudged on, Krepth in the lead again. Judging by the density of the trees and the thickness of the trunks around them, Arii guessed they were about an hour from the main population of Evergrave. The treetop city was in the heart of the forest where the trees grew thickest. She stole a glance over her shoulder at Elijah as he moved a few paces behind her, perhaps just checking that he was still following. He had not looked at her since he had awoken her that morning, and she had to suppress the temptation to ask how he was faring. His hair danced on a gentle breeze as he surveyed the impressive trees around them. She wondered if he had been this far from Viridya before.

"Get ready to see what a well-run court looks like, and take notes, Your Highness," said Krepth, glancing over his shoulder. Gods, it was as if the Shifter were trying to get a rise out of Elijah. So far, Elijah had kept his tone careful yet respectful in the face of Krepth's taunting and condescension, but his eyes hinted at a slow-brewing storm of anger.

"Don't fucking call me that," Elijah growled, finally snapping.

Krepth skipped and turned, arms outstretched as he gestured to the area around them. "Alas, you are the true 'King of the North', right? With that comes the title!"

Arii was almost at the point of killing them both when the sound of a roar echoed amongst the trees.

They all stopped, bodies freezing in the afternoon light.

And then they heard the screams.

Arii whirled, her eyes narrowing at familiar voices carried to her upon the wind as trees crashed nearby, and from between two pine trees came three figures.

Tikkani, Emerson and Quinn.

Hot on their heels was a Kryvern.

"Argh, shit…" whispered Arii as she moved, hearing Krepth and Elijah snapping into action behind her.

Tikkani was first to spot them, the girl's face twisting into pure relief, and Arii knew she was seconds away from a full-blown panic attack. Rage blurred Arii's vision, mingling with her own feeling of relief at seeing her friends alive. She drew the sword she retrieved from the guards earlier, before sprinting across the uneven forest floor towards them.

"Arii, thank the Gods!"

As the recruits approached, Arii reached out her hand, calling upon her magic to throw a large fallen log at the beast. The wood crashed against the Kryvern's head, causing it to stagger in its pursuit.

During the distraction, Elijah took that chance to bring his sword across the beast's chest. The Kryvern bellowed and swiped a claw – but Elijah was swift, dancing out of the way.

"The scales are too thick! You need to penetrate the eyes or the skull!" Arii yelled.

Or he could use his magic, she thought.

She briefly wondered if she should hang back and allow the situation to escalate, then perhaps Elijah would have no choice but to use it. A terrible image of the beast's iron claws skewering him had her backtracking the thought. Now was not the time to convince Elijah to use his magic.

An arrow whizzed overhead, embedding in the Kryvern's shoulder.

Then another skewered its eye, blood exploding across the nearby ferns.

There was a deluge of arrows, pouring like deadly silver rain from the treetops. As they pierced the animal, Elijah and Arii retreated to the others, roars of fury and anguish ricocheting off the woods surrounding them. Whining in agony, the beast hurled itself to the side before fleeing into the woods.

And then they were surrounded themselves by arrow tips and spear heads.

Arii stood perfectly still, the others following suit as figures emerged from the trees. The people directing weapons at their hearts were lean, thin, and their footsteps were almost silent on the fallen leaves.

And they all had delicately pointed ears.

Shifters.

"Just in time, Iniq, thank you for your assistance."

Krepth's voice broke the silence. Arii wondered where he had disappeared to, but her thoughts quickly left her mind as she spotted a familiar face. Even as she poked her spear menacingly into Elijah's chest with teeth bared, the woman was lovely, with dark hair and dark skin — rich and brown. Her hair was pulled back from her face and into a tail, one large braid combing from her scalp and into the thick tresses. A loose side fringe framed half of her stunning face and thickly-lashed vivid green eyes.

The woman did not lower her weapon, her intense glare pinned on Elijah. Like the others who held weapons around them, she was dressed in cloth and leathers that paid homage to the colours of the forest around them, along with a thick leather belt around her middle and knee-high, pressed leather boots. The difference between Iniq and her soldiers was that she donned a finely made bow nestled with a quiver on her back, gilded markings shimmering upon the dark oak. A weapon unique to the head of the eastern guard.

Tikkani lifted her hands to the sky, her face streaked with grime and tears, her hair a mess. Emerson looked no better; his own hands lifted in surrender. Quinn was on his arse, hands up, as a male Shifter towered over him. They all looked exhausted, dirty, and as if they had been through hell.

They also *smelled* like hell, too.

"You can lower your weapons now," persisted Krepth, his face splitting into his usual shit-eating grin.

The woman named Iniq did not budge. Her spear tip never left Elijah's chest, and she studied the male with a sneer on her face as she finally said, "This one, he smells off."

Elijah's brows rose and his lips parted, but Arii spoke first. "That's not the way to greet a guest to Evergrave, Iniq."

The woman's green eyes slid to Arii, before her harsh expression changed completely.

"Arii!"

The woman lowered her weapon and threw herself at the Fury, wrapping her arms around her shoulders in a swift embrace. The mood in the air melted from tense to calm within a split second, and the Shifters began lowering their weapons as Iniq held Arii at arm's length, studying her intensely.

"You're alive, thank Nyx!"

"Takes a bit more than a leap of faith from a waterfall to kill me, Iniq."

"Thank the Fates for that," she said, grinning enough to show sparkling white teeth. Iniq released Arii before motioning to the others to down weapons. Forest green eyes slid over Arii once more, before surveying her motley crew. Iniq smirked as she said, "You all look like shit."

Quinn flopped on his back at that, letting out a long groan.

"Suppose I'm just chopped deer liver?" muttered Krepth as Iniq arched a brow in his direction. He looked unimpressed at the cold reception delivered by the people of his home.

Iniq tilted her head, lips pursing. "*All* of you look like shit." A pause, "Hello, Krepth. Back so soon?"

Arii could recognise tension instantly after being surrounded by it for the last few hours, and there was definitely a hint between Iniq and Krepth. Knowing her childhood friend, he was in the bad books with the warrior. She made a mental note to find out the reason for it, even though it was none of her business. Alas, she was a nosy bitch.

"Come, let us get you all to Evergrave – you look like you could use a bath and clean clothing. You stink of lake water, among other things." Iniq announced, and Arii did not miss the look she shot at Elijah, before the small battalion began leading them through the forest.

LUC & EMERSON

CHAPTER FIVE

LORCH

It was impossible, well and truly impossible.

The Kryvern, a violent and unpredictable beast, was sitting on its haunches before his father like a dog.

Lorch was positive that no one else had ever seen something such as this. The beast's head lowered as Valdis stood with hand raised and amulet clutched in his palm in the castle gardens.

More caravans from Bonemire had begun to arrive as the sun set, and soon the gardens were filled with cages and people. Not to mention Kryverns, tens of them.

At first, Lorch had been fearful – the castle staff mirroring his own uncertainty as the animals were brought in cages. His father insisted he wait, allow him to show him just how much he had discovered in the last few weeks. And like a good son, he swallowed his fear and waited.

As Lorch's eyes roved over the beast, he noted signs of an incision on the animal's chest, the scales missing and the angry flesh beneath stitched together. The wild animal lowered its body to the grass, its head resting on its iron claws like an oversized, obsidian-scaled puppy. All there was needed to complete the picture was for its tongue to loll.

Lorch suppressed an insane chuckle of laughter. This was madness, absolute and sheer madness.

Valdis turned to his son, his eyes glinting blue before fading. "See, they are all under my control. No need to fret, my son."

Something shivered down Lorch's spine. He knew what he was

witnessing here was against everything he had been taught. Magic was evil, magic was unnatural. Magic was dangerous and unpredictable. Not even those attuned to it had full control, not really. The image of glass littering the throne room floor came to mind, the shock to his body as he recovered from the blast of Elijah's magic.

As he watched his father turn back to the Kryvern, he thought of all he had read about the history of Fythnar – about when the Fae reigned over the land with magic. Magic and the power it brought with it was said to bring about madness. Was this what it had been like back then? This very behaviour seemed to be against all they stood for, all that his *father* stood for. Lorch had always known his father was not a nice man, but this was beyond what he thought he was capable of.

Again, things manifested around him that he was unaware of until they chose to expose themselves, such as the news about his sister.

Stupid, naive, blind Lorch Kruel. He was a fool, and he knew it.

Yet despite what he saw right in front of his eyes, he still felt a sliver of fear when he recalled what he had witnessed in his own home. Power like that which Elijah displayed was worth preparing for.

Lorch found himself staring at the amulet, now resting on his father's dark blue doublet. Crafted upon its surface were coils of smelted gold, encasing the stone in a decorative, gilded shell, showing off the stone's constant glow. Its rough-cut surface almost resembled the shape of a human heart ripped straight out of the chest.

His eyes lifted to the sea of movement before him as dusk faded to twilight. Strange sounds filled the cooling air, the dull glow of blue reflecting off the gold castle walls, a sea of twinkling lights hovering before him as Lorch climbed upon a nearby caravan to better view the repurposed field before him. It had been a flat expanse of grape vines, now cleared to house the seemingly unending parade of caravans.

His eyes adjusted to the fading light, revealing a rippling scene of dark bodies, all flickering with blue as they moved jerkily about. Then the sea of movement paused, as dark onyx eyes devoid of emotion turned as one to stare at him.

Slowly the army of undead began to smile, lips curling and eyes glowing.

And Lorch saw his father turn to mirror the exact same smile, too.

ARIIAYA

Arii did not realise how much she had missed Evergrave until she was back within the embrace of the towering pine trees. The town had not changed much from when she had lived there with her mother, the same rickety-looking bridges connected one treetop home to another, the same pulley system lifted them from the forest floor and swayed the makeshift elevator as two Shifter men tugged at the ropes, lifting them into the trees.

Now she had no fear of the height, no fear of falling as she once did.

A lot had changed since she had been here, for her anyway.

As they alighted on the solid landing of the first collection of homes, Tikkani practically cawed with relief as she stepped from the caged platform, sinking to her knees. Arii knew she was a split second from kissing the solid slats of wood before Quinn had the girl's arm around his shoulders – lifting her up and helping her the rest of the way.

It seemed a fear of heights can affect soldiers too.

Iniq and her crew led them through the treetop city as eyes appeared all around them from the homes carved into the trees. Curious eyes, mostly, but she also noticed looks of wariness and perhaps anger. She would think about that later, for now they were in dire need of a decent meal – and a bath, especially the recruits as they tagged along behind them. They smelled like sewer water, and she was curious to hear how that came about.

"Freya has had some rooms prepared for your arrival," said Iniq as they stopped in a small clearing, two tree trunks ahead showing moss green painted doors. Arii's attention skipped over them, a feeling of sudden yet fleeting sorrow pulled at her heart. In the middle of the platform clearing was a metal pit, a small pile of chopped wood resting neatly to the side. Above them hung vines with silver lanterns, all flickering with firelight – along with more solid looking fixtures on the trees, throwing sparkles of gold.

As the light of the day faded, Arii remembered sitting by the fires with Krepth, drinking warm milk stirred with cinnamon. Until she had introduced it to him, the boy had not tried the combination before. It became their nightly ritual as they shared stories by the fire – mostly fantastical made-up stories that Krepth had dreamed up. His mind was a complicated, superb labyrinth of daydreams, and she missed his storytelling.

Now, as her gaze drifted, she saw her friend was studying her with eyes the colour of the leaves around them. "Welcome home." Krepth said with a small smile.

Arii felt her heart constrict.

"Emerson?"

The party turned at the sound of a new voice, and suddenly Emerson flew to embrace a young man ever so slightly taller than himself.

"Luc!"

"Thank the Gods, you're alright? Are you hurt?" Luc planted his hands on Emerson's biceps, holding his partner at arm's length to assess him.

"I'm fine, just a bit scratched up," said Emerson, visibly slackening in Luc's grip as a look of happiness dashed across his tired features.

As the two spoke and embraced, Arii surveyed Luc quickly. His skin was a deep brown, his hair as black as the night sky – tipped with silver like stars. His dark eyes were wide with concern, his face now completely rid of the roundness of boyhood. It was then that Arii recognised the boy from her childhood – Lucada Limus, brother to Iniq. Grinning, the Fury clicked her fingers together in recognition as Emerson and Luc turned her way.

"Lucada! By the Gods you have grown. You're a man now."

Luc's face split in a grin as he placed his arm around Emerson's shoulders, the two turning to face her.

"It's been a long time, Ariiaya! I should thank you for looking out for my Emerson. Like a bloody guardian angel."

Emerson snorted a small laugh as Arii chuckled, and it was obvious how relieved the recruit was as he leaned into his partner's side. She had always liked Luc. He was kind, genuine and a fun spirit – not taking many things too seriously. Quite the opposite to his sister, who was all seriousness and duty.

"He may be older, but my brother is still as annoying as ever," said Iniq.

Luc's look of mock outrage was half-hearted as he said, "Come on sis, my jokes aren't that bad!"

Iniq rolled her eyes. "Thank the gods you're here to preoccupy him, Emerson. It was becoming unbearable." Then she waved her hand in the air to draw everyone's attention. "Now, the water is hot, go and bathe. Afterwards we will have dinner by the fire. I trust you all like roast chicken?" She nodded at their eager responses then motioned at the two green doors. "You'll have to share rooms, but it's better than sleeping on the forest floor."

Arii watched as her friends began moving to the cottage on the left. She could not help but notice that Elijah had been silent beside her the entire time.

She turned and found his eyes were already upon her as he said, "You go ahead. I'll wait until you are done."

And risk him fading into the night? Gods no.

He must have noticed the look on her face, his own becoming unreadable as his arms folded against his broad chest. "Are we to argue about this, too?"

Yes, yes they were.

They had gone hours without butting heads, and she felt it was a tradition they were not soon to break.

"And leave you alone to brood and change your mind about being here? Not a chance."

"Am I some sort of prisoner now?"

"You're not a prisoner, Elijah."

His eyes were narrowed, jaw twitch returning. "Sure feels like it."

Arii suppressed a drawn-out groan. She was tired, hungry, and smelled foul. She was not in the mood to argue right now. Swiftly, she grabbed his forearm and began pulling him towards the door. "Well, at least wash up before dinner, you stubborn brute."

Surprisingly, Elijah did not protest as she threw open the door to the cottage and dragged him inside.

She was sure to get an angry tongue-lashing by Krepth later for how this looked, but in that moment she did not care. She slammed the door behind them before turning to face Elijah, who said, "You're scary when you're hungry."

Despite the jest of his words, they did not match his somewhat blank expression.

Oh, he had not seen scary, not really.

She crossed her arms over her chest, mirroring his look. "It's a Fae thing."

He winced ever so slightly as she moved past him to click her fingers over the candles and wall sconces around the room, igniting the wicks to flame.

"Is it a Fae thing – or an *Arii* thing?"

She ignored his comment, waving her hand in his general direction. "You are covered in blood."

"*You* are the reason for that. Besides, so are you," he pointed out.

"And you stink."

"Again, so do you."

"When are you going to tire of being an insufferable pain in my ass?" she called, throwing her arms up.

A twitch of his lips. "When you do me the same courtesy."

She shrugged. "Don't hold your breath," she said as she busied herself, not meeting his eyes. The room was just as she remembered it. The golden wood carved kitchen, the tapestries depicting forest animals draping the walls, the purple cushions on the carved sofa.

Then, unwillingly, her eyes conjured the image of her mother's final moments as she lay on the bed, her brow dotted with sweat, her skin so pale it had almost been translucent. Arii stood fixed to the spot, staring at the crisp white cotton sheets as her shoulders began to curl inward of their own accord.

Perhaps she should not have chosen to come in here first. Perhaps she should have stayed outside. She could feel her walls rising, her heartrate accelerating before quickly slowing as she practiced steady breaths.

One… two… three.

I feel nothing.

She withdrew, allowed years of practice to take hold of those emotions and press them down. She distanced herself from the man in the doorway, from his heavy gaze that was becoming curious, even as he watched on in silence.

ELIJAH

Elijah watched as Arii's demeanour slowly changed, her stare lingering on the bed nearby, her shoulders drooping and a breath methodically passing in between her lips. Counting, she was counting.

Before he could move closer, or ask what was wrong, she disappeared into the bathing room, as if in retreat. The sound of splashing water and the rustle of cloth could be heard, as if she was on a mission to distract herself, and perhaps put distance between them. His attention drifted to the bed, then around the small, cosy room as his mind replayed their brief conversation. Had he said something to offend? Perhaps, but it was hard to tell with Ariiaya. She was like a firecracker with an invisible wick, and he was not always sure what would set her ignition alight. It was not becoming clearer as he got to know her, either.

Then something came to mind, and he took a step forward. Her actions, paired with Krepth's 'welcome home' words earlier, had him speaking before he could catch the words.

"This place… this room. Is this where you grew up?"

Arii paused, her back turning rigid. Slowly, she turned, her expression dark. For a small moment, Elijah wondered why she looked so angry. Then her features changed, her purple eyes gazing over the room. He saw sadness in their depths, memories of ghosts, and he felt his arms fall to his sides.

"Yes," she replied simply.

Then, that sadness was gone as quickly as it had appeared, replaced with unjustified anger.

"Will telling you about my past convince you to use your magic?" she snapped.

"Unlikely."

"Well then, you won't mind if I end this pointless conversation quickly and submerge myself in a hot bath." Arii quipped, irritation pouring from her in waves. Elijah was not sure what had brought on the anger, but he was beginning to see that when it came to anger and Ariiaya, there was not much time between.

"Is this truly about my reluctance to use magic, or is something else eating your insides?" Despite what he gave away, Elijah could not deny the exhaustion lacing his bones, and with that exhaustion came his own irritation. He was normally very good at keeping his emotions in check, but when it came to the woman before him, he was finding that control was becoming paper thin. Now, as it had been since they had escaped the castle, magic roiled beneath his skin, jittery and wild like an untamed beast. It bubbled inside, coaxed forth with his annoyance at her words. "Will you give it a rest with the magic? I will not be using it, end of story."

"Perhaps I'll submerge my head in the bath so I don't have to hear another word of your pathetic whining!" she barked, swiping a bar of soap from the wash basin.

Elijah followed her, stopping in the doorway as he growled, "And I'll hope with a fierceness that you don't possess the power to speak under water! Honestly, though, it seems anything is possible at this point."

Arii sent the bar of soap careening at his head, cursing as he snatched it from the air.

"I'm growing more and more weary of your level of maturity, Ariiaya."

"Gods, you are insufferable!"

"Present company is wearing off on me, then," he uttered.

She pressed the heels of her hands into the sides of her temples as she groaned, and he could not help a small dash of feeling as her tone dulled, as if she was close to admitting defeat. "Please just use the bath I have fixed for you, or leave me to it, because I cannot find the energy to argue with you anymore today, Elijah."

He could see a hint of vulnerability. He watched as she pressed back the emotion that was shimmering just below the surface of her deep violet eyes.

So far she had given no indication that she wished to do him harm. But he could not rule out any potential plotting. She was an assassin, a user of magic, a Fae… a murderer. He was sure more blood coated her hands than he could ever realise.

And yet something deep within him trusted her. Perhaps because of what she had sacrificed in bringing him here, perhaps it was something else. But he did. The thought had his frustration vanishing.

He moved towards her slowly. The candlelight stroked her features as his hand lifted to her face.

She sucked in a breath, swift and sharp. He noticed she did that often when he drew near – as if she were steeling herself, preparing for something. She made to pluck the soap from his hand, and his eyes took the opportunity to skim her face, counting the dried flecks of blood like freckles across her cheek, the dark wings of her lashes rimming her deep violet eyes. He saw simmering flames there, deep within their depths that he was almost certain she would slaughter him for noticing.

Below her jawline, her pulse was a steady, noticeable thrum.

Hell, he could not help but be drawn to her even now when her eyes stormed with a look of bordering on murder.

Her angst, her fire… was it because she was back where she grew up? This place held memories for her, memories that brought forth feelings that she obviously couldn't control. He knew this after a brief discussion with Nem just after they had retrieved Arii from Bonemire. The Fury had let it slip, and now thinking back on the moment, he was not sure why it had come up. She had history here and not all of it was pleasant.

The mystery that was Ariiaya Trillia – the Violet Assassin – was slowly unfurling, and he knew that it was against her wishes. He knew she preferred he know nothing of her past, and nothing about *her* for that matter. She knew how to push his buttons, no doubt about it, but despite her uncaring façade – Elijah knew deep down she did care. She would not have returned to Viridya if she didn't.

Just how much was still yet to be seen.

So, before she could move away, he lifted a hand to cup her cheek.

ARIIAYA

It took all of her self-control not to move, not to breathe, as he touched her. Even now, she could feel his magic humming around them, stoked alight by their argument. Her frustration was still at the forefront of her mind when the words left her lips of their own volition. "You *need* to learn about your magic, Elijah."

She surveyed his expression, unable to read it clearly in that moment. Suddenly, his fingers moved to pinch her chin, raising her head as his grey eyes pierced hers.

"I'm getting a little tired of you telling me what I *must* do." His jaw slid forward, his voice low and dangerous. "You expect me to set aside years of a mindset so ingrained in our society that the very mention of what I am – what *we* are – has people quaking with fear? I have spent years fearing what I am, killing those who could be the very thing that *I am*." His lip twitched, the only outward indication of emotion that she could detect in that moment. In his eyes though, she could see a hint of sorrow. "For most of my life, I, as well as everyone else, have been educated so thoroughly that the Fae are evil, wicked, dangerous beings with too much power. So much so that they didn't care who they hurt. To learn I am one of them…" he almost choked, and she narrowed her eyes. "I have never hated myself as much as I do now."

"And you believe all that you are told? What about proof?"

He remained silent, assessing her before uttering, "It is before me."

She stiffened, knowing he was implying what he saw her do to the soldiers in the clearing. Alright, perhaps it wasn't her best decision, but those soldiers could have killed them, too. She knew her profession made her look terrible, but she was trying to make things right. She tried again.

"You shouldn't base an entire population on what you know about me, I am not a good example for what Fae are like, Elijah. Do you not remember your true parents, or your siblings? They were Fae. Won't you give their memory a chance? From what I have been told and read about them, they were far from wicked or evil."

"My memory is still clouded, not enough for me to remember them clearly."

She sighed. "Valdis upholds a faith of fear and bigotry, passed down from a very long line of forefathers. Perhaps somewhere in the beginning something did happen that began this violent chain of events. I'm not discrediting that some of the Fae did treat humans as lesser beings. But don't you think killing all Fae just because some 'might' hurt you is somewhat wrong?"

Elijah's tone was careful as he said, "I've hunted and killed countless Fae, Arii. I would not have been ordered to do so if they did not pose a threat."

"Did they fight back with magic, though?"

"They were not given the chance."

"What if they weren't Fae, then?" she whispered, a feeling of ice shivering down her spine.

"That was not a risk my superiors were willing to take," was his reply.

Gods, she knew there was much to discover about Elijah's past, and she wasn't naive enough to believe it filled with golden sunshine and frolicking puppies. Elijah was a soldier, someone trained under the harshest conditions to take the harshest orders without hesitation, and she knew he had been loyal to the Red Guard, so loyal that he was posted as personal bodyguard to the King – a job they wouldn't just give to *anyone*. He had known no different. Like her, she believed when it came to free will, they had none.

With the feeling of his eyes upon her and his fingers at her chin – which she had not thought to loosen – Arii tried again. "If not for the orders, if you had the choice, would you still have done it?"

His voice was low and deathly calm, canines flashing as he hissed, "Yes."

Well, she had a lot of work ahead of her, far more than she had originally thought.

Fucking *splendid.*

Her eyes fixed on his as his scent washed over her. Lake water was most prominent, but just beneath that was the usual pine and woodsmoke. Despite his harsh reply, she saw something akin to regret in his eyes, just a tiny flash, like he wished to take the word back. Because of that look and the gentleness with which his fingers dropped from her chin, she found herself pitying him… no, pitying them *both.* They had both been raised to believe they had no choice in choosing their destinies, covering their own hands in blood so others did not have to.

With a low exhale, Elijah stepped back from her, his throat bobbing, his entire look hinting at a tugging exhaustion that they both began to feel as the silence stretched.

Having him here, in the place where she had begun to lose her humanity, was almost too much. She had lost far more than that in this room all those years ago, and now as they stood in the place where her magic awoke, her insides roiling in confusion and lingering desire from his touch, she felt it was almost a cruel twist of fate.

Her walls began to erect once more, slamming up between them.

"Don't use up all the hot water…" she hissed, before slipping past him and leaving, the door slamming behind her.

INIQ

CHAPTER SIX

ARIIAYA

"What is in this? It's fucking amazing!" moaned Tikkani as she shoved another chunk of roast chicken into her mouth. Beside her, Emerson stilled, spoon hovering at his lips.

Iniq did not seem to mind Tikkani's crude praise of her cooking. If anything, it made the Shifter grin. "Secret herbs and spices," she replied, tucking into her own meal.

"If you can call salt, pepper and rosemary *secret*," laughed Luc.

Iniq shot her brother a withering look. "Quiet, boy."

"Well, I like it!" continued Tikkani, shovelling another bite and looking thoughtful. "Hmm, rosemary…"

They sat around the metal cauldron on thick pillows, the silence broken by the soft crackling of the fire and gentle scraping of forks against wooden plates. Emerson, Tikkani and Luc had caught up on the time they had spent apart, and Luc filled them in on his apprenticeship as a wood carver. Everyone was bathed and clad in clean clothing, and the atmosphere was calmer now. Arii listened in on Krepth and Quinn discussing the history of the Shifter people, one she knew from her childhood growing up in Evergrave. The Shifters were once Fae, and a very long time ago a small congregation became bored, and – using their magic – discovered a spell that allowed them to shift into animal form. Delighted and devious, those Fae used the power to sneak into the halls of the gods, where they had stolen three precious artifacts that appeared to be nought but glittering, expensive trinkets – when in fact they were three objects of great power.

The first was The Locket of Dreaming – an adornment said to

aid the user in traversing the dreams of others – alive and dead. The second was the Sword of Power – a weapon made of unbreakable steel and said to be the ultimate conduit for magic. The third was The Cloak of Protection – said to be unpierceable by mortal blades and untouched by time, never to fade.

The gods were furious when they discovered their prized possessions missing, and fell upon the mortal realm, their anger so palpable that they caused catastrophic events to unleash around them. Vicious storms, locust plagues and bringers of endless nights, the gods hunted until they discovered those who stole from them. Those Fae were struck with a curse, a curse that rendered them little more than humans – severing their magic, their strength, their immortal grace, and leaving them with but a lick of power and a limited ability to shift into an animal form that the gods would choose upon the birth of their future children.

The curse, and the theatrics that the gods wrought in their mission to find the thieves, left them weakened as they returned to their own realms.

The magical objects? They were never recovered, for the Fae were a stubborn race, refusing to give the whereabouts of the objects, and as the curse took hold and their bodies recovered, they found their memories of the past fading away. So, the whereabouts of the objects of power were forgotten, and forgotten still to this day.

The group listened eagerly, but despite the storytelling, the air between Arii and Elijah though was noticeably tense.

No one mentioned it, they all knew it was wise not to, lest they have their heads bitten off.

Quinn placed down his plate and stretched, fingers twining above his head before patting the swell of his stomach.

"That was delicious, Iniq, thank you." He eyed the Shifter, his grin far wider than necessary. No doubt he would attempt to pursue the warrior woman, she was his supposed *type* after all. Arii wondered if he was successful in nabbing a woman like Iniq, would he be able to handle it?

Probably not.

Iniq leaned towards Elijah, her hair slipping forward over her shoulder as she held out a platter of chicken thighs, "More?" she asked simply, her expression stoic still, but far less unfriendly than it had been upon their arrival. Arii could see the gesture for what it truly was – an olive branch without unnecessary words.

Elijah nodded, taking a thigh, "Yes, thank you."

Arii's mood was still sour, but the small exchange had her insides uncurling ever so slightly. She could tell by the way he nibbled at his food that Elijah was no longer hungry, but he took the offer anyway – for what it truly was. One of peace.

Somewhat satisfied, she put down her bowl and murmured to Krepth that she would return shortly. While her friends conversed, she took the opportunity to head up the nearby, rickety bridge to a slightly more elevated section of the town. Her steps were sure and swift, barely noticed by the residents as she headed towards sounds of birdsong.

Arii reached a heavy door in the trunk of a dark, aged pine tree and pushed it open. She didn't need to read the carved sign featuring an eagle in flight and the words *Evergrave Postal Service, you bring 'em, we send 'em.*

As she entered the shop, the jittering of cages and squawking of birds assaulted her ears. She pressed the door closed behind her, just as a male voice shouted, "Close th' door behind you, lady."

"Scribe, it's been a long time." Arii greeted, unable to help a smile.

The man was old, tall and thin as a twig, his rich red hair lined with grey and pulled back from his face. He balanced a pair of glasses on the bridge of his nose, and as he spun to greet her, he pressed them closer to his wide, grey eyes. "Miss Trillia! My gods, haven't you grown! What can I do for you, little violet?"

A pang of grief touched her heart at the nickname. She swallowed it down as she passed cages stacked from floor to ceiling, housing an array of chattering coloured birds. An abundance of neatly labelled pigeonholes and letters filled much of the space too. Scribe sorted through high stacks on his desk, seemingly oblivious to the overpowering smell of birds and their excrement, and their excited cries and fluttering. Arii decided to keep her visit brief.

"I need to send an urgent letter." She hesitated for a moment. "And it needs to go directly to Castle Viridya."

Scribe's brows shot up. "I'm unsure if the north is taking outside correspondence at this time."

"Then send a bird that can get in without notice, I'm sure you have something small and agile." She pushed a finger into the cage of a motley grey owl which twisted its head to an impossible angle, yellow eyes wide as it hooted. "I recall you had such birds."

"I do…" he said cautiously, eyeing her over his glasses as he pulled out a fresh page of parchment and a quill. "But what in Nyx's name could you possibly wish to send to Viridya?"

She did not meet his eyes, pulling her finger from the cage as the owl attempted to peck it. "That is my business alone, Scribe. Isn't your establishment renowned for its 'We won't ask if you don't' policy?"

"Times are tense, Arii. All I'll say is to place your pen and words with caution."

He pushed the writing supplies across the small available space towards her, throwing her one last glance before moving away to attend to some birds perched nearby, gently and skilfully attaching little messenger tubes to their ankles.

The parchment was small, and she knew that what she truly needed to say would require far more paper, but for now she kept her message brief. Dipping the nib of the quill into a nearby pot of ink, she wrote quickly.

Lorch,

It was never my intention to hurt you. I know that I did, and for that I am truly sorry. But fate has other plans, and if we allow this darkness to further manifest then we will all suffer fates worse than death. Please, help us turn the tide, for a brutal storm is coming and better you be with us than against us.

Arii.

She knew there was so much more that could be said – that should be said – but she couldn't risk more than those few simple sentences to fall into the wrong hands. There was no guarantee that the note would ever make it to the King, but she had to try.

Folding the note into a neat square and passing it to Scribe, the man curled it up to slot into a tiny cylinder attached to the leg of a miniature, sand-coloured bird with intelligence glimmering in its beady eyes.

"Thank you, Scribe. I owe you."

The man waved a hand. "Don't mention it."

Arii hesitated at the door on her way out. "These birds… they're not…" her words fell away as the man tilted his head, catching on to her unspoken meaning before he let out small chuckle.

"People? Nah, just regular birds. We leave the much heavier loads to our kin." He winked.

With a small smile, she left the shop and returned to her friends.

"Where have *you* been?" said Krepth, his tone light but laced with suspicion.

"Visiting some old friends. You aren't my only friend, Krepth, as much as you think so." She plopped back down on the crimson pillow beside him, swiping up her plate to continue picking at her meal. Krepth snorted.

She tried not to twitch under Elijah's analysing gaze, which she could feel from across the fire. Noticing a smudge of black ink on her fingertips, she subtly moved her hand to cradle the bowl, hoping he had not seen. Chances were that his eagle eyes had not missed it, but he didn't say anything as the group continued to eat and converse.

The trees rustled above on a gentle breeze, branches meeting and shaking limbs as Krepth placed down his bowl and turned to Arii, firelight dancing over his sharp, clean-shaven cheeks. "When you are ready, Freya is waiting to see you." His green eyes lifted to Elijah. "Both of you," he added.

Arii knew they could not put off seeing Freya much longer. She was not afraid of what the woman had to say – she trusted Freya. She was afraid of what Elijah might say or do when they met with her.

So far, he had not put up a fight on their way to Evergrave, but she knew he was still reluctant about the whole situation. He still refused to use his magic, speak about it, or even acknowledge it – as if it didn't exist. Everyone knew that was not the case though, the tang of it was on the air whenever he was near. When she used her own, he looked like he wanted to spin around and stalk away. She understood his reluctance, but he had to learn how to control it sooner rather than later, lest it eat him up from the inside. She was sure that a repeat of the throne room was possible.

She could not allow him to combust here like he had in Viridya.

Without looking at Elijah, she stood and announced, "Alright, let's go then."

†

Arii and a stern-faced Elijah followed Krepth across the swaying platforms, passing townspeople along the way. She noticed their curious faces as they paused in their evening routines, seeing that none of their gazes followed her.

Every eye was on Elijah.

His face was emotionless save for the little crease between his drawn eyebrows, most likely uncomfortable with the attention. Everyone knew by now who he was, and what his existence meant for Fythnar.

Hope.

They approached a pair of large, elaborately carved wooden doors, and Krepth pushed them open to reveal Freya Bloom's throne room. The space, carved into the forest's largest and most remarkable tree, was an impressively high ceilinged, warm room. Intricate features of flowing vines and leaves, combined with woodland creatures in stories were masterfully engraved into the wood of the walls.

Arii had seen the room a few times before, and every time she felt breathless from its beauty.

Freya Bloom sat upon a beautifully-carved throne of oak atop a dais, beneath a stunning chandelier made of carved the same oak that looked like the horns of a majestic deer. Her hair was longer than Arii remembered, the snow-white waves falling below her breasts, her chin raised and eyes glittering. She was dressed in a gown as dark as midnight, the cotton laced with silver thread in patterns resembling those on the walls around her. Despite the passage of time, she did not appear to have aged a day. Her dark eyes were fixed on them as they entered, and under her heavy gaze Arii dropped to one knee in a motion of respect.

Elijah made to do the same, but Freya's hand lifted quickly as she said, "No, you do not bow to me – Eliverus Herington. You bow to no-one."

Elijah stiffened, gazing up at the woman with the voice of gentle windchimes, and he visibly shivered, as if someone had dropped cold water down his back. Against her words, he dropped into a bow beside Arii, and Arii tilted her head to look at him through her curtain of hair.

"I am no king, Your Highness…" he said, his deep voice ringing against the walls.

Behind them, Krepth snorted lightly.

Freya's head tilted, like an owl on a perch. Her eyes slid over the man, over his dark hair and light eyes as he lifted his head to meet her gaze. She stood and slowly paced down the dais towards them.

"You have your mother's eyes," she said gently, dipping to rest on her knees before him.

Never had Arii seen the Queen of the East on her knees before a man. On her knees before *anyone* for that matter. Freya's fingers cupped Elijah's cheeks as she surveyed his face and he stared back, his expression pained.

"You knew my mother?" he whispered.

Freya smiled. "Yes, I knew your parents well. I can see them both in you. Your father's strength, your mother's sincerity. Eliverus, I cannot tell you how happy it makes my heart to see you alive."

With a gentle touch, she motioned for them to stand, before turning to Arii.

"Ariiaya, my sweet child – it has been far too long since you visited."

Arii felt her cheeks turn pink as she watched the Queen, a strange feeling blooming in her chest. "My apologies, Your Highness."

Freya smiled again before motioning them to follow her to a large oak table nearby. Perched on top were cups and a teapot, the spout steaming with the scent of lavender tea.

"Now, I heard what happened, but I feel it best to hear it from you two." Freya took a seat, motioning for them to join her. "Things cannot be misconstrued straight from the horse's mouth."

Arii sat quickly, smiling thankfully as Freya handed her a cup of tea. Elijah hesitated, but joined them and nodded thanks as Freya also handed him a cup.

"How does an assassination assignment turn into a rescue mission, Miss Trillia?" Freya said, lifting her cup to her lips.

"Well, erm…"

Elijah's eyes were fixed on his cup as Arii tried to formulate a believable story.

First, I fell for the King, then his bodyguard. My discovery of his true identity was mere coincidence.

Arii bit her lip and glanced away.

Freya noticed her reluctance, saying gently, "Well, we have you to thank, Ariiaya." She turned to Elijah. "If the power I felt is any indication of what resides within you, Eliverus, then we have much work to do."

Silver eyes lifted from his cup as Elijah's jaw clenched. "If you mean my magic... I'm not using it."

Argh, here we go.

Freya's brows rose in surprise. "You'll need it when you take back your throne."

"I do not *want* the throne."

Arii slid forward in her seat, shooting Freya an apologetic look. "Freya, don't bother. I've been trying to convince him since we escaped Viridya, but he's as stubborn as a mule."

Elijah fell silent, his face dark as he surveyed his cup with unnecessary intensity, as if the tea leaves were about to float to the surface and rise against him too.

The Queen's face was gentle as she spoke. "The North is spiralling into ruin, Eliverus, and has been for years. Now more than ever your land – your people – need someone to lead them back to the light. Do you not wish to take back what the Kruel family stole?"

"What did you say?"

The air rippled around them as Elijah's eyes narrowed. Arii felt the hair on the back of her neck stand on end as Freya said, "Valdis Kruel was the one who organised the night raid that killed your family, Eliverus."

The chandelier above them rattled as Elijah whispered, "You are lying."

"Why would I lie about such a thing?"

Arii swallowed, feeling sickness swell in her stomach. The news did not come as a shock – not really, now that they knew what Valdis was capable of. It seemed the scheme had been in the works for quite some time.

Freya's voice was firm but gentle as she touched her fingers to the back of Elijah's hand. "If you do not stand up against them, I fear that many more will suffer a fate like that of your family, and many more will be subjected to the evil that has been inching its way across the land."

"I... I can't," was all Elijah could manage, his voice twined with anguish.

From the doorway, Krepth chuckled darkly before moving towards them. "Perhaps he needs a little motivation?" said the man, and he grabbed the front of Elijah's shirt and yanked him up from his seat.

Arii felt the air crackle around them as Krepth snapped his arm back.

And punched Elijah square in the jaw.

The events that happened next were a blur, so fast even her Fae eyes had trouble keeping track.

Magic drenched the air, the chandelier shuddering above them as Elijah's head turned, eyes narrowing in an acidic glare at Krepth, his eyes flashing blue.

And then Krepth was lifted off his feet by invisible hands and sent flying across the room. The Shifter hit the polished wooden floors before righting himself in a rush. Suddenly a flash of light enveloped his body as he streaked forward, shifting on the fly. A massive black wolf appeared and speared through the light, its black mass of fur headed straight towards Elijah. As they collided, Elijah's hands grasped the wolf's jaws and wrenched them wide as the beast roared and snapped at his face, before they crashed to the ground in a violent tangle of limbs and fur.

Arii was up and at the two as they wrestled on the floor. "Stop it, both of you!"

The air was thick with magical tension, and apart from the little bit he had used to throw Krepth across the room, Elijah still refrained from using it. She imagined the power was raging within him, and he was holding it back with a fine tether. She felt she could almost choke on the air as Freya joined her, the Queen's look troubled.

They would not kill each other, would they? Krepth knew how important Elijah was to the future of the land.

"Krepth, that is enough," snapped Freya, her voice dripping with authority.

Almost instantly the wolf halted his attack and leaped away from Elijah. Light flashed and Krepth was once again a man, crouched and rubbing his jaw.

Elijah stood and rubbed his own jaw, his look incredulous. "What the hell is wrong with you?"

"You aren't the King yet, mate..." hissed Krepth, his eyes filled with fire. "And until you grow some balls and step up to the plate – I'll continue to be a thorn in your side." Krepth stood, wincing and clutching his ribs. "Not just the north is under threat of being consumed by darkness, Eliverus, but all of the other courts too. I will not stand by and watch you wallow in your aversion to magic when you have the ability to do something about it!"

Elijah lurched to his feet. "What makes you all think I can do anything about the darkness? Magic is the cause of it all. Magic only makes everything worse!"

"Despite what you have been told, Eliverus, magic can also make things better – when used for good." Freya reasoned.

Elijah ran a hand through his hair in frustration and turned his back on them, shoulders quaking.

"What is inside me feels *far* from good."

Arii paused, her hand raised to touch him, but thought better, letting her hand drop before whispering, "Let us help you, Elijah."

Her voice had him turning, his eyes seeking hers. She almost collapsed at the look of helplessness in their depths.

What was before them now was scary – a murky sea with monsters beneath. But it also had the potential to reveal a glittering, untapped world of possibility once the murk was cleared away. No longer would the truth be drowned in a sea of lies. She was determined to clear the haze and reveal to him the wonder of magic.

She placed her fingertips against his bicep – the briefest of touches – and she hoped he could see the sincerity in the motion as she said, "It'll get easier – the magic, I mean. You'll see."

All she had given him since they arrived was frost and made a mental note to do better. Her mind skipped back to their conversation earlier, to the way he looked upon her with scorn – a look she knew to be forced. Elijah had enough awareness to tell that what he had been ordered to do was wrong, and she believed, despite his words, that he was a good person deep down. She could not treat him as an enemy any longer.

Elijah's eyes slid over her face as they stared at one another, the room around them fading in colour. He trusted her enough to reveal his face once, and she hoped he could learn to trust her now.

"You will need the support of each court if you wish to stand a chance against Valdis, and in order to take back your throne," said Freya as she approached them, seeming unfazed by the moment in time that was just theirs. "It may not be what you want, but it is what needs to happen. You must do this, Eliverus, for your people. For your family's memory. For Fythnar."

Elijah's eyes drifted closed as Freya spoke, and Arii felt the heaviness ease from the room as he regained hold of himself.

"What do I need to do?" he finally said, and Arii released her breath.

"You will need to travel to the South Court, and then to the West – Jero, Thogan and Kadec will expect your arrival – but they will not lend their support easily. As you can imagine they have had issues of trust since the Kruel family's reign began."

Arii broke her gaze from Elijah to turn to Freya and Krepth, the latter's eyes narrowed yet resolute. Freya stepped forward and lifted her hand to cup Elijah's cheek. "Return to me here once you have their symbols of loyalty – for *my* task will be your last."

She offered him a smile before brushing her hand over Arii's arm and turning to retreat to her own quarters.

The three of them stood in silence, watching the Queen depart. As she disappeared from sight, Elijah's hand lifted to his jaw, for the hurt that had been pounding there moments ago was gone.

⸸

Leading the way through the lantern-lit, relatively busy streets of Evergrave, Arii cast her eyes over the treetop city. It had expanded and become far more populated since her time here as a child. The same curved, thatched roofs offered protection from what elements rained down from the thick canopy above, ornately carved wooden pillars holding the structures securely in place. The bridges connecting parts of the city felt sturdier now, and there were far more shops and stalls than she recalled. The weeping branches of the willow trees seemed longer, the wildflowers sprouting from knots in the trees thicker and more vibrant. Fireflies flittered in the air as people and animals went about their nightly rituals.

Arii paused by a stall offering thick, heavy cloaks, the colours ranging from light cream to forest green to midnight black. She fingered the sleeve of a deep blue cloak, noticing tiny sparkles laced into the fabric that reminded her of the night sky. Her eyes travelled down the cloak, noticing that it slowly lightened to a soft blue at the end. It was stunning… and most certainly out of her price range. Besides, she wasn't here to shop. After making potential progress in the throne room, Arii was eager to return to their rooms and prepare to depart the forest city.

With a small sigh, Arii turned to catch up with Krepth and Elijah, but jerked to a halt before she could run into Krepth. Behind her, the stall clerk spoke.

"Ah, Mr Hallier! Good to see you, lad. Your young lady here seems to be eyeing my one-of-a-kind stardust cloak."

Krepth gently swatted away a firefly that had briefly perched on his nose. He sniffed, then offered the stall keeper his trademark roguish grin. "So she is. How is business, Shriv?"

Shriv shrugged as he adjusted a tan coloured cloak on a hanger. "Could be better but could also be worse too. I ain't one to complain."

"How much for the cloak?" Krepth said, digging into his pocket.

"One hundred silver," Shriv said, without missing a beat, watching as Krepth pulled the drawstrings of his coin pouch.

One hundred silver? Arii almost gawked at that price.

Striking green eyes lifted, gazing through thick lashes, "Come now, Shriv. Can't you offer a little discount, for old times' sake?"

The man sighed, "Righto, I guess I can offer somethin', you did help recover my cart of exotic Kryvern skins after all." As he spoke, Arii noticed an array of coin pouches on a table nearby, the scales polished and the drawstrings made of fine crimson ribbons. Kryvern skin coin pouches? She hadn't even known there was demand for such a thing.

"Eighty silvers, then. But no lower, this cloak is unique – none other like it."

Krepth grinned, fishing out a gold piece as Arii's mouth opened in protest. Placing the coin in the man's palm, Krepth lifted a finger to halt her as Shriv shuffled off to get some change. "Ah, call it a welcome home gift, little Fury. I insist."

"But…"

Shriv dropped silver coins of change into Krepth's palm before he folded the cloak neatly and handed it to Arii. "Take good care of it, and it will take good care of you."

Elijah watched the exchange impassively, standing like a guard just outside the stall.

"Thank you, Krepth," Arii said weakly, eyes dropping to the beautiful cloak as she rubbed her palm over the soft yet durable fabric. Krepth draped an arm over her shoulders, placing a loud, theatrical kiss on her cheek that earned him a grimace.

"What are brothers for, hm?" he said as they continued on through the bustling streets.

Arii couldn't help the smile that tugged at her mouth, "I'm still angry at you, though." She could feel Elijah's presence behind them, and knew he was following. Thankfully without further argument.

"I know," Krepth said, grinning wide.

She was yet to understand why Krepth seemed to despise Elijah so, but for now chalked it up to the fact that the man had served the very family who had let the land spiral into ruin. Elijah had been nothing but gracious, even though he was recovering from the crumbling of the world he knew.

People still watched him with wariness as they approached their lodgings, and a little brown cat with wide green eyes watched with a flicking, agitated tail. Even the animals were wary of this new Fae male.

"Bet you still wish you wore your hood, huh?" Arii tossed over her shoulder as Elijah moved beside her. They crossed a wide, sturdy bridge, passing under a baroque archway, leaving the thick of the city behind.

"More than ever before…" he muttered, and in that moment, Arii could not blame him.

FREYA

CHAPTER SEVEN

ARIIAYA

"Of course we are coming with you," said Quinn the next morning as Arii filled two packs with supplies. Quinn was towering over her as she worked, closely flanked by Tikkani, Emerson and Luc.

"Absolutely not," she snapped, shoving a waterskin into the pack with a little more force than what was necessary.

"Come on, you guys need all the help you can get!" said Tikkani, her face fixed in an expression so resolute and serious that Arii thought the girl might blow a vein in her forehead.

After their return from the Queen's throne room, Elijah and Arii had settled into the two beds in the room they shared. He had lain with his back to her, but she knew he was not sleeping. Or at least, not until the moon had reached its zenith in the sky, and light filtered through the window to wash his form in moonlight.

She had watched the gentle rise and fall of his shoulder for a long time before she drifted to sleep, wondering what was going through his head.

Three tasks. They had three tasks to complete before they could go back to Viridya and face Valdis.

And Lorch.

Her dreams had featured the young King, his chest cracked open and a glowing crystal heart beating within. She screamed and wailed in agony as she clutched his heart in her hands, Lorch's lifeless eyes gazing up into nothingness.

No, he was not dead. He could not be dead.

Thoughts of leaving and going back to help him had entered

her mind dozens of times, the temptation eating at her insides like maggots. It was only when the recruits told her that he was alive and well that she pressed the thoughts back. It was hard to believe he was well, but Emerson insisted he was alive and looking unharmed just before they left, and he also added that Lorch had been beside his father most of the time.

Hate coated her tongue with bitterness. Valdis had his claws sinking into his son, and Lorch was allowing him to do so. Surely, he would see that what Valdis was doing was wrong. She felt she had known him well enough that he would know right from wrong. She hoped beyond hope that he was just putting up a ruse in order to survive.

In the morning, Arii raised her head from her chore of packing when she heard light laughter. It was such a strange sound to her ears, and she looked over to where Elijah was chopping wood. Three children, aged around five or six, watched on with wide eyes as he brought the axe down through the wood without a hint of effort. At first, he ignored them, but soon their little exclamations of awe had him tilting his head. Arii was sure the children had seen wood chopping before, but perhaps not by a Fae.

A dark brow rose on Elijah's face as a blonde-haired child approached, his little hands lifting to the axe. "I wanna try!" said the boy, seeming so small next to the muscled warrior. Elijah crouched before him, offering the handle. The boy clutched it with both hands and wobbled. Elijah kept his fingers on the flat edge of the blade, obviously fearing the boy may topple over from the weight. Slowly he showed the boy how to bring the blade down on the wood, and the boy squealed with delight.

Arii had never before seen the look that passed over Elijah's face. His eyes softened, the skin around them smoothing and the little crease between his brows disappeared as he spoke to the boy, his voice lost in the sound of the children cheering.

Elijah was smiling. Genuinely smiling – rare cheek dimples and all.

A little girl with hair just like the boy approached his other side, and

Arii watched as Elijah poked the girl's nose affectionately, causing the child to giggle.

Oh good gods.

"Oooh be still my heart… and my ovaries," whispered Tikkani as her face appeared beside Arii's, her eyes fixed on the scene before them.

Arii inched back and glared, but Tikkani straightened and touched a finger to the side of her nose. "Your secret is safe with me," she grinned, before heading back to her brother.

Arii huffed, blood rising to her cheeks as she ducked her head and continued to work with much more rigor this time.

Until a scream split the air.

Arii was on her feet in a flash.

She twisted to come face-to-face with Tikkani's wide eyed look of terror.

And a blade at the girl's throat.

A figure had materialised behind the elf, silver hair flashing as they tossed back their hood and glared with striking blue eyes. Nemesis.

"Nem, what are you doing?" Arii breathed, before sounds of scuffling erupted all around them. Emerson was thrown to the ground by a blonde-haired Fury wielding dual blades – one pressed to the boy's throat and the other at Luc – the latter knocked down to his knees, teeth bared in a snarl in his attempt to protect his partner. Arii recognised Claire, one of her sister Furies.

Quinn was clutched in the arms of fiery-haired Devina, the woman's eyes wide and glittering with devious excitement.

Dread pooled in Arii's stomach as she glared at the three Furies, her sisters in arms – sisters who she had betrayed when she had leaped into the waterfall in Viridya.

"Let them go!" she snarled as her hand slid to her dagger.

"Uh uh, Violet Assassin, I wouldn't do that if I were you," hissed Devina as Quinn struggled in her arms. She pressed her face to his cheek and inhaled, her eyes drifting closed as she scented his fear. "Where is the male?"

Arii's eyes slid to where Elijah had been moments ago with the children, and she blinked.

He was gone.

Nem followed her gaze, before the Fury pressed the blade harder into Tikkani's neck, causing the girl to whimper. Her voice was deadly calm as she said, "Hand yourselves over – peacefully – and no one will be hurt."

"Aww, but the Fates said we could kill everyone else!" pouted Devina.

Nem shot the woman a glare. "As a last resort," she retorted, her attention moving back to her best friend.

"Nem, you know what is happening in Bonemire. You know what is being done there. Help us." Arii stopped short of a pleading tone, despite her urge to.

Nem's brows narrowed, but Arii could see the uncertainty in her eyes when she replied, "We have our orders, and they must be obeyed."

"Even when those orders are wrong?"

Nem hesitated, and Arii noticed. She could get through to her, she knew it.

Devina and Claire on the other hand – they would be a much harder quest.

"Did you tell them what we saw, and what was done to me in Bonemire? Or did you keep that information to yourself?" Arii motioned to the two women as they held her friends in check. "We cannot let Valdis destroy this land, Nem. We cannot let him cover this world in darkness. What do we do then, who do we serve when the Gods desert us? Because they will not watch over a land with no one left to pray."

Claire was first to speak. "You tell lies, lies so that we won't kill your lover and this entire town!"

"Elijah is our last hope against Valdis!" Arii yelled.

Claire's eyes narrowed as she growled, "I've heard enough lies!"

Emerson's eyes snapped shut in preparation for the strike. Dread flooded Arii's gut and she inched forward as the Fury continued, "Eliverus was supposed to be dead, and soon that is what he will be –"

The woman's speech spluttered to a halt with a cough and a choke, and Arii's eyes widened as the blonde dropped to her knees, her mouth working as if she could not get air into her lungs.

Behind her stood Elijah, and his face was expressionless save for the crease between his brows, and the silver fire of anger in his eyes.

Claire choked, her nails scrabbling against the floor as blood spurted from a wound on her neck. Arii watched in shock as the woman flopped to her side, a dagger straight through her windpipe.

Nem and Devina's eyes darted to Elijah as he helped Emerson and Luc to stand, before stepping over the dying Fury.

Devina screeched, just as Quinn's elbow speared into her gut and the scene exploded into chaos.

Arii used the distraction to fly at Nem, who pushed Tikkani away just as their daggers clashed.

Behind her, Elijah was upon Devina with his own blades. The four danced and parried, steel whizzing through the air and clashing in the morning light.

Red hair flew in a fan as Devina twisted and stabbed at Elijah, who matched her stroke for stroke.

"You! You're the King's shadow, his hooded lapdog! Ah, how I have been awaiting a rematch," she hissed, spearing her dagger at his gut. Elijah was swift, grasping the woman's arm and wrenching. Devina grunted and dipped into a complicated twist that should have dislocated her arm, but instead it caused her to end up behind him, dagger aiming for his spine. Elijah jerked, catching her arm and wrenching the weapon from her fingers.

"You retreated before I could kill you last time. That won't happen again," Elijah retorted with a hiss, twisting and catching her head in his hands.

Devina's hand came up between them, and Elijah was thrown back as she punched magic into his chest.

Arii's concentration was momentarily severed as she heard Elijah hit the pile of chopped wood. Nem took that chance to punch her fist into Arii's gut, and as Arii doubled over, Nem's knee flew up, connecting with her face. Cartilage crunched and blood spurted from Arii's nose as she reeled back, hitting the deck on her backside.

Nem's expression was pained as she stepped toward her friend. "I'm sorry, Arii – I truly am."

Both of their heads suddenly snapped to the sound of frenzied screaming.

A bird was clawing and flapping around Devina's head, screeching and swiping at her face in a frenzy. The bird – a brown hawk – cawed angrily, dodging her hands as Devina tried to seize it.

Elijah leapt up and shot forward to bury his fist in Devina's stomach, punching the air from her lungs. He had his knife at her neck and her head back in an instant, his fist tangled in the fiery tresses of her hair with a movement so quick it could have been easily missed.

"Wait!"

He jerked to a halt, seconds away from slicing the assassin's throat.

Nem had her daggers raised in supplication, her expression drawn. She slowly lowered her weapons.

"What the fuck are you doing, Nemesis?" Devina choked, earning her a swift jerk of her hair by Elijah.

Arii wondered the same thing, eyes wide and nose streaming crimson rivulets down her mouth and chin, but she remained silent as her shoulders sagged with relief.

"I saw the horrors of Bonemire with my own eyes, Devina. What they were doing there was sick, and against everything we stand for. I won't sit back and watch as our world descends into darkness!" Nem cried, facing up to Arii. Her eyes were wide, her expression fierce. "Fuck orders, and fuck fate!"

Her daggers hit the floor as if punctuating her words as she held her hand out to Arii. With a sigh of relief and pain, Arii clutched her fingers and allowed the woman to help her up.

"I'm sorry about your face," Nem said, wincing.

Waving her free hand, Arii's chuckle muffled against her palm,

"Glad you have seen sense, Nem."

Elijah reluctantly let Devina go with a growl. The Fury placed a hand to her neck, her eyes murderous as she turned on them. "You are all fools!"

"Oh, come off it Devina!" yelled Nem is an unusual display of frustration.

"I'll have plenty of chances to kick your arse after we save Fythnar," said Arii, dabbing at her nose with her sleeve. Devina remained silent, stewing in her own pot of hate. Silently, the woman turned and leaped over the railing, leaving the group staring in her wake.

"Typical Devina, running when things get tough," drawled Arii, her voice muffled by blood-soaked cloth.

"She will return to the Sisters, no doubt to tell them of my desertion." Nem whispered as she knelt by Claire, her fingers gliding to the woman's pulse.

Tikkani approached, followed closely by Emerson and Luc – the latter with hands linked and their faces flushed but unharmed, their eyes mirroring sadness as Nem brushed her fingers over the dead woman's eyelids.

Elijah shifted where he was, sheathing his blades, his voice low as he whispered, "I'm sorry, Nemesis."

"Claire knew the risks when we left." Her head tilted to look at the man. Her words did not change the look of pain and regret in his eyes. "We all did."

Tikkani suddenly spoke up, "Hey, where is Quinn?"

The hawk landed before Elijah, wings flapping as it squawked. They all stared as white light flashed around the animal, manifesting into the form of a man.

As the light faded, Quinn knelt, head bowed, in the bird's place.

✝

"When were you going to tell us that you were a *godsdamned Shifter*?!" yelled Tikkani as she paced back and forth in front of

Quinn. The young man sat with ankles crossed as he leaned against the railing, looking completely nonplussed.

"Eventually, I guess."

"Eventually?!" the girl screeched.

Arii watched on as the two recruits bickered, her violet eyes cataloguing the way they interacted as Nem placed her hands on her face and swiftly snapped her broken nose back in place. Arii suppressed a colourful curse that would have made Tikkani blush, before Nem's fingers glowed with gentle, healing white light. The scuffle with the Furies had only spanned a few minutes, and shortly after Devina's retreat, Iniq arrived with a few guards in tow. Luc explained the situation to her, for he was the only one who could quickly douse her anger at not being present to protect them all. And the fact that the Furies had snuck passed her guards unseen. Arii had been quick to explain Nem's switch of sides before the warrior could skewer her best friend.

"So, you're heading south first, then west?" said Nem.

"Yes, that's presuming we can gain the Southern Court's support." Arii's eyes danced to Elijah as he joined them, hefting one of the packs onto his shoulder. That was when she noticed that his hair was shorter. The sides had been neatened, no longer covering the points of his ears, the top slightly longer and sweeping over his forehead and into his silver eyes. His new hairstyle showed off his strong jawline, pointed ears and rugged features.

Gods, he looked remarkably sexy, somehow more so than before.

He noticed her stare, his expression changing to… abashed? She could swear his cheeks flushed as he lifted a shoulder. "Freya insisted I cut my hair… she said the people need to see my face – and see my ears."

"You let her cut your hair?" gasped Arii, dumbfounded.

"Actually, Iniq did it." He rubbed his nape, eyes drifting away.

Arii's stomach twisted in knots at the thought of anyone else touching his hair, especially another woman. Then she stomped on the strange feeling quickly, horrified at herself. He was not *hers*, she had no silly Fae claim over him.

"Many will recognise the late King in your features now you're no longer hidden. You look good," said Nem, offering a smile as she stood – severing the awkward tension. Arii could have kissed her for it. Her words were true, too. Arii could see the likeness of the man she had seen in the tomes she had searched while staying at the castle. Elijah looked like his father in his early years.

"Something tells me we will need more than an impressive dance with daggers to sway the leaders of the other courts," said Arii, dipping to retrieve her pack.

Elijah huffed, disappearing into their rooms, possibly to check they hadn't left anything, or just to space between them as awkwardness entered the air.

Nem hitched her own pack as they were joined by Tikkani, Emerson, Luc and Quinn.

"Ready to go!" chimed Tikkani. As she eyed Arii's dark look, she ducked and scooped up her own pack. "We are coming with you, Arii, like it our lump it."

It looked as though the argument about Quinn's heritage was over, for now.

"So am I," said Krepth as he approached, his own pack on his shoulders. He was clad in traveling leathers, same as they all now wore.

Arii stood quickly, her gaze sliding over her friends as the gathered before her. She felt her heart squeeze in her chest, an unfamiliar feeling of pride pressing in on her. Accompanying was something else… the feeling of fear.

She could not allow any of them to be hurt, or worse. She had spent the last hour trying to convince them not to follow – to stay here where they would be safe. That was unless she and Elijah failed – then nowhere would be safe.

With a resigned sigh, Arii turned to see Elijah watching them all, his face unreadable.

"Alright, let's go."

⸸

"This mead tastes like Nymph piss. Now I remember why I avoid this shithole," sighed Krepth, and despite his complaints, lifted the tankard of amber liquid to his lips once again.

"You know what Nymph piss tastes like?" exclaimed Tikkani as she took a seat, followed by the remainder of their group.

Krepth's brows waggled as he grinned at the girl, and she nodded a thanks to the serving maid who placed a few more tankards on their table. With a look of disgust at Krepth's imaginative feedback, she pushed her own mug in Quinn's direction.

The trek from Evergrave had taken several hours, and by the time they arrived in Trader's Bay, the sun was high. The town was just as Arii had left it several months ago – run down, stinking and filthy.

Elijah had surveyed the town with a look of carefully withdrawn shock, and Arii assumed this was due to the state of the sodden port town.

Thankfully, he and Krepth had not spoken for the entire journey, the time mostly filled with Quinn's chatter and Tikkani's random questions about what he could do in his bird form.

"So, the day that plump ol' mean Maggie in the kitchens complained that a bird had shit on her clean washing *five* times – that was *you*?"

"What do you take me for, some kind of animal?" At Tikkani's pointed look, Quinn's lips slowly spread in a wicked grin, "Yeah, that was me."

Arii was as surprised as everyone else that Quinn was a Shifter, but then again her life was nothing but surprises lately. She shifted her gaze to Krepth as the man chugged from his tankard, as she asked him, "So, you're sure the ship will be here soon?"

Krepth nodded.

"And you're sure we can trust the crew?" she continued.

Krepth put down his drink, a hand pressing to his chest in mock pain. "Little Fury, do you doubt the calibre of my connections?" Arii gave him a deadpan look, which only made the Shifter grin. "Of course we can, the captain and her crew are long-time friends of mine. I'd trust her with my life."

Well, that was good enough for her.

"How long will it take to get to Erstonia?" said Emerson as he sipped water. Beside him, Luc tucked into his roast beef as if it were his last meal. Arii had noticed that Emerson never touched a drop of mead – or anything alcoholic for that matter. Tikkani joked that he was an angry drunk, but Arii knew it was because he in fact had a sensitive stomach.

"It should only take a few days to arrive on the southern continent, as the crow flies – or should I say as the hawk flies," Krepth shot a pointed look at Quinn, who leaned back upon his chair and stifled a belch behind a closed fist. Continuing with a cough, Krepth said, "If we do not run into any complications on the way, that is. The journey to the castle will take another day through the snow fields. I hope you all packed something warm to wear."

Luckily, the Shifters in Evergrave had provided fur-lined coats for them all.

The Southern Court was the only court she had never visited. If the stories were true, Jero Vox and his brother Thogan were twins, just like Tikkani and Emerson. She had also heard that the southern continent was blanketed by miles of snow, colossal mountains and harsh terrain – along with their own assortment of deadly creatures. Apparently, the cold kept the Kryverns away, but there were sure to be other beasts in their place. The journey was not going to be easy.

"Perhaps the harsh southern continent will help you find your balls, Eliverus," Krepth sneered as he lifted his mead to his mouth.

Arii's brows rose as her eyes darted to Elijah, who was nursing his own tankard.

She noticed he had not touched a drop. The man's look was dark, his eyes narrowed.

Argh, here we go again. Krepth was playing with fire, and she idly wondered if the man had a death wish, or perhaps he had a strange plan in his head. With Krepth, she never really knew.

"Or there could be an unfortunate *accident* to your own balls, Krepth," Elijah retorted, finally taking a drink.

Tikkani barked a laugh, followed by Quinn and the remainder of the group as her laughter eased the tension.

Arii smiled slowly in the dim, flickering light of the tavern as the group continued to converse.

And that was when she heard a voice.

'You are leading them all to their deaths, Ariiaya Trillia.'

Startled, Arii glanced to the right, then to the left – but the sound, it did not come from either side of her, nor front, nor behind.

It came from within her mind itself.

'More lives mean more graves,' the voice said.

She sensed a peculiar feeling of cold fingers dashing along the base of her skull – long nails pressing into the sides of her brain and squeezing. Her teeth clenched inside her closed mouth.

'Do not make a sound, lest you wish for those around you to suffer...'

Heeding the warning, she remained silent, eyes dropping to the drink she nursed. The voice was undoubtedly female – melodic, entrancing and as cold as pure ice.

Was she going mad?

'Good,' cooed the voice, its tenor flat and devoid of emotion.

Scrabbling at her mental defences, Arii attempted to shut out the presence – but an immense power shuddered behind her eyes, threatening to squeeze her brain like a ripe pumpkin, causing her to suppress a groan of pain.

'I would not bother, Fury... Your mind is like a sponge – soft and disappointingly pliant. I must admit, I hoped for more of a challenge.' There was the tiniest hint of bravado in the voice, but the tenor disappeared as quickly as it had appeared.

'Who are you?' thought Arii, hands shaking with anger, pressed against her knees under the table.

'I am your doubts. I am your impending failure. I am your anger.'

Arii swallowed harshly, eyes lifting as a bead of sweat formed, trailing down her brow.

Her eyes met silver as Elijah watched her across the table, the simple knit of his brows showing that he possibly felt her unease. The others continued to speak, laugh and throw down their meals as she battled silently with the voice in her mind. Her nails bit into her palms, the pain dragging her attention ever so slightly as the presence began to fade upon a whisp of dark smoke, claws leaving marks upon her consciousness as it whispered words she would not soon forget.

'I am your fear.'

Then it was gone.

Leaving Arii with a whole lot of unanswered questions and a temple-splitting headache.

VALERIE

CHAPTER EIGHT

ARIIAYA

A short time later the group gathered on the docks, looking up at an impressive ship with red sails. The vessel was surprisingly neat, the lower hull riddled with barnacles, but the remainder of the wood was polished to perfection. On the front of the ship was a woman carved from wood, her hair fanned out behind her and her arm outstretched, clutching a sword. The painted silver of her weapon glimmered in the afternoon light as the crew bustled on board, preparing the vessel for departure.

Painted in gold on the bow were the words *Murderous Lust*, and Arii found she instantly liked the ship.

From the main deck a woman gazed down at them. She wore the typical garb of a pirate, knee length boots and black pants weathered from salt air. Perched on her head was a wide-brimmed pirate hat that looked to have seen perhaps every inch of the sea. She wore a vest, arms left bare, her entire right arm covered with a story of tattoos. All she lacked to paint the final picture was a squawking parrot upon her shoulder. Arii also noticed that the woman was young, perhaps the same age as herself. And she was absolutely drop dead gorgeous – in a sea swept and harsh kind of way.

The woman leaned over the raising, lifting a hand in greeting. "Krepth, you son of a bitch – get your arse up here. We are losing precious daylight!"

Krepth motioned for the group to follow as they trailed up the boarding plank. Once on the deck, the woman threw her arms around him in a very enthusiastic show of affection. With her arm looped around his waist, Krepth turned to make introductions.

"This is Captain Valerie Gray, our very experienced guide for the voyage to the south."

Valerie grinned as she stepped forward – clutching her hat before sweeping into a bow. "Greetings, landlubbers. Welcome aboard the *Murderous Lust*."

Arii's eyes catalogued the woman, her hair a dirty red, her eyes a gentle hazel, her skin suntan and her nose dusted with a smattering of freckles. A breeze toyed with her hair as she brushed it back, the tips of her ears showing round and pierced with a few simple silver loops. Human, it seemed.

"Landlubbers?" whispered Luc from the corner of his mouth to Tikkani, who shrugged with a look that mirrored his confusion.

"Pirates, strange folk that's for sure," murmured Emerson, scratching his chin.

After Krepth's quick introduction to each of their little group, Valerie's eyes fixed on Elijah as the Shifter swept a hand his way, "And this is Eliverus Herington."

"Shut the front sails! You're *the* Eliverus Herington?"

"Are there any others?" drawled Elijah, his voice devoid of humour.

Valerie smirked at that, before bellowing over their heads, "Gunner! Show our guests to their cabins!" She eyed them all, "Now they ain't nothing like your fancy castle lodgings, but they'll do."

A man with sea-matted locks approached as Valerie chuckled, "You'll need to bunk with one another, though. There aren't many cabins but it's better than sleepin' on the poopdeck!" Valerie slapped a hand on Krepth's shoulder. "We have so much to catch up on, Krepthy. Come, get settled and I'll tell you all about our last haul from beyond The Boundless Sea!"

✦

"Ohhh Krepthy," sighed Arii mockingly, fluttering her lashes as they headed down the narrow, rickety steps towards their cabins. Never had she heard her friend referred to in such a way, and she latched onto the hilariousness with two eager hands.

Krepth dashed his fingers through his hair, teeth flashing in a wide, wicked grin, "Are you jealous, little Fury?"

"Gods no!" she chuckled, making to thump him on the arm before he slipped into a nearby cabin. Arii rolled her eyes before entering the cabin allocated to herself, Nem and Elijah. It was small, but had enough space for three sleeping bunks, a thin table, and an accompanying chair. At the end was a porthole with a view of the open sea.

"How is Emerson?" Arii asked, her expression turning to concern as she threw her pack on the bottom bunk and glanced at Nem. As soon as the ship had shown signs of movement, Emerson had turned as white as a ghost and complained he did not feel well. Shortly after, the boy was up on deck, leaning over the railing and hurling his lunch into the sea.

Nem sighed and tilted her head. "It's going to be an extra-long journey for the boy, unfortunately."

Arii winced in sympathy. How strange that the recruit, who grew up in a fishing community, had such a bad case of sea legs.

Tikkani on the other hand had found an instant friendship with Captain Valerie. The girls bounced back and forth insults that would have their mothers turning in their graves, joking and bantering like they were long lost friends. It seemed Tikkani had finally found someone who loved a good curse just as much as she did. Perhaps part of Emerson's sickness came from the fact that there was now two Tikkanis on board – and he had no way of escaping them lest he take a leap into the sea.

Elijah headed to the deck after offloading his pack, insistent that he help prepare the ship. Arii guessed he wanted to get busy, preoccupy himself under the constant stare of Valerie's crewmembers.

Once alone, Nem turned to Arii. "So, are we going to talk about… well, the last week of events?"

Arii stiffened, shooting her friend a glare. She was met with bright, narrowed eyes as Nem continued.

"That was a huge risk you took, heading back to Viridya with a theory that could have backfired. If Elijah was not who you thought he was, you could be a head upon a pike on the castle walls right now."

"Well, it's lucky that I'm always right."

Nem rolled her eyes, before her expression grew serious. "He has had a long time to hate magic, what makes you think he is willing to face Valdis, and oppose the people who took him in, and raised him no less?"

"He is here now, isn't he?" snapped Arii.

"From what I have witnessed, he is unwilling to use his magic."

"If he did not wish to be here, Nem, he would not be. Elijah is a Fae – you and I both know he would be back at the castle if that were his true wish."

Nem sighed, running a hand through her hair. She paced, and Arii felt a sense of trepidation before Nem paused before her. "He remains because of you."

"Don't be ridiculous."

"When have you known me to be ridiculous, Arii? I see the way he looks at you."

"He hates the Fae, Nem. *We* are Fae."

"If he truly hated Fae, we wouldn't be here, speaking about this, would we?" she reasoned gently.

Arii's mouth snapped shut, unable to formulate a retort that was not a filthy curse. She spun, busying her hands with something – anything. She could feel her friend's eyes on her back, like a weight pressing her shoulders inward, accompanying the shadow in the back of her thoughts since the invasion of her mind in Trader's Bay.

"The Fates were not wrong when they said to guard your heart, Arii. But they were wrong about everything else."

Arii slowly turned to face her friend, her expression twisting as Nem said, "Free thought and strong emotion do not make us weak – they only build a foundation to help us become stronger."

KREPTH

"Hoist those sails like your sister's panties, and get that anchor tied down tight! If I see a lick of movement, I'll lash you up in my quarters and spank your arse until we get to the south!" hollered Valerie as the crew whizzed around her, pulling on ropes and climbing ladders as she headed for the helm. "Weigh anchor and hoist the yardarm you jackanapes!"

Once at the wheel, she held onto her hat as a sharp sea breeze whipped its rim into a frenzy.

"That doesn't sound like a bad punishment to me," Krepth said as he leaned against the railing, his dark hair dancing around his face as the ship headed for open waters. Salt was most prominent to his sensitive nose, but there was also a promise of adventure on the salt air that had his insides quivering with anticipation, messing with his dislike for the dark male with silver eyes trained on his little sister. Ariiaya was not his sister by blood, but she was in every other right that mattered. She had no one else to protect her, and he knew she would argue she did not need protection. But that was what a big brother was for.

He did not trust Elijah. *Eliverus.* The King's lapdog. He wondered why the man continued with them on their journey. He was not shackled to Arii, he was not a prisoner – although Krepth would argue that he should be watched far more closely than he currently was. Was he gathering intelligence in order to slip from them and return to the gilded castle?

Valerie grinned widely, before casting her eyes over the crew once more. On the deck below, Emerson held onto the railing as he fought back another hurl, Luc by his side. Elijah and Quinn helped pull the ropes with Gunner, lending their strength as the vermillion sails snapped in the wind. Tikkani looped ropes against the railing, fully investing her attention on a couple of knots that Gunner had taught her quickly.

Valerie placed a spyglass to her eye, surveying the expanse of sea ahead of them, peeling Krepth's mind from his surveillance of the dark-haired Fae. "Looking good – perfect skies for smooth sailing."

Krepth could not agree more. He watched as gulls swooped ahead, riding the sea breeze as the ship coasted over water like polished glass. A bell tolled nearby, signalling their departure from Trader's Bay.

He turned his gaze back to Valerie. Despite Arii's mocking, Krepth kept his lips sealed to the fact that he and Valerie had no romantic history. They bantered, they flirted, but never had they shared a bed. Their friendship thrived off the possibility of a romp, but never crossed that line, for they enjoyed the dance they shared.

Would he sleep with Valerie if she offered? Perhaps.

But it was not Valerie whom he wanted.

Krepth had his fair share of women and preferred to keep things casual to allow his worries to be lost to the pleasures of carnal sin. The women he chose wished for the same, and that was the way he had always preferred it.

Until a silver-haired Fae female entered his life.

Nemesis had always been an enigma to him, her disposition stoic and her heart clearly guarded. He knew that was mostly due to her memory loss and the harshness of her upbringing, but he could not help be drawn to her even though all she showed him was the barbs upon her rose. She was beautiful and deadly, and more often than not he found himself wondering for his sanity in his pursuit of her. Some would argue that their history meant that they were friends, but their friendship was a strange, awkward one wrought with tension.

When it came to Arii, he could see some of the ice melt away from Nem's composure.

Perhaps that was why he liked her? Or perhaps a little bit of why.

Krepth sighed, and Valerie turned, a dimple flashing as she winked at him, and he let his roguish grin rise to cover any hint of deep thoughts.

"Let's head below deck and get some grub." Valerie said as she motioned to a crew member to take over the helm.

"Gods, I love it when you talk like that." Krepth laughed, trailing after the captain as they headed down below.

ARIIAYA

Below decks, the group came together over a dining table in the captain's personal quarters. The room was a decent size, enough to squeeze them in. Lanterns swayed above, throwing light across the room. Rolled up parchment, heavy chests and packed bookcases surrounded them, a heavy wooden desk and chair stationed under a line of wide windows.

Valerie had the cook whip up a feast of roasted beef with thick gravy, lightly charred carrots dipped in honey, steamed peas and potato mash. The crew dug in, impressed with the offering.

"So Eliverus, what have you been doing this past twenty years?" said Valerie casually, leaning back in her chair and tilting her ruby-encrusted glass of rum his way.

Elijah paused, before pushing his plate away. He looked uncomfortable as the table's attention turned to him. Under their gazes, he cleared his throat and spoke. "I was the King's personal bodyguard."

Valerie's jaw dropped. Gunner slammed his mug of rum on the tabletop as he exclaimed, "Pig's arse!"

Elijah's look became glacial. "No arses about it…"

Another female crew member leaned forward over her meal. Lyda's skin was a deeply tanned amber, her hair the colour of raven wings, sheered short on the sides and left long on top. Her eyes were striking and strange, one a deep emerald green, the other almost pitch black – making her gaze twice as intense as her fork hovered in Elijah's direction. She exclaimed around a mouthful of mash, "You were the King's lackey?! After what happened to your family, how could you stand to be in the presence of such a spoiled little brat?"

Arii felt the air crackle with pressure around Elijah, causing her hand to find his under the table. As soon as her fingers curled around his, the pressure paused, and his eyes slid to her. He gave her a look from the corner of his eye as he said evenly, "I had no memory of who I was until recently."

"And *they* never suspected who you were? Goes to show their level of awareness outside their own gilded lives." Lyda shoved her fork into the small mountain of potato on her plate. "Fascinating!"

Valerie's best friend, Lyda Wild, was reportedly known as 'The Wild One', according to the crew. An interesting moniker, thought Arii, just as the woman leaned her chair back, lifted her fork, and fired a glob of mash directly into Gunner's eye.

Gunner cursed, and Lyda howled with unhinged laughter, almost tipping backwards on her chair. Quinn grinned, lifting his own fork in excitement at the possibility of a food fight – only to be stopped by Luc's subtle hand on his arm as he shook his head.

"And all it took was a little Fury to open the floodgates before whisking you away from all you knew. I'll bet you've had a lot to process," continued Lyda, righting herself with a wide grin.

Elijah's eyes slid to Arii once more. "Yes, you could say that."

Captain Valerie gestured to her tattooed arm as she said, "Well you've got one hell of a journey ahead of you, Your Highness. By the end, you may just have a story worth tattooing."

The table turned to look at her, and Arii felt Elijah ease as the attention moved from him.

Tikkani asked, "That's some serious ink, what is your story?"

Valerie winked as she said, "Perhaps I'll tell you sometime. Krepthy knows all about it."

Krepth huffed a laugh from the other end of the table, his mouth full of peas. Valerie placed her boots on the table, causing Emerson to jerk in his seat nearby. "Got some more stories to tell you, Krepthy. Make sure you come to my rooms tonight with an open mind."

Arii swore she saw Nem stiffen in her peripheral vision, which did not make sense to her. Her fingers slid from Elijah's, feeling that the moment had passed. Though she would not admit it to anyone, it had felt strangely good to grasp his hand.

Her eyes lifted and she saw him offer a hint of an appreciative smile.

It had those damn butterflies taking flight in her stomach once more.

The group fell into a comfortable conversation, discussing Valerie's recent haul from a small island just off the west coast. Quinn insisted no such island existed, which resulted in Valerie clearing the table to slap down a huge canvas map. All the while, Tikkani watched the conversations with wide, awe-struck eyes.

"I think I'm going to be sick..." whispered a small voice. Emerson suddenly fled the room, hand over his mouth as the ship dipped over some particularly large waves. Luc remained in his seat, eyes shining with sympathy. "Poor Emer, he gets violently seasick." He swallowed. "I would follow him, but er... I'm afraid I'd be hurling over the side too if I hear – or smell – any hint of it."

"The boy needs to try some of this rum – that'll put hairs on his chest!" barked Gunner, knocking back the remainder of his tankard, gold rivulets running down the sides of his mouth.

Arii gazed after Emerson, the unfamiliar feeling of sympathy rising once more. The ship rolled then, causing them all to waver in their seats.

"I'd better go check on him," said Arii, rising from her seat as another wave jolted them.

"I'll join you," said Lyda, following as she headed above deck. "Feels like the sea is angry, no doubt there will be a storm shortly," she said as she headed for the main mast, clambering up the ladder towards the crow's nest.

Arii approached Emerson, leaning over the railing and quaking with heaving wretches. She rubbed the boy's back in soothing circles. When he turned his head, she saw his expression change from pathetic to surprised. "Arii?" he whispered.

"Hey, landlubber," she said, offering him a small smile.

He attempted a smile, before he was sick again.

Beyond, the sea raged – waves reaching for the grey skies as the *Murderous Lust* ducked over a large crest of water. Arii briefly wondered if Elijah could have been the cause of the sudden storm, but quickly dismissed it. He had not been angry at dinner, had he? It was hard to tell anymore, apart from a shift in the air. Elijah seemed to have a much better grasp on his control of late.

Perhaps it was only when he was alone with her that he let a little of that control slip.

The ship heaved violently, and Arii gripped the railing, one hand holding Emerson. Water rose and lashed across the deck as Lyda yelled from above, "Storm's coming, get below decks!"

Arii tried to pull Emerson back from the rails, but found the boy was holding on with both hands –so tightly his knuckles were bone white.

Another wave of water smashed against the hull. Arii could hear Tikkani's voice over the roaring of the waves as their friends emerged on deck. Crewmembers dashed about, preparing for the storm.

"Emerson! Arii!"

Arii attempted to dislodge the boy from his death hold on the railing as spray soaked them. "Come on Emer, let's get you bellow de–"

Water flew across the deck, liquid fingers grasping their boots like a vengeful water spirit, and Arii felt the deck slide from beneath her feet.

"EMERSON!" screamed Tikkani and Luc in unison, just as another wave crashed over them, tearing Arii and Emerson from the deck and into the ocean.

LYDA

CHAPTER NINE

ELIJAH

"Oh Gods, Emerson! EMERSON!" wailed Tikkani as she ran for the deck. Elijah's arms came around the girl, and she struggled madly, her hair whipping around her as he pulled her back to cover.

"Tikkani!" growled Elijah as the girl flailed, her eyes wild. Luc had the same thought, blindly attempting a dash towards the deck – only to be stopped by Krepth. The young man's limb flailed, but Krepth's hold was firm.

"Let me go!" Luc yelled, just as Tikkani screamed, "He can't swim!"

Elijah's teeth clenched as Lyda bellowed from the crow's nest. "Overboard, two bodies overboard!"

Two bodies…

Arii.

He was swift, pressing Tikkani into Nem's arms as she emerged behind them. He bolted onto the sopping deck as the wind droned like an angry beast and he felt the chaos of the sea far beneath his feet. The storm had come on quick, and they were by now a good couple of hours out to sea.

Captain Valerie pushed past the group, heading for the helm to take control of the ship while bellowing orders to her crew. "Fix the rigging, you rusty ingrates – ensure all loads are strapped down tight or I'll cleave you all to the brisket!"

Elijah's eyes raked the raging sea below, searching for any sign of Arii and Emerson as he removed his cloak. Panic pinched his insides, fearing the longer they were out in the tempest, the harder it would be to bring them back aboard.

"You can't go in there!" yelled Krepth over the roar of the wind as Tikkani and Luc clutched each other within the cover.

"The fuck I can't! Arii and Emerson are down there!" Elijah bellowed, jerking away angrily as Krepth grasped his arm. "Don't touch me!" he snarled.

"Something is approaching, Cap'n!" yelled Lyda from above, pointing to the raging sea beyond. "From the western side!"

Eyes widening, Elijah saw two heads break the surface.

Arii and Emerson, bobbing just above the raging surf.

Behind them, a colossal shadow loomed beneath the waves.

Elijah's yell of warning was lost to a boom of thunder.

ARIIAYA

Air shot down her throat as Arii's head broke the surface, gasping and spluttering as salt water assaulted her from all sides. She bobbed, her head jerking around to see the *Murderous Lust* in the distance, snapping back to see Emerson's head slip below the water a few feet away.

"Emerson!" she yelled, hands spearing through the waves as she swam for him, inhaling a breath and diving. Salt stung her eyes as she kicked towards his descending form, his exhaustion apparent as his limbs kicked feebly. Her hands clutched his arm, dragging him swiftly towards the surface.

As they gulped down air, Arii could hear voices from the ship – the cadence of their calls wild and urgent, as if in warning.

Before she could think, the water beneath them darkened, and she heard Emerson's wail of fear as a riot of bubbles danced on the surface, like a school of hungry, carnivorous fish swarming about them.

Oh, this was not good.

Emerson began to panic, clutching at her shoulders. "Arii, I can't… I can't swim!"

Oh, this was getting better.

"Hold on to me!" she yelled, coughing as she took in a mouthful of sea water, but yanking the boy as she began swimming awkwardly back towards the ship.

And then the water erupted around them.

Arii felt a sold mass hit her from below as something emerged from the depths, shooting them out of the sea. Emerson screamed, and she grabbed his clothing as they slid on a sodden platform of dark emerald scales. He jerked to a halt, dangling over the edge of a massive snout.

Emerson twisted, coming face to face with a jaw full of teeth as the creature breathed a gush of hot breath, causing his eyes to snap shut.

Arii's head turned to see two large golden eyes, irises shrinking to narrow slits as the beast's growl reverberated beneath her.

Sea drake.

She let thoughts flee the chaos of her mind and inhaled a swift breath as Emerson yelled, "ARII!"

On the exhale, his tunic slipped between her fingers as she let Emerson fall.

The boy screamed, dropping several feet before hitting the water. Arii's lips curled back as she snarled right into the drake's eyes before she spun and leaped into the sea in Emerson's wake.

ELIJAH

"Sea drakes, two of them!" bellowed Lyda as another of the creatures breached the surface, scales glittering and long serpent bodies thrashing against the ship's hull. The crew flew about the vessel in a frenzy as Valerie yelled, "Ready the cannons!"

Quinn sprinted across the deck, skidding to pick up a lead ball and following Gunner to the cannons as he jerked open the heavy latch.

Elijah discarded his sword belt, his attention only partially on them as Tikkani flailed wildly, her movements frantic with worry as she screamed her brother's name.

Nem twisted the elf to face her and cracked her palm across the girl's face. It was harsh, but the Fury would not be able to protect her or Luc – or any of them – in their hysterical state. Tikkani's head snapped to the side, her hand clutching her cheek in shock.

"Help the crew! We will save your brother!"

Luc nodded wildly, face leached with worry as he pulled Tikkani towards the crew's commotion.

"We are no help to them back here, Tikk!" he called. As if in a daze, the girl followed.

Nem dashed to Krepth as he grabbed Elijah again, who threw a punch at the Shifter's head. Krepth ducked, his grip never faltering as Elijah struggled.

"Damn you, let me go!" he roared.

"You won't be any use in the water alongside them–" Another fist flew by his head as Krepth dodged. Elijah knew inside he was panicking, his blows not as precise as normal, fortunately for the Shifter.

The ship jerked, and a terrible roar sounded from above. They looked up just in time to see the tip of a tail – before it smashed against the side of the ship. They all stumbled as the *Lust* tipped dangerously, shards of a snapped mast raining around them. The storm had picked up in earnest now, cool rain hitting the deck like marbles.

"You need to use your magic!" bellowed Krepth.

Crash.

Ropes snapped and splinters flew. Above them a colossal head appeared, serpentine and glittering with deep emerald scales. Seaweed dangled from between its serrated teeth as the sea drake hissed. If the beast were not threatening their lives, Elijah would have thought the animal majestic and beautiful, in a terrifying way.

His face twisted with anguish. "I… I can't!"

Below, he could just hear Arii and Emerson's yells. He turned to face the beast as it roared, the air around them sparking with energy. His shoulders shook, his silver eyes wide as he stared up. He doubted himself, afraid that this power boiling inside him would explode forth and disintegrate them all.

Magic was evil, chaotic, unpredictable. Ever since he'd destroyed the throne room, he had felt unstable – physically and mentally as he battled the newly unleased beast. He hardly knew himself anymore yet also felt like he'd found a long-lost friend.

Nem suddenly flew forward, her hand grasping his. He jerked at the contact, eyes snapping to hers.

"Save them, Elijah! You can do this." The determination... the hope in her eyes had him sucking in a breath. He didn't know her well, but enough to know that she would be diving into those waves to save her friend if she thought there was a chance.

There were no other options.

He stared at her, hair whipping around his face before his expression changed.

Then, Elijah turned and sprinted towards the front of the ship.

ARIIAYA

Arii's legs kicked wildly as she struggled to keep herself and Emerson above the rolling waves. There were times when the water pulled them under, and she wondered if they would surface again, her eyes stinging and her limbs growing numb from the cold. She would not let Emerson die – she would not let any of them die. Not like this. They had trusted her enough to follow on this quest laced with peril, to help in any way possible.

'They follow you out of friendship. Pity they will all die.'

The voice returned with a dark caress and sharp teeth.

It could not end like this.

She would not allow it.

The telepath – whoever she was – sure knew when to pop into her mind. Arii pushed back, earning her nothing but laughter. Then suddenly the wraith retreated, taking some of Arii's energy with her.

Above them, one of the monstrous sea drakes roared as it smashed its tail against the *Murderous Lust*, tipping it dangerously. Her heart threatened to stop, her stomach clenching in tight knots that made her efforts to remain afloat much harder. Everyone she cared about was on that ship, and it was minutes away from capsizing.

Arii lifted a hand above the water and threw a ball of magic at the animal's neck.

Then another.

And another.

The magic was a tiny snap against its scales, but the beast's head slowly turned in her direction. She was sure the beast was glaring, if that were possible.

Now what, genius?

Arii clenched her teeth hard and Emerson harder as the serpent's jaws opened wide and it let out a screech, spraying water like needles against her exposed skin. It began to move in their direction.

Think. THINK!

She lifted her hand again, magic spluttering to life on her palm as she shook sodden hair from her eyes.

Suddenly a massive burst of energy snapped against the sea drake's head and it jerked, scales dislodging from its hide and showering the ocean surface like falling coins in the dim light. Then another burst of magic had the serpent's head twisting back towards the ship just as her own magic spluttered out.

Arii and Emerson made collective sounds of relief, elation filling Arii's chest as she saw Elijah up on deck.

She would have known his tall, dark-haired form anywhere.

Throwing out a hand, he sent another burst of magic against the beast's neck, causing it to bellow with anger. Elijah's arms snapped out, his face twisted in a snarl as his magic erupted around the sea creature, haphazard spears of crackling blue energy unlike anything Arii had seen before.

This was his magic. Wild, untamed, powerful… dangerous. And this without a lick of training.

The serpent let out a long, enraged cry. Suddenly a second beast broke the surface near the ship and Elijah changed trajectory as magic thundered to life upon his palms – his hand flying to shoot a blast of power, causing the second creature to jerk back.

His power was incredible, his hits random and uncoordinated. Every single eye on that ship watched on in shock, fascination, and awe. He held the sea beasts at bay, but he would not be able to keep this up for long. Magic had limits, and Arii had no idea when he would hit his.

From the helm, Captain Valerie called over the crashing ocean, "Keep them distracted, Eliverus. I'm turning this baby on its side!"

Thunder boomed overhead, followed by a snap of lightning – searing the sky and highlighting the chaos. One serpent broke from the surface, spearing at the ship. Elijah threw up a hand, magic erupting and halting the thing in its tracks. Sparks from his power caused fires to erupt, shooting across the sea and devouring the rum escaping from holed barrels in the hull of the *Lust*. Liquid fire fell from the beast's hide, dripping like golden starlight upon the dark surface of the sea.

Valerie threw her weight into spinning the wheel and the ship began to turn sharply. The *Murderous Lust* spun, the crew on board holding on for dear life as the vessel turned, as fast as a vessel of its size could – diving swiftly until its right side faced the creatures.

Shutters lifted and cannons snapped forward.

"FIRE!"

Deafening shots of gold lit up the grey as every cannon on board erupted. The beasts screeched, cannonballs hitting their mark as plumes of blood misted in the open air. Tikkani wailed, pressing her hands over her ears as Luc and Quinn plugged their own ears with their fingers.

"Eat lead you bastards!" roared Valerie, slamming her fist against the wheel as the creatures' pained cries split the air. Her head whipped to a crewman, drenched red hair sticking to her face as she yelled, "Load again!"

The crew were relentless, swiftly re-loading the cannons with trained efficiency. Lyda cackled from the crow's nest, punching the air to the chorus of serpentine screams.

One of the beasts had fared better than the other, head dipping towards the ship – towards the helm where Elijah stood. Nem was swiftly beside Elijah, throwing her hands up. Her magic spun around the burning rum that raged upon the waves, and with a jerk of her wrists the fire rose and hit the closest creature in the eyes. Her distraction worked momentarily.

The captain's yell split the air once more.

"FIRE!"

The second volley thundered the air, fire erupting as cannonballs sailed between ship and beasts.

Slowly, the sea drakes began to retreat with sounds of pain, slipping beneath the waves.

Arii watched it all, legs beating the waves despite turning numb a while ago. She had watched the whole thing, every second that Elijah stood on the deck, arms outstretched as the air raged with his power. Using his magic, the magic he had refused to touch for so long.

He had done it. They had done it.

Her lips curled as she heaved Emerson's head above the surface, feeling an unfamiliar flame of pride flicker in her chest. Pride, and relief that the attack was over.

She knew he could do it.

And gods, it had been spectacular.

Her eyes lifted to a speck in the sky – a bird – as it dipped towards them, and realised it was Quinn. He dropped a line of rope, and Arii clutched for it desperately. Quickly she looped the noose around Emerson's middle, pulling the knot tight. The boy was exhausted, his head barely above water as she clutched his cheeks – forcing him to look at her. "You need to paddle, Emerson! Keep your head above the waves."

Quinn squawked above them, looping circles as if crazed. His cries pierced her ears with a sense of urgency. The rope pulled, and Arii felt relief as they began to head back to the ship. Her head bobbed, hair in her eyes – stinging and red rimmed from the salt water as she held on.

Then something grabbed hold of her boot and pulled her violently beneath the waves.

Water speared down her throat as she was dragged deeper and deeper under the sea.

Arii's body jerked, her eyes wide as a glitter of scales shimmered around her, followed by drifting plumes of crimson.

Blood.

She floated in the centre of a sparkling, liquid obsidian world, surrounded by flashing scales, her heart a riot in her chest as she fought against panic. Teeth flashed, and she jerked as the mass flew past, sending her body spiralling out of control. Instinct took over, and she brought up her leg, snatching the dagger from her boot as the sea drake turned her way again. Air bunched in her cheeks as Arii threw a punch of magic behind her to propel herself at the shadow, face twisting with rage as she thrust the dagger into the sea drake's eye.

As the shadow screamed past, a massive fin slammed against her guts, sending her spinning wildly once more. She choked, her fingers losing grip of the knife as it dropped into the abyss below. All she could see was darkness, clouded red with thousands of tiny glimmering bubbles. Salt water assaulted her eyes and flew up her nose, and she choked again.

So, this was it then. After all she had been through – she was to die right here, drowning and falling into the darkness of a sea so boundless it had no end in sight.

At least she had seen Elijah finally using his magic, and she felt a strange peace settle over her. He would see that magic could be used for good, could be used to defend others against danger. He had already seen how it could heal and change lives. She hoped what he had seen so far could outweigh the bad, and that he realised how he could use his power to bring change to a land in such desperate need of hope.

Despite his brooding nature, his reluctance, his fear – Arii knew Elijah had a good heart.

A strong heart. The heart of a King.

Thoughts of his face fluttered before her eyes as she sank into the void, bubbles trailing in her wake, her limbs drifting aimlessly. She remembered his gentle touch as they kissed at the School of Fate, the way he whispered her name like a prayer and a curse. He had challenged her to look beyond what she could see in front of her.

He had changed her.

He made her want to be better, to look for a future. He made her want to live in a world filled with colour.

If this was how things should end for her, then she took comfort in the fact that she may have helped just a little bit.

Above, a shockwave rippled against the shimmering blue, and suddenly a form was spearing through the water, straight for her. Her lips parted, her lungs giving out just as Elijah's features came into focus above her. Grasping her face, he pressed his lips to hers. Air rushed into her lungs, causing her body to jerk, filling her with lifesaving air.

Elijah was giving her his air.

Saving her life.

Arii's hands grasped his shoulders, and they floated together in the middle of a dark, ominous world – nothing but the feel of him under her fingers, the pressure of his lips on her own as he forced his breath into her lungs. His grip was almost painful, his arm snaking around her middle as their lips broke apart and he jerked on the rope tied around his waist.

As they broke the surface, Arii gasped loudly, gulping down air. Her vision darkened around the edges, her limbs numb with exhaustion. Elijah's face bobbed before hers, his hair smoothed back, water glistening in the short, dark hairs of his beard. She could see his lips moving – but his words drifted away on a howling wind.

The last thing she felt was his arms securely around her as she was lost to the darkness.

CHAPTER TEN

ELIJAH

"I've removed as much water from her lungs as I could. She will need to rest but I'm sure she will wake in no time," Nem looked across from Arii's sleeping form to Elijah, seated nearby. "She's stubborn. So much so that even death knows she's not done with this world."

Elijah's eyes did not leave Arii's face. He had not left her side since they hauled her, limp and unconscious from the sea, refusing to change out of his sodden clothing until Nem threatened to cut the cloth from him herself – with or without his permission. Reluctantly he had changed, but he did not dally long before he was back in the room, watching while Nem's healing touch fluttered over Arii's still, pale body.

Nem had muttered about how much of a pain in the arse he was, and no wonder Arii liked him so much. Her words, whether he was meant to overhear them or not, had blood rushing to his cheeks and neck. Arii always seemed to be one tick away from shoving a blade through his chest, and the woman saw *that* as fondness for him? He shuddered to imagine what Arii might do if she designated someone as an enemy.

Now dressed in dark cloth pants and an off-white tunic, Elijah looked and – admittedly – felt like completely different man. Salt-wind-swept hair, cheeks tinged pink and a glimmer in his eyes. He knew that Nem could see a change, but he did not care. He felt changed. Not only because he had almost lost two people who, strangely enough, he was beginning to consider his friends, but he had tapped into the magical side of himself that had lain dormant for the majority of his life.

He was changed whether he liked it or not.

Gods, he had been so close to losing her.

They *all* had been.

Elijah was observant, partly by nature, and partly as a soldier and guard. He saw the way the recruits acted around Arii, hesitant as if creeping around a sleeping bear – yet energised as if her very presence had them feeling safe enough to let their walls down.

The same could be said for her best friend, Nemesis, who wore a cold mask of indifference most of the time, but it softened when Arii's flame was near. There was an unspoken respect between them, which told Elijah they had been through a lot.

Then there was Krepth. Yes, he was a hot-headed ass, but he saw a brotherly love there that had him reining in his anger when Krepth insulted him. He was protecting her, and Elijah could not blame him.

He would do the exact same for his own sister.

Thoughts of the dark-haired, wide-eyed girl came to mind – ghosts of memories past that he tried desperately to bring into focus. What he did remember of Ghila was that she was quiet and softly spoken, yet when she spoke, it was for a reason, and those words were measured and eloquent. She was just like their mother. All grace, all nobility – despite her tender age, he knew she would have made an incredible duchess. His thoughts lingered around a memory of her singing – her voice like a haunting song. He recalled her delicate fingers flecked with paint, smiling gently as they painted portraits together in the shade of a willow tree. They had shared a passion for art.

Grief fingered at his gut, a loss he didn't realise he felt so deeply, from such fleeting memories.

Krepth paused in the doorway, clearing his throat and casting his green eyes over Arii before they slid to Elijah. Elijah expected a smart-arse remark from the Shifter, and he was sure Nem did too by the slight stiffening of her shoulders, but he surprised them both by saying gently, "You saved us today, mate. Thanks."

Nem's brows rose, and he could not help the light twitch of his mouth that betrayed his own surprise, before offering Krepth an incline of his head. As quickly as he had appeared, though, Krepth was gone.

Elijah knew that gratitude would have been hard for the stubborn male.

"He's right. You put aside your fear to save us today. If not for you, we would probably be at the bottom of the ocean." Elijah's expression softened ever so slightly as Nem continued, "If they hadn't been trying to rip our ship apart, I'd say those sea drakes were beautiful."

"They were," Elijah agreed, "and to tell you the truth, I had believed their existence was myth and myth alone. Now I feel a fool for thinking our journey would be smooth sailing."

She flashed him a small grin, and he returned it with his own. "Nice play on words."

"Thank you."

Nem slowly stood, before dropping a hand to the man's shoulder. "The entire journey is bound to be riddled with obstacles, but one of those has already been dealt with. You used your magic, and honestly, I thought *that* would have been the greatest one."

"Well, the situation forced me into it," he grumbled.

"Be that as it may, we are all grateful to you, Elijah." With a gentle squeeze, the Fury slipped from the room – the soft click of the door sounding in her wake.

Elijah shifted to prop his elbows on his knees, before resting his forehead against his palms.

When he had stood on the deck of the *Murderous Lust* against the sea drakes, he had reached into a part of himself which he had been fearful of touching for as long as he could remember, a part of him that was always there, just beneath the surface. He had no idea what he was doing, but when he reached down into the rippling silver pool and grasped the power between his fingers, the rest seemed to come naturally. It could have been the adrenaline, the fear for Arii and Emerson in the dark sea below them, or the crew of innocent people around him, but as he threw that charged power in the beasts' direction, Elijah had felt a thrill unlike anything he had ever felt before.

It had felt good, like stretching a tight muscle he did not know needed stretching.

He would not admit that to anyone, and definitely not to Arii. He could imagine the smirk on her face, her hands on her hips as she exclaimed a cavalier *told you so.*

He had been so close to losing her. And until that moment he had not realised how much he did not *want* that to happen.

How far he had drifted in the space of only a few weeks.

Their conversation as they had stood in her childhood home only days ago returned to his mind.

"If not for the orders, if you had the choice, would you still have done it?"

"Yes."

That single word he had uttered in the heat of the moment had become the single word he had regretted ever since. He had wanted to inflict pain, his own inner demons reaching out for someone to blame for the hurt and confusion he felt inside. He had never regretted a moment more than that one, the weight of his words like a dark mass in his chest. It wasn't true, and she had almost died thinking he wished that upon her and her kind.

Their kind.

While in the service of the King, he had followed orders blindly, blanketing his ears to the whispers of doubt that rose after every mission. He had wanted was to prove that he was a loyal soldier, a man with purpose. But truly, in his heart he was lost. With every order, every stroke of his sword, the darkness yawned wider, threatening to swallow him whole.

Elijah's eyes lifted from his callused palms to look at Arii, so peaceful on the small cot. Without her scowl, without her cocky grin, sharp tongue and even sharper blades, she seemed like any other human woman. But she was not.

She was a Fae. Strong, fearless, resilient, foul mouthed and incredible.

She challenged him, and an undiscovered part of him was thrilled by that, as if he were searching for someone like her all along but hadn't truly realised it.

He realised then that he did not want her any other way.

ARIIAYA

Arii began to stir, lashes fluttering as she regained consciousness. Vision blurring, she lifted her hands to paw her stinging eyes, stifling a cough as she tasted salt on her tongue. She remembered filtered, musky darkness all around her, the drone of her eardrums as they compressed beneath the water, liquid shooting up her nose as she drowned.

And then he was there, breathing life into her lungs.

Elijah.

"We have *got* to stop meeting like this," she forced past her parched lips, wincing as new pains began to bloom over her body. As her vision focused and consciousness fully took hold, Elijah moved to sit on the end of the narrow cot, his intense stare focused on her.

His lips twitched in a small smile.

Gods, she wanted to see that smile more often, preferring it over a scowl.

"Only *you* would take on two sea drakes while trying to save a friend from drowning. Are you mad?"

"I think you know the answer to that question, Elijah."

A knowing smile reached his eyes then, and she had to keep from melting into the cot. Before he could agree that she indeed possessed qualities of madness, she faltered and whispered, "Emerson?"

"He's fine, shaken… but fine. Tikkani and Luc are with him."

"Thank fu–" She froze, eyes widening as they fixed on him fully. "You used your magic!"

Elijah shifted, his expression turning uncomfortable. "Yes."

"You saved me, you saved *all* of us."

"No, Captain Valerie's quick thinking saved us – I just provided a distraction."

"Elijah–"

He leaned forward; his silver eyes dark as he said, "I had no idea what I was doing, for all we know I could have been simply tickling the bellies of those beasts."

Arii's laugh quickly turned into a snort. "Oh, you were definitely doing damage. If you learned to control your magic, I think you could have turned those overgrown sea snakes into fish food."

His head tilted slightly, and a strange look passed over his face. Arii suddenly felt self-conscious under his heavy gaze. "What?" she asked gently.

Elijah's face was dead serious as he said, "I almost lost you."

Cue the crazy stomach butterflies.

"I'm surprised you didn't let them eat me… one less thorn in your side," she said, shifting as heat bloomed at his words.

Elijah's look turning stormy as he leaned toward her, "I need you, Arii."

His words had her pausing, her eyes dropping to his mouth, his lips that had saved her. Arii had never needed saving before, had never *wanted* saving. Why was it that he continued to do so – despite all the trouble she caused him? She swallowed audibly; her attention drifted back up to his eyes. He hated her kind, had admitted so back in Evergrave. Spindly fingers of doubt held on to that thought, no matter how hard she tried to send it away.

Elijah's hand lifted to brush a damp lock of hair behind her pointed ear, his fingertips caressing her cheek as he murmured, "Who will teach me to control my magic?" he added. Breath locked in her throat, making it difficult to speak.

Oh, his magic… *right.*

Shivers shot down her spine at his touch, at the fire that skimmed along her skin. Her fingers lifted to take his hand, to study his strong fingers. Her fingertips glided over his palm as she spoke. "So… now you're willing to learn?"

"I might be open to it, yes," he whispered, his attention on her fingers as they danced along his palm to his wrist. She could feel the power thrumming beneath his skin, his magic fluttering restlessly underneath her fingers as her eyes lifted to his face. He was still reluctant to admit what he was, the colossal potential he wielded, but she felt a renewed sense of purpose to help him get there, despite what he had admitted in Evergrave. She would confront him about it again, but for now – while he was looking at her like this – she decided that would be a conversation for another time. Perhaps a time that involved some wine. Lots of wine.

She felt the beginnings of confidence, a golden pinprick of light against the darkness. His words hinted that he was not as immovable in his beliefs as she had first thought.

"I won't go easy on you," she whispered, her voice coming out gentler than she had intended.

"I wouldn't want you to, nor would I expect you to."

His voice was as quiet as her own as she drew his fingers to her mouth without thought, touching the tips to her lips. The air around them hummed, and she could feel a shift in the salty fibres as the ship groaned beneath them. Gently, his index finger brushed the bow of her lips, and Arii felt heat begin to pool in her stomach.

Not to mention other places, too.

Alone, they were finally *alone*.

He stroked his thumb over her bottom lip, and she saw his eyes darken like the sea beneath them. Her breath stroked his thumb as she rasped, "Water?"

Elijah was still for a moment, staring at her mouth before snapping out of his trance. Letting his hand drop, he rose to pour her a cup of water.

For a time, the only sounds were the crashing of waves against the hull, the creak and moan of the wooden structure around them and the thud of boots above. Voices sounded as the crew went about repairing the damage to the *Lust*, Captain Valerie's barked orders a muffled sonance. Arii surveyed Elijah's broad back before he returned to hand her a banged-up pewter cup.

"Thank you," she saluted with the cup, "and thank you for saving my life – again."

His lips twitched in the hint of a smile, but his eyes remained dark. "I guess you can call us even."

She downed the water quickly, her throat completely and utterly parched. "No, I'm pretty sure you have saved me three times now." She began lifting fingers as she spoke, "The bandits on the road, Bonemire and the sea drakes."

He quirked a brow at her, taking the cup for a refill. "I didn't save you on the road. You were more than capable in getting yourself out of that situation… I just did not know it then."

"True, true."

She downed another offering before handing it back to him with a thankful smile. She paused. "Wait, when did I save you?"

Elijah took a seat on the bed once more, his fingers curling around the cup as he stared into the trembling liquid. "In Viridya… when I destroyed the throne room and you tossed us from the waterfall." He paused to glare at her sideways. "Perhaps that reckless act cancels out your rescue attempt, which means I am two notches above you on the tally."

"Come off it!" she chuckled.

He smiled, before his expression turned to utter calm. "Perhaps you have been saving me every day since we met. I just didn't realise it until now."

Arii's smiled faded as Elijah leaned toward her, his eyes glowing in the murky light from the small window. His lips brushed hers, and she felt the beast rising under her skin once more. Her body, her lips, responded immediately. Slowly, *oh so slowly*, his hand slid to cup her nape as he brought her head forward.

Like the night at the School of Fate, his lips brushed hers delicately – almost as though he was afraid to take the leap. Was he afraid? Or was he hesitant because, just like last time, she was recovering from another near-death experience?

Arii's fingers lifted to slide into his hair, tugging at the thick strands as his scent washed over her. Sea salt, mild soap, and a rogue spiciness that she was coming to know was just *him*. Fire ignited in her stomach, slithering to her nerve endings as she pressed forward, deepening their kiss – opening her mouth to him. Weeks of pent-up frustration and emotion began to surface, snatching her breath as she brought her other hand to his bicep, nails digging into the fabric of his shirt. Beneath her fingers, his muscles tensed.

Everything was building, everything she currently felt and had been feeling for weeks. The need, it was like an insatiable ripple in a river before a raging waterfall. Arii had known for a long time that she wanted Elijah, truly wanted him since the night he had helped her slay the bandits on the road. Much of their time early on was filled with hot bickering, but despite the fact that she could not see his face, his voice and deadly grace alone had her spine tingling and her toes curling, speaking to the beast beneath her skin.

She had to hold back with Lorch, had felt there was an itch that could not be scratched, no matter how hard she tried. She did not regret sleeping with Lorch, *gods no*, not for a moment. But she did regret the pain in his eyes the last time she saw him.

What she had felt with Lorch was the beginning, a tiny gap in the gates holding back her emotions.

Now, perhaps she could open those gates a bit wider, but as that thought manifested, she also felt hesitation. Old habits had her internally withdrawing, unsure of how she was supposed to feel inside since she had suppressed her feelings for so long.

Even now, as Elijah kissed her like she was made of glass, his comments from Evergrave lingered in the shadows of her memory. No matter how much she trusted her gut feeling that the venom in his words did not match the uncertainty in his eyes, she couldn't shake the little fingers of doubt that pricked her.

Despite that, in this moment, she wanted him.

She pressed closer, deepening their kiss and allowing the thin sheets covering her to fall. Someone had changed her from her sodden clothing and into a cotton shift. Despite her state of undress and the lightness in her head, she pressed her position – their lips never parting as she pushed Elijah back against the wall next to the cot, propping herself on his lap. Beneath her, she felt his body shudder as his hands buried in her hair, and she braced her hands against his broad chest. She caught his bottom lip between her teeth and heard his sharp intake of breath.

"Arii, you need to rest..." he rumbled, his voice tinged with gentle disapproval.

"Outside of the castle, you no longer tell me what to do, Master Wolfe. Besides..." she nipped his lip, "...you started it."

She pressed her weight against him, and a small groan escaped him. It clawed at her insides, the Fae within her rising and her pulse quickening. His hand slid to her lower back, and she skimmed her lips against his once again.

"You said you needed me..." she dipped her head to his neck, placing a gentle kiss just below the lobe of one delicately pointed ear. She felt him stir against her, felt the hardness of him press against her inner thigh as he groaned again. That sound alone almost had her spiralling, let alone the feeling of him so close to where she wanted him.

She circled her hips, the motion possessively wanton, stoking the fire within them both.

The lanterns above flickered and swayed, before the entire ship quaked around them. His hand moved to grip her upper thigh, fingers skimming the exposed skin, just below the hem of her sleeping shift.

Gods, she wanted his fingers higher – wanted them all over her body. He was so powerful, not just his body but the magic he harboured inside. It made her quake, not with fear, but with incredible, incomprehensible need.

"Arii..." he murmured, the tone of his voice causing her to gently pull back to look at him.

Her breath left her lungs, just like she was once again being dragged under the sea as she stared into his eyes, dark with desire yet glowing from within. She could hear the suppression in his voice, feel his muscles bunching under her fingers as he wrestled with himself.

He wanted her, just as much as she wanted him and that knowledge had her straightening her spine as a smile played at her lips.

She felt… powerful. Desired. Needed.

She doubted he needed her like she needed him though – like a dry field in need of rain, like life giving air to her lungs. Within the turmoil of her mind, he was a beacon of light, showing her the way forward. His destiny also gave her purpose, keeping her from returning to the emotionless shell she once was. How had the land's most deadly assassin changed so much in such a short amount of time? Perhaps Nem was correct, and Fae were not supposed to suppress their emotions. She *had* felt stronger lately, stronger with the knowledge that she now had others to guide and protect, and it was not just herself against the world.

Suddenly Elijah flipped her on her back, bed springs squeaking beneath as his weight pressed upon her. His lips were on hers again, and this time they were rough, claiming and hungry. Her nails skimmed under his tunic, pulling it free from his britches, clutching at the ragged ridges of the scars on his back as he pushed against her more urgently. She groaned into his mouth, and he swallowed the sound as if it were doused in honey.

His head ducked to her neck, his canines skimming the sensitive skin there, a hot sigh dancing across her collarbone.

"Elijah," she whispered, her breath a swift hiss. He was all around her, the air she breathed, the fire in her veins. The room shook as he sucked her skin, causing a low moan to roll from her lips, her hips undulating in kind.

Whatever this was, whatever was causing the inferno storming within her, could only be answered by him and no other, she realised.

Elijah exhaled a shuddering breath, then moved aside to gaze down at her, his chest rising and falling just as rapidly as hers. He seemed to be waiting for something, frowning slightly as he studied her face.

The ship shuddered again, groaned and dipped, just as Elijah inhaled another sharp breath. Sweat had begun to bloom on his brow.

Was he the cause of the quaking ship?

Above them, Captain Valerie was bellowing at her crew to find the cause of the disturbance, swearing that if there were more sea drakes she would leap into the sea and wrestle them herself. They had only known the woman a day but Arii felt her words – although maniacal – were somewhat serious.

Blowing out a breath, Arii's swollen lips began a sultry smile, thinking it best to distract him lest they end up sinking into the sea – as much as it pained her to be the one to stall their heated moment.

"Do you know what the mead in Trader's Bay and making love in a boat have in common?"

Elijah blinked, eyes aglow, throat working on a swallow as he murmured, "What?"

"They're both fucking close to water."

Slowly, the quaking began to ease as Elijah blew out a shuddering breath – her crude joke spearing through the haze of their desire. The ship subsided to gently rocking, and the yelling from above abated. After a few moments, he spoke, but his words dropped away at her triumphant smile, "You are…"

"Crude? Vulgar? Sexy? So incredibly tantalizing that I could make you sink this boat without realising it? Yes… yes, I know."

Perhaps one day they would indeed cause mountains and seas to shake with their ecstasy.

Literally.

But not today.

He swallowed thickly as she shifted to her knees, pressing a hand to his chest as her lips brushed his jaw line, and then settled against his lips once more as she whispered, "As much as I want… *this*, I don't think we should risk the entire ship's crew…"

Elijah's hand cupped her cheek as he blew out another shaky breath, "I think that is wise…"

She could have sworn she heard pain in his deep voice – either pain that they had stopped or that he now understood he could wipe out a ship full of people with barely a thought.

She shifted from his lap to lean back against the pillows of her cot.

"Not just a pretty face," she whispered, only a little of her own pain showing. Deep inside, though, she felt that pain in her soul. She was burning from within, every inch of her tingling with unsated desire.

Alas, it was not their time *now*, either.

Thank the Gods, because the door flew open, crashing against the wall as Krepth stepped into the room, eyes narrowed and expression utterly livid.

CHAPTER ELEVEN

ARIIAYA

"Are you *trying* to capsize us?" Krepth thundered. He stopped short, head tilting and nose twitching in a way that reminded her of his wolf form, a predator scenting prey. Then his eyes narrowed, and his gaze darted to Arii.

The Shifter's acute sense of smell told him what words would not, as he scented the sea salt mixed with desire in the air.

Ah shit.

As Elijah stood from the bed, Krepth was before him in a second – his hands grasping Elijah's tunic, yanking him up as he snarled in his face, "Keep your traitorous hands *off* her!"

"Krepth!" cried Arii, leaping up from the bed.

Krepth slammed Elijah against the nearby wall, his fury palpable. Elijah snarled himself as he retaliated, throwing his arms up to dislodge the Shifter's grip. Arii knew where this was headed and she slid between them, her hand flying up to press against their chests as the two males bared their teeth like dogs fighting over the last strip of meat on the carcass.

The ship moaned beneath them, and she felt that now familiar shifting weight upon the air, a crackle, snap and shudder that signalled Elijah's power.

"Are you mad?!" she roared at Krepth, violet eyes promising violence.

"You've held nothing but contempt for me since we met! Have I not proven that I'm on your side?" Elijah bellowed at Krepth over Arii's shoulder.

Her fingers pressed against his chest as she shot him a look that promised he would not be spared from her violence if a fight were to break out. Arii shoved them both again, but felt her voice was falling upon deaf, testosterone-filled ears. "Stop it!"

Krepth snarled, the sound entirely lupine, before taking a step back. "It isn't a matter of what side you're on, mate, it's what's at stake should you fail." His eyes swept over Arii, not missing her state of undress. She fought a blush, absently tugging at the thin straps of her shift.

Gods, he was unbelievable! This was far beyond a brotherly need to protect her now.

Something else was wrong, and she was determined to figure it out.

Arii threw another narrowed-eyed warning at Elijah before spearing a finger into Krepth's chest. "You, me – on the deck, now!"

The Shifter threw one last venomous glare Elijah's way before slipping from the room without more fuss – which Arii thanked the gods for.

She found her folded clothing and dressed quickly as Elijah remained leaning against the wall.

"Arii."

She straightened to look at him as she tugged on boots and tightened her belt. They remained silent for a few moments.

The mood of the room had instantly changed with Krepth's anger. She could feel herself withdrawing back into the comfort of her steel walls. When she was with Elijah, she found that much of her control slipped through her fingers like sand, and her awareness of the world around them dimmed. It was dangerous, and she had to get a hold of herself. She should not have allowed him so close.

"Vanquish those emotions lest they blind you like a bat."

Klotho's words rose unbidden from her memories, dragging up doubt to dash away the remnants of heat from her skin.

Arii's violet eyes did not meet his as she said, "Perhaps you should check on Emerson." Her words were dismissive, bordering on cold, and she did not need to look at him to see his concern.

Sliding past him to head up on deck, Arii whipped her hair into a swift braid as she stomped up the stairs.

Krepth was standing with his attention to the sea, his arms crossed over his chest and his dark hair dancing in the wind. As she approached, he did not turn to face her, almost like he *couldn't*.

"Explain what in the world that was all about?" she hissed, anger still lacing her nerves and sending tingles to her fingertips. She itched to grab her blade and find something to stab.

When he finally turned to her and his expression changed to sorrow, Arii felt her stomach sink. She barely heard him as he whispered, "Arii, there is something I haven't told you."

She stepped toward him, seeing his moss-green eyes shadowed with pain. "What is it?"

"It's my mother… she…" he paused before saying gently, "She was taken by Red Guard soldiers from the market in Trader's Bay, just before I returned from Viridya."

Arii's mouth turned as dry as dust as she pictured the raven-haired woman with eyes the same shade as the man before her. How had she not noticed her absence when they were in Evergrave? Gods, she was so caught up in her own world that she was missing the finer details of the people she was doing this all for.

Her friends and their families.

"No," she whispered, more to herself than to him.

Krepth ran a hand through his hair as he turned to the sea once more. "She was taken to Bonemire." His voice lowered an octave, venom coating his words as he hissed, "Herington knew she was there – yet he only got *you* out."

Arii's mind was a whirlwind of questions as she rested a hand on his arm. "Your mother was in Bonemire when Elijah and Nem saved me? Krepth, there were many innocent people in Bonemire – it was only luck that we escaped without raising an alarm–"

"–He could have at least tried to get her out! Get them *all* out!" Krepth snarled, spinning on her.

So, this was why Krepth held so much anger towards Elijah – not only that he had served a twisted tyrant and an immature king, but that he was involved with Bonemire somehow.

She truly believed Elijah had not known about Bonemire prior to her rescue. She forced her mind back to when he swept her through that grim courtyard, past cages of bodies and crystals. The place had been thought to be a training ground, where the dregs of society were taken to earn amnesty by serving the Crown.

Had he seemed surprised? Had he seemed sickened by what they saw? Her brain almost hurt trying to remember, as if it did not want to. As hard as she tried, she could not remember anything save the relief and the exhaustion she had felt.

Another little seed of doubt bloomed a bloody flower in her mind.

"But… how could Elijah have known?"

The man scoffed. "Do you not think the King's bodyguard would have access to the papers of those being sent to Bonemire? He has more knowledge about what was happening there than you realise." He drew out his next words through clenched teeth. "I. Do. Not. Trust. Him."

"I thank Nyx that he got you out when he did, I truly do, but he could have saved many more lives!" he continued, fists balling.

She swallowed back the bile and doubt, and stood stubbornly by her original belief. "If he wished us ill, we wouldn't be standing here arguing right now. That's why he's here now, to learn how to use his power to save them all, save the entire land."

"Sure, and once he has a firm grasp of his magic, he will run straight back to Lorch. He served under that family for almost twenty years, Arii! Maybe he is taking advantage of your newfound feelings to gather information about the other courts and their weaknesses. Once he has what he needs, once he has a grip on his magic, what makes you think he won't go back and aid them in their sick plot to wipe us all out!"

"He won't!"

"How do you know?"

"I just know, alright?"

'How well do you truly know Eliverus, Ariiaya?' whispered the wraith, slithering into her mind like an eel. *'Is there truly more between you than a war of fire and ice?'*

Arii swallowed, willing the voice to leave her alone. Strangely, the wraith departed, but not before whispering, *'We are never truly alone, Violet One. Not when our minds are here to trick us.'*

Sea wind whipped her braid as she blinked rapidly, then thrust her attention back to her friend, staring into his eyes as Krepth said with dead calm, "You're going to get hurt, Arii. I can't let that happen, I can't lose you too," his voice ended on a pained whisper, his face twisting in anguish. "I don't even know if my mother is still alive. She could be one of those... *things.*"

Some of her anger ebbed away as she clutched Krepth's face between her palms. "We will rescue them all, somehow," she whispered as Krepth leaned his forehead against hers, a fine mist of sea spray around them as his eyes closed. "Just... try to keep things civil, Krepth. He *is* the future King. That earns a little respect." She swallowed. "I trust him."

He huffed a laugh in response, and she could feel just a tiny bit of his anger drift away on a sea breeze. After a heartfelt pause, she continued, "Krepth, you've always trusted me..."

"I trust *you*, little Fury. Herington though – that will take the moving of a mountain."

She smiled ruefully as she said, "Something tells me that if you keep on prodding him, you may just cause that if you aren't careful."

The Shifter's mouth tilted in a grin as the air around them lightened, the wild sea breeze taking their remaining anger with it – for now.

"Or if *you* aren't careful," he purred, flicking her nose teasingly. "Do we need to speak about the birds and the bees, little Fury?"

"Argh, no." She knew what he implied, and it made her unable to meet his eyes.

"I don't say this often, nor do I say it lightly, little Fury, but... be careful."

"I know, I know," she murmured in stubborn response. With

a playful shove, Arii stepped away and turned her gaze to the sea. Beyond, the waves rolled like wings, and Arii's attention rose to the darkening sky. Stars began to flicker in the obsidian blanket, peeking through a wash of deep purple as the day bordered on night. On the breeze came a chill not present before, perhaps a sign they were approaching the freezing southern court.

"Mosey your arses below deck and get some shut eye, you lacklustre mob of ingrates!" called the Captain as the crew began to finish up their tasks. Hips swinging and hat fluttering, Valerie sauntered towards them, her face splitting in a grin. "Good to see you up and about, Arii, and also good to see you ain't walkin' like a sand crab. Do us all a favour and perhaps refrain from rolling between the sheets with your hunk of a future King until we reach solid land, heh?"

Arii's eyes widened as her cheeks flushed deep crimson.

Sand crab?

Krepth leaned over and slapped a hand against his knee, and Arii noticed he was struggling to breathe as the Shifter wheezed with laughter. "Sand crab! Nyx's tits, Valerie – where do you get lines like that?"

Valerie's grin remained as she slid her arm around Krepth's waist. "My little black book isn't just for cataloguing my conquests, Krepthy. Care to join me? I may just let you sneak a peek."

Krepth's deep laughter fluttered in their wake as they headed below decks, leaving Arii alone to stare out to sea.

Her hand lifted to her cheek, the skin hot and flushed after Valerie's crude remarks. It took a lot to make her blush, and only once the woman had disappeared below decks with Krepth did the meaning behind her words register.

Elijah's power was obvious to them all now, and one would assume such power could be applied to the bedroom, too.

Arii's fingers probed her slightly swollen lips, heat still rising up her neck.

Could Elijah have truly sunk the ship if they had allowed things to continue further?

He was not in control of his power yet, and the true extent of his abilities was still a mystery – not just to her but to Elijah too.

A slim form slid into the space beside her and Arii tilted her head to gaze at Tikkani, as the girl sighed deeply. "The sooner we get to land, the better. Gods, if I see another ship after this, I think I'll feed myself to a fucking Kryvern. Or better yet a sea drake." She leaned her head against Arii's shoulder and said, "Thank you for saving my brother, Arii."

Arii allowed her to rest there, her own eyes drifting closed. "Don't mention it, kid." Her words were short, yet amiable as they stood in companionable silence, watching a flock of gulls caw and swoop on the sea's surface.

She should tell Tikkani that this was why she had not wanted them to follow – the dangers they would no doubt face along the way. Yet in that moment she could not voice her fears. She was happy they were here – sharing this adventure, no matter the perils.

"Let us head below. Tomorrow we will reach the Southern Court, and we need to be rested and ready." Arii said, and she led the elf below deck.

†

The room was flickering with candlelight as Arii entered, gently closing the door behind her.

Her entry cut off a hushed conversation between Elijah and Nem from where they lay in their separate beds.

Elijah was covered with a thin cotton blanket, his arms folded behind his head as he stared at the ceiling. Nem was on her side, head propped up on a palm, causing her silver hair to fall in a curtain against her pale skin.

Arii paused as she sensed tension, violet eyes sweeping the two Fae with thin suspicion. "What's going on?"

Nem inclined her head in Elijah's direction as she said, "We were just discussing the future."

Elijah's eyes rolled as he huffed, "Nemesis was asking questions which I believe are irrelevant."

"Irrelevant? How is 'What is the first order you'll give as king' irrelevant?"

"It is irrelevant because I'm not going to be king."

Nem sighed heavily, falling onto her back and pulling up the sheets as Arii sat on her own cot, sliding off her boots. Nem continued. "Here I thought we were making progress. You can't escape your fate, Eliverus."

Elijah loosed a breath through his nose in response, silver eyes tracking Arii's movements. "I will learn to use my magic to help fight against Valdis." His voice was low, gentle and monotone as he added, "But I will not be ascending to the throne."

He was not going to change his mind easily, Arii knew that. She also knew how incredibly stubborn he was. Just agreeing to work on his magic was a colossal leap alone.

One step at a time.

"Get some sleep, both of you," said Arii, earning her two sets of rolling eyes.

"Yes, mother," drawled Nem, turning her back to them as she nestled into the squeaky mattress. Arii lay down on her side, facing Elijah as he stared at the ceiling. His eyes slid to her in the dim light. "How are you feeling now?"

The question had her pausing, studying his face as her cheek pressed into the pillow, her voice dropping as she said, "I'm fine. Fae recover far quicker than humans."

His lips twitched. "That is true. I often had to hide my injuries lest someone see how quickly they healed. Colleen noticed though…"

His voice trailed as his smile slowly faded. Arii felt a pang in her chest, knowing thoughts of his adoptive mother were occupying his mind. Slowly she propped her head on her palm, her voice serious as she whispered, "We will get her out, Elijah. We will get them all out, I promise."

Not only did she mean Colleen, but her words extended to Lynnera, Hawke and Sybell too.

And Lorch.

Gods, she hoped he was alright. She hoped they were *all* alright.

Elijah remained silent, eyes drifting to the ceiling once more as the ship rocked beneath them. Arii took that as an end to the conversation. Lifting a hand, she snapped her fingers to snuff out the candles, plunging them into total darkness save a dash of moonlight from the window beyond.

GUNNER

CHAPTER TWELVE

ARIIAYA

The glowing orb of magic bobbed on her palm between them as Arii lifted it to eye level, her gaze meeting Elijah's. The morning was crisp, the sky overcast with clouds as the *Murderous Lust* skimmed across a calm sea. In the distance loomed snow-capped mountains and land dusted with white.

The Southern Court.

They had about an hour before they were to reach Skaald, the harbour town located on the shore of the frosty continent. Arii had never been to the snow-covered port, but she had heard the inhabitants were gruff and harsh. She was not sure how their party would be received, but for now she had Elijah's magic to worry about.

"Do you know how magic works?" she enquired, head tilting ever so slightly.

"Can't say that I do. Unfortunately, the laws of magic were not compulsory knowledge growing up in the north." He paused, eyes lifting from her palm to her face. "But something tells me I'm about to get a lesson."

"Magic is not infinite, Elijah, and that is something you'd best understand. It is a force we borrow from everything around us, and in turn we give a little back. One's magic is only as strong as the soul within." A pause, before nodding towards him. "Tell me, what did it feel like when you reached into your magic?"

Elijah's eyes slid back to the magical orb, his jaw working as if he were searching for the best words. After a moment he blinked, swallowed, and let the answer roll. "It was like… a pool. A pool of water that only I could see." His brows knitted as he added, "The water, it was not like normal water though… it was–"

A small smile, a flash of teeth as Arii finished, "Like tar? Liquid yet glutinous – right?"

"Right. Last night, against the sea drakes… I could grasp it – but it would slip through my fingers like oil."

"With practice it will get easier." She bounced the orb as she spoke. "That pool, the magic within it – it only goes as far as your soul will allow. For some, the pool is deep, and for some it is as shallow as a chamber pot." An assessing glance. "But, all magic has a limit – all pools have a bottom – and the closer you get to that limit the longer it takes to recover afterward."

Elijah eyed her, and she could see an intensity in his gaze that raised goosebumps on her skin as he whispered, "My pool… I could not touch nor see the bottom."

Endless power… surely it was not possible? She knew he was strong – incredibly so – yet she was sure his magic had a limit.

Finding that limit was going to be a challenge, it seemed.

"Reach within yourself and just pinch at the power. It's very much like when you grasped it against the sea drakes – only this time you only need a tiny bit."

Elijah's brows fell as he studied the ball of magic on Arii's palm, his look uneasy. They had found a spot just to the side on the main deck, sitting on two crates as the crew bustled around them. They had been sitting like this for hours, hours which only became more weighted as they tried and tried again to tap into Elijah's magic.

Once again, he splayed his fingers and locked his eyes on the space above his palm as the sea breeze whipped his hair. Arii stared at his hand, fighting an urge to watch his handsome face instead as a shadow of concentration drifted across his features. When nothing happened, like the hours spent up until this point, she saw the coat of frost settling over his features as his feet shifted slightly – as if he were having trouble getting comfortable.

"It's not working," he said in agitation before he jumped to his feet.

Her free hand speared out, grabbing his fingers as she snapped, "Elijah, control is not going to come overnight. And it is most certainly not going to come if you give up!" Frustration picked at her insides like crows to a carcass, and his lack of fortitude ground down her patience. Funny, normally he was the one with the unflappable composure, not the other way around.

With a huff, Elijah sat back down as Arii hissed, "Now, fucking concentrate!"

If her crass tone fazed him, it didn't show. Elijah's stare was like steel as he shifted and brought his attention to their hands, her fingers still firmly grasping his. With a deep inhale through his nose and a long breath out his mouth, Elijah's fingers began to squeeze, applying pressure and Arii's eyes lifted to see his gaze fixed solely on her.

She became aware of a weight on her shoulders, a shiver tickling her fingertips like thousands of tiny needles – but it did not hurt. Her lips slowly parted, her eyes fixed on his as he moved his hand to her wrist, before sliding his fingers down her arm. Fire danced where his fingers touched, and slowly that touch travelled back to her palm, his index finger following the lines on her skin. Finally, his hand lay flat in hers, palm against palm.

Momentarily mesmerised, she tried not to shudder visibly at the prickles of need popping along every nerve ending in her body.

Elijah flipped his palm to the sky, resting his hand upon hers, and slowly a sphere of magic began to form.

It was not like hers though – Elijah's sphere was tinged blue and glittered with crackling energy – like a tiny electrical storm raged within the confines of the ball.

Both of their eyes widened at once, and Arii couldn't help the breathlessness in her voice as she said, "There you go."

Elijah's breath rushed between his lips and his eyes lifted to hers, a glimmer of carefully concealed wonder in their depths that had flutters alighting in her belly.

"All you needed to do is concentrate on the magic," she added.

He smiled, his next words totally unexpected. "But I wasn't

concentrating… not on the magic anyway."

Arii caught her bottom lip between her teeth as she studied the sphere, her fingers curling around his wrist as Elijah added, "Perhaps I *can* do this."

"Of course you can, Elijah," she said encouragingly, shooing the butterflies that his earlier words created in her stomach and hoping her cheeks didn't betray her as a small smile lit his dark features.

They stared at one another for a small heartbeat.

"Land ho!" called Lyda from the crow's nest above, breaking the moment forming between them as Valerie bellowed from the rear of the ship, "Prepare to dock and throw anchor!"

The magic faded with a fizzle, and with a last glance, Elijah slowly stood and headed to help prepare the ship, Arii staring in his wake.

"Now that is the arse of a king."

Arii's brows lifted to Tikkani as the girl sidled up beside her, golden eyes glimmering and brows waggling suggestively. She grinned as she studied Elijah's broad back.

"Oh, for the love of all that bleeds..." Arii groaned, and Tikkani cackled, hoisting a thick loop of rope over her shoulder.

"For a Fury, you sure do blush a lot! It's adorable!"

"I don't… blush."

"And water isn't wet. Come on, Arii." Tikkani grinned impishly, before skipping to join the bustle.

Arii's hands flew to her heated cheeks as she gave a last glance at Elijah.

Well, she wouldn't admit it out loud, but gods, Tikkani was right. He *did* have an exceptional arse.

With a drawn-out sigh, Arii headed to help Quinn secure the cannons as Gunner hummed a merry tune. The man's sea-salt locks wavered around his lightly bearded face as he whistled; "Oh me lovely had bosoms aplenty – oh me lovely had legs for days. Round me cheeks her thighs did quiver, ohhhhh me lovely did taste as sweet as–"

"Gunner, prepare anchor and flag down the dock before our arrival!" barked Valerie from the helm as the *Lust* began to slow. "And for the love of all who have ears – shut your gob before I shut it for you, eh?"

The man ceased his singing, jovially humming along instead. His eyes sparkled as he muttered to Arii, "She won't show it bu' the captain *loves* my singing."

Arii had to wonder if the man was mildly delusional, or perhaps still a little drunk from breakfast.

They prepared the boat to dock, the crew moving around the deck with trained proficiency.

Quinn hummed Gunner's tune for the half hour that they worked, and Arii was seconds away from throwing him in the bay when bells began to toll from the docks, welcoming their arrival. The wind whipped across the decks, the air holding a snapping bite. Luckily, they had all dressed in thicker clothing lined with fur – but that did not stop the shiver shooting down Arii's spine.

"Hell, it's cold!" groaned Tikkani as the group gathered on deck.

"Strange choice of words," said Emerson as he appeared beside them.

Luc soon followed, his lips lightly tinged blue against his dark skin as he shivered. "Yeah, isn't h-h-hell filled with fire?"

Arii surveyed their faces – then paused on Emerson, glad to see a tiny bit of colour had returned to his cheeks. The boy's golden eyes met hers and he offered a tiny smile as he clutched Luc's hands and brought them to his mouth, breathing and rubbing them to bring warmth.

She smiled back before sliding her gaze to the harbour town ahead.

Skaald was a large town with well-maintained docks filled with fishing vessels rimmed with an array of fishing nets. Arii recognised the Vox family crest upon the hull of many of the ships.

The crudely painted design of a white bear's head, a mark of the south.

Gulls dotted the sky, cawing and resting on the railings of the docks – alighting in flight when a fisherman passed by, before returning to their post to continue their ear-grating symphony.

Rugged-looking people dressed in motley-coloured furs and skins paused to watch the strange ship glide in, their faces weathered and eyes narrowed in suspicion. Not one man was without a beard, Arii realised. Every man on the dock looked rough and haggard, as though they had never known a shave.

The women looked just as tough. Hair braided back from severe, strong faces, eyes glittering with mistrust. Arii wondered if anyone in Skaald ever smiled.

A man with a long, dirty blonde beard paced down the dock, his hand lifting in greeting as the ship glided to nestle beside a smaller fishing boat. Captain Valerie's hand lifted in response as the crew busied about dropping the anchor and readying the gangway.

"Ahoy!" she called as she headed down the gangway to the dock, her hands meeting the man's in a friendly shake. "Captain Valerie Gray of the *Murderous Lust*. Many thanks for allowing us to dock, good sir!"

The man's face lit up in a smile under his beard. *Ah, so they can smile.*

"Welcome to Skaald. I am Herold Fir, the dockmaster," he said, his voice thickly accented. "Yer ship doesn't bear any particular marks of concern – so that allows you harbour without a fuss," he said, lifting a hand to shield his eyes against a ray of sun. Arii pondered his words, and Krepth answered her unspoken question, "He means that our ship doesn't bear a crest from the north."

Ah, so that explained the looks of unease on the faces of the townspeople. Would they have been denied a dock if their ship bore the crest of the north?

"Be you just visitin', Captain Gray? Or are you lookin' to trade wares?"

Valerie slapped a hand to the man's shoulder before waving towards her ship and crew. "Needin' a place to rest the night. Point us in the direction of your closest tavern, Herold. My crew are needing a good meal and I hear nothin' beats the stew here in Skaald!"

Herold smiled widely again. "Right you are. Follow the road to the right along the docks. The Breezy Maid – you will not miss 'er.

They'll receive you gladly if you tell 'em Herold sent ye'."

"Brilliant," sighed Valerie, flashing a grin before cupping her hands around her mouth to shout at the ship. "Hurry your arses, you stinking fishslappers. I'm starving!"

"Does she ever call you anything nice?" whispered Emerson to Gunner as the crew began to depart the ship. The crew looked dishevelled, but there was a new light in their eyes at the promise of their feet on solid ground and alcohol to wet their tongues, a much-needed morale boost.

"Gods no! If Cap'n Valerie calls you something nice – then you know you're truly in trouble," said the man, grinning as they headed towards the tavern.

NEMESIS

"What are you afraid of?" Krepth whispered as his lips paused inches away, their faces so close their breath danced in the salt air between them. That same salt drifted in the rays of light streaming in the porthole windows around them, and if her mind were not focused on the unwanted attention, Nem would have thought the sight almost ethereal – in a damp, fish-stinking way.

Her back was against the wall of the cabin she had just finished clearing, her fingers curled around her dagger and she inhaled slowly – as if a sudden movement might raise the wolf behind his eyes. Pupils dilated in orbs of emerald green as Nem's lip curled over her teeth, her face shadowed within her hood.

"Fear is for the weak, Krepth. And I am anything but weak."

Fingers splayed on the wood behind her, his lips twitched into the lopsided smirk she knew so well, and he inhaled deeply – scenting his prey. "I don't doubt it, Nem. But why do you continue to deny what is so clearly forming between us?"

"And *what* is forming between us exactly?" she shot back.

"Come now, silver moon…"

Her body shuddered at the nickname – a name that he had only uttered when they were alone. Which was occurring far more frequently of late.

"Step back, Krepth – or I may just accidently gut you…" she snarled, baring her fangs, suppressing the feeling of fire in her gut as his deep, complex scent caressed her senses. Thick woods, pine and moss, all enveloped by a rugged wildness that brought forth a curiosity she'd rather deny. She hid her feelings beneath a mask of anger instead.

When he didn't budge, Nem pressed the tip of her blade into his gut with a hiss, "Did you not sate your desires with the little pirate captain last night, wolf?"

He blinked slowly, before leaning back and glancing down at the knife at his stomach. His voice held a note of hurt, and even through her anger she knew it was genuine. Her stomach twisted of its own accord.

"Sate my desires? Nem, you know me better than that."

"I do not. I'm starting to think I do not know you at all," she breathed, nudging the weapon deeper. She had never dealt with invasions of her personal space well, even before meeting the wolf Shifter, and as always the male did not seem to catch on to her hints – no matter how glaringly obvious she made them. Nem knew that *her* scent, however, would be giving him mixed signals.

Despite their years of friendship, there was a tension between them. She found him irritating at the best of times, yet she could not help the ribbons of want fluttering in her stomach.

He was charming, charismatic and easy on the eyes, and he had a wild glint in his eyes that sang to something deep withing her, a thirst for… more. More from life beyond the occupation she had been forced into. Even though she had no memory beyond her emergence upon the sandy shores of the west of the continent, she had a little flame inside that remained alight no matter how much she tried to douse it.

A little flame of desire to know her truth.

Where had she come from? Where was her family, and did they still live?

Who was she, truly?

Krepth brought her back to the present, his smooth voice cracking through her reverie. He had the nerve to look wounded at her words. "Nem."

"Get out of my face, dog. The crew is docking," she growled, before sliding under the arch of his arm and moving swiftly from the room, leaving Krepth staring in her wake, eyes dark and shadowed with a deep hurt.

ARIIAYA

"Okay, yes, you're right," moaned Tikkani as she spooned hot stew into her mouth. "This is the *best* stew I have ever tasted!" She paused, shooting a glare her brother's way as he opened his mouth to speak, swallowing hard before pointing her spoon in his direction, "Don't tell me not to speak with my mouth full, Emer. We are in the south after all! This is the land of little manners and more barbarity!"

Emerson rolled his eyes before continuing to eat his meal. He had not spoken the words out loud, but he had not needed to.

"I'm always right," nodded Valerie as she downed a mug of mead. She drank almost as much as the men who had begun to drift closer to their group in the tavern – haggard and weathered individuals of the township. After a few minutes and tension, the men had begun to chatter and warm to them – all because of Valerie. She had a way about her that made others comfortable, an air of nonchalance and a quick whipped tongue that had the townspeople's defences dropping, causing them to laugh along with her crude jokes and easy-going demeanour.

All the while, Tikkani watched the woman with wide eyes and a grin that never left her face.

Arii swore she could see a hint of stars in the girl's eyes. Chuckling, she spooned her own meal and glanced at the silver-haired Fae beside her, brows raising as the hearty meal slid down her throat and warmed her insides. Nem's meal sat untouched before her, her eyes staring into the dish as if something may emerge and curse her.

"You haven't touched your food, Nem. What's wrong?"

Aqua eyes lifted and her expression turned glacial. "Nothing."

"Nyx's arse it's nothing."

"Just drop it, Arii," hissed Nem, looking away and angling her body in a way that had Arii's brows narrowing. Fine, she would drop it –for now.

Arii looked at Krepth as the man leaned back in his chair, his eyes on Nem before Arii asked, "How far to Erstonia?"

Krepth tilted his head, a lopsided grin tugging at his mouth. "Provided we don't get caught up in any snowstorms – I'm thinking we will be there in two days. Limited stops of course." His eyes drifted to Nem once more, and Arii swore she saw a shadow pass behind his eyes before it was gone.

"Herold has put us up with some horses, and Valerie was kind enough to part with some supplies from the boat," Elijah said, his deep voice drifting from a few seats away.

Krepth tipped his mug in Elijah's direction as he said, "I don't see any reason to delay. As soon as we are done here, we should get moving."

Arii felt some tension ease from her body, silently contented that the two men were keeping things civil. They hardly met each other's eyes, but they were not trying to beat each other up, and for that she was thankful.

"I disagree, your trek is set to be a harsh one. Get a few hours rest here before sunrise," said a bearded, surly looking man with a hint of pink cheeks.

"Gerald is right, we have a couple of rooms left, just enough fer all of ye, methinks," piped up the Innkeeper nearby.

"I'll bunk with Krepthy," winked Valerie.

Krepth shot her a grin.

"Luckily, Skaald has a good supply of horses for all of us," Valerie added, "for in the 'morn, we will be coming with you."

Arii's brows lifted in surprise as Elijah said, "And what of your ship?"

Valerie leaned back on her stool as she replied, "It'll be me, Gunner and Lyda. The rest of the crew will remain here until we return." She slid forward, her elbows on the table as she stared directly at Elijah. "If what we witnessed on the *Lust* against the sea drakes is any indication of what you can do, Eliverus – then that is a story worth bearing witness to. I want to see it unfurl before my own eyes, and not through some bard in a tavern who may skew the truth in song. I may even add new ink to my other arm once this is all said and done."

And just like that, their group went from eight to eleven in the blink of an eye. If Elijah could convince others to join their cause without trying, Arii wondered what kind of following they could amass if he actually put his mind and effort to the task.

The spark of hope flickered into a small flame within her ribs.

Only for the wraith's earlier whispered words to rise in her mind, drenching her with a feeling of cold water.

'More lives mean more graves.'

Elijah crossed his arms over his chest, leaning back in his chair with a look of reluctance. She fully expected him to refuse, so she was surprised when he simply said, "Alright. What do you know of our destination?"

Valerie's grin was wide as she arched a brow, hazel eyes glittering in the dim light of the tavern. "I know plenty, far more than you, I'll wager. We will not weigh you down–" She pressed a hand to her heart and lifted a hand in the air. "–pirate's oath."

Krepth tsked and chuckled. "Pirates have oaths? I find that hard to believe. Aren't you all cut-throat bastards?"

"There is still much for you to learn about pirates, Krepthy." Valerie's look turned mischievous, causing Krepth's eyes to drift down to his mug of mead. Arii felt Nem shift beside her.

The silver haired assassin kept her own attention anywhere but on their group, brooding silently in her own thoughts.

Arii catalogued the scene to her memory bank to investigate later. Nem was not the only one who could push for answers about the men around them.

"I have been to Erstonia. Jero and Thogan know me – maybe it will provide easier access to an audience." Valerie said, sculling the remainder of her drink before slamming down the tankard.

"Right, let's finish up and get a wriggle on to bed, shall we? I'm close to murdered."

The group was quick to agree, chairs scraping wood in a sudden chorus. The crew of the *Lust* hurried back to their ship on the tailwind of a promise that Valerie, Lyda and Gunner would be back at first light.

The Innkeeper showed the rest to their rooms. "And this be yours. Pardon that you do not get your own room, Your Highness." He patted a hand against the tired wood at the end of the hall, glancing at Elijah, and then at Arii over his shoulder – the last to be allocated a room. If Elijah was surprised that the man knew of his identity, he didn't let it show. Arii guessed Valerie had let that information slip.

Arii poked her head over Elijah's broad shoulder and said, "Let me guess… there is only one bed?"

"No, room's got two, miss."

Arii clicked her fingers together and muttered, "Darn."

LYNNERA & HAWKE

Chapter Thirteen

SYBELL

Sybell wondered how long she had been locked away in the castle dungeons.

Weeks?

Months?

Surely it had been months. It felt like months.

She shifted on the thin mattress, groaning at the ache in her shoulders and hips.

It was quiet, naught a sound but the consistent *drip drip drip* of a lavatory drainpipe conveniently situated outside her barred cell window, mixed with the hushed voices of her parents in the nearby cells. If they spoke too loudly, one of the guards would rap his sword against the bars and exclaim that if they did not shut their mouths, his sword would do it for them.

Arsehat.

She knew that *he* knew that if he touched them even with the tip of his weapon, Lorch would have his head. Even though they were being held captive, she knew her brother cared for their welfare, deep down. She held on to that belief within an inch of its life, even though he had not shown any indication that that was the case. But, what did she have if she did not keep some semblance of hope, no matter how small?

Eventually the melody of dripping water was replaced with the sounds of *them*.

The undead.

The first of Valdis' experiments had been brought in late one night, a slight, thin woman wearing the attire of a noble, torn in places and soiled with dirt. Her hair was unkempt around her hollow cheeks, her movements jerky as a group of guards placed her in the cell across from Sybell. She did not protest or fight them, just stood in the corner of the deathly cold cell as the guards dispersed.

And that is where she had remained.

For hours.

For *days*.

Head tilted down, her mouth agape – eyes unblinking and as black as oil – a dull glow of blue pulsed from her chest. It lit the cell, before plunging it back into darkness, every few seconds or more – mimicking the slowed down, steady staccato of a beating heart.

But Sybell knew that no heart beat within that woman's chest. No, encased in her chest was a chunk of magic-infused crystal, reanimating her from death.

Nothing but a mindless puppet.

It had taken everything not to think of Ingrid, her dearly departed lover and friend who had succumbed to the same horrid, unimaginable fate. A mindless corpse, a thing that held no remains of the sweet girl she had known and loved. Sybell had worked tirelessly to pick up the pieces of her fractured heart, bestowing a curse upon each shard as she vowed to deliver retribution one day.

That could not be done in this cell, though.

As the days ticked by, more people were placed in the cell with the first woman – all standing, glowing, mouths agape, eyes like voids and all swaying ominously. Men, women… young, old… skin ranging from pale to dark. All with the pallor of death.

It freaked her the hell out, to her very core.

She tried to keep her back to their cell to avoid looking at them, but nothing kept the feeling of unease from their unblinking eyes and deceased presences at her back.

Now, she shifted to sit, running her fingers through the tangles of her dirty blonde hair. Gods, she reeked. She needed a bath… hell she would kill for even a wet cloth to wipe some of the grime away.

She had been close to begging a guard at one point. But no, never would she beg, no matter how desperate she became.

Sybell shifted to the bars, curling her fingers around the cool metal as she craned her head to the cell adjacent, pressing her cheek against the grimy metal as she whispered, "Father."

Movement flittered in the darkness, and soon she could see Hawke's face. Gods he looked tired. Below his eyes were dark bruises, his cheeks covered in a rugged, unkempt beard. "Syb?" he whispered back.

"It's going to be tonight," she said simply, causing him to shift and grip the bars of his cell harshly.

"No, no, we discussed this," he began vehemently.

"We did, and those discussions ended with me not changing my mind. I'm getting us out of here."

Down a little further came her mother's voice – a whisper in the dark. "Sybell, there must be another way."

"Has another opportunity presented itself in the time we've been down in this shit-infested dungeon? No!" she hissed, scooting back in her cell as she clutched the hem of her dress, tearing away fabric and using it to tie a braid in her hair. Swiftly, she knelt and grabbed at her blouse, loosening the fastenings on the front to the hasty whispers of protest from her parents.

She would not suffer another *godsdamned* moment in this place across from swaying, disgusting, glowing dead bodies that reeked like graves left open and forgotten.

Perhaps it was time to *beg*.

"Excuse me, guards? Guards!"

Blue light flared in the cell across from her – yet the bodies did not move beyond swaying.

Boots fell upon the stone, and soon a guard in crimson uniform paused at the door of her cell, "What?" he snapped. He did not wear a helmet, perhaps feeling it was not needed down here.

"Please… sir. It has been so long since I have bathed. Please…" she shifted to the bars, remaining on her knees as she adjusted the front of her blouse subtly. Glancing up through thick lashes, she shifted to press her arms against her breasts, pushing them up as she dashed a hand along her collarbone to brush the braid over her shoulder.

The man's eyes glinted, a small smile tugging at his mouth as his brows rose ever so slightly.

Perfect.

"I cannot arrange a bath for you, miss…"

Before her entire demeanour could change to that of anger, the man leaned forward, his eyes pinned to her cleavage as he whispered hoarsely, "but I can arrange for a wet cloth, perhaps a small bucket of water… I'm afraid these can only be offered in my office, though."

Of course, away from prying eyes.

Bile rose in her throat, but she swallowed the burning heat harshly.

Retaining the false demeanour of a helpless maiden, Sybell shifted to stand, pressing her breasts harder against the bars for extra emphasis as she mewed quietly, "Oh would you, please? I'll do *anything*."

She could feel her father's seething anger, and her mother's quiet horror. "No, Sybell!"

Her parents' reactions only spurred the man on as he smirked, moving towards her cell door while turning ever so slightly to shoot a vulgar smile at her parents.

What would an assassin do? thought Sybell.

Then, she knew exactly what they would do – what *Ariiaya* would do. She did not know the woman well, but something told her she would grab the problem with her own two hands – and tear it apart until it no longer existed.

Sybell launched her hands through the bars, looping an arm around the man's throat – taking him by surprise. Before the man could sound a warning, she yanked him back against the cell door, the back of his head thumping the metal as she secured her hands and squeezed his throat into the crook of her arm. To better her chokehold she wrapped her legs around his waist – catching his arm in the process. The other scrabbled at her elbow in an attempt to free himself. His short nails scraped and tore at her skin. Teeth gritted, she held on with all her might as the man gurgled and spat against her flesh. Her muscles screamed in protest, weakened by lack of food.

Hold.

His free hand came up to catch her hair, yanking harshly, tearing a chunk of golden strands from her scalp. She angled her head and bared her teeth like an animal as she hissed a curse, but she did not budge. No, she would not allow him to break free. If he did, he would surely torture her – or worse.

He would harm her parents.

Hold.

She could feel the man shaking, could feel the heat rising up into his face, and against her skin his cheeks turned red.

Then blue.

Then a sick shade of purple.

She pressed her lips to his ear, her breath a deadly hiss as she whispered, "If you *ever* touch a vulnerable woman or even *think* about doing so ever again, I want you to remember this moment. The woman you choose may show you far less mercy than I – or deliver you a fate worse than death." Sweat beaded on her brow as the man jerked, eyes rolling back into his skull. "Now tell me *that* is worth getting your tiny little prick wet."

As his movements began to lessen, Sybell stole a glance across the space ahead and into the opposite cell.

And wished she had not.

The corpses were watching her.

Every… single… one.

Black eyes unblinking and chests glowing, they stood motionless and quivering – yet they did not move to help the guard. There was a feral, almost hungry look about them, as if the violence excited them.

She shivered uneasily.

Easing herself down, and then the guard, Sybell swiped an arm over her sweat-drenched brow before grabbing the keys from his belt. Swiftly unlocking the door, she dashed to her mother's cell – and then her father's – unlocking the doors. Before Hawke could speak she growled, "Chastise me later, father, we are getting out of this *godsforsaken* place. *Now*."

Sybell was surprised there were not more guards on patrol. Surprised yet thankful. It was clear to her – and noted by Hawke – that Valdis did not think they would find the means to escape.

Joke was on him.

They crept through the halls, keeping close to the walls as Hawke lead them towards the stables under cover of darkness. It had to be close to midnight, if not just past. The air held a crispness that was unusual to her, though she had to admit she was rarely up at this hour. Well, since Ingrid's death she had found herself waking far more often during the night, covered in sweat with a scream lodged in her throat as the remnants of a nightmare faded. But before that, Sybell was sure she had been the biggest fan of sleep that existed in this miserable land.

Pausing with a lifted hand, Hawke ventured a peek around a corner, before motioning them to move. "It's clear, and if we move swiftly, we may make it to the stables without anyone seeing us."

"Where are the guards?" Lynnera whispered, her hair the most unkempt Sybell had ever seen it.

"Valdis is distracted by building his army with people who do not cost him as much, and the majority of those who still breathe have been sent to retrieve Eliverus. The corpses, they do not eat, they do not drink – but they are still not truly reliable enough to be left unattended."

"Gods, he has truly gone mad."

"Does it really surprise you, mother? The man has been unhinged for as long as I have memory." Sybell took her mother's hand as the woman frowned.

Lynnera sighed as she said, "I knew he was a troubled soul, but I never thought him capable of… this."

Lacing fingers with her mother, Hawke pressed a finger to his lips. "Let's go."

They moved, gliding swiftly over the moonlit path towards the stables. Sybell swallowed curses as her bare feet hit the stones, placing that pain in the back of her mind as a flicker of hope bloomed in her chest.

The stables.

They were so close to escape.

Hawke believed there would be trouble at the gate and he had armed himself with the guard's sword and knives before they exited the dungeons. He was confident they could escape on horseback if they prepared carefully.

Entering the stables, Sybell almost breathed a sigh of relief as they passed over the threshold, glancing back at her parents as she led them into the stall of a beautiful brown stallion she knew well. Swiftly, Hawke lifted a nearby saddle, placing it upon the beast's back as Lynnera quickly worked on the girth. Sybell stroked the animal's muzzle, making hushing noises as she bridled it before leading it from the stall. Hawke ducked into another stall, emerging with a mare.

Before they could get any further, a voice drifted from up ahead.

"Where do you think you're going?"

With a gasp, Sybell's head lifted to see Lorch emerge from the darkness of a nearby stall, pausing by the exit. He was dressed casually in a dark blue tunic and brown pants – his cheeks dusted with light stubble and his hair slightly unkempt. His eyes, though, were distant and cold.

"Brother… please."

Lorch lifted a hand, silencing her as his eyes drifted over his mother and Hawke.

Sybell's hands fisted by her sides, and her heart lurched as she prepared herself for a fight. Her eyes danced around, looking for his guards.

Lorch's hand drifted down, and he sighed, "I am alone." His voice was heavy with exhaustion.

Heavy with burden.

Lynnera stepped forward, hands grasped pleadingly at her chest.

"Come with us, son. We can all escape this place, escape the horrors happening here."

"No," he whispered simply.

Sybell stepped forward, gesturing pleadingly back to her parents. "You will let them die here? You will let them be taken and tortured, and made into those… things?" Her face twisted as she growled, "What the hell has happened to you, Lorch? The brother I knew would never allow all of this to happen. What is happening here stands against everything we have ever believed in, ever been taught."

Lorch's expression was stricken. "No… I… I cannot leave. It's too late for me." As he spoke, he moved to unhook the latch on the gates behind him, pushing them wide, "But it isn't for you."

Hawke's voice was a rasp from behind. "You're allowing us to escape?"

"I am merely turning a blind eye. Be swift, I must get back before they notice I am gone."

As they moved forward to pass him, Lynnera embraced her son – tears tracking the grime on her cheeks. "Please come with us," she whispered weakly.

Lorch pressed his face into her neck. "Heavy is this wretched crown. Without it, father does not have the full support of my armies. The longer I wear it, the longer I have just the tiniest bit of control. Here is where I must remain, mother. I'm sorry."

In his own way, Lorch was bracing his own defences. Sybell grasped her brother's shoulder and lifted her chin. "I knew you were still in there somewhere. Take care, brother."

"Go," he whispered, stepping back.

Sybell took her mother's hand as the woman protested again, tugging her along as Hawke moved to help her mount.

Swiftly they disappeared into the night on horseback, and Sybell vowed she would return. She would save her brother, knowing he was not completely lost to them. She just hoped he could hang on long enough, and not allow the darkness to take him completely before she had the chance.

Now though, now she had to find Ariiaya.

VALDIS & LORCH

CHAPTER FOURTEEN

LORCH

Lorch crumpled the parchment in his fist, his knuckles turning white as he leaned against the desk of dark mahogany wood in his private study. A puddle of discord swirled in his stomach as he replayed the letter's message over and over in his head.

Soon after he had returned from the stables, a messenger had arrived with the note, and after a quick interrogation, he gleaned that no one else had seen its arrival.

The more he thought about it… about *her*, the more his insides rebelled. His heart – the traitorous thing – wanted to savour the note, keep it close, keep it intact. But Lorch's mind was stronger, it seemed, and with a cry he hurtled the ball into the nearby hearth, the parchment becoming food for the flames dancing there.

It was all an act, it had all been but an act. He knew this to be true despite what she had written on paper.

Lorch clenched his teeth as tears of frustration pricked at his eyes. He would not let them fall though. No, the iron barrier he had erected around himself would not allow leaks to form.

His mind brought forth images unbidden, despite the fight to keep them away. He remembered her smile, which seemed to reveal itself to him alone, severing her own carefully composed defences. He remembered her touch; sure and strong, as she took her pleasure from him under the shimmering chandelier in his royal chambers. Her eyes held him captive within their violet depths, keeping him pinned like a mouse under the claw of a cat.

It was only after he had learned she was a Fury that all these traits made sense. She had been created to entice, moulded to slide under your skin like a sharp blade.

And that was exactly what Ariiaya Trillia had done. She had slid beneath his skin so deep that remnants of her scent still played at the edges of his memory.

His father had said shortly after his return from visiting The Fates that Ariiaya had been sent to kill him. *Him.* But she had not done so.

Why?

Initially Lorch thought perhaps she had felt the same way about him. But after thinking on it – obsessing over it – he could not get past the pleading he had seen in her eyes as she faced him in the throne room. Her hands had lifted, and he knew that she had been seconds from pulling a weapon to defend Elijah.

A weapon against him.

He had been so stupid. And with that knowledge, he had vowed to take the hurt and fashion it into his own weapon. He had never before thirsted for revenge, but neither had he felt heart-crushing pain like this.

A weapon that his father provided in the form of an iron-gilded, magical gem in a necklace.

"Sorry to interrupt, Your Majesty – but your father requests your presence in the meeting chamber. He said your council is ready."

The gentle, feminine voice nabbed his attention. A woman stood in the doorway, her chin tilted up. Her hair was swept back into a braid, but he could tell that the brown tresses were thick and only just wrangled into submission. There was a softness to her face, yet a keenness to her evergreen eyes that paused his words as they rose. Her simple moss-green apothecary's robes featured a leather pouch at her hip, accentuating the curves of her body. She was beautiful, and he had not seen her around the castle before.

His hurting heart gave a little lurch.

Until he spied the pointed tips of her ears, causing his eyes to narrow in suspicion.

Normally a soldier would bring summons from his council, not an apothecary.

"Who are you?" he asked bluntly.

Those keen green eyes blinked once, a tiny shift in her feet the only tell of her discomfort, "Celadine Clover, Your Highness."

"My father trusts messages to healers now, does he – Celadine?"

"He requested I bring you a tincture for your headache and thought it prudent for me to bring you the message too." A pause, before she tacked on, "Your Highness."

It was like his father to be thrifty, he supposed.

"Ah, of course." He stepped forward, taking the little vial from her outstretched fingers. He turned it over in his palm, not moving to consume it.

When silence pulled between them, the healer was first to speak. "The council, Your Highness."

Ah, his council. A bunch of miserable, crusty old fools. He had never cared for their company but his father insisted on gaining their cooperation to construct their defence against whatever the other courts may do when they ultimately chose to stand with Eliverus. It was inevitable, his father said.

"Thank you, Miss Clover. For the tincture and the message."

With a small nod and a curtsy, the apothecary fled the room.

Lorch sighed, swiping his crown from its perch on a red velvet pillow nearby, replacing it with the vial. Nestling it upon his head, he stopped by a nearby mirror. The terrible visage looking back at him forced him to hesitate. Sunken cheekbones cradled large bruises beneath his eyes like black voids, copper hair pushed back into a semblance of the flawless wave he was famed for. His lips were chapped with dry crevasses that could rival those in the Dragon Teeth mountains. His brows narrowed in hatred of what he saw.

"You were a fool for letting them go," he said aloud, a slightly deranged laugh escaping as he thought about the faces of his mother, sister and former commander. A weak moment where he had allowed his heart to call the shots. No, he would not do so again.

He watched the lips of his reflection hitch up, his voice dull. "It was for a purpose, was it not?"

Yes, yes, it was a calculated move. They would find Ariiaya and tell her that there was still a goodness in him worth saving.

They would return for him.

And then he would crush them all.

Another laugh escaped him, and it sounded crazy to his own ears. Perhaps he was becoming just like those calculating, crazy old fools on his council. Misery had become venom in his veins, and misery loves company, they say.

His face held a wide smile now, chapped lips tearing to bleed. He dabbed the tip of his tongue at the wounds as he moved alone through the golden hallways to his council chambers. Only a few of the wall sconces were lit, leaving the hall frightfully dark, but he found he liked it better this way.

As he took his place beside his chair at the circular table made of deep mahogany and topped with a large covering of pure gold, his eyes roved the men of the council. Those men stood now, each one bent at the waist in respectful bows. Council meetings were just a back and forth affair of trading suggestions on how they could better fill the royal coffers. Most of the time he would just let his father handle it, enabling himself the time to sit and daydream.

Not this time though. This would not be like their normal meetings.

He nodded to his father, who stood tapping his foot to one side.

"Thank you for gathering here tonight. Not much notice was provided, and I know this is not our usual time of day for discussion but as you all know, these are not usual times." Lorch stood, placing his hands on the cool wood.

Each of the five older men nodded and took their seats, all plastering looks on their faces that they hoped hid the fact that they would much rather be in their warm beds. Lorch knew that the weather had become unusual of late. Where they normally sweated through hot, sunny days and balmy nights, now things seemed to be growing colder. Much, much colder.

He had also noticed a strange, black matter gathering on the outside of his castle. The stuff pebbled on leaves and petals in his usually immaculate gardens. To the touch it was as hard and cold as black ice. Some had even begun to gather on the banks of his secluded pool, and on the leaves of his favourite willow tree.

He had heard whispers from his servants – when they didn't think he was listening – that it reflected their king's bitter, broken heart. Some said it was a sign from the gods that their land was teetering on the edge of total ruin.

With this and the sickness that reports told him were running rife through the towns of his court, Lorch was coming to think they might be right. The gods were angry, and he had a sneaking suspicion he knew why. He used to pray to them – to the gods and goddesses of darkness and light – but it had been a long time since he had knelt on his knees in the castle prayer room, for his belief had become an afterthought long ago.

He owed the gods nothing.

"Of course, Your Highness, we are at your every beck and call," the man closest to him said, a plump man with two chins and a rather large nose. His hair was receding, the line above his brows moving further and further towards his scalp with every meeting. He had been on the council for decades, his word heavily influencing the other men around their table. What hair he had left was surprisingly voluminous, and sandy blonde in colour.

The same colour as his fair, plain daughter.

She had been as meek as a whipped foal, and as uninteresting as the sole of his shoes… yet he had still bedded her, back when he enjoyed the simple pleasures that a plain noble woman could bring. It was like accepting a glass of cheap wine just for the sensation of getting drunk.

Until he had *her*, and everything changed.

Arii.

Now… now he craved the rich, more luxurious wine, and would settle for nothing less.

He had not been with anyone since. He couldn't be with anyone again. Not until his soul quenched its thirst for vengeance.

Lorch sat as his father began to speak, fixing his attention on the scar that was stark against Valdis' rugged face in the firelight. He used that feature as an anchor, pulling himself from the thoughts of Ariiaya's skin, her heady scent, her moans of pleasure…

"You all know of the returning blight of the Fae with the emergence of the supposed lost heir, Eliverus Herington. By now you would have also seen the forces we have been amassing on these very grounds. For the longest time we have lived in relative harmony with the south, east and west – but we strongly believe that a time of calamity will soon be upon us. The Fates have foretold of chaos on the horizon. You all saw the destruction that the Herington Prince reaped upon our own throne room. He cannot be allowed to become a reason for the other courts to band together and usurp our throne. Our monarchy has challenged the fibres of this society, but we are strong, its people are strong, and because of us, they did not need to fear the Fae."

Valdis paused, sweeping his gaze over the councilmen, before adding in a severe hiss, "But that could all change if we do not have your unwavering support."

"You have always had our support," piped up the man furthest adjacent to the King's hand, his grey hair parted in the middle, bushy eyebrows drawn, "but there have been rumours afoot that the King's army has been amassed using…" he swallowed, almost choking on the word, "magic!"

Murmurs erupted about the table, fingers fidgeting and voices mingling. Lorch couldn't help but let his eyes skip to his father as he laced his fingers together and leaned forward, drawing his lips to his fingertips. Many different scenarios had played through his mind prior to tonight, quiet contemplations on how the council would react to his father's unorthodox – no, sacrilegious was a better word – method to amassing their army and gaining the power they now had.

Lorch did suggest not telling the men, but his father begrudgingly insisted they needed funds to bring in more people to create more soldiers, as many of those who worked in Bonemire had been struck down with the sickness that was gripping the land. That too, his father blamed on the discovery of the Fae heir and the imbalance his existence created for Fythnar. They also needed to weaponize the soldiers, armour them in hopes it would prolong the carnage they could cause – even though the things were already dead. Weapons and armour cost gold, and even Lorch knew that their coffers were not overflowing as they once were.

Gold won wars, too.

The importance of this meeting was not lost on him, so he kept his mouth firmly shut and his face expectant as his father did the talking, like every other time they gathered here. His father's tone, his face, *hell*, everything about him demanded attention – demanded obedience, and fear. Sometimes, Lorch found himself wondering what things would be like if his father sat upon the throne, and not himself. He had to admit, things would probably not be so different, for he always relied on his father's counsel above all else.

"Those rumours are true," said Valdis coldly, pausing as voices rose, "But sometimes it is necessary, for the sake of survival, to fight fire with fire. We need gold in order to keep creating soldiers, enough that whatever is thrown at us will be like waves breaking against shores of iron."

The youngest of the five councilmen shifted in his seat and said, "Even with our support and gold, we do not have enough to feed an army the size of which you have already amassed, let alone a larger one."

As if Valdis had been expecting this observation, he motioned to the door, and two soldiers entered. A third man hobbled in tow, the clink of iron chains proceeding his movements. They did not need to be magically inclined to feel the shift in the air, the strangeness that followed his entry. He did not walk nor sound like the others. Lorch kept his head still but watched and waited for what was to unfold.

He wanted to see the councilmen's reactions, but mostly it was because the presence of an undead soldier still knotted his stomach.

The afflicted man was dressed in a red guard uniform, just like the men accompanying him, but his was spattered with blood, which had been hastily wiped. His head tilted as if too heavy to carry, skin far too pale, his eyes glazed.

Two of the five councilmen flew to their feet, one being the man who had spoken first. "What... what is that?"

As the words left the man's lips, the undead soldier's head snapped his way, as quick as a striking asp. His hands flew out, moving to attack. Before cracked, pale fingers could tear and claw, the soldiers yanked the undead man back. His teeth snapped together like a tethered dog, rabid and unhinged as a high-pitched shriek tore from his peeled back lips. The councilman mirrored the sound with his own, but suddenly the soldier stopped, then stepped back, arms falling limp at his sides.

His eyes, though, remained wide and unblinking, fixated on the councilman who had fallen back on his seat with heaving gasps of terror.

Lorch swallowed audibly.

"To answer your earlier question," Valdis subtly tucked the amulet back into the neck of his tunic, where Lorch knew it remained always. His father never removed it, even to bathe. "These men... they do not eat, they do not need to bathe, they do not need to relieve themselves. They are the perfect soldiers, swift, fearless, relentless. And they all answer to me."

All five councilmen were staring now, all with open looks of pure shock and horror. Valdis had not let them see the amulet. He believed the less people who knew of its existence, the better. They could not allow the key to their army to fall into someone else's hands.

Even Lorch's hands, it seemed. Never did he let Lorch hold it, not even for a moment.

"This is madness!" began one man as he slammed a hand against the table, then winced and checked that the undead soldier was not going to react. When he was met with a slightly swaying, blank faced stare, he gathered the courage to continue and turned to Lorch. "Your Highness, you condone this... necromancy?"

Lorch spoke around his linked fingers. "I do, Councilman Jerico."

"And what will we do with them when the war is done?"

Valdis moved closer to Jerico, his look all predator in its grace. He had hardly made a sound as the man voiced his grievances, to which the other councilmen nodded in agreeance.

"When it is all done, we will have plenty more land to spread to. With your help, I have plans to erect more facilities like Bonemire, where we can house our armies until they are needed again," answered Lorch.

"More land to spread to?"

Lorch suppressed an outward wince. Hells, he had not meant to say that. Perhaps it was best to let his father answer the questions. But what was done was done, and so he waved a hand in a look of nonchalance as he answered, "War, which is inevitably coming, will no doubt cause weakened borders. I have the land's best interests in mind when I say that I will not hesitate to join our courts with the others in a matrimony of peace and prosperity. It is time for order to be seized, and for the land to be ruled under one monarchy."

He had discussed this with his father a few nights ago – the prospect of a land united under one rule. Lorch had listened eagerly as Valdis explained his grand plan, and found himself agreeing. If the entire land was under one rule, then everyone would have access to all the resources they needed. No court borders, no withholding of trades. Not to mention town taxes all coming into one large coffer.

Lorch had to admit, it was a brilliant plan. It would be a bloody, harsh battle, and order was sure to be difficult to maintain, but with the magic his father wielded, and the possibility of further discoveries, he could not fault the plan.

Once, Fythnar was a land undivided, an archaic time when civilisations were just beginning to rise. As populations grew, and magic ran rife, small groups began to take charge, and towns began to form with communities of different folk. Humans, Fae and elves established separate societies and things became tense. And messy.

So, four of the most powerful families rose, and an accord was written and the courts established.

An invasion had not been attempted in hundreds of years, and the last time one court attempted to do so, they were quickly put back in place by the ruling family in the north, the great ancestors of the Herington line. Lorch did not have much interest in ancient history, but as far as he knew the court who had attempted to invade were the barbarians in the south – raiders who thirsted for the rich, green lands that their neighbours lived upon. He didn't blame them, he imagined living in freezing, snow drenched lands year after year would get tiresome. In a way, Lorch supposed history could be repeating – their land was in turmoil – but this time, they would break down the barriers rather than keep them.

Jerico blanched, "You speak of… mass invasion."

"Correct."

"What of simply defending ourselves?" said one man.

Furious voices began to rise.

"This is ludicrous," fired another.

"I cannot condone this!" said Jerico, flying to his feet, chair screeching and falling behind him. The air was tense now, filled with the rising staccato of angry voices. Lorch could see that they were quickly losing this battle, quickly losing the support of the only means for obtaining the funds that they needed. His mind whirled, grasping for something to sway them back, but his father was quicker.

Lorch had not even seen him move.

Valdis – while the men spat and argued – slipped behind Councilman Jerico and drew a knife to the man's throat.

The room hushed swiftly to silence.

"These meetings, though they may seem necessary, truly are not," he said, his tone bone dry. Dangerous. "They are but a formality… a chance to allow you all the impression that your opinion matters in the grand scheme of things." He leaned forward, lips to the man's ear, but he did not lower his voice. "In truth, though… we do not need you. Not really."

What was his father doing? They needed the council's wealth, didn't they?

"We will, however, close this meeting with a warning, Councilman

Jerico, one that your great sacrifice will encourage the other good, devoted men to continue their support, as they have done for years."

The man quivered, "Sacrifice? What, what sacrif–"

Before he could finish, Valdis's hand jerked, deftly sliding the blade through the man's throat and showering the dark mahogany and gold table in a torrent of red. Jerico gurgled and clutched at his throat as Valdis stepped back smoothly, allowing the man to flail and teeter back towards the guards who watched on with blank expressions.

Every set of lungs had hitched in horror, four sets of eyes wide and brows drenched with enough sweat to pass as waterfalls. Valdis had the attention of the room, even Lorch's own unwavering attention, and he realised he was holding his breath, too.

"I had hoped measures such as this would not be necessary – that you were all smart men. But alas, we must resort to threats upon your safety… and that of your families." Valdis wiped his blade on a white linen napkin, looking thoroughly bored and not as if he had just slit a man's throat. "Continue to support us and no harm will come to you, and as always, you will remain under the protection of House Kruel. Should you waver…" His hand lifted and pointed towards Jerico, who had fallen to his knees as he bled over a deep blue rug. One of the councilmen made a small sound of distress.

Valdis snapped his fingers.

The guards let go of the chains, and in a swift blur of movement, the undead soldier was upon Jerico, tearing through the man's clothing and into flesh so quickly, so violently, that Lorch had to swallow down bile. Jerico's screams were keening and warbled with his ruined throat, and they only spurred on the mindless beast as it tore him apart.

The closest councilman flew from his seat to be violently sick upon the floor.

"What has been discussed in this room will not leave it. To speak of our discussions or against what has been trusted to you today will be seen as treason, punishable by death." Valdis snapped his fingers once more, passing his other hand over the amulet as the blood-soaked, possessed beast of a man stood and lumbered back to the guards, who – with shaky hands – retrieved his chains.

His father had each of their councilmen by the balls, and Lorch was coming to terms with the fact that this was swiftly becoming a monarchy which ruled with fear. Fear was a powerful emotion, one which made people do almost anything.

"You are all dismissed," Lorch finally said, his voice far calmer and stronger than he felt, and he was thankful it did not waver as the men all stood, bowed, and hurried from the room. The guards retreated too, taking their expressionless and wobbly charge with them. Lorch glanced at the cobalt rug, but did not linger on the ruined mess that was once a man. "Well, that's one way to do it," he mused, dryly.

"Desperate times call for desperate measures, my son. Soon, the entire land will be begging for your mercy, for your protection and your power." A smirk played on his father's lips, his voice dropping, almost as if his thoughts were taking him away.

He lifted a hand absently to the amulet, tucked safely against his skin. "Soon, everything we have worked so hard towards will come true, and the gods themselves will tremble at my feet – the feet of a mortal man. I will be a law unto myself as I will usher in a new age of men."

A dash of doubt passed over Lorch like the fingers of an ice wraith. He repressed a cold shiver.

It was not lost on him that his father had not spoken of them collectively that time.

JERO

CHAPTER FIFTEEN

ARIIAYA

Arii watched Elijah buckle the saddlebags against his mount's flank, casting his eyes over the impressive animal as he ran a hand over its thick fur. Herold had provided them with large, hardy Fjord horses – massive beasts built for trekking the harsh winter terrain. Their manes were cropped short to prevent the strands from tangling and freezing together, their necks thick and their coats coarser than the horses they were used to. In comparison to the animals back in Viridya, they were almost twice as large and twice as hard to handle. Herold insisted that with a steady hand, the animals would be at their beck and call.

Tikkani grumbled as they led their mounts along the road, heading west. The day had just ticked over mid-way, and the sun ducked behind grey clouds as the group prepared to mount. They were leaving later than originally planned, but after the last few days' events, Arii could not blame the fatigue that kept some of their group in bed until the last moment.

"I've been meaning to ask, Tikkani – what's with your aversion to horses?" Arii asked as she tugged the reins of her beast, tossing her braid over her shoulder and twisting the leather straps around her knuckles for a better hold. Her cloak draped the horses' flanks, cobalt blue fabric glittering.

"My father once had a work horse named Butternut. Butternut was straight out of the fiery depths of hell." At Arii's puzzled look, Tikkani continued, "Any chance she got, she would bite me. Tell me, have you ever been bitten by a horse? It fucking hurts."

"I don't think I have ever heard the words butternut and hell in the same sentence before. Nay, come to think of it, I don't think I've ever heard anyone name their horse Butternut, either." Quinn mused as he weaved a braid into his mount's short mane. It was neat, leading Arii to believe he had practiced the art many times, no doubt while making small talk with a woman the morning after.

Luc laughed, unable to hide a snort, "Did you seriously just weave the word *nay* into a conversation about horses?"

"Caught that, did ya?" Quinn winked, earning a loud, exasperated groan from Tikkani.

"You're a real fucking wordsmith, Quinn, now can we please get going?" snapped Arii as Emerson nodded in agreeance. Ahead, she swore she heard a deep chuckle from Elijah.

"And that makes all horses… bad?" reasoned Luc from his own horse – a light, grey steed with white spots. There was a light blush to his brown skin – thanks to the cold – and he shifted his scarf higher to cover his chin. "That seems unfair," he added, shivering.

Arii knew Luc to have an affinity for animals. He often tended to the stables in Evergrave, and his knowledge of all matters of bird and beast made him a source of information in the city. She was not surprised his tone held a tinge of defensiveness. "Did you perhaps tug on Butternut's mane or forget to brush her down after a long trot?" he asked, lips pursed.

"They can't be trusted!" said Tikkani, arms motioning to her horse theatrically. "One moment you're feeding them a carrot then BAM, your hand has two less fingers!"

"You're not missing any fingers," Luc observed, grinning as Emerson rolled his eyes, having heard the story and possibly other variations of the tale many times before.

"No, but it *could* happen," she surmised defensively.

"If we avoided doing things in life for fear of losing fingers, Tikkani, many other interesting things would be avoided," retorted the leopard Shifter.

Tikkani tilted her head quickly, waving a hand toward her brother as she said, "Speaking of avoiding things, and I guess the topic of fingers brings the thought to mind too but–" Emerson stiffened a fraction before the words left his sister's lips, "When's the wedding?"

Luc stifled a chuckle behind a closed fist as Emerson's face slowly turned tomato red.

"Tikkani, for gods sakes," he muttered, ducking his head and nudging his mount into a steady trot to get ahead of them.

In his wake, Tikkani clucked her tongue, eyes dancing with mischief as she leaned towards Luc. "Still hasn't given you an answer, eh?"

Luc sighed, "No, but I'm not pushing, you know that."

"He will say yes, you know."

Luc smiled, and Arii spied not a hint of doubt as the young man whispered, "I know."

The weight of the importance of saving their land increased with the knowledge that a wedding might be on the horizon. It was strange… not often did Arii look forward to anything, but a union of love between two important people in her life? The anticipation was a warm fire in her heart. And it stoked her determination that little bit further.

Valerie headed the company, dressed in simple traveling clothes instead of her pirate garb. She looked strange without her hat, her orange locks fluttering as she nudged her steed with her heels, clicking her tongue. She was not without her hat though, the garment fixed firmly over her saddlebags.

Following closely was Elijah, silver eyes glancing over his shoulder at their group before they began a thunderous trot. The group was wrapped up to their chins in fur scarves to better protect them against the increasing cold as they headed inland. The air was already biting, and Arii wondered just how cold it could get.

Their procession thundered along the moist dirt road, one used for transportation of carts to and from port to city, heading up a steep incline before leveling out with a sweeping view of the white land ahead. Mountains of behemoth proportions shadowed the snow-dusted landscape, drenched in white as far as their eyes could see.

Arii had never been so far south, and the view reminded her of a valley of sweetcakes dusted with too much sugar. The air was beyond chilly now, and she nestled deeper into her furs.

Valerie lifted a hand, signalling directly between two of the largest mountains in the distance as she called over the rising wind. "Between those two mountains is Erstonia. May not look far but trust me – this is harsh terrain. Keep close together and we will be fine."

Tikkani shivered atop her mount as she said, "Nyx's fucknuckles, it's bloody freezing!"

Quinn shot her a look. "You're in the south," he said incredulously, grinning as Tikkani rolled her eyes and pulled the fur up to her eyes.

Emerson looked at home atop his Fjord as he brought the animal next to his sister's, bumping their flanks as he said, "You always said you wanted to visit the south. Are you regretting your words now?"

"Y-Yes." The young woman shivered.

They all grinned as Tikkani murmured a string of profanities into her scarf, thankfully muffled by the thick fur as they continued on.

After a few hours of travel down a harsh valley of white, the group settled into a small enclave of trees, the bases relatively clear from the snow which stayed piled on the thick branches above. Gunner, Quinn and Elijah gathered as much dry kindling as possible to set up a small fire. The horses nuzzled the snow, finding grass beneath to graze on as they all huddled around the crackling fire, the sky darkening above.

Lyda munched on jerky, offering a piece to Tikkani who reluctantly reached a hand from within her cocoon of fur to take the snack. Gunner stretched out his legs, groaning as he massaged his thigh. "Too bad it's faster on horseback. My legs can't straddle like they used to."

"Tell us something we don't know," chuckled Valerie, chewing a piece of jerky while arching a brow. "You are reaching past yer' prime, Gunner!"

"Ey! I'm still all good in other parts!" he defended, grabbing at his crotch before Lyda threw a hand up to halt him.

"Tsk, there are younguns here, Gun," she chuckled.

"Who are you calling younguns?" exclaimed Quinn as he warmed his hands before the fire. The flickering flames highlighted the flop of his messy brown hair and the sharp lines of his jawline and straight nose. "Just because we are younger than you doesn't mean we are inexperienced in the art of *love*."

"Oh gods, here we go..." murmured Emerson to Luc as Quinn cleared his throat before launching into a story about his most admirable conquests that made Gunner chime in eagerly, sore thighs momentarily forgotten.

"Are you warm?"

Elijah's voice was lowered, only for her in that moment, and Arii felt those familiar butterflies awakening at the sound, the gentle concern in his words.

Arii's eyes slid to Elijah as he joined her sentry position by the tree, his cheeks tinged pink and his silver eyes flickering in the dim firelight. Arii had been quick to take up guard duty nearby, forgoing her spot by the fire to watch over their party. Nem had the same idea, perched on a fallen log, sharpening a dagger while keeping a keen watch on the darkening world around them. Every now and then, Krepth's eyes sought her out, and Arii had noticed.

She pulled the cloak around her, grateful for the gift as the frigid air licked at her skin with icy tongues. Hardly ever did she remove the cloak, secretly loving the subtle sparkle in the midnight blue material, the piece quickly becoming one of her most prized possessions. It was strange, but when she wore the garment, she felt different, somehow... safer.

But, she had chalked the thought up to mild fatigue and partial paranoia – feelings that came with their present predicament.

All she could manage in response to his gentle query was, "I'm fine, thank you."

Elijah's eyes drifted from her to the group, watching as they conversed. After a beat of silence, he spoke again, in barely a whisper as he said, "They're a strange bunch."

Arii watched each profile in the firelight, surveying the new faces and the old. They were a strange bunch – but they were her strange bunch. In that moment she felt strangely protective.

"I don't think I could live with myself if anything were to happen to them," she admitted quietly, before glancing at the man beside her once more. Thinking the words was one thing, but admitting them out loud to someone? It had been easier than she had thought.

Her voice had wavered though, causing Elijah's attention to drift back to her, his arm brushing against hers as he said, "It's alright to feel protective, Arii."

"I'm not… used to feeling anything."

He inclined his head in the group's direction, crossing his arms as he murmured, "I have lived with humans for a long time, feeling is not something I'm unfamiliar with – but like you, I felt I had to suppress certain emotions. I suppose it was a deep seeded fear of being different – my body was different, and so I was sure my mind was too. Only now – after spending time with you – do I realise that we feel just as much as humans do. Perhaps even more than they do, if we allow it."

Was he finally accepting that he was a Fae? As much as she wanted to dismiss his words – tell him that she did not feel as strongly as a human – she could not bring herself to do so. She knew he was right, and deep down she had known the truth for a while.

Elijah continued, speaking so freely that she was afraid that if she moved, or responded, he may just cease. And she was intent on listening to what he had to say, absorbing this little bit of information about himself that he was offering. "My… friendship with Lorch was the only thing keeping me from wholly compressing into a dark cocoon within myself. If not for him, I think I would be nothing but a weapon for his father to wield."

She glanced up at him, and she knew he spoke the truth. Who was to say that Valdis would not have used Elijah as a weapon? The bodyguard's skills were impressive, especially when he was thought to be but a mere human. She held her tongue, not feeling they were yet at a point where she could ask him about his past – about what he had done in the name of the crown. Arii was not naive; she knew that Elijah had honed his deadly grace and skills through practice, just like she had.

She had no doubt his hands were just as stained with blood as hers were.

Her mind drifted back to his prior words as she looked at him sidelong. "Do you truly believe Lorch is just standing by, watching while his father brings forth darkness with the very magic they all fear?"

Elijah's jaw twitched, clenching as he said, "I believe Lorch is smart enough to play along – to make his father believe he is a spineless pawn to be moulded as easily as the snow beneath our feet."

"You don't think he… will be tempted by his father's lies?"

Elijah was silent for a time, the sound of the group's laughter reaching them before he spoke.

"I know Lorch. There is no way he would be standing idly by. He is smart – he will be laying low."

A shiver speared her spine, a feeling of dread as she glanced back at the group, watching as Tikkani leaped at Quinn, throwing him to the ground as the group roared with laughter. Tikkani shoved fistfuls of snow into Quinn's face as the young man laughed. "You're too hot to handle, huh? Let me cool you down then!" she bellowed, shovelling snow down the front of his tunic – his laughs turning to high-pitched squeals as the two wrestled.

"Have you remembered much about your family?" Arii enquired, rubbing her hands together and fighting the urge to shift closer to him.

"Small details, yes. My brother, Brohem, he was older than me but unfortunately not wiser. He did not take his prince hood seriously, and it is strange but as my memory returns, I see a resemblance to my brother in Lorch." A wistful smile. "My sister, Ghila, had a face of beauty that would bring men to their knees, and she held herself with such decorum, despite her young age. She was sweet, she was incredibly kind. She embraced being a princess."

Arii's heart tugged at the emphasis he placed upon the word 'was', as if it were sinking in that his family were truly gone. "They sound… wonderful, Elijah."

Elijah's expression softened ever so slightly, that tiny dimple on his cheek making an appearance that sent her heart into a fluttering frenzy.

Nearby, Quinn chuckled as he gently pushed Tikkani, causing the girl to fall back on her backside with a thud. It seemed their little play fight was over, for now. As he stood and brushed snow from his front, he offered her a hand. She took it, shooting him a smirk. There was undeniable attraction between them, and Arii couldn't help but believe they'd make the perfect pair if they could get beyond their anxieties of how the other would respond if they made a move.

Elijah's head tilted as the group continued to chatter, and Arii felt the air shift around them as his hand lifted to touch her arm, his voice low as he whispered, "Do you hear that?"

Arii reached her senses out beyond their camp. She heard the sound of paws thudding on snow, followed by the eager panting of an excited animal.

Suddenly, Elijah was shooting forward like a blur, dagger flashing as a white mass of fur speared at their group, jaws wide and glittering. Just in the nick of time, his dagger lodged into the animal's side as he threw his weight against a giant white wolf, intercepting it just a few feet away from Tikkani and Quinn.

The group's laughter and their campfire had drawn the attention of snow wolves.

Two more white forms flew from the darkness as the group scattered.

"Look out!" yelled Quinn as Tikkani ducked, throwing himself to shield her body as another wolf flew over their heads, jaws narrowly missing them.

Nem drew her daggers, flinging the weapon at one of the beasts as it leaped at Lyda – her blade embedding in its neck before the beast hit the snow, writhing as death claimed it.

Arii skidded across the snow, shooting out a hand and punching a burst of magic into the chest of another wolf, its rabid snarl turning to a yelp as it careened across the clearing to crash into a nearby tree.

Blood glittered starkly like rubies on the snow as the group fought and felled the beasts.

Valerie drew her curved sword, bellowing obscenities, lodging the weapon into the chest of one of the beasts as it clamped its sharp teeth on Gunner's leg, his yells echoing through the carnage as more animals joined the fight. A flash of light signalled Luc's transformation as he Shifted, a large black panther entering the fray and knocking the wolf away from Gunner. He twisted, fangs glinting as he yowled and swiped with clawed paws. Emerson was not far away, nocking an arrow in his bow and letting it fly with trained precision, felling any beast who got too close to his lover.

How many of them were there? Their numbers seemed endless.

Arii did not have time to count as she twisted to Elijah. He sheered a blade through one wolf's throat, before twisting and gutting another before it could latch onto his arm. The beasts were huge, three times as big as Krepth's Shifter form. Their bodies were lithe and corded with muscle, long muzzles tapering from thick necks and barrelled chests, narrowing at the flanks, ending in a large, bushy tail. Snow white fur glittered as if tiny diamonds were encrusted in the very fibres, long claws as black as onyx. They were relentless, savage and rabid – their eyes a vivid blue like the many mineral springs they had passed on their travels.

She had never seen wolves such as these before.

"Didn't think to tell us they had oversized snow mutts in the south, Valerie?" yelled Arii as she dodged a flying set of snarling jaws, slamming her fist into the wolf's side before following through with her blade.

"May have just missed that little detail." Valerie yelled back as she ducked a careening white blur. The woman twisted and slid into a spread legged stance next to Gunner and Lyda as the group began to press back, forming a semi-circle as more beasts appeared from the darkness.

They were severely outnumbered.

"Group up! Press your backs together and don't let them get behind you!" called Krepth, brandishing a torch and thrusting the flaming tip at the faces of the snarling beasts. Saliva dribbled from the gaping jaws of one wolf, its stalk slow and languid as piercing blue eyes swept over them, a hungry snarl ripping from its maw.

Krepth tilted his head in Elijah's direction at the head of their group as he murmured from the corner of his mouth, "Now would be a good time to dip into your bag of tricks, Your Highness."

The growing group of wolves stalked forward, eyes alight with hunger before lowering on their haunches in preparation to strike.

Then they sprang, jaws opening impossibly wide.

Elijah's hand snapped out before him, fingers splayed.

Arii felt the shift in the air – the wind that had been sweeping over them suddenly stilled as the world slowed in motion, tiny fragments of snow rose from the ground and drifted into her eyesight with crystal clarity – tiny diamonds shimmering in the flickering camp firelight. The hairs on her arms stood on end as crackling energy sizzled against her skin, a thrumming hum beginning to vibrate in the earth beneath her boots. Her attention drew up, breath whooshing from her lungs at what she saw.

Above them – levitating as if frozen in mid leap – were the snow wolves.

"Holy fermenting hell…" whispered Gunner, clutching his leg as the ground began to quake in earnest beneath them.

Arii's eyes snapped to Elijah, his hand still outstretched, his face twisting and lips pulled back over his teeth. Sweat bloomed and beaded on his forehead before her eyes, and then she noticed that he was beginning to shake.

"Get back, all of you!" she yelled, moving to grab Tikkani and Quinn just as a resounding boom shook the clearing. Their party scattered, hitting the snow as a shuddering explosion struck their backs.

Magic slammed against them, rocketing out and crashing into the wolves as they dangled in mid-air. Canine bodies flew, smashing into the snow and rock all around them.

Slowly, the group began to rise from their positions as they recovered, looks of surprise and awe plastering every face as they watched the beasts limp away in defeat.

Then all eyes turned to Elijah.

He stood in a perfect circle of cleared snow, moist dirt beneath his boots, his shoulders shaking as his hand dropped to his side, watching the beasts in their retreat. His breaths were shallow, chilled mist clinging to the heat of his breath as Arii approached, attempting to clasp his hand before yanking away as static sparked between their fingers.

"Ouch!"

Elijah suddenly spun, eyes wide as he grasped her shoulders. "Did I hurt you? Is anyone hurt? I just grabbed the power and just... pulled. I wasn't thinking."

"Elijah, it's alright – nobody was hurt," she said quickly as the others hesitantly joined them.

"That was bloody brilliant!" crowed Valerie, slapping her palm against Elijah's broad back. "Remind me not to get on your bad side!"

Arii's eyes swept Elijah's face; his eyes fixed on her own as the group recovered.

For a small moment she felt melted to the spot – lost in the mercury depths of his eyes as the others blurred around them. She swore she could see a tiny spark in those depths, a shadow of a smile tugging his lips.

As quickly as it has appeared, it was gone, as if it had never been.

Damn mind, playing tricks.

"Well perhaps you could reach back into that pool of yours, Herington – we have company..." growled Krepth, drawing Arii's attention.

Just beyond the flickering light of the campfire was a man.

He stood silent, broad shouldered and harsh-looking, covered with thick furs and a long beard. He watched them silently, dark eyes and expression unreadable.

Slowly from the darkness came two more figures, both men – both just as weathered and harsh.

Southern men.

The group tensed, slowly reaching for their weapons once more.

Before they could draw steel, the man lifted his hand in a placating gesture. "We mean no harm." His voice was low, as ragged as the harsh terrain around them as he added, "We were on patrol when we heard the sounds of your group under attack." His cool blue eyes were set under two thick, bushy eyebrows – his gaze never once faltering from Elijah.

"You," said the man, jerking his chin in Elijah's direction, "You used magic."

Elijah stepped forward then, lifting a subtle hand to pause Arii as she began to move with him. It took everything within her not to growl at the way the man glared at Elijah. She eyed the men with a scrutinizing tilt of her head.

"I did," confirmed Elijah.

The man nodded, as if the admission pleased him, turning to his men before bringing his attention back to the travellers. "You are not from the south – obvious as you would not have lit a fire where the wolves like to hunt." The man's beard twitched as a hard smile appeared upon his features. "From the north, I assume?" By the unquestioning way the man's eyes slid over their odd group, Arii guessed he knew exactly who was within their traveling party.

"They are expecting you in Erstonia, Eliverus Herington. Word was brought ahead from the east that we were to expect your arrival. Come, we will accompany you to the castle."

Elijah stole a glance back at the group, meeting eyes of uncertainty as they began to gather their scattered array of belongings amongst the cooling corpses of snow wolves.

When his gaze met hers once more, she gave him a slight tilt of her head – enough of a confirmation that they would follow. She would not drop her guard though, and she knew Elijah would not either.

Slowly the group began to retrieve their horses, trailing the rugged men into the freezing night.

THOGAN

CHAPTER SIXTEEN

ARIIAYA

Elijah headed their procession, following in the tracks of the three southern guides. The men were mostly silent as they travelled, only speaking occasionally to glean some more about their crew.

After some careful persuasion, Arii eventually learned the man whom had spoken first was named Aaren, and the two men shadowing him were Christoph and Klohem – border men in service to the Vox family. They patrolled the valley, and for what Arii was unsure. So far, they had only encountered the snow wolves, and what other beasts roamed the land they were yet to discover.

Arii could feel tension radiating around the group at the appearance of the strangers, who had set her on edge. She watched their every movement like a hawk, her expression as cold as the surrounding snow. As the hours passed without a fuss, she began to relax a touch, her eyes often roaming to Elijah's broad back, watching his keen gaze as it swept back over their surroundings. She could tell he too was watching like a bird of prey.

The group napped in the saddle – not the most comfortable place to sleep but the less time they paused the better.

They travelled for a day and a half, stopping halfway to rest in the shelter of a cave – a high mountain shelf mostly shielding them from the biting wind as the moon passed overhead.

It took all of Arii's effort, combined with Nem, to convince Elijah to stop and sleep. He needed to be alert when they entered Erstonia, and magic recovered with rest. They had no idea what they would be faced with there, or what the Vox brothers would demand in return for their support against the north – if they graced them with a meeting at all. Elijah relented, albeit reluctantly as Arii and Nem kept watch, their party resting for a few hours before dawn bathed the white world in mild orange light.

On the second day, the group reached a gentle decline into a snow-covered valley. The trees hung low, branches frozen solid in bows of respect. Arii could see the outskirt of a river, the arctic waters running gently between frosted riverbanks. Snow began to fall around them as the colossal mountains loomed ahead, tiny clinquant diamond specks dusting her cheeks and eyelids.

Beside them, Tikkani leaned her head back and opened her mouth, poking out her tongue to catch the snowflakes.

Arii smiled as Emerson laughed beside her. Hesitantly, she lifted a hand and allowed the powdered snow to bunch on her outstretched palm.

"Before this journey, I had never seen snow. The north never gets cold enough," Quinn whispered. White dusted his lop of brown hair and stuck to his lashes like sugar.

Arii flipped her hand, allowing the powder to fall.

"Plenty of time to frolic later, the castle is naught an hour away from here," called Aaren over his shoulder.

Arii had only ever read about the castle in textbooks. Nothing compared to seeing the incredible, formidable structure in the flesh.

As they rounded a road atop a precariously thin ledge of mountainous rock, the castle suddenly came into view in the hazy distance before them.

It was a behemoth structure, a city of solid stone walls nestled in the side of the mountain as if the gods themselves had carved the construction. Tall turrets of stone reached like fingers into the sky, snow-dusted rooves scattered in amongst the safety of the thick walls. The architecture was harsh and square, and yet as the mist cascaded from the mountaintops – brushing the highest towers and causing the filtering sunlight to dance over the grey masonry – there was a rugged beauty to Erstonia that Arii had never imagined. She could not help but stare along with the others.

Birds drifted overhead, sunlight catching and reflecting off the rolling, snow-capped mountain ranges beyond the city as they followed the alpine path towards the front gates. Either side of the entry stood two bears carved from stone, at least twenty feet tall, heads lifted to the heavens and jaws open wide, standing like sentries with glittering eyes made of crystal.

The gentle *clop clop* of their mounts' hooves on the stone path echoed over the space as they progressed beyond the statues.

"I have *got* to get me one of those!" Quinn called, his neck craning as they passed.

Arii had to admit – the stone bears *were* incredible.

Aaren rose a hand as they approached the entrance, the men atop the wall waving in response before the gates began to open. Arii could hear the crank of metal, the sound of stone grinding against stone.

If the castle of Viridya was impenetrable, then this place was surely its cousin made of stone. Twice as sturdy, and twice as impossible to sneak in to. She thanked the gods that they had an invitation and didn't need to infiltrate their way inside.

As they entered the city, Arii could not help but feel like they were being watched.

Her head tilted, catching glimpses of faces in the windows of the houses they passed; curious people exiting their homes at the sound of their mount's hooves on the damp cobblestones. The structures were cold grey stone, their facades blanketed with snow, small piles collecting upon windowsills and on the timber coverings, stalactites of ice glittering from surrounding overhangs.

The people were weathered and dressed in furs, covered in the thick skins of bears, wolves and other southern creatures. Their faces were wary, their hair long and pulled back, braided away from their strong faces. The men all had thick beards of varying lengths, and Arii supposed that was to help protect their faces and necks from the freezing temperatures.

Arii had heard the people of the south were harsh and standoffish, described in texts as barbaric and brutal, so when they were greeted with nothing but wary stares she was not at all surprised.

Aaren and his companions showed them to the stables, where they handed their horses over to some young stable boys before being led towards the highest structure on the highest slope the city.

Heavy wooden doors swung wide as they entered the throne room of castle Erstonia, the warm air within greeting them as their group followed Aaren's lead. Arii's head craned to absorb everything, blinking in astonishment as the trailing snow crunched under their boots.

The throne room was a colossal, cool grey space lined with flickering dark steel wall sconces and thick stone pillars forming arches across the ceiling. Dark blue drapery lined the walls, embroidered with the symbol of the south – a snarling white bear – the material fluttering as the door closed behind them. The only light – apart from flame-lit lamps and a small firepit in the middle of the room – was a small, circular window with stained glass just a few feet above the dais.

Her assessment of the room paused on that dais, where two men sat regally on identical, dark stone thrones, carved with thick, sweeping detailing.

Jero and Thogan Vox, twin Princes of the south.

The first man, apparently the eldest by only a few minutes, was Jero. Built like a brick outhouse, he had muscles the size of tree trunks, an impressively shaped beard the colour of deep sand, and thick shoulder length hair framing his face. Peeking from the curtain of his locks was a tattoo – arching just above his right eyebrow and sweeping beyond his hairline. From what Arii could see, the pattern resembled many of the beautiful and rugged details scattered throughout the stone city. He eyed them with dark hazel eyes under bushy eyebrows, and despite his thick facial hair, Arii guessed the man to be around Elijah's age.

His brother, Thogan, looked almost identical – only his sandy brown hair was swept back into a tail with a leather thong, the sides shaved close to his skull and tattooed with the same thick yet beautiful tribal patterns as his brother, though on the opposite side.

Two sets of hazel eyes scrutinised their traveling party as they finally reached the foot of the dais.

Jero leaned forward, arm muscles bulging as he stroked his beard. Arii had at first believed the man to be wearing a one sleeve tunic – but upon closer inspection she realised his entire left arm was covered in dark tattoos.

Thogan had his opposite arm covered in the same story of ink as his brother. They both wore dark leather jerkins, thick belts with steel buckles and thick, heavy knee-high boots.

Arii did not know much about the twins, only that they were strong and harsh men, just like the people they watched over.

Aaren bowed respectfully, and the group bowed shortly after.

"Your Highnesses, I have for you Eliverus Herington and his accompanying party from the north. There are a few more than Freya Bloom had stated in her letter, but I believe Captain Valerie Gray and her crew are not strangers to us."

Jero held out a hand, flicking his fingers in a standing motion as Aaren finished.

"Please, rise – all of you," said Jero, his voice deep and harsh like thick gravel. His tone held a lilt of an accent, not unattractive. It made Arii think of water crashing against smooth stones, harsh yet strangely mesmerising.

As they stood, Jero pushed up from his throne, closely followed by his brother. The man approached Elijah to brace his big hands on his shoulders. They were almost identical in height, Arii noticed.

"Welcome, brother. It has been a long time."

Elijah was silent for a moment, before he cleared his throat as he said, "Thank you for your hospitality, Prince Vox." He nodded to Thogan before continuing, "But I must apologise – have we met before?"

Arii gnawed her lip, feeling some tension build under the stares of the southern Princes.

Elijah's brows narrowed, his questioning look causing Thogan to say, "So it is true, you have no memory of your past?"

Elijah simply nodded, and Jero's brows rose, his head tilting as he surveyed the dark-haired man before him.

"Well, this is somewhat awkward – but please know that it was upon peaceful terms, as our families were once allies."

Arii noticed Elijah's throat bob at the mention of his family – faces he was only beginning to remember through the haze.

Jero smiled, causing his eyes to crease at the edges as he said, "Come, let us all dine in our great hall, and I will tell you of a far simpler time. Perhaps it will help jog your memory."

⸸

The long tabletop was covered with an incredible array of food, and Arii was unsure what to try first. Many of the dishes were roasted meats – thighs, too large to have come from regular chickens, roasted with green beans, bay leaves and rich gravy, along with large racks of beef ribs drizzled with a red wine sauce. There was boar meat sliced on a bed of warm mushrooms and broth, leeks sautéed in goose fat, and crisp roasted potatoes and carrots cut into thick chunks sprinkled with herbs. Around the feast were seasoned vegetables, the greens bright in dark wooden bowls. Southern people did not appear to have big appetites for sweets, Arii noticed, but there were small offerings of figs soaked in whisky. The meals were hearty, made to warm them up from the inside.

Fires roared in hearths on every wall of the room.

Beside her, Quinn spoke around a mouthful of roast. "I think I found my new favourite court!"

Tikkani make a *tsk* sound from beside Quinn, her eyes never leaving the brawny Princes at the head of their table as she hissed, "Quinn, don't speak with your mouth full!"

"Oi, you do it all the time!" he shot back, grabbing a drumstick and slamming it into his mouth – like some kind of wild animal.

"Not in front of *royalty* I don't," she growled, and Quinn jerked in his chair as she mashed the heel of her boot into his foot.

"Ow!" he moaned around his food.

On Arii's other side sat Krepth, his forest-green eyes tracking the conversation happening just a foot away, just as Arii was.

The air around them was not uncomfortable. Surprisingly the Vox brothers had been nothing but hospitable so far. She could hardly believe their luck – perhaps gaining their support would not be as hard as she had initially thought.

The room was filled with chatter, so much that Arii was not sure where to focus her attention. Initially it was on Valerie, Lyda and Gunner as they gushed over the tenderness of the boar meat, but her mind was like a scurrying mouse – weaving in and out of conversations as if through tunnels in the walls. To focus herself, she tweaked the starlight blue hem of her cloak between her fingers, mind briefly drifting back to the discussions of gods back in Evergrave. During the attack of the snow wolves, one of the animals had taken hold of her cloak in its teeth, before yelping to quickly set it free. In the chaos of the moment, she hadn't paid it much mind, but now, she wondered if there could be more to the cloak than just a simple piece of clothing.

The gods had been an afterthought in the north for as long as Arii had been alive. There, majestic and spotless buildings of faith stood neglected, gradually decaying. Cursing – and sometimes praying – to those gods seemed to only pass people's minds in the heat of a moment, and true worship of them had dwindled to small groups of a faithful few. She wondered if the magical objects stolen by the Fae long ago had taken away some of the gods' power, leaving them weakened and only able to communicate through inanimate objects such as The Tapestry of Life.

She was not even entirely sure what gods still remained, and which had faded to dust with time. She often found herself cursing to Nyx – the goddess of night, but she had heard utterings to Hemera, the goddess personification of day. Arii knew there was bound to be more than just night and day, but thoughts of gods and goddesses and their large family trees caused a headache to form between her eyes.

Jero leaned back in his chair, wiping the side of his mouth with a thick grey napkin before stroking his beard. "Gods, Herington – you do look a lot like your father. Your eyes though, they are your mother's."

Elijah glanced up from his meal, his body tensing despite the Prince's friendliness.

"I have been told that before. You knew my parents?"

Thogan smiled, holding up his mug as he said, "We were young when we met your parents, but they left a lasting impression. Tyverus and Hannera were fast friends with our parents." Thogan's look slowly darkened as he leaned forward in his seat, gaze locked on Elijah as he whispered, "Not a day went by that our parents did not speak highly of their northern friends. Up until their last breath they insisted someday we seek retribution for their deaths."

Elijah's voice was low, careful as he said, "And yet you remained here in the south…"

What he was insinuating had Arii's hairs standing on end. Despite his birth right, Elijah refused to fight for the throne – for what was rightfully his. It surprised her that he spoke so boldly. It was obvious that now that the snow was settling, Elijah was perhaps seeking someone to blame for his family's demise.

"What happened to your family was abhorrent, Eliverus. What the Kruels did to them will forever live in the memory of all who knew your family. But we could not mass an army and strike the north, no matter how much we wish for retribution."

Krepth spoke then, pointing his fork in Jero's direction. "Why? Your hesitation has aided in the slow decay of a once thriving dynasty."

Arii shot her friend an incredulous look as Jero's face became dark in response. "What is happening in the north is no fault of ours, Shifter."

Krepth's brows arched as his expression mocked horror. "Oh, my apologies – I guess hiding behind your stone borders like little snow babes was the best course of action then."

"Your court did the exact same, closing off from the north. Yet you question us?"

Krepth began to stand but was halted by Arii's steady hand on his chest.

It was clear that things, despite being hospitable, were turning tense, understandably. She was sure that these Princes had not welcomed guests from the north in a long time, and even though they had good intentions, they were still learning to trust. Slowly she stood, her purple eyes dancing over the table.

"What everyone did in the past is now irrelevant," she said, her voice steady as her eyes met Elijah's across the table. "What we do *now* is what matters." Her gaze darted to the two Princes as she leaned on the table, hands resting upon the dark mahogany surface.

All eyes were fixed on her, on her determined expression and slowly baring teeth.

"We have been given a shred of hope, a surviving Fae with magic so powerful that he may just be able to restore balance to a crumbling land. It is only a matter of time before the darkness that Valdis Kruel is bringing forth will reach your borders, and then what?"

She motioned to Elijah. "Eliverus has incredible magic. Help him learn to control it – and lend aid in the fight to save the entirety of Fythnar. This is not just the north's fight – it is *all* of our fight. South, West and East too!"

Jero leaned back in his chair, carefully considering her words.

Her eyes met cool silver once more. Elijah's stare was smouldering, his brows low and expression unreadable. She broke away, attention sliding to Jero as he finally answered.

"We have had reports of what was transpiring in Bonemire, and reports of armies being moved to Viridya in droves." He glanced at Thogan, meeting a small nod before continuing. "I'm afraid we cannot just *give* you our support, though."

Arii stiffened, her gaze narrowing. There it was.

Jero lifted a thick hand before adding, "Eliverus must also earn the approval of our people if you wish to have the support of our armies. We do not force any of our people to enlist or fight in our wars – they *choose* to do so, out of love for our nation and the cause they fight for."

Elijah spoke, his voice rough as he ground out, "And what does that mean?"

Thogan spoke after a beat of silence. "If what your group says is true, you are formidable with a blade – and the magic you have displayed so far could shake mountains. To prove yourself, we require you to undertake one of our longest standing traditions. You will need to enter the Permafrost Arena and fight against our most fearsome warriors and beasts. That will earn the respect of our people."

Valerie's whisper was barely audible from across the table as she said, "Well fuck, it was nice knowing you, Herington."

Permafrost Arena? thought Arii.

As if reading her thoughts, Emerson piped from down the other end of the table, "The arena is a warrior's way of rite in the south – a place where people fight to the death in the name of honour. It is said the snow is permanently stained red from the bloodshed there, and you can hear the roar of the crowd echo across the mountain passes. Once, the cheering was so fierce that it caused a landslide, burying a nearby town under snow."

Thogan picked some food from between his teeth as he chuckled, "Your knowledge is admirable. Only the best warriors leave the arena. Conquer it and you will have unquestionable loyalty – ourselves included. A king needs to show strength. This will not only earn our support but show us your backbone. Physically and magically."

Elijah rubbed the bridge of his nose as Arii plopped back in her chair, her legs no longer able to keep her upright as the severity of what they were saying coiled in her gut.

"I'll do it."

Arii's wide eyes shot to Elijah, as did the entire table. She could feel the tension thick in the air around them. Elijah was talented in battle, she had not seen anyone fight like he did. He could conquer an arena of the best warriors in the south.

Right?

Apprehension spoiled the feast in her gut.

Jero clapped his massive hands together as he exclaimed, "Aaren, send word to prepare the arena and notify the townspeople. In three days' time, history will be made in the Permafrost Arena!"

Hazel eyes sparkled with eagerness as Thogan added, "This will be an event worth witnessing."

CHAPTER SEVENTEEN

ARIIAYA

A man slammed his boot upon the tavern table, lifting a jug of beer into the air as he addressed the full room of eager faces before him. Clearly a bard, the man clutched a much-loved lute as he launched into his story.

"The earth shall rumble and the heavens shall part, for the arena craves blood and blood is what it shall receive! Prepare yourselves, brothers and sisters, for the Permafrost Arena shall once again make history!"

The air was sizzling with excitement, along with the thick, mingling scents of food and liquor. The large tavern was a bustle of merriment as townspeople ate and drank, accompanied by thumping, wild beats of crude instruments from the bard and his crew as word of what was to come reached every crevasse of Erstonia.

"Our gods will bear witness, for none shall wish to miss this. Will the arena taste the royal blood of the fabled 'Prince who was lost', Eliverus Herington, seemingly snatched from the jaws of death to finally appear here today? Or will the finest warriors in the south finish what fate started many years ago?" The crowd cheered. "Will he survive and emerge triumphant? Will he be deemed worthy by the gods of the arena?" Barks and hoots reverberated the tavern windows. "Should he be found unworthy, though, may his cooling corpse become food for the wolves, and may a thousand black crows descend upon the arena to feast upon his entrails!"

Arii remained silent as the group conversed around her, taking up a table in the corner of the busy place. It had only been a few hours since they had parted ways with the Princes, and even though the smartest thing to do would be to rest, Valerie had insisted they pay a short visit to the city tavern, explaining that she had friends there.

"Gods, these people are so barbaric," said Tikkani around a snack of dried jerky, a piece stuck between her front teeth as Luc nodded enthusiastically. She suddenly stood, throwing her hands up before bringing them down upon the table as she roared, "I love it!"

Her outburst earned her a startled look from Luc, who blinked rapidly. Beside him, Emerson pinched the bridge of his nose and squeezed his eyes shut. After their feast in the stone castle, Arii wondered how the girl could be eating again so soon.

Had Arii not been so preoccupied by the rampant chatter of her friends, the cheer of the tavern patrons and the way they spoke with such disconnect about the fight to come, she too would be showing amusement as Tikkani hoisted her tankard into the air, a boom of cheers shaking the cutlery upon their table.

Nem nudged her knee against Arii's, pulling her from her musing. "I know that look – you're contemplating murder, aren't you?"

Forcing a wry smile, Arii said, "Unfortunate that I'm severely outnumbered here. If you fight with me, surely we can even the odds?"

"You worry for him, for Elijah." Nem hedged, staring in that intent, unblinking way that told Arii that she was also in no mood for jokes.

Arii watched as a serving man slammed down more tankards upon their table, her gaze not meeting Nem's as she said, "We cannot know what he will face. We have but a few days to prepare, and he still has not yet grasped a stable enough hold on his magic."

Nem's brows drew and she too launched her gaze elsewhere as the conversation of the table drifted towards them. Their travel party sat with Aaren, who had been assigned their guide for the duration of their stay in Erstonia. Quinn conversed with Gunner, Krepth and Elijah, the latter who despite the weight of the day seemed at ease. Arii wondered if Elijah truly grasped the gravity of the situation he was about to enter.

Lyda leaned across the table, her smile wide, dark hair tussled, her eyes shimmering bright as she inserted herself into the conversation. From what Arii could gather, they were discussing what animals they would be if they all could shift.

Not everyone was obsessing over the trial as she was, it seemed.

Arii sighed and pressed thoughts of the arena back as she promised herself she would worry later.

"Gunner would be a boar. You know, unkempt and smelly, likes water and mud," said Lyda, earning her a wave of hands from Gunner as he objected.

"Bollocks, I'd be one of those proud and powerful Fjord mounts! Sturdy as stone yet swift as lightning, not to mention being hung like a–"

"Please," yawned Lyda, drawing out the word, "Can we not converse about anything without you bringin' up the size of your–"

"I'd be a fox. Cute and cuddly with the very real possibility of turning rabid at any given moment," chimed in Tikkani, prompting the others to raise their voices and talk over one another. Arii felt a smile spreading her face, her eyes meeting Elijah's over the table. He held a small smile too, his cheeks-tinged pink from the food and warmth. Lingering for a little longer than necessary, she passed her attention back to the group as Lyda leaned across the table and pointed a fork at Krepth, before motioning the utensil towards Quinn as she changed the subject. Lyda often did that, skipping about conversation as thoughts entered her head.

"So, I'm just speaking hypothetically here, but hear me out, kay?"

Krepth's brows rose and he leaned back in his seat, gaze curious as he swallowed his bite and folded his arms behind his head in a look of nonchalance.

"Let's say you were lost in a forest, loping along with pains in your guts so dire you felt you were but minutes from keeling over dead from hunger. Then there, upon a log you spot a nice, juicy lookin' bird, none the wiser to you – the hungry wolf – but a few steps away." She slapped her hands together, capturing the attention a few haggard men nearby who listened eagerly. "You catch it, you eat it, but not before the knowledge hits you that the bird–" She paused, pointing the fork at Quinn once more, "was another one of yer' Shifter brethren."

Krepth slowly righted his posture, face coalescing to mild shock as a snort sounded from Valerie nearby. Everyone recoiled as Lyda asked, "Would that be considered cannibalism?"

The entire table launched into conversation as her question stoked a fierce debate.

Nem's head tilted, looking thoughtful as she reasoned, "It's a valid question."

"Well, I guess it could be considered cannibalism…" flailed Krepth, his almost speechless hesitation uncharacteristic.

"Why am I the one who gets eaten?" cried Quinn.

Valerie laughed like a crow, thumping the table before coughing, "Cannibalism?! Trust Lyda to think of such a thing."

Lyda raised her fork into a salute. "That's me, the philosophiser."

"I'm surprised you know such big words, Lyds!" laughed Gunner, taking a sloshing swig of beer.

Tikkani waved her hands, her voice raising above the others as she shouted, "Oh, I know what Valerie would be! A sea drake!"

Thoughts of eating one's brethren aside, the group continued to throw about theories of what each member's spirit animal would be, their voices melding into a din as Arii pressed a hand to the side of her head.

A tankard of water was placed before her, causing her eyes to lift to Aaren. "There is plenty of mead, beer and wine if you like it, Miss – yet sometimes plain ol' water is best."

Arii took the water gratefully, "Thank you, Aaren."

"Don't mention it. Strange bunch you've brought into our walls, but they no doubt have good value."

She laughed, "You have no idea."

Aaren lifted his mug, taking a sip before placing it down and dashing away the froth from his top lip with the back of his hand. His southern accent was thick, but she had no trouble catching his words as he said, "Don't worry about your King. From what I saw in th' clearing against the wolves, the gods watch over young Herington. They will no' abandon him when he enters the arena."

"You believe an outsider will win your battle games? A man your entire court knows nothing about save for the fact he should be dead."

"And that fact alone proves he be' blessed," Aaren reasoned.

Arii shrugged in response. She did not disagree with the man, but she couldn't seem to shake the fingers of doubt prodding at her insides at how little she knew of the arena and its combatants.

If life had taught her anything, it was to always expect the unexpected.

Aaren cocked his head towards Nem, "So, yer' name is Nemesis?" Nem's eyes slid to him, as he added, "What were yer' parents thinkin' when they named their child Nemesis? I mean no offense Miss Rion but it's bizarre."

Nem's silver nails tapped against the goblet she nursed, "I named myself," she replied simply, taking a dainty sip of her wine, her striking eyes fixed on the man.

Arii thought back to when she had asked the same question. At the beginning of their fragile alliance, Nem handed the information over reluctantly as they cleaned training weapons in the courtyard at the School of Fate. *When I washed up on the shore with no memories to fill my head, I was lost, afraid, and alone." She paused as Arii's brows lifted, halting in her task. Rays of dawn peppered her pale skin as they ran oiled cloths over their weapons.*

"Do you know what it's like to have nothing to think back on, no thought in your head except empty, mindless buzzing? I knew not where I had come from, who my family was – if I had a family at all. I did not even know my own name." Nem continued unfazed, her voice monotone. "So I swore the world as my enemy, and I its nemesis…" a small shrug, "Anger was all I had in the beginning, and I was so angry. Angry at the world, angry at whoever left me there, angry at myself for not remembering… the name just stuck."

The few words that Nem offered seemed to satisfy Aaren as his brows lifted behind his mug of ale, his shoulders bobbing in a shrug.

Arii was jerked back to the present as Tikkani suddenly said, "An owl, definitely an owl," which drew the attention of the group, Nem included. To blank looks, the girl hiccupped and grinned, seemingly still tuned in to the earlier conversation. "Nem would be one of those owls with silver feathers like knives and talons that could rip your face right off the bone."

Silence.

Emerson slapped his forehead, the sound punctuating the awkward moment.

Then Nem laughed.

A low, twinkling sound like bell chimes on a breeze.

The music started up again, and voices blared to life as conversations flew back to where they left off. A strange feeling, one that was becoming constant around her friends, rose in her chest once more as Arii's gaze travelled from Nem's small side smile to the others.

Tikkani tilted precariously in her seat, and Elijah's hand subtly curled around her bicep to keep her from falling from her perch. He gently pressed a mug of water in front of her, dashing her liquor cup away while her eyes fluttered with drowsiness. She could see the concern in his stoic mask, but there was a tinge of amusement there too.

Her friends laughed and continued to converse, and Tikkani dashed the cup to her lips, unconcerned as she chugged the water down.

Elijah's eyes met Arii's, and she knew as soon as his brows creased that he saw what she was fighting to hide in her own eyes.

Instead of continuing to wallow, Arii grasped her previously abandoned mug of mead and threw it back to her lips, downing the entire thing whole.

✝

The next morning Arii was intensely grateful that she had not flailed overboard on the drink, as she, Elijah, Tikkani and Nem took their places on an open-aired training ring in the army courtyards. Now though, as she dashed her oiled cloth over one of her daggers –

she wished she had had a few less drinks as the ghost of a headache danced behind her eyes.

With it, an ugly sour mood reared its head as memory of what was to come resurfaced.

Elijah busied himself dashing a whetstone over his sword nearby, the sound slowly grating on her. She was but a moment from questioning how much sharpening a blade truly needed when Tikkani's voice deflected the ire that Elijah did not deserve in that moment.

"The Violet Assassin huh? Rumour has it that you eat your victims once you finish killing them, like some kind of wicked spider," said Tikkani as she secured the head on the arrow she had just finished fletching. Nem choked on a laugh nearby.

Arii blanched, unable to hide her look of surprise at the entirely random train of thought that her friend was riding. "That's new, where did you hear that?"

Elijah hesitated in his task, the sing of stone against steel a consistent cadence in the air, but those movements slowed as Tikkani piped, "It's true then?"

"Well, it depends on your definition of 'eating her victims'," Arii waggled her fingers in the air, resembling quotation marks. "Figuratively… literally…" She paused, her gaze meeting Elijah's, which had locked during her speech. Then she whispering saucily, "Sexually…"

"And I'm out!" laughed Tikkani, pacing the ring to where Nem tested her own weapons.

"You started it!" Arii called after her.

"You are incredibly immature," Elijah said, continuing to draw the stone on steel, but his attention was not fully focussed on his task anymore.

"I'm only providing more information for those interested. Besides, you only touch the surface of the monikers and rumours that follow my name. I've been called far worse."

"Huh, such as?"

She lifted her hand and began to tick off fingers. "Bitch… Hellion…

Heartbreaker–”

"Rapscallion, heartless wench…" he broke in with the flash of a smile.

She gasped, placing a hand over her heart. "Whoa whoa there Your Highness, I'm sure you've had your fair share of names over the years too."

"Enlighten me, Hellion," he prompted with a lift of a brow.

She glared, then she stood suddenly, drawing the attention of Nem and Tikkani nearby as she called out, "The hooded virgin with a face like a dropped sweet cake."

He blinked rapidly, the look hysterically comical on his rugged features. "Where in the world did you hear that?!"

Arii's pointed canines flashed as she grinned wickedly, "True then? The part about being a virgin? Because I can tell you the other part is untrue." She grinned, leaning in and attempting to snatch a spare whetstone from beside his thigh.

His fingers snapped around her wrist, and Arii's eyes lifted to meet dark silver. She once again noticed the dark flecks of black in amongst the grey, like an inverted starry night.

"Wouldn't you like to know…" he whispered, low and deep.

Tension sizzled and had Arii's attention been anywhere but on the rare, slow and languid smile forming on Elijah's lips, she would have noticed Tikkani's raised brows as she hitched her chin in their direction while grinning at Nem. Arii's voice dropped an octave to match his as she breathed. "Mmmm… yes?"

Elijah leaned in close, breath against her ear, lips grazing her jawline ever so slightly. She sucked in a breath and held it as he murmured. "In your dreams, perhaps."

As if it had never been, the tension snapped like a violin string pulled too taut, and he leaned back to continue with his task as if they had never spoken.

"Ha ha!" cawed Tikkani, slapping her knee as Arii's face mirrored a shocked look. "Get a room, you two. I can see the snow melting around you!"

Krepth paused nearby, eyes like daggers as he hauled a bag of supplies towards the stables. Arii hadn't even noticed his arrival, far too preoccupied with very inappropriate thoughts of Elijah placing her in very compromising positions that suggested he had forgone virginity many years ago. Their eyes locked for a moment, and at his protective expression, she glared in response.

She wiped the look from her face swiftly as she passed the whetstone over her dagger with perhaps a little too much force, deciding to ignore Krepth. She found she enjoyed this light-hearted banter with Elijah, and she would not allow an overprotective brother figure to ruin what little fun they found themselves having.

"You wound me, my friend."

"We are friends now, are we?" Elijah probed.

Without looking at him, she continued her task with gusto. "Never said we weren't. Now, let's get some practice in before the sun falls."

The sun moved across the sky, and by the time it had reached its zenith and begun its descent, it was just Arii and Elijah left in the ring, sparring and dancing like times past. The routine continued on the days that followed, in amongst some small spurts of leisure time with their friends at the tavern.

For two days they trained in preparation for the Arena. Two days of intense, sweat laced exercises and thrown curses in the training ring as Arii once again snapped at Elijah, her teeth baring as frustration flared through her insides like wildfire. Frustration, and perhaps a little bit of anxiety, too.

His movements were swift and precise, but she knew he was holding back when it came to his magic.

As they glared at one another across the snow-covered outdoor training ring, Arii pointed her sword towards his chest as mist gathered before their panting, open mouths.

"Try again, and this time – for Nyx's sake – do not hold back!"

Arii knew it would take more than two days to coax Elijah's full potential of magic. That could take weeks. They did not have that kind of time, and tomorrow he would be in a frozen arena facing the most fearsome warriors of the south.

He could not lose; they could not afford him to.

Arii knew that if he were to lose, he would not come out of the arena alive.

At first, she had argued with him to let her fight by his side in the arena, which he had refused and reasoned that it would not be allowed, anyway. He had met her anger-fuelled response with a stubborn set of his jaw and crossed arms, his gaze dark and intense.

So, she threw her frustration into their sparring.

His further reluctance to dive fully into his magic had her teeth grinding together. What small progress they had made on the *Murderous Lust* seemed to have backtracked suddenly, and it had her almost steaming from the ears like a boiling kettle.

He had a small chance at winning without his magic, but she knew he ultimately had to show the people his magical strength and power. It was what they were expecting, she was sure of it. They had seen warriors fight with tooth and nail before; but a male Fae, perhaps the last, fighting with magic? That would surely sway them. And that meant accepting everything within him – magic included.

Elijah had dipped into the magic a few times, throwing blasts of power her way which she avoided, or met with her own magic.

The crackling blue blasts were but a snap of what she had seen him use against the sea drakes.

Arii thrusted forward, sword spearing towards Elijah's chest in a blur. He blocked, before she swept her foot out to trip him, and angled her fist to punch a blast of magic at his gut. Elijah leaped, twisted and thrust his palm out, deflecting the attack straight back at her. Her eyes widened in surprised as she was knocked back a foot, the magic slamming her into the dirt and punching the breath from her lungs.

"Better," she coughed, as Elijah stalked towards her.

Flipping back onto her feet, she rocketed forward, twisting in a blur to appear behind him, her palms slapping either side of his face as she willed her magic forwards.

Just as quickly, Elijah's hands snapped to clasp her arms as he dipped to toss her over his shoulder. She twisted, hitting the snow-covered stone with a grunt. Her hands flew out, palms outstretched and with a crack of power, Elijah's body flew across the ring, hitting the ground a few feet away.

Suddenly she was atop him, her thighs straddling his as her blade pressed against his throat, her face twisted in fury. "You're still holding back! You cannot hold back tomorrow, Elijah – you will *die*!" she screamed in his face, her voice wavering on the last word as her anger – her fear – erupted.

Elijah gazed up at her, his expression unreadable as the blade pressed deeper into his jugular. He did not make a move to fight her, his voice gentle as he said, "You have seen me fight, you have seen what I can do, Arii. I hold back now because I have no idea what this power inside me would do if I lost control." His brows narrowed as he added, "I don't want to hurt you."

Arii leaned down, her nose inches from his as she whispered, "You never have to hold back with me, Elijah."

His lips pursed as he drawled, "The only one to regret those words will be me – when you're a red smear upon the snow."

"That is my risk to take. Everyone is expendable, Elijah. Everyone except for *you*."

"Don't be ridiculous," he retorted.

"I'm not, it is the truth!"

Frustrated at their lack of progress, she eased off him, allowing him to rise as she sniped, "It's getting late, you need to rest before tomorrow."

She did not meet his eyes as she gathered the various weapons they had been using throughout the day. She could feel his presence as he paused nearby, surveying her back as she hoisted a bag over her shoulder, the weapons within clinking together.

"Ariiaya," he started, but she ignored him, striding in the direction of their rooms without looking back.

CHAPTER EIGHTEEN

ARIIAYA

The Vox brothers had placed them in comfortable lodging, small stone rooms adorned with warm wooden furniture and large crackling hearths, which always seemed to be stoked and flaming whenever Arii returned to hers, no matter the time of day or night. She was sure they had housekeepers who ensured the fires were constantly lit, or they would all suffer frostbite.

As the moon lifted in the sky beyond her window, Arii stared into the flames in silence, sitting barefoot and cross-legged on the floor before the fireplace.

Dressed in just a light woollen tunic and loose canvas pants, she felt that anything more covering her body would surely cause heat stroke. The room was hot – but after being out in the elements all day, it was not exactly unpleasant.

Her mind drifted, watching the flames dance. What kind of warriors would Elijah face in the arena tomorrow? From what she could glean from Aaren, southern warriors were unlike any else in Fythnar. They were brutal, they were used to the cold, and they had incredible strength. Christoph had exclaimed that their top warrior, Vax Bloodborne, had faced five giant bears alone in the mountains and had killed them all with his bare hands.

Then he had drank their blood… allegedly.

The last part she was sure was an added flourish, but Arii was not willing to find out. She had also heard word that people were traveling from all across the south to attend the event, not having had anything so exciting happen in years.

Her friends seemed just as worried as she was about the possible outcome of the day ahead. Nem had taken a liking to Elijah, although she did not admit it outright, and Arii knew this when Nem voiced the same tone of anger at Elijah facing the arena alone. But she also had a confidence in Elijah's abilities that Arii could not quite fully muster herself, despite seeing what he could do.

"Elijah is incredibly fierce and strong, Arii. I think we need to give him a little more confidence. What he needs is us believing in him," she had said, holding a firm stare as Arii felt her insides crumble.

It was not that she doubted his combat prowess... no, she did not doubt that part of him.

What was this feeling then if not doubt?

As she considered her inner turmoil, a knock sounded at her door, pulling her from her thoughts.

"Come in," she called, continuing to stare into the dancing flames. She heard the door open and footsteps enter the room. Normally she would not just allow anyone into her rooms without first gleaning who they were, but she knew who approached before he had even lifted his hand to knock. It was a strange sense – a feeling of anticipation that her beast gave off – that told her who it was.

The steps hesitated nearby, before a solid form eased into the space beside her. Her head tilted as Elijah stretched his legs out, boots angled away from the fire as he leaned back.

"I'm surprised you knocked," she said, her gaze never leaving the hearth.

"I'm surprised you invited me in."

They sat in silence for a time, both watching the flames flicker up a log, the embers skittering as the flames fluttered merrily. It was soothing.

"I understand why you're frustrated." Elijah said into the silence, breaking the gentle sound of crackling from the hearth.

"Do you?"

"Well, my magic doesn't seem to allow for mind reading, unfortunately. So, I've had to go off gut feeling and the signals you have been quite literally screaming in my face for the past two days."

Her head slowly angled, eyes narrowing as they met his. Elijah's expression was placid, the firelight playing across his strong features. Before she could speak however, he said into the air between them, "You're afraid."

She slowly turned to him, brows rising. "Afraid?" she echoed, not masking the surprise in her voice.

Was that what this was, fear? Was she afraid of what was to come? Of course she was afraid, who would not be afraid of a darkness bringing forth an army of undead.

But that was not the kind of fear he was speaking of, was it?

As she studied his features, studied the gentle depths of his silver eyes, across the sharp ridges of his cheeks and up to the thick, dark tresses of his hair to the hint of his delicately pointed ear – she realised the feeling she was experiencing was completely different from all that.

She was afraid of losing him.

And afraid of the intensity of her growing feelings toward him.

Was she ready to admit that to him, though? She had been dashing emotions away for so long that now that she was faced with them, she was unsure of how she would handle the possibility of rejection. Being conscious of her own feelings and the possibility of being hurt emotionally was a foreign concept to her, and now that she was allowing things to slip through the cracks, she was facing the strange realisation that you didn't need to be physically wounded to feel true pain.

Arii's gaze lowered to his lips, a breath sighing free. "Well, it's either that or I could just be hungry again..."

Elijah's lips quirked at that. "Well, you are particularly foul when you're hungry."

"Am I not foul all the time?"

"A lot, yes, but not all the time," he replied gently.

She smiled then, unable to help it, and his face slowly began to coalesce into an expression she had only seen a handful of times before.

"You know, you should smile like that more often…" he murmured, lifting a hand to brush his thumb over the little crease between her drawn brows.

Fire sparked in her veins at the touch, her eyes drifting closed as his finger glided down and along her jawline. "You are so beautiful when you smile," he breathed.

She wanted to snort a remark about always being beautiful, but as his fingers gently pinched her chin and his face closed the short distance between them, the words dissipated halfway. His lips brushed against hers, and she felt as if the very floor beneath her may just fade away if she did not hold on to something. So, she slipped her fingers into the hair at his nape, pressing forward to deepen the kiss.

It was like breathing in the smell of a forest in spring, his scent heady and complex. She could taste sweetness on the back of her tongue – magic – and her heart rose in tempo as his canines brushed her bottom lip. She could feel his hesitation, and even now, he held back. Perhaps it was due to hiding the parts of him that gave him away as a Fae for so long, always leaning back for fear of discovery.

He no longer needed to do so, and especially not with her.

Slowly she moved to sit on his lap, her thighs straddling his as she buried both hands in his hair. Beneath her, she felt a rumble in his chest and a swift inhale of breath that had her toes curling. To entice a reaction like that – with hardly any effort on her part – had a shiver of heat trailing down her spine.

Pressing his back to the side of the bed, she felt one strong hand caress her cheek, the other sliding along her abdomen and around to her lower back.

"What are you afraid of?" Elijah whispered between heating kisses, causing her to pause and lean back to gaze at him.

"What?"

Elijah's lips curled at her reaction, his fingers trailing down her neck in a touch so gentle it caused shivers to cascade down her spine once more. He did not seem to mind repeating himself as he leaned forward – brushing his lips along her jaw to her neck, sending the butterflies within her stomach into a frenzy.

"What..."

His breath fluttered over the sensitive skin of her neck.

"are..."

He brushed the tip of his nose across her jaw.

"you..."

He paused, fingers sliding into her hair and angling her head, before teasing the lobe of her ear with his teeth as he whispered, "... afraid of?"

Oh Gods.

Had he any idea what he was doing to her? Heat flamed across her skin, the room suddenly feeling far hotter than before, almost suffocating. With a swallow, she replied with a breathy, "I don't know what you're talking about."

He chuckled, the sound stoking fire to all her nerve endings as he sighed against her skin.

Was he waiting for her to admit to something?

Suddenly he dipped down and swept her into his arms, causing a squeak to erupt from her lips, her eyes widening in surprise. As they met his, she noticed they were dark, the silver depths shimmering with amusement.

"Alright, I'm afraid you're going to drop me on my arse," she cried.

"Try again," he murmured as his lips crashed against hers, sending her thoughts spiralling into an abyss.

All she could think about in that moment was his firm arms around her, the strength behind his kiss and the thrumming of his heart beneath her fingers as they braced against his chest. The feeling returned in full force, that fear of never feeling that reassuring thrum again – of his soul being sent to rest with the goddess Nyx in front of a sea of people in the Permafrost Arena tomorrow.

Her fingers clutched his nape as he moved them to the bed, gently setting her upon the featherdown covers and pressing his body against hers. He broke the kiss, gazing down at her with such intensity that it punched the breath from her lungs

Slowly he lifted a hand, and without breaking their stare, he snapped his fingers…

…and the lock on the bedroom door snipped shut.

At the sound, her beast rose within her, rousing with a purr, scraping against her defences as she hooked a leg over his hip, and flipped him on to his back. He grunted, still seemingly unused to tumbling with a woman almost as strong as he was, as she shoved him onto the mattress.

"You're learning," she whispered, leaning down to place her lips against his throat.

"I have a teacher who rides my arse all day."

"Oh that is amusing, as I thought you loved to ignore all forms of advice from your said *teacher.*"

His hands slid beneath her tunic, fingers skimming the skin of her back as he rumbled, "Perhaps she needs a lick of patience… she has a fiery temper that could rival a Kryvern."

"Maybe she just wants to ensure you don't become mincemeat under the mace of a southern warrior tomorrow. Perhaps she cares if you come back to her alive."

"Arii…"

She paused, leaning back to gaze down at him. His chest rose and fell under her hands, his cheeks flushed and eyes dark as she surveyed his expression. Her heart constricted as she burned his face to memory, eyes flicking over his features in the gold firelight, solidifying it in the forefront of her mind where – more often than not – he remained almost daily.

What if he died tomorrow? What if she never heard his voice again, or felt his gentle touch or tasted him upon her lips? Yes, they butted heads a lot, and he had her temper rising without much effort on his part – but that was them. They rebounded off one another – yet they always returned, like a string was tethering them to one another. He also challenged her when it came to her emotions.

Saving their land lost some of its appeal if he were not battling in it with her.

With far more hesitation than she normally felt, she shifted to unbutton her woolen blouse, plucking one button at a time as he watched – his gaze unblinking. She shrugged the garment down her shoulders, the golden light dancing across her body as his eyes swept over her.

Elijah's throat bobbed as his eyes drank her in, his lips parting ever so slightly.

"I'm not… used to feeling like this…" she whispered as he sat up, his face level with hers as he skimmed his knuckles down her arm. Goosebumps pebbled; her eyes fluttering closed as his lips brushed her own.

"And what do you feel?" he murmured against her lips before they were whispering along her jaw. If she did not know any better, she could have sworn he was trying to get her to admit what she felt inside. He seemed to be doing that a lot lately. He knew it was hard for her, and he somehow knew that in this moment she was in the middle of a battle within herself. Like when she pushed him to take control of his magic, Elijah was doing the same with her emotions.

One strong hand slid up to rest between her shoulder blades, the other skimmed up her stomach before cupping her breast, causing her thoughts to fall into a muddle.

Arii felt her lips move of their own accord as she admitted, "I feel… fear." Her eyes opened to gaze into liquid silver, her breath hitching; "Fear so deep it is settling in my bones."

Elijah's brows narrowed but his eyes softened as the words cascaded from her lips like an untapped fountain, and her eyes suddenly burned with unshed tears, hot angry tears that she struggled to contain.

"I'm afraid not for the fate of this land for once, but afraid you won't come back after tomorrow. All I feel is… inconceivable fear that… I…" She was lost for words, struggling to articulate exactly how she was feeling inside.

How did she feel about Elijah, truly?

At first it had been curiosity, then slow admiration, and then it had twisted into inconceivable, burning desire. And now, it was something far deeper than she was willing to admit out loud, something truly foreign to her.

How could she feel so fiercely, so quickly, after so long of not feeling anything at all?

Elijah must had noticed her struggle, because his voice was barely a whisper as he slid his hand to the nape of her neck and placed a kiss to her tender lips. "I know how hard it is for you to articulate your emotions into words, Arii. You don't need to hold them back any longer, especially not with me."

Funny, that sounds a lot like what she had been saying to him in the training ring. She swallowed thickly as his warm breath skittered across her collarbone.

"Enough talk…" she exhaled.

His teeth against her neck once more caused her thoughts to scatter, a small sound escaping her throat, causing him to smile against her skin again.

"It was worth a try…" he chuckled darkly.

At the gentle pressure of his hand on her breast and the hot fire coursing to the core of her, her spine relaxed and her head tipped back as he placed kisses down her neck to her collarbone, causing her senses to alight with sparks. Her fingers found the buttons of his tunic, and she knew suddenly that the time for words had passed.

Thank the Gods.

She practically tore the buttons free, revealing his firelit chest and battle sculpted torso.

Oh sweet Nyx, she had forgotten just how extraordinary his body was.

He shrugged out of the tunic, tossing it aside as their lips clashed again, tongues dancing as she felt him press forward – deepening their kiss, his mouth claiming hers with far more passion than he had allowed himself to display before. She felt as if a small tether had severed, as if he was finally realising that he did not need to hold back with her. Finally, he was perhaps taking his own advice. He could be a Fae – strong, fiery and passionate.

As Fae, the only limits they had were those they set for themselves.

And she had to let go of her own.

She sucked his bottom lip between her teeth, feeling satisfaction as he groaned, feeling the stirrings of him against where she wanted him most.

Suddenly his head dipped to her breasts, and she had to slam her mouth shut as he took her nipple between his lips, drawing upon the tip and causing her back to arch as she hissed a pleasured curse. The coarse hairs of his beard scraped against her skin, intensifying the feeling.

Elijah smiled against her as he tilted his head, eyes smouldering in the firelight as the walls shuddered around them. He took the second peak between his teeth and gently flicked his tongue against her sensitive flesh.

Hot fire speared to her core as she moaned his name. Static snapped in the air around them as she pressed herself closer, fingers digging into his shoulders as he kissed her skin, skimming a trail of fire up to the tip of her chin.

"You're so incredibly bewitching..." he murmured, locking eyes with her once more.

Where had this man come from?

The Elijah she knew was gruff, standoffish and brooding, not at all someone she imagined whispering sweet words that made her toes curl and the space between her thighs ache with need.

Suddenly he flipped her on to her back, pressing his weight against her, causing her to curl a leg around his hip to pull him closer, feeling almost desperate in her need to have him as close as possible. A window nearby shuddered, rattled as if something shook the earth momentarily. Oblivious, they continued, lost in their exploration of one another.

"Elijah..." she ground out as the fire in the nearby hearth danced wildly, as if a breeze has somehow picked up. Something tugged at the fog of her consciousness, but it was quick to dissipate as his teeth found her neck again and her lashes fluttered closed.

She sensed magic glittering in the air. It whispered over the bare parts of her skin like butterfly wings, raising gooseflesh in its wake despite the heat of the room.

She must have made a sound, because Elijah paused in his worship of her body to brush a lock of hair across her collarbone. It caused her to shiver.

She was not shy, she was not afraid to fight for what she wanted, and she wanted Elijah like nothing else. But as her heart slammed against the cage of her ribs and her hands fluttered over the scars of his back – Arii realised this almost felt like their last night together.

It could very well be their last night together.

Oh, how she wanted to have nothing between them, their skin coming together so she could not tell where she ended and he began. She knew he felt the same, could feel the evidence pressing harshly against her inner thigh, straining against his pants.

But was she ready to say goodbye?

This almost felt like a goodbye.

As her body tensed, Elijah leaned back fully, gazing down at her with a question in his eyes. Tenderly, he brought his hand to her cheek, brushing a chocolate strand of hair from her eyes. "Are you alright?"

Gods, was she so easy to read?

Arii bit her lip before confessing. "If we do this, then I feel like it'll solidify the fact that you may not return tomorrow."

Elijah's brows drew, worry lines forming. His lips parted, but she pressed a finger to his mouth.

"I will not make this our goodbye. I will not, because when you return to me tomorrow – alive, I swear to the gods and all that will listen that I will give everything to you."

A shadow passed across Elijah's features as his eyes slid across her face, as if trying to guess a riddle.

She continued. "Every scrap of me, every *godsdamned* fibre – it is yours." She swallowed thickly, violet eyes growing glassy as a phantom pain bloomed across her chest – thoughts of her time in

Bonemire flickering across her mind as she continued. "Because I can't enter the darkness again without you, Elijah. Whatever is on the horizon – none of it matters if you aren't there to face it with me."

Admitting the feelings that were causing her heart to race helped her to feel lighter, yet a shadow of anxiety remained. She did the best she could in that moment to keep her emotions in check, but the words were out in the air now, and couldn't be brought back. She felt strange, as if admitting some feelings aloud made her insides churn uneasily.

Before she could delve into the reasons, Elijah's throat bobbed, and he inhaled deeply – gathering her scattered attention. His silence had the anxiety within her raising its head higher. She had never felt so… open, like the pages of a book. She had always kept her cover snapped shut, a lock clicked tight upon her emotions. Now, lying beneath the possible future king of Fythnar, she felt her soul uncurl like the petals of a moonflower, bathing in the silver moonlight of his awed stare.

"Then I'd better survive tomorrow," he whispered finally, leaning to place a tender kiss to her swollen lips.

"Or I will come and find you in the afterlife and kick your perfect arse," she blew out a breath before nipping his lip, suddenly desperate to lighten the mood. He chuckled darkly against her lips, her heart stuttering at the decadent sound. She really liked his laugh, she realised.

"Perfect, huh?"

She nipped his lip again with a feline grin, "You know it is."

His grin faded, his expression growing serious. "Is that truly how you feel? Even after what I've put you through?"

"What in the world are you talking about?"

His thumb dashed along her bottom jaw. "I've fought you every step of the way since the beginning – yet you still… believe in me."

"They will all see what I see, Elijah. I can promise you that. You just need to grasp your destiny with both hands and show them that it is you who will lead them against the darkness. There is power in you unlike anything that has graced this land in over two hundred years.

You need to use it. See it as a blessing and not a curse."

As she spoke, she swore she could feel a breeze flutter across her skin and tickle her toes.

Had she left a window open?

"I will come back to you tomorrow – you have my word." His eyes opened slowly, and within their depths she saw a fire of determination that brought truth to his whispered words.

"Not just because I promised you my incredible body, I hope?" chuckled Arii.

He shot her a hot glare, before slipping from the bed. Wordlessly, he began to unbuckle his pants, causing Arii to stare with wide eyes.

"Close your mouth, little Fury – can't wear boots to bed, can I?"

Arii shrugged, sliding on to her side and watching with appreciation as he stripped and stood in his underclothes. She had to swallow and bite her lip for fear of gaping openly.

His body was battle scarred perfection, smooth, pale skin sculped over an incredible body made for war, making her decision to wait incredibly hard.

Stick to your word, Arii.

Elijah's hand motioned for her eyes to lift, and she was reminded of the time he had stared at her in her silver gown before the party on Winter Solstice.

"Can't a woman appreciate the gods' finer gifts?" she sighed lamely.

Elijah huffed, moving to dig out the coverlet as they slipped under the sheets, pulling the thick down up to cover their near nakedness. As they both moved to lie on their sides, faces inches apart with the fire dimming in the hearth, Arii's gaze tracked the lines of his face before resting on his eyes once more.

"Are you afraid?" she whispered into the dimming silence. His face was partly in shadow, the moonlight caressing the broad slope of his shoulder as his arm moved to drape over her hip. The motion was smooth, yet protective and she found she secretly liked that, too. It made her feel… safe. His hand splayed on her lower back, drawing tiny circles against her skin through the sheet as he murmured, "I'd be a fool not to be afraid."

She swallowed, eyes drifting closed as the adrenaline of their passion began to dissipate to a gentle hum in her veins. Like always though, that incessant pull towards him from between her breasts continued, and she had to chant in her mind over and over that she was making the right choice in not leaping off that cliff just yet.

"Sleep, Arii," he whispered, her mind on the soothing patterns of his fingers on her back as fatigue swept over her bones.

The soft mattress and the comforting scent of him made it easy to relax as Arii began slipping into a gentle oblivion.

Just as darkness claimed her, the wraith's voice returned, whispering, *'Heavy is the head that bears the crown...'*

CHAPTER NINETEEN

ELIJAH

Elijah watched Arii's face slacken with sleep, and wrestling with the raging firestorm within him. It felt like hours passed as the golden light of the hearth faded, and the moonlight slowly slipped over her fluttering eyelids. Her cheeks had remained flushed for some time, colour dulling as her features returned to pearl.

He was almost thankful that she had stopped their night from advancing any further. He was not sure what the beast inside him would do if he allowed it to take over. They were still getting acquainted, and something told him that if she had allowed things to continue, his effort at being a gentleman would have been decimated like the logs of wood now smouldering as ashes in the hearth. Gods, he had wanted to take her there, the temptation to bite her neck so strong that he almost admitted to her that what he feared most was himself.

As he watched her sleep, the claws had skimmed under his skin, purring with desire. It only ever happened with her – the heat, the wanting, the unfamiliar turmoil within him. He had always had such a strong semblance of control, but ever since she entered his life, it was as if she were trying to snap those tethers without really meaning to.

She confused him, well and truly perplexed him, and he was sure it wasn't all unintentional. Her eyes promised passion as her mouth delivered chaos, her gaze searing with desire, even as vehemence spewed forth in words. He could see it in her eyes, smell it on her skin, and feel it from her lips as they brushed against his that she desired him with the same burning and insatiable hunger as he desired her. She held him as if he would vanish into thin air, caressed his scars like they were divine gifts from the gods, and whispered his name as if it tasted like chocolate. They were like fire and ice – her wildfire flames tangling with the blizzard shrouding him until they were dangerously close to becoming a superstorm.

Was this almost uncontrollable need to have her part of being a Fae? Perhaps this was normal. He had no idea. He did not feel like this around any of the other Fae that he had encountered. Nem, Devina… no, no-one else coaxed the beast like Arii did.

It was like a cord coiled within his chest, tugging in her direction wherever she was near, and sometimes Elijah swore there was a vague familiarity between them… so distant, so… strange. As if they could have known one another in another life, another reality. When they were like this – tangled in each other, exploring one another – he couldn't shake the feeling that her body was made for him, and his made for hers. They just… fitted. He was not sure how to explain it. And he would not be explaining it to her. Elijah knew Ariiaya well enough now that he knew such talk would make her withdraw.

He had to tread with care when it came to her emotions, he had learned that the hard way, coming under the fire of her heated glare too many times to count.

Elijah's mind drifted, his gaze sliding to the nearby window. Dark clouds housed stars, pitch black beyond the frost-fingered window.

"Are you afraid?"

Arii's question lingered in his thoughts like a black stain. Yes, he was afraid, but not for what he would face tomorrow. His fear was that this power inside him, this… wild, immense power… would not be enough to rise and become the saviour everyone wanted him to be. The saviour this land needed. Everything he knew about magic had been shattered into a million pieces, and he was still trying hard to surpass the mindset that it was nothing but evil.

Evil.

His mind drifted to Lorch, to thoughts of what his brother was enduring in the castle. Despite his confidence that Lorch would not cave to the darkness, he could not help but feel doubt. Valdis was persuasive when he wanted something, and that something was a kingdom on its knees before him, shrouded in darkness and riddled with death. He had tried to imagine what a conversation with Lorch would entail in their current predicament, but if the headhunting soldiers in Amberbourne were any indication – he assumed it would bring nothing but heartache. Valdis would be wasting no time in pressing his dark and twisted influence on his son – the son he had used as a marionette in a political game of power, tugging at the strings while remaining in the shadows.

His insides churned with disgust that he had never thought more about what was clearly happening right in front of him, for years. Decades.

His fingers splayed on Arii's skin and he pulled her closer into his embrace. Her gentle sigh tickled against his chest and the soft murmur of his name upon her lips washed him into an unfamiliar feeling of tranquillity.

The fire within ebbed to smouldering embers as his eyes drifted closed.

In that moment, Elijah felt a sense of peace he had never truly felt before.

⸸

"Are you fucking kidding me?!" roared Arii the next morning as Nem helped Elijah strap some lightweight armour over his clothing. The outfit was thicker than he was used to wearing, insulated for the freezing temperatures he was about to face outside, yet light enough to move relatively freely.

His silver eyes tracked Arii's stalking figure as she paced the room, the anger radiating from her like a furnace. "Not even a dagger? They expect you to go into the arena unarmed?" she continued, hands chopping the air in her frustration.

Krepth lounged nearby, tipping his chair on its two back legs as he chuckled. "Perhaps they want to see what he can really do," he offered unhelpfully, before adding, "Perhaps it's the motivation you need to really delve deep into that magical pool of yours, Herington. Perhaps you might touch the bottom this time?"

"Can it, mutt!" snarled Arii, pausing in her tirade and sending a glare his way that would have sent him careening from his precarious lean if looks defied physics.

"Krepth is right, Arii. They obviously know how skilled Elijah is with blades, from his history as the King's bodyguard, but they know nothing of his magic's potential," said Nem, pulling a strap on Elijah's shoulder and looping it through the buckle.

"It's what I would do," murmured Elijah, his eyes fixed on Arii as she whirled to face him.

"You agree with this?!"

"I don't have a choice," he said calmly.

He wanted to ease the fear and frustration he could clearly see bubbling to the surface as Arii continued her pacing, but it appeared he was having the opposite effect. She only seemed to be getting more agitated, hands balling into fists then loosening… over and over, as if she needed something to squeeze. By the dark looks she gave Krepth, he surmised Arii was envisioning the Shifter's neck between her palms.

Nearby, Valerie laughed as she leaned against the wall. "This might be worth inking on my free arm. Rattle the arena and leave them speechless, Eliverus. I'll be up there rooting for you, and I'll see you when you return." With a grin and a wink, Valerie left the room.

"That's the attitude we should all be adopting," commented Krepth.

Arii ground her jaw in response but remained silent and seething.

Through the solid doors to the arena, a boom of voices sounded as a massive crowd cheered in response to something on the grounds. Situated in a room connected to the Permafrost Arena, Elijah had been given an hour to prepare. The arena was located behind the castle of Erstonia, and rather than travel around the mountainous ranges, the Vox brothers had created a tunnel under the mountains, directly to the colosseum-like structure. The trek to the arena was a story in itself as their group had followed Aaren through eerie, lamp lit tunnels.

How the Princes had managed to create such awe-inspiring tunnels, Elijah had no idea.

The thought left his mind as Arii's frustrated growl sounded once more.

Nem placed a hand on his shoulder before whispering, "Good luck." Then she walked from the room without a second glance. She was a woman of little words; Elijah was coming to know and appreciate that fact.

Krepth stood, his voice unusually low and serious as he added, "Try not to die," throwing a glance Arii's way before following Nem.

That left him alone under a gaze of violet fire.

Elijah tilted his head as the crowd roared again, sunlight filtering through two small windows nearby and lighting Arii's hair as she paused before him. Her face was harsh, her eyes narrowed and her jaw set. He knew that it was not just anger that ate away at her now, it was fear. Fear for someone else. It caused heat to radiate from her in waves, pulses shivering from within her very being.

"You could slip a dagger into your–"

"No, that would go against the rules."

"Rules? What fucking rules?"

"Arii..." he warned.

"We have no idea what sort of foes you're going to face out there, Elijah. You could be walking into a trap," she snapped, teeth baring enough to show fangs.

His expression remained stoic as he crossed his arms upon his chest. "You said last night that you believed in me. I do not think that changed overnight."

She speared a hand through her hair in frustration as his gaze fixed on her, seeing the struggle she was trying so hard to hide.

Slowly he stepped forward, placing a gloved hand on her arm, moving her to face him. "And as I said last night, I will come back to you. *That* has not changed overnight."

Her lips dropped into a frown as her eyes began to soften, and he saw raw emotion glittering in their amethyst depths as he leaned forward, placing a gentle kiss to her lips. A sound escaped her, and he felt her hands sliding to clasp the nape of his neck, deepening the kiss as his arms curled around her, holding her tight. The moment felt… fragile, like a slight breeze would carry it off on the wind.

What was between them now was new, unexplored, hesitant – yet Elijah could not help but feel it was right.

Suddenly the double doors to the arena shifted and began to part with a thunderous groan.

Arii's eyes bore into his as she whispered, her voice rising before the sound of the crowd became deafening, "Don't hold back, Elijah."

Their hands held firm, before sliding apart and Elijah headed for the doors, the roar of the crowd almost drowning out his words, his silver eyes glinting as he growled, "No longer…"

⸸

The thundering bellow of the crowd was deafening as Elijah paced onto the ice-covered area, eyes sweeping the colossal spread of bodies filling the stands. Drums thundered in time with his footfalls, a booming melody that had the crowd rising in anticipation. Clouds cloaked the sky in grey, casting the stadium in mild light as a chilly breeze swept plumes of snow across his boots.

Above the crowd perched a platform with an uninterrupted view of the arena below. Upon it were two thrones, occupied by Jero and Thogan, flanked either side by Aaren and a number of stern guards. He also spied two smaller figures beside Thogan, a woman and child. The little girl, hair braided to her waist, looked to be inching on her toes to see the arena. The woman kept the girl's hand firmly clutched in hers as she leaned toward Thogan, speaking with words Elijah was too far away to hear.

Did Thogan have a wife, and a child? He would have confessed to being astonished that they would let a child witness the bloodshed that was undoubtedly about to erupt in the arena, but he had decided during the previous several days that the people of the south were not faint of heart – and neither were their children.

To the side was additional seating for the Princes' guests. Elijah spared a glance, seeing the familiar, concerned faces of his friends.

The Permafrost Arena was a behemoth of a structure with high walls and ruggedly carved pillars, accommodating thousands of bystanders in staggered tiers of seating with incredible views of the circular space below. Snow blanketed everything in alabaster, hints of cold grey stone here and there, the seating only cleared of the cold stuff hours before the first guests began to arrive.

As Elijah's eyes swept the snow before him, he remembered what Emerson had said while they dined with the Princes a few nights ago. The snow on the arena floor was deeper than the white dustings on the surrounding stone walls, indicating a darker floor beneath the most recent layer of snow, hinting at the very real potential of blood-stained earth beneath.

The drums thrummed in a long-beating tempo as Elijah paused near the centre of the arena. Far across the arena, another set of double doors began to open, and four fur-covered, solid-looking bodies emerged into the overcast morning light.

The drums ceased as a deep, resonating voice boomed, "All hail witness to Eliverus Herington – long lost heir to the Northern throne, thought to have been killed twenty years ago. Now, he comes to prove himself in the Permafrost Arena, in hopes of winning our support in a bid to take back his birthright!"

Elijah's features frosted like the ice around his feet, his hands balling to fists by his sides.

"Facing Eliverus will be some of the more fearsome warriors in the north, forged from this very arena! Frisk Bjorn the Fearless, Feras Coldstone the Heartless, Rune Voltox the Giant Slayer and Vax Bloodborne of the Frozen Peaks. Now, watch as history is made here under your very noses – for only one warrior will leave this stadium alive!"

The crowd roared, and Elijah's eyes skated over the four men in quick assessment.

Frisk – the first man – was smaller than the others, his build lean, his hands hovering over two white bone daggers at his hips. Like all the southern warriors, he had a thick beard and blonde hair pulled back from his face. Elijah imagined he would be the swiftest of the four and one to keep an eye on.

Second came Feras, a stocky man with thick arms bare to the elements and smattered with ink. His nose twitched above an impressive moustache, his top lip curling in distaste as he hoisted a mace, slamming the shaft against his upturned palm. He would surely rely on his weapon, and Elijah noticed the way the man leaned slightly to his left – perhaps keeping weight off an old injury.

The third man, Rune, was a taller, skinnier man with short hair and a thinner beard than the others. His eyes were almost so light that they resembled snow, and they skimmed over him in similar assessment, as he clutched a bow in his long fingers. Elijah knew he would excel at distanced combat – but perhaps up close the man would struggle when it came to strength.

Lastly was Vax, a giant of a man with rippling muscled arms and a dark, thick beard, his eyes deep set and his brows drawn low. His head was bare to the sky, shining like a newly polished stone. He hefted a sizable great sword, his lips curling back to bare yellow teeth in a grimace that hinted at madness.

Elijah knew he was the one to watch.

Boots shifting, fists uncurling and eyes narrowing, Elijah drew his mind into focus, slamming closed any thoughts of beyond the arena, sliding into a state of consciousness he knew intimately. It was a state of mind he had learned to delve into early in his training, a place where nothing but the foe before him mattered, and the remainder of the world faded away.

It was where he retreated before he was forced to kill.

The four warriors began their march forward, weapons raised. The crowd pulsed, the cries dying down as the men sized each other up.

"No weapons, eh? Now that is interesting," drawled Rune, fingering the feather tips of an arrow as he moved to Elijah's left.

"What you gonna do, kill us with yer bear hands? That is more Vax's style!" crowed Frisk with a chuckle, his southern accent thick as tar as he unsheathed his daggers, twirling them around his palms.

Elijah didn't bother to inform them that he hadn't been allowed to arm himself, and after appraising their weapons, he had to admit that Arii may have been right. This may just be a set up.

Vax barked a laugh from Elijah's right, causing his eyes to dart to the man.

"He doesn't look so tough," hissed Feras, lips twitching as his head tilted.

Beneath Elijah's skin, the beast rose its head, sparks glittering to his fingertips as the group began to pace a wide circle around him.

"Enough talk," growled Vax, the deep tenor of his voice causing the three warriors to move.

Around them the crowd roared.

Snapping into action, Elijah shot forward in a sprint, boots crunching on the snow just as Rune nocked an arrow and let it fly. It whistled over Elijah's shoulder, narrowly missing his neck as he ran at the marksman first. He would have a hard-enough time taking the others down without the threat of arrows in his back.

Rune's eyes narrowed in realisation as he swiftly levelled another arrow. Elijah snapped out a hand, delving into the pool of his magic and drawing the power to his fingertips as a crackling blast of magic speared from his palm and at the marksman.

Rune dove into a roll, narrowly avoiding the blast.

Elijah's eyes darted to the left as silver flashed, causing his boots to skid in the snow as he dipped backwards. Daggers whirred a hair's breadth from his nose as Frisk's twisted features and violent snarl suddenly appeared before his face. Narrowly avoiding a blade to the guts, Elijah twisted and dodged as the man's arms flew in a blur, silver streaking in search of flesh.

Their movements were like a snap in the air, the two men dancing, ducking and weaving in trained ferocity. Elijah's movements were on the defensive, weaving in between Frisk's attacks, and when a split-second of weakness presented itself, he landed a swift blow to the man's jaw before spearing a hand up in an attempt to disarm him of his daggers. Frisk was nimble, jerking back to avoid another blow.

A whirr sounded, and Elijah snapped up a hand just in time to deflect an oncoming arrow with a swift burst of magic.

"Aha! A magic user, who would have thought!" squawked Frisk, moving swiftly to attempt another slash across Elijah's torso. With a grunt, Elijah punched a burst of magic into the man's chest – throwing him a few feet away.

The warriors were cocky and obnoxiously loud, no doubt to appease the roaring crowd.

Head whipping, body following suit, Elijah continued his sprint in Rune's direction as the man's fingers clutched for another arrow from the quiver on his back.

Suddenly, Elijah was before him, one hand coming up to slam the bow to the side, before landing a heavy hit to Rune's guts. The man recovered surprisingly quickly, fist heading for Elijah's face, which was quickly blocked by his forearm. Rune twirled, using the bow as a batten, the wood whistling through the air as the warriors fought.

Their movements became fiercer, blows heavier. Elijah ducked a flying punch, catching the man's arm on his shoulder and pulling up before the sound of a pop was followed by the man's agonised howl.

Vax's roar announced his arrival, great sword cleaving through the air as Elijah and Rune both jerked back – the sword parting the snow to hit the dirt with a thump. Whirling, Vax recovered his heavy weapon, and Elijah threw a burst of magic at the hulking man, throwing him back. The attack only bought him a slither of time though, for the man recovered astonishingly quickly.

Rune attempted to nock another arrow, but with a dislocated arm the movement was impossible. Elijah's hands groped Rune's skull as he spun to stand at the man's back. With one swift jerk of his spine, the man folded back, bowed like the weapon he favoured, his face twisting in surprised rage.

Do not think…

Do not feel…

Crack.

With a swift twist of the skull and a pop of his spinal cord, Rune's lifeless body dropped to the snow, mouth slack and eyes staring to the grey clouds above. Elijah dipped to the man's body, his fingers fluttering over the fallen warrior's face to gently close his eyes, murmuring a swift prayer under his breath. Blowing out a breath, Elijah slowly stood – mist clinging to the warmth.

The crowd boomed, people thundering their fists against the battlements as Feras charged – mace flying through the air, following his angry yell.

Narrowly avoiding the weapon, Elijah stepped back, hair flying as he ducked another pass. He shot forward, delivering a swift uppercut to the man's chin – sending him flying back as Frisk darted around his comrade's flailing body – daggers whistling towards Elijah's torso again.

Although they were not Fae, the men were strong, their movements precise and sure – landing blows that he had no doubt would result in bruises – and it stirred the beast beneath Elijah's skin, clawing forth in need of retribution, eager to be let out from its cage. The men dipped and dove in a death dance – Elijah's Fae speed giving him a swiftness that the mortal men lacked.

But he was outnumbered and had barely touched the surface of his magic.

Silver tore through his leathers, hot pain simmering as the blade made contact with the skin just below his ribs. Lips curling, canines bared, he spun – sweeping a leg out to topple Frisk, before slamming a pulse of magic against Feras' mace, in an imitation of a shield that Arii had been trying to teach him to manifest for weeks.

He did not have time to feel proud of himself.

Seeing Feras' eyes widen in momentary distraction, he took that chance to clutch the handle of the mace – before bringing up his open hand to smash against the stocky man's face – a sickening crack telling him he had just broken his nose. Feras' head snapped back, blood arching as the man went down.

Elijah snatched the mace, pirouetting before flinging it into Fisk's chest as the man converged upon him in his comrade's falling wake – a throaty grunt his only reply as the smaller man staggered back.

"Bastard!" roared Vax, his great sword coming down hard.

The mace was heavier than the weapons Elijah normally preferred to use, so his reaction was slower than usual, gloved hands slipping on the shaft as he lifted the weapon to deflect Vax's blow. Vax's heavy sword sliced through the shaft like butter, causing the wood to shatter. Elijah felt the shock run up his arm as the weapon cleaved in two, his body jerking back as Vax threw his sword in an arch, bellowing with rage.

Barely dodging, Elijah jolted to the side, slipping into the man's defences, throwing a punch into the giant's kidney. It was like hitting one of the solid castle walls. Shockwaves reverberated up Elijah's arm, sending his teeth into a chatter as Vax cawed a laugh, a meaty hand shooting out to clutch his throat. Elijah barely had time to brace as the man threw a volley of heavy strikes into his stomach, knocking the wind from him. Before he had the chance to recover or retaliate, the giant tossed his body like a sack of potatoes, sending him flying.

The crowd went into a frenzy, demanding blood, their cries shuddering the stadium walls.

Above, Arii shot forward in her chair, screaming his name – the sound lost amongst the chaos.

Blinking, Elijah sat up shakily, causing stars to burst like a supernova before his eyes as he fell forward, dropping to all fours. His gloved hands slammed against the moist ground, his tongue sweeping across his teeth, and he swiped a glove across his bleeding mouth, spitting blood to the snow. Pain bounded in his skull like loose wasps, white-hot fury coiled in his gut, sending electricity through his veins. Elijah was pretty sure he had landed on his head.

The boom of voices faded in and out around him as his eyes slid to his hands, fingers gripping the snow as something began to writhe in his chest, surging from deep within.

Later he would recognise the feeling, a feeling he had only ever felt once before when he was just a boy.

The overwhelming need to survive.

As his ears rang and blood tinged his tongue, thoughts of his parents drifted across his mind's eye – breaking free of his carefully composed defences.

Their faces covered in blood.

Eyes devoid of life, chests never to rise again.

Elijah had not re-witnessed their deaths before. That particular memory had been pressed so deep in his subconscious that he had begun to believe he may not have truly seen their demise, but there it was, wavering before his eyes now when he could not afford to lose focus. He suddenly grieved for what the child in him had witnessed, the horror that he knew was still locked away in his mind – as if it were trying to shield him even now. Taking that grief, he moulded it into anger, anger that pulled violently upon his reserves of strength.

These men were not the source of his grief, but as snowflakes swirled about him, he regarded them as obstacles to his path.

He could hear boots heading his way – knew the three warriors were closing in as the world around him began to slow.

Many more could end up like his family if he did not prevail. Countless lives would cease and for them death would not be the end – they would be made to roam and inflict more pain like mindless shells.

Suddenly, Elijah realised that he could not allow that to happen.

The earth beneath his fingers began to tremble.

Above him, the sky began to turn a deeper shade of grey, the clouds spinning as freezing air speared down his throat, cold starlight spreading across his chest as he exhaled. Magic sizzled through his veins, and for once he welcomed it.

Eyes widening, Elijah tore off his gloves, slamming his open palms against the sleet floor as the taste of magic overtook the metallic tang of blood on his tongue, coating his mouth and sending shivers down his arms.

He fell into the pool of his magic, and Elijah did what he had feared to do for so long.

He let go.

With a roar, he sent magic thundering into the earth, a hulking shard of rock piercing from the surface just inches away from Vax. The man lost his footing, falling to the side as another fragment of earth rose like an arrowhead, slamming through Feras' guts and impaling the southern warrior like a melon upon a thick pike.

Blood exploded across the snow.

The crowd's tenor changed; cries of awe mixed with outrage.

Elijah did not have time to think as Frisk's blades were once again heading for his face.

Rolling, he dodged as the man's blurred jabs flew now without rhythm, frenzied, one catching the fabric of Elijah's shirt and the other carving a line across his neck. Magic sizzled along Elijah's fingertips, writhing though his muscles and lacing around his heart like a glittering shield. Hands a blur, magic a pulse thrumming through his veins, Elijah's hand flew with the speed of a striking snake as his fist – crackling with energy – slammed into the man's solar plexus, sending him careening to slam against one of the risen crags of earth.

In a blink, Frisk was disarmed, and Elijah took his blades, the steel glittering as he melded the two together into a shimmering javelin of ice and speared the magic-made weapon through the man's stomach – burying the glittering crystal blade so deep it pinned him to the rock, leaving the man open mouthed and gaping. Feebly, Frisk clutched at his gut, blood dribbling from his lips as he gurgled, confusion mixing with fading light in his eyes.

Elijah threw the man a regretful look. These men were warriors, born and bred to fight yet they had no need to die today. Remorse fluttered through him as Elijah rested a hand upon the man's shoulder.

"You die for a cause far greater than you know. Rest easy upon the stars, brother." Elijah murmured as Frisk coughed, teeth grimacing in a soft smile as the man died.

Three down, one to go.

Elijah slowly turned to face his last opponent, face set hard, silver eyes glowing.

Nearby, a flurry of snow began to twist unnaturally as something began to materialise.

ELIJAH

CHAPTER TWENTY

ARIIAYA

Gods, he moved exactly as he had back at the castle – like death itself gave him wings.

Arii stared; her eyes wide as her heart hammered in her chest.

He had let go, finally let go and embraced the magic he had been dabbling in for so long. But she knew what they saw now was just skimming the surface of what Elijah could do. Whenever she was near him it felt like something were thickening the very air around them. Gentle magic did not do that – gentle magic did not allow someone to manipulate the very ground beneath them, causing it to shudder and splinter.

Arii's eyes slid to a flaring of snow as it whipped in a mini tornado near the other end of the arena – and suddenly dread coiled in her guts.

No… it could not be.

"Arii, what the hell is that?" cried Tikkani, pointing towards the slowly coalescing form of a giant ice creature. The sudden sickeningly sweet taste of thick magic invaded Arii's taste buds and her senses peaked to high alert.

Snow crunched under the boots of her comrades, all of which had risen from their seats. Arii did not need to see the faces of her pirate friends to know that they watched the arena in awe, their bellows lost in the boom, while Emerson and Luc gasped at the scene developing before them.

"What the fuck?" yelled Krepth, and Arii followed his gaze to where the two Princes stood.

Jero and Thogan were both standing, arms outstretched, eyes glistening with light as magic sizzled around their outstretched palms.

Magic users.

Fae magic users.

Arii did not have the time to think, her mind dashing back to Elijah on the arena floor as ear-splitting roars reverberated around the stadium, the sound almost metallic and unnatural. Her eyes widened at the sight of enormous, crudely-cut ice sculptures given life, glittering like diamonds in the winter light.

Standing at the end of the arena were two colossal bears made of ice.

ELIJAH

Elijah remembered the brothers' passing mention of warriors and beasts in the Permafrost Arena… but he had been expecting creatures of flesh and blood.

Not ones made of magic and ice.

Vax's voice called over the grunts of the forming animals, his face lit with madness as he lifted his sword to the heavens and bellowed, "You wield magic, boy – but can you conquer it?"

Elijah's lips curled back in a snarl as his eyes darted to the bears – two behemoth crystal forms heading their way. Slowly, he began to unbuckle his armour, letting the metal slide from his shoulders and hit the snow with a metallic *crash*, leaving him in nothing but undertunic and leathers as he rolled his neck and shoulders. He tore the material from his arms, tossing the bloodstained cloth to the snow – leaving his muscled arms bare to the cold – welcoming the stinging chill. The bite on his skin narrowed his focus as he blew out a breath.

Now he understood partly why the Vox brothers had detached themselves from the north. They were Fae, and they had magic. Two things that the north hunted and hated. He guessed their parents had kept their children's secrets well-guarded.

Boots skidding on the snow, he ducked into a fighter's stance, and threw his hands into his magic again, fingers clutching at the churning pool in desperation.

The magic fell through his fingers like water, as if evading him.

Gods, what was happening?

He did not have time to ponder though, what little sun was left in the sky was spearing through ice as one of the bears thundered his way – roaring with animal anger as it charged. Elijah spun, sprinting for one of the crags he had brought forth from the earth. He tore up the jagged spear of stone, fingers scrabbling as he twisted, using the stone as leverage. His muscles bunched, screaming at him, but he pushed all feeling back and leaped.

Leaped straight at the creature.

The beast flew by, slamming into the crag with a solid boom as Elijah landed on its back. His fingers slipped against the ice, fingernails cracking and breaking. A curse slid from his teeth as he struggled to find a hold that didn't send him plummeting from the beast's back.

All the while, he threw his mind into the pool of magic, mentally groping as it wavered and recoiled. Still, it did not come to him.

Desperation began to rise. Had he finally drawn upon too much? Had he hit the bottom of his stores of magic? He didn't believe so, for the shimmering pool was still before him – he just could not grasp it.

The bear threw its head back, bellowing with rage. Its twin thundered ahead, glittering ice claws swiping across the back of its brother – screeching like nails down stone. Elijah jerked, narrowly avoiding the swipe, scrabbling further up the bear's neck towards its head.

Suddenly, Elijah felt his body jolt, his perch sliding from beneath him as he was thrown from the creature's back. He snapped into a roll, skidding across the snow and recovering just in time to flip backwards as his face almost met the blade of Vax's great sword. He had not even noticed the man, his attention focused on the ice bears.

Elijah spun, slamming his boot into the man's arm, causing the warrior to bark with pain – seconds before he rolled away from a raging animal of ice, jaws snapping in the air where he had been moments ago. It was a precarious, flailing, dangerous dance that Elijah was sure was a grand spectacle for the audience. He was running out of time, and strength. He needed his magic, and in the heat of the moment he decided to draw upon just a touch. Attempting to disarm the southern warrior, Elijah pinched a slither of magic and formed a small blade, burying it into the warrior's thigh. Vax roared, eyes wide as Elijah arched in a swift somersault, narrowly avoiding beheading by Vax's blade.

Then he was slammed in the side by a colossal paw, sending him flying across the arena.

He hit the snow-covered dirt hard, the breath whooshing from his lungs. He had been outnumbered before, but now he was surely outmatched. Slowly he stood, recovering his breath in gasps as snow began to fall like icing sugar. White flakes rested on his shoulders and touched his eyelashes like tiny fingers.

Ahead, Vax approached, seemingly in slow motion.

As Elijah exhaled, Arii's voice burst like starlight through his mind.

All you need to do is concentrate.

Magic is part of your soul, accept it fully without doubt and it will not hesitate to aid you.

Stop holding back!

Pressing back everything but the need to defend, Elijah emptied his mind until it was just him and the rippling pool of his power. Changing tactics, he tenderly coaxed the magic to him. For so long he had pushed it away, fought against it, *hated* it – even without the knowledge of what it truly was. He had seen its destructive capabilities, but he had also seen what else it could do.

Heal, bring life, create things from nothing.

In the hands of the right person perhaps magic could do more than bring about fear. It could change lives, for the better.

Now, he caressed the power, brought it forth and *asked* it to do his bidding. Unlike before, he had grasped at it haphazardly – plucked it forth unemotionally.

Now, he begged the shimmering essence within himself for help.

Not *for* him – but for those who relied upon them *both*.

The iridescent magic flowed forth, filling his body, his mind. Elijah suddenly realised it was not a pool before him… but a glittering lake of writhing, rippling luminescent power.

The magic engulfed his soul in glistening light.

Then he was moving, his body a blur of exploding sparks and snapping magic – a vortex of shimmering light as his body *disappeared…*

And snapped back into existence a foot in the air behind Vax Bloodborne.

The man's eyes widened in surprise, mouth popping open as Elijah dropped upon his shoulders, boots digging into the man's hips as Elijah's arm slid around the man's neck, snapping into a chokehold that had his muscles bunching and veins popping to the surface of his skin.

Vax began to flail, sword jerking in an attempt to dislodge as his face began to turn red. Elijah grimaced, hold never slipping as the warrior's spittle showered his arm and Vax choked, snow raining on them as the bears thundered their way.

Magic whipped up in a vortex around him, and Elijah willed forth another massive crag from the earth with nothing but a thought, his eyes darting to the closest bear as the magic impaled the creature through its middle – ice shards exploding over the nearby crowd.

By now, the people of the stands were on the edge of their seats, the sound an incomprehensible boom. Elijah swore he could hear cheering in amongst the thunder.

Vax dropped his sword to snatch a knife from his boot, stabbing it up and into Elijah's side – the blade passing through his skin and searing pain into his gut.

He uttered a pain-filled curse but did not let his grip cease.

Vax began to tire, his face turning purple as he dropped to his knees, eyes rolling back as he slid into unconsciousness. When he felt the man slacken, Elijah released his hold and let the man fall to the snow face first, his giant body slamming to the blood-soaked dirt with a heavy *thud*.

With a huff and a growl of pain, Elijah tore the knife free, throwing it down as blood seeped through his parted fingers.

It was time to end this.

Elijah turned to face the last creature, swiping snow from his eyes as he broke into a dead sprint, heading directly at the beast as its massive paws quaked the ground beneath his feet like an oncoming stampede. Arms pumping, Elijah coaxed the magic forth, light erupting from within his chest as he let the power envelope him in its embrace – nerve endings alight as he leaped, stars exploding around his body and snapping it into nothingness.

Reappearing directly above the bear, he dropped onto its neck and slammed his hands on its skull, his fingers shattering the ice. Pain tore up his hands and into his arms. He could hear a high-pitched screech as the magic billowed forth from within him, glittering specks of snow rising around them like suspended diamonds as gravity ceased for the tiniest of moments.

"This is for the north," he uttered savagely, eyes aglow with lightning as he commanded power to punch into the beast's skull – light erupting within the animal's eyes before its roaring body reared back…

And its head exploded into a glittering shower of light and ice.

ARIIAYA

A shockwave followed the explosion of the ice bear, a wave of power that had the entire audience of the arena falling over one another, including Arii, their friends and the Vox brothers.

Jero and Thogan slammed against their seats as snow hit their faces. A fine mist drifted in the air, leaving the arena in fog as Arii recovered first, throwing herself forward against the balustrades.

"Elijah!" she screamed, unable to see him.

'Death, it is imminent. For you, for him, and for everyone you hold dear.'

Arii shook her head against the voice of the wraith, snarling, "Not now!"

The mist began to drop, and she saw a halo of cleared snow, rings of ice scattered across the floor.

Krepth attempted to grab her arm, her name cracking from his lips like a whip – but he was too slow. She vaulted over the stone lip, dropping to the snow-covered floor below. Boots hitting the earth, she snapped into a roll, leaping into a sprint towards the wavering form ahead.

Her body collided with Elijah's just before he hit the ground. She grunted, his weight a shock as she held firm, his name all she could muster as she guided him to his knees.

"Elijah!" she called again, slipping under his arm and wincing as static flared across her skin at the contact.

"I promised you…" he mumbled as she lifted his face to stare into his steel grey eyes.

"Hush, you great big *incredible* brute! Hush," she demanded, her hands moving to check his wounds. "Let's get you into the warmth."

As she spoke, Nem appeared on Elijah's other side, helping to hoist him to his feet.

Arii's body shook with relief. He was alive… and he had *won*.

Above, the crowd's voices melded into one as they thundered, fists pumping to the sky as they roared a war melody into the frosty air.

"Herington. Herington. True King of the North!"

†

Elijah winced in his sleep under her glowing palms as Arii brought the healing magic to her fingers, watching as deep wounds began to knit. He lay shirtless upon the bed they had shared the night before, blood a crimson stain upon the white sheets as his stomach flexed beneath her hands. His brow was beaded with sweat, the pillow drenched, his chest rising and falling with his heavy breaths as he slowly returned to consciousness.

What they had all witnessed in the arena, Arii was sure word would be cascading across the land like water down a crystal stream. Elijah had emerged victorious against the south's greatest warriors and colossal beasts made from magic and ice.

She assessed him as his muscles began to relax. His head was tilted, his gaze fixed on her as her fingers began to retreat from his skin. She had not noticed he had awoken.

The air was thick, the raging fireplace crackling furiously as her eyes skidded over Elijah's face – relief mixing so violently in her stomach that she felt ill.

He had done it.

He had finally let go and embraced what he was.

Now he needed to embrace *who* he was.

They were leaps and bounds ahead of where they were yesterday, there was no denying that. If he truly did not want what was to come next, he could have spread his arms and allowed the warriors of the north to take his life right there in the middle of the arena.

Yet, he had fought, and he was alive – his beautiful, dark features flickering in the firelight as they stared at one another in silence.

"Nice to see you," she whispered, watching as a weak smile tweaked his lips. Her slowly warming heart squeezed in the confines of her chest.

"I must look like hell – the Gods know I *feel* it." Elijah croaked.

She helped him sit up against the wooden bedhead and handed him a tankard of water as she said, "You used a lot of magic. For someone who has been suppressing it for twenty years, you can expect to feel like shit."

He huffed a laugh, downing the water.

"You were… incredible," she whispered honestly, her violet eyes wide and unblinking as he rested the mug on his lap. He was silent for a time, staring into the cup with a strange expression.

"You don't think… they'll fear me, do you?"

The question had Arii pausing as she cleaned her hands in a pail of water, her eyes drifting to the fireplace, watching the flickering inferno within as she shifted through what she should say.

"No, you don't understand how different the other courts are to the one you grew up in. Magic was once embraced, revered and used to protect. Your kind of magic has not been seen in a long time, yet the people here did not seem surprised by it – nor did they seem to fear it."

She tilted her head to look at him, drying her hands on a scrap of cloth, her thick hair dashing across her cheek as she continued, "Well, you saw what the Princes did. Perhaps your kind of magic is not as rare as we first thought. It has been kept secret, waiting for the chance to be brought forth to make a difference."

"Jero and Thogan… they're Fae?"

Arii's brows narrowed at his words. "Yes, it seems so. They've kept it a well-hidden secret, one which I'm sure Valdis would love to discover," she said with venom. She worried her bottom lip between her teeth as her eyes lifted to meet his. "We have some hard-hitting questions for those bastards."

Elijah contemplated her words before she suddenly said, "Elijah, I don't mean to alarm you but… you *teleported* across the arena. Do you have any idea how insanely cool that is?"

He chuckled in earnest then, the deep rumble causing her toes to curl.

A knock sounded at the door, causing Arii's smile to fall. Nem entered, her silver hair pulled up into a bun, accentuating her high cheekbones.

"If Elijah is ready, Jero and Thogan wish for an audience." She blinked, her look almost bird-like in its cool assessment as she nodded towards him. "Glad to see you alive, Elijah."

His answering smile was gentle as Nem ducked from the room.

Arii turned back to her charge, surveying his body quickly before she busied herself with tugging down her sleeves, eager to look anywhere but his bare, perfectly sculpted torso.

"Thank you," Elijah murmured suddenly, sliding next to her on the bed. His words were low, and she knew they held much more meaning than just the healing of his immediate wounds. She faced him, feeling the heat thrumming from his bare skin as she gently wiped a cloth over his still-damp forehead.

"Don't mention it," she whispered, eyes fixed on his as the feeling of his fingers dancing along her arm had her suppressing a shiver of desire.

With a jolt in her stomach, she realised she would always be utterly and inexplicably infatuated by him. She could no longer deny the feelings growing within her.

Without looking back at him she said, "We shouldn't keep them waiting."

She heard him move to her, his broad form taking up her vison as she straightened to hand him the neatly folded clothes and whispered, "I'll just step out for a moment."

His deep chuckle was a honey caress against her insides.

"Don't be ridiculous," he said, gently taking the clothes from her and beginning to dress.

"You can't blame me from at least trying to respect your privacy," but she paused as her eyes drifted over him as he turned slightly – the scars so vivid against his back that she felt her beast rise, snarling at the thought of his past. That need to fight, to protect, flared within her as she surveyed the carved muscles of his back, the ripple of his arms, power lacing every little movement he made.

It had taken every fibre of her being not to leap into the Permafrost Arena to his aid; and taken every ounce of willpower not to turn on the Princes and *make* them end the fight. When she had realised that he was expected to fight without weapons against fully-armed foes, she had nearly burst into flames of pure fury. Convinced it was a trap, the only one able to restrain her was Nem.

She stayed with him now, overwhelmed by relief that he was here, alive.

Elijah shrugged on a thick cotton tunic, buttoning the front before snatching a coat from the nearby chair as he said, "Let's go."

✝

"You have questions, Eliverus. That we expected after revealing our magic in the arena. Speak, if it pleases you. I can see you are upset," said Jero from where he and Thogan sat on their ornate thrones, twin sets of hazel eyes unwavering. Elijah stalked below the dais, his body tense with anger as he paused and turned towards them. Arii, Nem and Krepth backed him, faces set.

Moonlight filtered down upon them from the window above, tinging his dark hair in silver. Despite the clear, star flecked night outside, Elijah's face gave the impression of a midnight storm.

"How? How have you remained hidden all these years?"

"'Tis a fair question," drawled Thogan, picking at food in his teeth as Jero stood up to approach the group.

"We have our late parents to thank for our secrecy," said Jero, crossing his arms. "They were always very private, preferring my brother and I away from the public eye. When the uprising began, we were pressed into further secrecy. My magic awoke at a younger age than my brother's, you see. We learnt to hide the telling features such as our ears and canines, and most importantly… the magic simmering in my veins." Jero tilted his head as he paused at Elijah's side, nodding at the man's own pointed ears. "Perhaps our parents had a foresight for the chaos that was to come?"

"*The Time of Darkness* saw not just the northern court tumble into ruin, but all other courts too," said Krepth. "Keeping hidden would have kept you alive for only so long. Your people obviously know of your magic, but they do not fear you. How?"

Arms crossed, Thogan spoke from the dais, "Tell us, Spymaster, how much do you truly know about the uprising within the other courts?" Krepth's brows narrowed, and his mouth opened to reply, but Thogan continued, his voice low and gruff.

"The insurgents waiting in the shadows here in the south were quickly thwarted thanks to a few carefully placed pieces on the chessboard, but it was not without bloodshed. Our parents lost much that day, close advisors, friends, family and..." Thogan paused, hard features turning even harder as Jero lifted his hand, brushing back his cloak to reveal his heavily tattooed arm. "Our parents sacrificed themselves to save our lives. Their blood – their *magic* is what kept our land from falling under the same malice as our northern brethren."

Arii's head tilted to survey Jero's arm, as did the others, gazes dancing over the bold sweeping spirals – similar runes carved into the stone walls throughout the castle – before pausing on the faces of two people, their eyes life-like upon Jero's skin. The man's face, so much like his sons', had an impressive beard and thick brows, his arms wrapped around the shoulders of a woman whose mouth curved in a soft smile. Her long, sandy hair was draped in waves over one shoulder and fashioned into braids of war close to her skull on the other. Despite her strong face, her eyes remained kind, and Arii saw the resemblance now as she shifted her attention back to the Princes.

"I am sorry you had to discover your magic in the way that you did, Eliverus." Thogan's russet eyes shifted to Nem, and then rested on Arii, and she found herself almost fidgeting under his gaze. "We are aware of the unfortunate method of awakening magic in the north, and we know that the Fae are now far and few between. Discovery of magic was once an enchanting, eye-opening experience that filled the host with wonder and light. Most often than not the event would happen at a young age. Sometimes later in life. Now it seems the quickest and most sure-fire way is with pain and soul-altering trauma."

"But… is that not the only way?" Arii asked, surprised but fiercely curious. She stepped forward, gnawing on her bottom lip as she surveyed the Princes.

"My own magic manifested the first time I laid eyes upon my daughter, Frida," said Thogan, a small smile lightening his otherwise harsh expression. "When I saw her, it was like a light entered my heart and a fire ignited in my soul. My magic awoke when my heart did, and it was not prompted by suffering."

Arii swallowed, her mind spinning with the force of a tornado.

Magic could be awoken in other ways, *better* ways.

She recalled the child and woman who had remained beside Thogan's perch when they watched Elijah in the arena. The girl bore a mix of features from her parents and had a fierceness in her little eyes that told Arii that she would one day be a warrior like her father. Now, thinking back, if she had not have been so wrapped up with worry for Elijah, she would have taken better notice of the girl's little pointed Fae ears.

"What of your magic?" Elijah prompted, nodding to Jero.

The man only smiled and said, "A story for another day."

Gleaning Elijah's raised brows, Arii could tell that he was just as curious as all of them at the Prince's words. But the man continued, casting aside their curious thoughts for now.

"We have a firm belief here in the south… A belief that not only applies to my brother and I, but to the whole of Erstonia." Jero's head tilted to Elijah, and Arii was unable to look away as a flicker of light dashed across Jero's pupils. "Magic will always remain, no matter how hard people try to snuff it out. You see, Eliverus, magic is not just within us, but also in the very air we breathe. You can erase a person or being, but you cannot erase their magic completely."

"It remains when the user has long departed," said Thogan, leaning back in his chair.

"So, you're saying that your parents sacrificed themselves to release their magic… into the air?" Krepth's voice and expression was incredulous, his brows riding high.

What they spoke of was an entirely different sort of magic – powerful magic born of sacrifice. Magic brought forth and born of *love*, emotions far fiercer than pain or trauma. And by the look in Thogan's eyes, and the power he and his brother had shown in the arena, she knew it also to be something different to wield. It was not clutched and projected from fingers, like the magic she and her fellow Furies wielded. No, the magic they spoke of was but a fable – unconfirmed and unspoken of, especially where she grew up.

Her mind skipped back to her detainment in Bonemire – the feel of the cool stone floor beneath her cheek, the rancid smell of mould and rot as moonlight bathed her broken form through the tiny, barred window. She recalled the aching, seemingly endless agony after Valdis' torture, the bruises hiding just beneath her skin, the feeling of black hopelessness riding upon a whirlwind of pain. Slowly, through the haze, she had thought about the people she had met, the people she… cared for.

Despite the iron manacles suppressing her magic, a spark had danced upon her fingertips. It existed when it shouldn't have. At the time she had thought nothing of it, brushing it off as a trick of the mind. What they spoke of now was self-sacrificial magic. Magic empowered by emotion, empowered by *love*.

But Arii felt old beliefs resurfacing, as years of manipulation won the fight in her mind.

It was a load of–

"Horseshit" spat Arii, crossing her arms, her expression pinched. "Such magic, it doesn't exist."

Elijah remained silent, watching on with an unreadable expression as Jero waved his hand towards her.

"Ah, you are one of those Fury assassins, yes? Your disbelief does not come as a surprise, you have been conditioned to push your emotions aside and shut off your thoughts. The perfect killing machine. A soldier without questions need no answers."

"Emotions cloud our judgement and distract us from casting magic properly." Arii turned her gaze to Elijah, her chin lifting as she narrowed her eyes. "Our wayward heir to the throne here is proof of that." Her purple eyes were vivid in the firelight as her lips curled, showing teeth. She knew she looked every bit the murderous Fury assassin in that moment, and she found she did not care.

Elijah's returning glare was stony as he growled, "What are you talking about?"

"Those windows above the throne room didn't stand a chance. When I told you who you really were, your emotions got the better of you – resulting in a whole lot of destruction."

"Ah, yes! That was the magic surge we felt a week ago. Such power!" Jero remarked, not bothering to hide the awe from his voice. "On the contrary to what you have been taught, Ariiaya, it could be argued that emotions play a part in strengthening the magic within us, too."

"Hmph."

"Your reluctance to believe this is to be expected," he continued, before a slow smile peeked from within his thick beard – a crescent of white teeth and sharp canines. "To see Eliverus' power unbound and fuelled by love. Now I would pay good coin to see that." Arii's cheeks flushed as the Prince gave her a strange, almost knowing look.

It caused her to swiftly glance away.

"Your show in the Permafrost Arena proves that despite many years of suppressing your true nature, you were born to wield magic, Eliverus. You were victorious over our best warriors and obliterated our own frost magic." Jero slapped a heavy hand upon Elijah's shoulder. "You have proven yourself and your strength. My brother and I, and the entire south, are by your side for what is to come."

Elijah nodded, his lips curling with a smile as he locked hands with Jero in a vigorous handshake.

Thogan stepped down from the dais, joining Jero. "Victory in the Permafrost Arena calls for reward, brother."

"Reward? Your support is reward enough. If anything, you should be angered that I killed your best warriors," argued Elijah.

"They are no longer our best warriors," said Thogan simply.

Jero nodded, casting his eye over the group before once again resting on Elijah.

"Allow us to gift you a permanent mark of our allegiance, by magic, by blood, by flesh."

The flames in the crude steel braziers upon the stone walls flickered in a dance, casting flurrying shadows across the throne room, his words ushering forth an air of magic. The Princes, in unison, placed their hands upon their hearts in gestures of respect.

"From now until the end, the south will kneel before the true King of the North and follow him into battle."

ELIJAH

CHAPTER TWENTY-ONE

ARIIAYA

An hour later, Arii, Elijah, Krepth and Nem made their way down a dimly lit hallway, the first rays of dawn shining through the small, thin windows.

Nem ran a hand down her face as their boots clapped against the rough stone floors. "Gods, I hadn't even realised the time. It feels like an age since the arena… yet it has only been hours."

Krepth paced ahead, spinning on his heel and dancing backwards, his face splitting with a sly grin as he motioned towards Elijah. "Come on, Your Highness, show us what the Princes gave you!"

Elijah kept his gaze forward as he murmured, "We have more pressing matters – like preparing to move on to Ayrith and the West Court."

"Come on!"

"Krepth, I'm as curious as you are as to what Jero and Thogan gave Elijah, but do you have any idea how long a trek we have ahead of us?" Nem groaned as they approached a heavy wooden door.

Krepth rolled his eyes, before ticking off fingers one by one. "First we need to cross The Ivory Plains, and if we have time we will stop by Lilidale for supplies, and then–"

"We need to survive The Wastes," interrupted Nem, pinching the bridge of her nose with a sigh. "Gods help us."

"The Wastes?" enquired Elijah as the group paused before the exit.

"Crossing The Wastes will be another test in itself. I would suggest we follow the coast, but that will add hours to the trek and we don't have the time." Arii's gaze was piercing as she tilted her head, honey tipped locks falling down her shoulder. "They say those who tread The Wastes will be faced with their greatest fears, for the very air is made of nightmares."

Spearing a hand through his hair, Elijah sighed as he said, "Well, no-one said any part of this journey would be easy."

"We should be prepared for the very real chance that we could lose lives there."

Arii's attention briefly turned to Nem and Krepth as the silver-haired Fury clamped her hand on the spymaster's arm and practically dragged him through the exit. If they had exchanged tense words while herself and Elijah spoke, she had not heard.

Those two had some real issues going on, issues she would need to get to the bottom of soon.

For now though…

"There is a very real chance we could lose far more than our own lives if we fail," she finished, casting her gaze back to Elijah, before jerking back a touch – the movement so subtle that she congratulated herself inwardly on her self-control.

Elijah stood close – closer than he had been mere moments ago. Despite herself, she felt her stone defences begin to crumble as her eyes met his, and in the dusty morning light she swallowed.

Hard.

"I know what is at stake, Arii."

"Do you, truly?"

His eyes were like silver fire, his fingers a whisper against her jaw. "Yes."

Gods.

Tingles prickled her skin, warmth igniting in her belly at his touch. Then her hand clasped his wrist, the air between them snapping with tension.

"Good, I'm getting through to you then," she said, barely a whisper.

For several moments they stood, mere inches apart, heated air between them.

Then she had to open her stupid mouth and sever the moment.

"What *did* the Princes give you?"

He blinked, her attempt at distraction successful, for now. "Ah, they gave me a tattoo," he replied, shrugging his shoulders, nonplussed.

"A tattoo?!"

"Mhm."

A bark of laughter escaped her at his aloof expression, turning into a very unladylike snort. "A tattoo?" she repeated.

Elijah's arms lifted to cross his chest as his expression became almost defensive. "Is my having a tattoo so odd to you?"

"No, it's just… That was the last thing I imagined them giving you! I thought perhaps an ornate carved battle-axe, a pretty ice paperweight or even a bear cub."

"A bear cub?"

She chuckled. "Huh, gods I need sleep," she groaned.

"Too right you do, you're inching on mad – madder than usual."

"Whoa there warrior – you're going to get me all hot in my leathers with that kind of talk."

"Argh, you are so strange… and inappropriate," he sighed.

Arii's face was all feline, canines poking her bottom lip as she motioned with a flourish towards his chest.

"You have not yet seen inappropriate. So, where is it? Don't tell me it's on your arse–" A pause, then a sly grin followed with, "Actually, please tell me it's on your arse."

"No, it is not on my *arse*. It's on my arm, if you must know."

"You'd think the reward would be something a little more… useful. Gold, jewels for trade – a weapon perhaps."

Elijah began to unbuckle the clip of his cloak. "Just because it is not gold or a weapon does not mean it is not useful," he chided, shrugging his tunic from his left arm.

Seeing his skin had her pausing, but before the glimpse of his neck and shoulder could cause those familiar butterflies in her stomach – she saw the gift left by the Princes upon his skin.

The tattoo covered his upper arm and flowed onto his pectoral, bold yet elegant black runes curling into an elaborate piece of artwork encasing the head of a snarling bear. It resembled the south court crest to an extent yet was not an exact replica.

Her fingers lifted, tracing the patterns along his warm skin, pausing when a shimmer followed where her fingers touched.

Magic.

"Alright, I concede – that is bloody incredible."

"I'll admit I was resistant at first, but Jero did say that this was a custom in the south. All winners in the arena receive this mark of their court – and when others see it, they will know that we have the full and unwavering support of the south." His eyes met hers as her fingers lingered. "I suppose this is the mark of loyalty that Freya spoke of."

"It doesn't bother you that this mark is laced with magic?"

Elijah was silent for a time, studying her face before his lips parted to reply–

Thump.

"Nyx's tits!" cried Arii, hand to her chest, whirling to the door behind them as another *thump* sounded from the other side. Throwing a questioning glance at one another, they swiftly threw the door open to the frosty outdoors, their boots crunching upon icy white snow.

Their eyes slid over the white-dusted courtyard, and Arii's hand hovered over the dagger at her hip, ready to spring into action at the drop of a snowflake.

A white projectile whizzed over her head, followed by a grunt.

Spinning, she twisted to see Elijah shaking snow from his hair like a rugged dog.

Laughter bubbled up her chest before bursting from her lips.

"HA–"

A snowball slammed into the side of her head, exploding in a puff of white.

And then another hit her back.

Then her backside.

The assault rained upon them from all sides, and before Arii could leap to anger at being taken by surprise, she heard laughter ringing from nearby, joyful and light.

Quinn peeled around the corner of a nearby stone statue, cackling like a madman as a sizable snowball rocketed in his wake and slammed into the back of his head, sending him careening and planting face first into the snow. Tikkani's laughter followed as she came into view, moulding a lump of snow in the palms of her hands. Her cheeks were flushed and pink, her hair sprinkled with white and damp with snow.

Her smile was like sunshine after a storm.

Soon the others joined her – Emerson, Luc, Krepth and surprisingly, Nem. Nearby she also spied Lyda and Gunner – the latter who was moulding something questionable into the snow, grinning as his companion cackled. Valerie stood, arms crossed and head shaking, but her amused expression couldn't be hidden.

Their friends, they all laughed. All had smiles upon their faces and they all looked… happy.

Despite the overwhelming danger they were yet to face, her friends all looked like tomorrow did not hold the possible threat of death.

No, for now they would live in the moment – live for the strange snow beneath their feet and small happiness a snowball fight could bring. Death was eternal, life was fragile and fleeting. In that moment, as their group gathered around her, Arii realised that all moments of happiness, no matter how small, needed to be savoured.

Arii turned to Elijah, hesitant as her gaze met his. Her hand dropped from her blade and she sighed, letting the tension melt into the snow beneath her feet. His answering smile was gentle, his hair dancing in the cool morning breeze as he stepped forward–

And dumped a handful of snow right on the crown of her head.

Stunned, blinking and opened mouthed, Arii stared at the man before her, unable to hide her look of pure surprise.

Then Elijah laughed.

It started as a bark, and then it slowly turned into a deeper sound, his canines flashing and the corners of his eyes crinkling as he chuckled. Unbidden, unfiltered, gentle and… carefree.

As if for a moment, just one small moment, the weight of the world did not rest upon his shoulders.

And it caused her own face to break into a full-blown grin.

"Oh, you are dead." Arii ducked, sweeping snow into a hasty ball as Elijah backed towards the group, hands lifting in defence, yet that rare smile remained.

The recruits watched on with wide eyes, unsurety upon their faces as if they were expecting a quick rise to anger – or that the head belonging to their only hope of salvation may just roll across the snow at any moment. Krepth's brows were raised high, staring at the back of Elijah's head as he whispered, "This should be good."

"She's going to kick his arse," Nem added with a sly grin.

"Place yer' bets," chuckled Valerie, as Lyda slapped a glob of snow into the captain's outstretched palm.

Then all hell broke loose as Arii began hurling snowballs at the group, cries and shrieks rising in the cool morning air.

Just for a short time all thoughts of the danger to come were forgotten.

For a short time, they were just friends battling with harmless projectiles in the snow.

And the only feeling in her heart in that moment was joy.

⸸

Soaked, laughing and exhausted, Arii practically skipped ahead of Elijah as they headed towards the wing of the castle where they were lodging. Spinning to face him, she grinned as she paced backwards exclaiming, "You have met your match in the battle of snowballs, Master Wolfe."

Elijah dashed his damp hair back from his face as he laughed, "For once I agree with you, Miss Clearwater."

"Oh good gods, please tell me someone witnessed those words! Did the almighty warrior of the Permafrost Arena just admit that he was bested? By a mere woman?"

"You are no mere woman, Arii."

She paused, biting her tongue between her teeth and almost causing a collision as he skidded to a stop before her. She poked a finger into the centre of his chest as she exclaimed, "And don't you ever forget it."

"That'd be incredibly hard to do, you remind me every waking moment we are together that you are unlike anyone I've ever met – let alone clashed snowballs with before."

"Oh, do you clash snowballs often, Wolfe?"

"Hardly, this is the first time I have ever experienced snow. Did you not notice how I was slipping and sliding in my boots? Quinn had better coordination than me."

"Liar," she chuckled.

He smiled, his eyes like liquid silver.

Her eyes passed over his broad shoulder, finally noticing that the hall beyond them was empty. She had not even noticed that the others had retired to their rooms.

A warm shiver dashed down her spine as she returned her attention to him, and she felt that suddenly there was something unspoken between them – something that needed to be said.

Or perhaps words were not needed.

She saw his throat bob, as if he too felt what she did.

She had not even noticed that her hand had moved from poking to splayed on Elijah's chest, his heart thunderous beneath her palm. Swallowing, she stepped closer, head tilting ever so slightly.

Could she take a chance? Dabble with fate once more?

Elijah's hand lifted to cover hers, so much larger than her own as his thumb traced a circle upon her skin. "Arii…" he whispered, his voice warm yet hesitant, almost tinged with a question.

Not here, not where others could interrupt them as they always did.

Wordlessly she laced her fingers with his before opening the door to her room, tugging him inside without once breaking eye contact.

She knew not if the fire in the hearth of the room was lit.

She knew not if the bed had been made, nor the window drapes drawn, or any candles lit.

All she could see was him.

All she wanted to *feel* was him.

And he did not protest as his back slammed against the now closed door, his hands on her hips as her fingers tangled in his hair, mouths colliding without a pause for breath. His scent, the heat of him, the taste of him – it was maddening, causing the beast within her to rise from its forced dormant slumber.

Her insides were a sudden riot of hunger, an inferno of anticipation and strangely – nervousness.

Sure enough those butterflies were back, taking wing in her belly like they always did around Elijah. Despite that though, she could not deny that her body – her soul – yearned for him unlike anyone she had ever met.

Including a young King with copper hair.

She pressed thoughts of Lorch back into a dark, familiar part of her mind, welcoming the all too intimate black void as she focused her entire attention on the man before her as he pressed her back, flicking his fingers to lock the door behind them with a gentle *click*.

All the while their lips remained locked.

Elijah's fingers dashed along the buttons of her tunic, a flutter of magic popping them from their homes.

Arii's hands slid over his shoulders, magic loosening his cloak, followed by his sword belt, and then the buckles of his leather vest. She pushed the garment over his shoulders before her hands flew to her own tunic, shucking it to the floor. Teeth and lips clashed as she pressed him roughly against the wood once again, bodies coming together with a sense of urgency.

His magic relieved her of her own weapons belt in a snap of blue light.

They broke apart briefly, breathing raggedly as Arii backed into the room. Her hands danced as she brought forth her magic, purple sparks causing candles to light and the drapes to snap closed.

All the while Elijah stalked after her, eyes dark with desire.

They both paused in the flickering candlelight, chests rising and falling, eyes locked, lips shimmering with fervent kisses.

Arii swore she could hear a faint humming, and she tasted the sweet sensation of magic upon her tongue. She could see it in his eyes – his magic, his power. It was just below the surface, hovering, waiting. It showed through the grey of his irises as blue light, their depths flickering yet smouldering.

Elijah's hand lifted; his fingers pinched.

Click.

The hearth came to life with flames and blue sparks, the golden light bathing the room with warmth.

Slowly, her teeth pinched her bottom lip.

They stared at one another for a few heartbeats more, the air heavy with heat and magic.

She closed the distance between them, fingers twining with the short hair at the nape of his neck as she pulled his lips to hers. Her heart hammered as his arms encircled her, one hand sliding to the small of her back – the other resting upon her cheek as he tilted his head and deepened the kiss.

Gods, he tasted like something made *only* for her, rich, heady and intoxicating.

Heat flared and she scrabbled at his trousers, unlacing the drawstrings as his hands made swift work of her own remaining clothing. Soon they were in nothing but their underclothes, not a sound but the steady yet heavy cadence of their breaths mingled with the crackling fireplace. His fingertips brushed her collarbone, before skimming a lock of her hair over her shoulder. Breaking the kiss, Elijah dipped his head to run his lips along her jawline – his breath hot against her flushed skin. She tilted her head to the side, groaning as his canines brushed the fluttering pulse just below her ear.

She felt him shudder, his entire body humming with pent up energy as his shoulders curled inward – shielding her in his embrace.

Gods, she wanted him to let go.

She wanted to let go.

She knew that it was a Fae instinct to bite – to claim. She had never experienced it before, and it was predominantly a male thing among the Fae, an overwhelming need to leave a mark upon his mate.

Mate.

It was a deeper connection than your typical wedded couple. To find your mate was the endgame. Lovers of the heart, mind, body and soul. She had never believed in it before.

Before she could think on it further – they were suddenly by the bed within a flash of light.

On the complete opposite side of the room.

Before she could register that he had used magic to jump the distance, the backs of her knees hit the bed and their mouths clashed again. Hands clutching, breaths mingling, Arii twisted – and he followed her lead. Crashing upon the mattress, she straddled his hips, canines tugging his bottom lip and hands splayed on his chest as she ground against him – breathing in his groan. Her fingers grazed the array of scars, the light thatch of hair on his chest, the ridges of his battle-honed stomach. The heat of his hands seemed to be everywhere – callused palms grazing, sure and confident, leaving trails of fire on her skin.

Breaking the kiss, she leaned back to stare down at the firelit warrior beneath her.

Her eyes drank him in, cataloguing every incredible inch to memory, branding this moment behind her eyes and hoping with every fibre of her being that time would not be a thief.

Elijah's eyes were almost black, cheeks flushed, hair unkempt and brushed back from his face – leaving no obstructions to her perusal. She could see he was doing the same, eyes roving her face before drinking the remainder of her in.

Slowly.

Oh, so *slowly*.

As his eyes met hers once more, he whispered, "Gods, why is it that I cannot stay away from you?"

Usually she would answer with bravado – but instead she simply said, "Maybe it is fate?"

His lips hitched up, "Fate? Or perhaps destiny."

As she inhaled a sharp breath at his words, he took the opportunity to switch their positions and pressed her back to the mattress, his weight almost sending her beast into a frenzy. She rocked her hips against him, and he pressed her deeper into the plush covers – earning him a breathy moan.

"I want to touch you, feel you…" he paused, before whispering, "…taste you."

Oh, Fates skin her alive.

At his words, she felt his fingers gently stroke up her thigh, pausing a few inches from where she wanted him to be. Waiting.

Despite his words, every movement he made was laced with respect, and she knew he would not proceed without being absolutely clear that she wished for the same.

She did not deserve him.

"May I?"

At his tentative whisper, her eyes met his – and her fingers trailed to rest on his bicep. "Yes. Gods yes."

He blew out a breath, as if he had been holding it in. At her consent, he leaned in and grazed his lips over hers as his fingers moved, removing her last material barrier.

Oh gods.

When his warm fingers found the spot, her back arched of its own accord – her body alighting with sparks. Pleasure swirled through her limbs, curling her toes as his fingers glided inside, teasing circles with his thumb that had her groaning his name. Her hands tangled in his hair, pulling his lips to hers again. His mouth swallowed her moans like rich wine as his fingers worked – gently at first, and then faster – working her body like a weapon he knew intimately, spurred on by her sounds of encouragement. When his fingers were suddenly replaced with his mouth however, she was sure she'd combust. The delicious fire of release was building in her stomach, her heart an untamed, wild thing in her chest.

She glanced down, and the sight of his fingers splayed upon her stomach and his head between her legs had her barrelling towards burnout, her pulse firing through her entire frame as that delicious heat rose to a crescendo – cracking like lightning as stars burst behind her eyes and release crashed through her like a thunderclap.

Upon a sigh she whispered his name – a prayer and a curse.

Elijah slowly moved atop of her, the sight of his glistening lips causing the ripples of heat in her gut to flare yet again.

"You are wicked," she sighed, body feeling languid.

"Again, I have a good teacher."

"Huh, can't say I can take credit for *that*. But – you can practice on me *anytime*… What?"

He was watching her then, something rising to the surface in the darkness of his eyes. "When you let go – when you let your barriers fall, I see you – the real you, Ariiaya. You're resilient, powerful, and incredible, but when you show your vulnerability, how much you can truly *feel*, it adds another level of strength to all of the incredible qualities that you already possess. You're just… so beautiful." A pause as his eyes swept over her – over her face, her body, *everything*. As if he saw deeper than her skin, saw things she could not. All the while, she remained speechless. "You may not believe this, but despite your past, you are *good*, and those who side with evil should fear a force like you."

Her heart shuddered at his gentle words, his heartfelt words.

Her fingers touched his lips, followed by her own and she halted his speech, whispering, "Not tonight, let's not think, please."

With a resigned sigh, his arms circled her as she drew him back to the mattress again. Her beast inside was insatiable, a shivering thing of boundless need as her hands explored as much of his firelit skin as she possible could – delighting in how incredible it felt to have nothing between them. "Allow me to return the favour," she whispered, taking him in her palm – earning her a low groan.

Where she was soft, he was hard – years of training honing his body into a thing of art.

Hers. Tonight, this incredible man was *hers*.

She caressed him, worshipped him, took all that she felt in that moment and tried her best to translate it into giving him as much pleasure as he had given her. His low groan had her eager to please him further, but before she could slide down and return his favour, her name on his mouth pulled her from her single-minded focus.

He flipped their positions, his big hand cradling her head, mouth trailing to the pulse upon her neck, and electricity shot to every nerve ending in her body. When the heat of his kisses and his caresses became almost too much, her eyes fluttered closed and his mouth paused upon her flesh, teeth grazing, seconds away from piercing. He groaned against her skin and she gripped his shoulders as he pulled her closer against him. His hand gripped her thigh, squeezing.

Yet he resisted taking that final plunge.

That final joining of their bodies.

"Gods, I… It's the strangest thing but… I want to *bite* you. Tell me that one of Nem's precise snowballs to my head has dislodged some sense from my brain."

Ahh, a true Fae male.

She groaned, toes curling at the admission as fiery, delicious heat pooled in her core.

"Then do it," she purred.

He pulled away ever so slightly as he whispered hoarsely, "That's a thing? Are you sure?"

Never had she been so sure of anything in her life. She wanted… no, she *needed* him to claim her, the feeling like life giving breath in her lungs. "Yes, it's a temptation that can happen – particularly to male Fae."

"I have so much yet to learn."

She waited with bated breath for a few moments more before his hand covered hers gently. "I have but a slither of control around you, and as much as I want *this*," he dipped his head, "I want to wait."

Her mouth prepared to open and protest, but he continued, eyes dark. "I intend to have you, *all* of you. When I take you, when we make that leap, I fully intend to take my time and savour you, Arii.

Savour every... single... inch of you." His gaze roved her face. "I can promise you now that it will not be in the borrowed rooms of another kingdom."

Surprise flickered over her features as his steel eyes met hers, and he added quickly, "You make it incredibly difficult to remain a gentleman, though."

She grinned impishly, skimming her nails along his stomach. "Don't beat yourself up, I've worn you down." She sighed a breath, placing a kiss to his shoulder. "But I understand."

As much as it pained her to pause so close to the main event, deep down, she wanted to wait too. These moments between herself and Elijah – they were different to any other she had shared with anyone else before. Heated, magnetic, passionate, bordering on cataclysmic, yet she too wanted to savour the moment when it finally came.

He sighed then, voice laden with sweet awe as he whispered, "I don't know much about the Fae..." His words teetered off as he pressed a feather light kiss to the sensitive flesh of her neck, hand cupping her cheek as his lips travelled against her jaw. "But perhaps our feelings – our love – unlocks true magic."

Instead of biting down, like she hoped, he leaned back to look at her. The absence of his warmth had gooseflesh rising. Instead of protesting, she paused as her eyes met his – dark in the firelight. Slowly his hand moved to her chest, palm resting against her drumming heart. His body loomed over hers, pressing in all the right places.

The magnetic attraction between them was like a forest fire, and she could see how much he wanted to let go – she could see it through the beads of sweat upon his brow, felt it in the thunder of his heart and saw it through the grey storm clouds of his eyes.

Within their tempestuous depths she spied something else – something perhaps mirrored in her own heart.

She looked at him then – *really* looked at him.

And she realised she had been falling from the moment she saw him in the library back in Viridya.

Falling in *love* with him. Falling in love with the last hope for their kingdom's salvation.

And it frightened her beyond anything she had ever faced before.

'Once again you allow feeble feelings to distract you, Violet Assassin.'

There it was again – the voice.

The wraith.

'You mew like a pathetic little kitten under his touch. Oh, how far you have fallen.'

It brushed her mind, like a passing thought – yet the words held a weight which she could not ignore.

'You... are... weak.'

The words were hissed, one by one, and they landed like blows upon her brain.

As if on instinct, she felt ice enter from the tips of her toes, traveling up her legs and into her thighs as a feeling of fire drenched her from the top of her head – spearing down, down, down as her breath punched from her lungs at the realisation.

She had known something was manifesting within her for some time.

But to admit it to herself, let it enter her heart as something far greater than just attraction to him...

Was she ready, truly?

Fire and ice collided within her chest, and old habits roared to the surface with a force so violent it had her hands slamming against the solid wall of Elijah's chest – magic rippling and rising forth from somewhere inside her that ran on pure instinct.

Fear was a wild animal, and her mind – in that moment – was nothing but prey.

Elijah's eyes widened at the sudden change in her, his own hands flying up rest on hers as he quickly realised what was happening.

"Arii!" he rasped, vocals thick with an emotion she could not place. "What's wrong? Look at me. *Look* at me!"

She groaned, lips peeling back to reveal her fangs as she hissed, "Get... off."

"I know this is a lot to process – we have been through much the last few days. What you're feeling – I feel it too."

Was she so easy to read, truly?

"I feel *nothing*!"

She was an assassin, cold blooded and cruel with everlasting stains of red upon her hands.

He was to be a King.

He deserved far better than her. Anxiety, self-doubt and pity took precedent in her mind as she ripped her hands from his grip, shoving him back. He let her blow land, sitting back to allow her freedom as she dashed from the bed and stalked towards her clothes on the floor. She heard the heavy thump of his feet on the stone and sensed him approaching, but that did not stop the words flooding out without thought, "I let this go too far."

"We need to talk about this," he gestured between them. "About us."

"What do you want me to say?" she hedged, not meeting his eyes as she yanked the still damp tunic over her head.

"Perhaps start with allowing me to get close to you, and I do not mean physically. When we are together, you let your walls come down – you *relax*."

She stiffened, her body seeming to lock up – the complete opposite of relaxed. Her mouth ran again, words with a bite of acid shooting from her lips. "I want to fuck you, that much is obvious. Why must you need more? I'm… I'm not *capable* of more."

"I'm not asking you to change. I only ask you to allow yourself to feel what is in your heart. Talk to me, Ariiaya."

Why, why did he press so hard for her to admit to her emotions? She had a hard-enough time containing them now, let alone combating what they were doing to her insides. What they were doing to her soul. What *he* was doing to her soul.

Admit them? No, she would not admit them.

To anyone.

She was beyond stubborn; she could thank her mentors for that.

"And what is there to talk about? I don't *feel* anything."

"That's a lie and you know it."

Her head shot up, and just as her lips parted to snarl an obscene curse, he was suddenly before her. He was smart enough not to touch her though, instead frowning intensely. Seeing his expression reminded her of when they first met. That frown was all she had been able to see from beneath his shadowy hood, and she remembered the feeling of wanting to drive her dagger into his chest.

That feeling was returning with stunning force.

He exhaled and lifted his hands, eyes softening as he said, "We can take things slowly. Not a few weeks ago you wished to kill me."

She blinked at that – thinking she had been a bit more subtle in her initial dislike of him. "I never wished to kill you… I only wished to stab you a little."

Elijah saw the distraction was successful and grabbed it with both hands. "Only a little?"

"Okay, *a lot*."

"Aren't you glad you didn't?"

"Right now, not so much." She could feel the anger slowly ebbing away, draining down her body and out through her toes. He had that effect. One moment he brought forth fire, the next moment a sweet soothing balm that tamed that firestorm he had stoked.

"Elijah, I…"

His hands gently glided down her arms to twine his fingers through hers as he murmured, "I should not have pressed. Whatever you are feeling, whatever *this*–" he gestured between them, "–is, we do not need to discuss it until you are ready."

Arii swallowed, feeling suddenly foolish against his compassion. They were so far from being alike – yet they were so similar that it had her almost suffering whiplash. How could he be so patient with her? Gods knew, if he had been acting the same way, she would have stormed out by now.

Patience had never been her strong suit.

"I'm not good at this," she admitted weakly.

"Obviously."

"I'm good at many other things though… like murder."

"*That* I can agree with."

"How can you want me…"

He blinked, as if her question shocked him. Truthfully, her question shocked herself. The filter between her brain and her mouth was a thin veil around him, it seemed.

"Despite the harsh mask you wear in front of everyone, I know that goodness fills your heart. Despite your upbringing and the training and the… suppression of your true self – I see you, Arii, the *real* you." He smiled, and the look he gave her was tender. "I believe what I said back at the School of Fate – you can feel with an intensity that surpasses that of human emotion. You no longer need to pretend with me."

He truly did see the good in her – despite the blood that coated her hands. Perhaps he saw what she did not, because truthfully in her mind she felt there was hardly a scrap of goodness in her.

She wanted to be what he saw her to be, someone who was good.

For him, she wanted to be *better*.

"What is that?" interrupted Elijah suddenly, and she followed his gaze over her shoulder to the dresser on the opposite side of the room.

Eyes narrowing, steps swift, she paused before the drawers as a strange feeling of dread began to tickle at the nape of her neck. Upon the furniture was a small square lockbox, which she could have sworn was not there when they had arrived in Erstonia. Her fingers hovered over the box, pausing as the sweet taste of magic danced across her tongue.

Elijah was a reassuring presence behind her as she opened the lockbox and stared at what was inside.

Laid upon a small pillow of red velvet was Lorch's golden thread and nestled against it was a small square of folded parchment.

Upon the parchment was one word.

Ariiaya.

DEVINA

CHAPTER TWENTY-TWO

ARIIAYA

"Well, I'll just point out the bloody obvious, shall I? We have been infiltrated by someone from the north." Krepth leaned back in his chair, picking remnants of breakfast from between his teeth as he watched Arii's furious pacing. "If you don't stop, little Violet, you will surely carve a path into the stone. Come – sit." He tapped a hand on the wooden chair beside him.

Shortly after discovering the string, Arii and Elijah had swiftly dressed, before notifying the guards that a meeting with the Princes was needed, all passion of their brief collision fizzling to embers and their conversation paused for now.

The strange appearance of the box had been the final knife in the event that murdered their mood.

"There is only one place where someone could have entered the castle undetected," mused Jero, stroking his beard as he leaned back in his chair, eyes tracking Arii as she paced the throne floor. "That is through our cemetery."

"That's morbid," whispered Luc, sitting alongside Emerson with their hands entwined. "What does it mean, Arii?"

The Fury lifted a hand, the glowing string dangling from her clenched fist as she growled, "It means the Fates are watching – even this far south."

"The Fates, or Valdis?" pointed out Emerson. "You left this particular string back at the castle, did you not?"

Arii frowned, eyeing him. "Yes. I'll admit I could have perhaps hidden it better but that fact that it's *here* is what concerns me now."

"The Fates are not our enemies, not truly. Although they reside in the north, they are welcome here in Erstonia," said Jero. "My thought is that the Fates are trying to get a message to you without drawing attention, Arii, if they are indeed the ones to leave the string."

"Was there anything else on the letter?" enquired Nem, perched on the corner of the heavy wooden table – as far as she could get from Krepth, Arii noted.

"My name, and the words 'We will meet where ends begin again'."

"That does sound like a message that the Fates would leave," reasoned Tikkani, worrying the end of her braid. She had a tinge of pink to her nose and cheeks as she shivered once, leaning towards the warmth of a nearby hearth.

"It does, but this thread was last seen in the hands of Lorch Kruel," pointed out Nem. "The Fates are the mistresses of riddles, so that makes sense."

Arii snuck a glance towards Elijah, who stood by the fireplace. He stared into the flames, characteristically silent yet she knew he was deep in thought, judging by the worry lines between his brows.

All she could think about was the letter she had sent to Lorch, and she wondered if this was a message in response.

A door nearby flew open as Valerie made her grand entrance, closely followed by Lyda and Gunner. "What did we miss?" said the pirate, dropping unceremoniously upon a chair closest to the pitchers of wine. Gunner swiped a mug while Lyda peeked out a nearby snow-dusted window.

"How do you feel about riddles, Val?" said Tikkani.

"Hate 'em," she retaliated, no hesitation in her reply.

"Oh, I love riddles!" grinned Lyda toothily. "Lay it on me."

That was no surprise, as the pirate often spoke in riddles, and that was when she was sober. While drunk, she was hardly intelligible. Arii passed the note to her, to which she held the parchment up to her nose, eyes narrowed in concentration.

"Ends begin again… I've never been good at riddles," said Quinn, munching on a piece of dried jerky. "Why must people speak in riddles? Out with it, I say!"

"Agreed," muttered Arii peevishly, crossing her arms.

Lyda's hand flew to the air, note clasped between her fingers, drawing the eager attention of everyone, before hope was rapidly dashed as she said, "Is this a bad time to admit that I can't read?"

Valerie hawked a laugh.

"I think Jero provided the answer before. Where do ends begin again?" said Emerson, to no one in particular as he clutched Luc's hand tight. All eyes turned to him. "When you die, where does your body go – ideally? I'd say whoever left you that message intends to meet you in the cemetery, Arii."

The group's attention was fully on the young man now, causing him to drop his chin meekly. "When we end, we go to the cemetery – to begin whatever comes next."

"The boy may be right." Thogan said, his deep voice breaking the brief silence.

"Well, no harm in taking a stroll to the cemetery to see if this theory is correct." Krepth announced, standing and stretching. "It could be a trap, though."

"Oh, I have absolutely no doubt it will be a trap." Nem pushed off the table, heading for the doors as the group began to move.

Perhaps it was the last remnants of adrenaline – or perhaps it was withdrawals from deviating from her regular line of work, but Arii felt restlessness seep into her limbs. She flexed her fingers by her sides, her lips curling into a smirk as she said, "I sure do hope so."

†

Arii was absolutely positive that her stubbornness was rubbing off on her friends. Short of locking them in their rooms, she could do nothing but sigh and agree when Tikkani, Emerson, Luc and Quinn all insisted they accompany them to Erstonia's graveyard. Thankfully Valerie, Gunner and Lyda had agreed to remain at the castle's local watering hole, quite happy to pick the brains of the town residents to see if anyone had seen anything strange – while sampling the beer on offer.

After arming themselves to the teeth with weapons – courtesy of Jero and Thogan – the group followed the Princes' lead through a crudely carved stone archway, dusted lightly with powdery snow. A handful of castle guards remained nearby, patrolling the perimeter.

The sun had just retreated behind the mountains, a rich sunset painting the sky with hues of orange and pink.

The graveyard was a haphazard smattering of tombstones, many covered in overgrown vines and ivy leaves. There were stone sculptures carved to the likeness of the person passed, as well as elaborately designed pieces that were bold but beautiful. Some had crumbled with age, and some leaned as if the dirt beneath could no longer keep the stones straight. Some also had old bones draped like necklaces, and the skulls of animals resting upon them – ram, elk and boar heads with thick, curling horns and tusks perched like morbid crowns for the dead. Names in a language Arii could not read were carved into each of the tombs, people long gone but not forgotten despite the wild, ruggedness of the misty place.

The trees, now they were unexpected.

Dark, almost black bases broke through the ice and snow, reaching with spindly fingers into the sky. Sprouting from their limbs were deep red leaves, hanging like the willow trees back at the clear pool in Viridya. Their arms twisted in odd directions; the red canopy above creating a light cover against the heaviest fall of powder from above. The floor was littered with leaves, scatterings of red against the snow.

Pausing by a hanging branch, Tikkani pinched a leaf between her fingers, studying the golden veins in the middle of the leaf. "These trees, they're beautiful. The leaves… they remind me of blood."

Jero glanced over his shoulder, "They should, for they were born of the blood of those residing in this cemetery. Our beloved feed the trees, keeping their memory alive well after death."

"Oh, what the fu–"

"Suppose it'd be safe to call them blood trees… literally?" chimed in Luc as Emerson slapped a hand over his sister's mouth, hissing for her to *hush*. She twitched away from the tree as if the person beneath it may just rise from the earth.

"Indeed. The blood trees began to grow thousands of years ago. The magic from those buried here could be the cause of their unique colouring," continued Jero, undeterred by Tikkani and Emerson's flailing. "It is also said that the sap that the trees weep resembles tears of blood."

Arii glanced up, watching russet rays of light break through the canopy to dance in patterns against the dark tree bark. Magic was thick in the air, its smell metallic, its taste – ancient. There was not a better word to describe the rich, burned sugar taste on the back of her tongue, as if toffee had been sitting in the back of a castle kitchen for far too long – stale and forgotten.

"There is someone up ahead," murmured Elijah, his hand already hovering over the pommel of his sword as the group entered a clearing.

Arii felt the mood of their group instantly tense.

The clearing was white, a circle of old, towering stone monoliths framing a central statue of a marble bear, its head lifted to the sky, jaws parted in a roar. At its feet stood a cloaked figure, hooded head looking up at the statue. Slowly the person turned, pale hands folding back the hood.

"You received my message. Good," said Klotho, her lips curled in a smile that did not meet her eyes.

"Klotho?" gasped Arii.

"You seem surprised, my Violet Assassin," purred the woman, resting her hands before her. If not for the dark cloak and darker air, the woman may have just faded into the snow, her skin so pale it resembled moonlight.

"The last order you barked was for my murder so, yes, you could say that." Recovering, Arii twisted a dagger through her fingers as she growled, "I'll give you a few minutes to convince me *not* to end you right here and now."

"Ahh Ariiaya, quick to violence as always."

"I am what you made me," she retorted.

Jero stepped forward, followed by his brother, dipping their heads in respectful greeting. Jero offered a hint of a smile, perhaps to ease the tension. "Sister Klotho, we welcome you. What can we do for the Sisters of Fate?"

Klotho dipped into a swift curtsy "Well met, Prince Jero." She nodded to his brother. "Prince Thogan. I seek an audience with my runaway assassin, if you do not mind. I admit I am not surprised that Ariiaya brought along her little band of misfits. Oh, how far you have fallen, girl."

"Something tells me you did not come all this way to pick me apart, Klotho. Spit it out."

"Must I? You defied your orders and turned your back on your sisters. You know this to be true, I need not elaborate."

"I did what I felt was right."

"Right? When have you ever cared about what was *right*?"

"Since I discovered Valdis is breeding a fucking army of undead to kill us all!"

Klotho visibly flinched at that. "Ah yes, that. It is not your place to question fate, Ariiaya. The Gods will set things right, in the end, but the thread given to you was destined for Lorch Kruel, and you failed."

"Was it truly?" said Elijah as he stepped forward, his face as expressionless as stone. "I have known Lorch for many years – he doesn't deserve the fate of ending by assassination."

"I will get to *you* next, *Prince*." The woman spat, as if a foul thing had touched her tongue.

Arii launched forward, teeth bared in a snarl. "You do *not* speak to him like that."

Her reaction gave Klotho pause, and the woman's golden eyes danced between them as her face morphed from scorn to delight. "Oh, now *this* is interesting."

"There is a point to this sunset meeting, am I correct? I don't think you travelled all this way to admire the trees and tombstones," interjected Krepth as a breeze picked up, dashing leaves across the forest floor.

Klotho's wide smile did not falter as her eyes swept the group, falling upon Nemesis. "I came to bring my pupils home. Come with me now without fuss and the punishments intended for your betrayal will be far less than if you resist." She paused, eyeing Elijah. "And Prince Eliverus must also accompany you. He will need us to guide him into his magic."

She spoke as if he did not stand before her, as if she had a claim to him – a claim the Fates believed they had to *all* who wielded magic. Arii knew – even though she hated to admit it – that the Fates were perhaps the best people to train Elijah to control his magic. They trained their assassins in the art, so it made sense.

So why did she feel a sense of dread in the pit of her stomach, as heavy as lead, at the thought?

Something did not feel right, as phantom fingers caressed the base of her spine.

'Give him to them. Relinquish your burden,' cooed the female voice, entering her thoughts unbidden.

No… that was not an option. She had trusted her gut every step of the way up until now, she was not about to ignore it.

"Don't do it, Arii. Klotho and the sisters have an alliance with Valdis. He gives them Fae, and they give him magic to fuel his nightmare machine, not to mention soldiers to do his dirty work whenever he calls," Nem said, glaring.

Klotho laughed, the only response to Nem's words.

And it confirmed Arii's suspicions.

"We do not need to be divided in this, Ariiaya. We can work together, be as we once did. Magic will return to Fythnar, and your fate rides on the side that you choose. Come *home*."

Arii did not need to glance back to tell Nem had the same unease about her as she did, either sensing the presence or mirroring the same agitation that she felt at Klotho's words.

She had always trusted the sisters, saw them as mentors, a strange sort of family – in place of those she had lost. They had never been motherly by any stretch of the imagination, but she assumed they had grown to become everything she knew. Perhaps she had never known better before.

Until now.

Now she knew better.

Subtly, Arii slid a foot forward as she whispered, "We are not going anywhere with you."

Klotho sighed heavily as she said, "I was afraid you would choose the path of nonsensical righteousness." Slowly she lifted her arms to the darkening sky, preceding the sound of crashing in the forest beyond. "Then you leave me with no choice… a shame."

Half a dozen cloaked figures flew from the forest behind their group, and Arii's eyes darted back over her shoulder as they were suddenly flanked.

Furies.

Arii heard a muffled curse and the sound of struggle, and she spun back to see that Klotho was clutching Nem to her chest, blade pressed against her best friend's throat. Anger sizzled down her limbs as Arii drew her second dagger.

"The Gods do not favour betrayal. Remember this when they do not stand to greet you at your end. We, the Sisters of Fate, do not favour betrayal."

To punctuate her words, Klotho's dagger slid through flesh as Nemesis' throat was opened to the sky.

No.

NO.

Red.

All she could see was *red*.

It bloomed across her vision as Nem fell to her knees, hands clutching at her throat to stop the red… red… red. Her silver nails coated in her own blood as she gasped, but it was no use.

It would not stop.

The blood would not stop.

Arii sprinted, unthinking, as the scene erupted into chaos. Behind her, she vaguely recognised Krepth's inhuman howl of anguish as she sped, daggers moving first, striking the air and narrowly missing Klotho as the woman danced back, amusement on her face. Her hands flew out of her cloak to call forth lightning with impossible speed, her hair fanning out from her face as the graveyard turned blue.

"Now!" Klotho demanded; her cry followed by the distant sound of shrieking in the forest beyond.

That sound was horribly familiar. It had been a constant drone outside Arii's cell in Bonemire. The sound haunted her dreams, coated her tongue with bile.

For the first time, Arii froze dead in her tracks.

The undead, they were here.

Impossible!

Swarming from the forest either side came the undead.

Klotho's hand shot out, and just like all the times before within the training arena of the School of Fate, she was once again hurling magic Arii's way. But this time Klotho's intent wasn't to teach a lesson... it was destruction.

Elijah was before Arii in an instant. His hands flew up, fingers splayed as the magic collided with his outstretched palms, and Arii swore he visibly slid back an inch in the snow. The magic parted and ricochet either side of his position, sparking fires in the closest trees. The snow melted around his boots, his fingertips smoking in the aftermath.

Klotho cackled madly, disappearing into the blood trees as the undead took over.

Utter chaos erupted, but one purpose broke through the haze of Arii's mind.

Nem, she had to save Nem.

"Go!" bellowed Elijah, "We will cover you!"

With a nod, Arii spun and sped for Nem, skidding in the blood-soaked snow to grasp her best friend's shoulders and roll her over, clawing the cloak and leather away from her wound.

Blood, there was *so much* of it.

As her fingers flew over Nem's throat, Arii tried to block out the screams – wild, distorted human screams – from how many, she did not know. Throwing healing magic into her fingers, she began working even as she glimpsed the scene, emotion thickening in her throat.

Her friends, including the Princes of the south, were forming a circle around her.

Shielding her and Nem.

Tikkani and Emerson nocked arrows to aim at the oncoming hoard. Beside Emerson, Luc's human form vanished in a flash to become a black panther with silver-streaked fur. He roared as Krepth's wolf crouched and snarled beside him, hackles raised. Quinn drew his sword, pushing back his hair from eyes glassy with dread.

They all stood their ground despite their fear.

She found Jero and Thogan – bear hide cloaks rising as magic doused the air around them.

Then Elijah.

He unsheathed his sword, the metal ringing in the air as he slid into his fighting stance, as awesome to her now as it had been in the training ring.

As Arii's eyes finally dropped to Nem – skin waxen and splashed with red – she focussed single-mindedly as she had done a thousand times before. She removed all thought and emotion as she pressed her hands to Nem's wounds, allowing her magic to take over.

CHAPTER TWENTY-THREE

ELIJAH

The undead charged into the clearing with no intent other than to rip them all apart. Their eyes were like streaking lights, mouths gaping impossibly – some missing jaws completely. Others were missing limbs, eyes, ears, even parts of their skulls.

Elijah had never seen a more frightening sight, and he had seen his fair share of battles.

They moved with mindless vigour, scrambling over statues and trampling over graves like scurrying mice.

Years of training took over as Elijah lifted his sword.

"Strike to decapitate! Removing their heads will stop them," he yelled.

The hoard was upon them within seconds.

Elijah's sword swung through the air, severing the heads of two living corpses as they flew at him with a shriek. Black blood sprayed the air as he threw out a hand, punching a flash of magic at another – sending them flying.

He chanced a swift glance at the recruits flanking him.

Tikkani was firing arrows like a madwoman, and despite the fear he could plainly see, she fought with incredible bravery. Beside her, Emerson dipped and fired an arrow directly through the mouth of an oncoming undead – before the corpse was set upon by Luc – jaws slamming down upon the thing's neck as he tore the head from its body.

A shriek got Elijah's attention just as fingers grasped his cloak. The thing jerked violently at his clothing, spinning him out of the garment just as a mass of black streaked by, taking out his assailant. Krepth's head lifted from the headless corpse, green eyes alight with feral rage, and Elijah nodded a swift thanks before the wolf took off again.

Jero and Thogan fought with magic, tearing corpses in two, setting spectral bears upon some and spearing shards of ice through the necks of others.

Everywhere Elijah glanced there was chaos.

They picked off the few undead that made it through their lines, narrowly preventing them from reaching Arii and Nem in the middle.

A thundering crash brought Elijah's attention to a particularly large afflicted, one who could have been mistaken for a giant. He walked with a heavy gait, tossing a broken piece of tombstone like a mace as he approached with an enraged bellow.

"This just gets better and better," Elijah muttered as he tossed his sword from one blood-soaked palm to the other, before sidestepping a blow from the man's makeshift weapon. The thing was slow with the heavy armament, giving Elijah plenty of openings to slice his blade along the man's arm, across his flank and then down his back as he danced out of the way.

Despite the maiming blows, the afflicted showed no sign of pain, nor any sign of stopping.

With a roar, the man flung his mace in Luc's direction.

"Look out!" bellowed Elijah – but there was no need. Thogan was suddenly before the black panther, deflecting the attack with his own heavy mace of magic and ice. The undead man staggered briefly – and that was all Thogan needed as he tore a sharp-edged axe from his belt and hurled it at the giant. The weapon tore through the thing's throat, almost completely taking off his head. It dangled to one side as the man toppled to the snow and leaves like a massive sack of bones.

Thogan met Elijah's eyes then nodded gruffly before moving on to the next assailant.

Tikkani's mouth hung open as she gasped, "Fuck my face hole, that thing was huge! Holy fucking knuckle fucks!"

"Oh my gods!" cried Emerson as he tore an arrow from the throat of an attacking woman, and nocked it in his bow before shooting the same woman through the eye, causing her to stagger. "Did you seriously just say that?"

"Do you really think I'll mind my language while we fight a fucking battle against the fucking undead?!" cried the girl as she tore a knife from her belt to cut the throat of an oncoming man who was missing half his jaw. All the while muttering "Ew ew ew!" under her breath. The thing gurgled, hands grabbing at her as she swiftly kicked him in the gut.

"Do you really want your last words to be 'holy fucking knuckle fucks'?!" cried Emerson.

Tikkani barked a mad laugh as she continued to fight off her attacker. "Wouldn't that be something!"

Her brother rolled his eyes dramatically.

"There are far too many comebacks to that statement about your face, Tik – none of which I will voice because most importantly… I like my face hole where it is," yelled Quinn, jerking his sword from the chest of a fallen corpse.

Tikkani grimaced as she tore her knife from the fallen man's throat to glare at Quinn. "Has battle forced a filter between your brain and your mouth, Quinn? *Now* I've seen everything!"

"You both have no filters…" Emerson lamented.

Elijah huffed a laugh as he slammed his sword through the skull of a fallen afflicted, watching as it flailed before ceasing its struggle. Trust Tikkani and Quinn to stir laughter in the heat of battle.

He took stock of the situation and despite their group fighting with everything they had, more undead continued to flood from the blood trees. He threw spears of magic in every direction and severed countless heads, but they just kept coming.

No matter how hard he tried to tap into the bottomless pool of magic he'd found in the Permafrost Arena, he could not replicate it. His inexperience clawed at him, dousing him in self-doubt so sudden that he could taste bitterness.

He could have saved them all if he hadn't been so stubborn about his magic.

With a sinking feeling of dread, Elijah quickly realised they were severely outnumbered, and as he took in the carnage the thought arose that they may not survive.

Bodies littered the graveyard floor, continuing to pile as red leaves fell from the canopy above in a slow, bloody rain. Screams rang out everywhere, the sounds of metal hitting bone rousing haunting memories of battles long past. Images shuttered behind his eyes, past blending with present as blood dotted his lashes. His heart thundered in his ears, the cadence resembling drums of war.

This – what he saw before them – was what the entire land would succumb to if he were to fail.

The knowledge had his shoulders buckling under the weight of the world.

"Eliverus!"

His attention snapped back to the present at Jero's voice. The Prince's clothes – like everyone's – was covered in black blood and gore, as he yelled, "There are too many!"

"Bring forth the bears from the Arena!"

"I'm afraid that is impossible, our magic is suppressed in the graveyard. You too will be affected."

Shit.

"You did not think to mention this earlier?" His blade tore through the chest of an attacking woman, her eye sockets empty, mouth agape.

"It should be common knowledge that magic is dampened in the presence of graveyards…" The man paused after smashing his mace upon a trodden corpse, splitting the skull like a ripe melon. "Ah, apologies my friend – of course you had no knowledge of this."

"There may be a thing or two I missed while growing up – yes," he muttered defensively.

"Remind us to give you a few lessons when this is over."

"If we survive, that is," chimed in Tikkani helpfully.

"Elijah!" came Emerson's yell as he let loose his last arrow to take out an afflicted woman as she came dangerously close to where Arii knelt. The thing clawed along the floor, dragging its sundered body forward, jaws impossibly wide and snapping.

Krepth leaped the distance, slamming the thing into the snow. With a flash, he returned to human form as he tore head from torso, roaring with rage. The Shifter tossed the head away, teeth bared in a shadow of his lupine self, his eyes glimmering with unshed tears as he returned to Arii and Nem's side. He drew a knife from his boot as he growled, "I hope you know what you're doing, little Fury."

The group backed up, tightening their circle as bodies continued to pour from the forest beyond.

"Quinn, I know this isn't the time but... I have something to confess," whispered Tikkani as the group pressed tighter, and Elijah could see tears tracking the gore on her cheeks. Beside her, Emerson joined hands with Luc, briefly back in human form.

Quinn's fingers laced with Tikkani's free hand as he whispered back, "Tell me when this is over."

Elijah's chest constricted as he glanced at Arii, her back arched protectively over her friend as thoughts tumbled through his mind. He had not the chance to tell her–

A howl pierced the sky.

"Finally," cried Jero as he lifted his axe into the air.

From the forest came streaks of colour, teeth flashing and tongues lolling as a chorus of massive paws thundered the earth. They leaped through the air; jaws wide as they collided with the undead.

Wolves.

They were giant, far larger than the wolves they'd encountered on their journey here, and far larger than Krepth's animal form. At least twenty tore their way into the crowd, drawing the attention of the undead around the perimeter. The wolves were vicious – tearing limbs and snapping necks, their long fur like silk in the moonlight, iridescent and shimmering.

Filled with new hope, the group began fighting once again and Elijah stole a glance back at Arii.

Her head was bowed, her body curled over Nem's and her hands were pressed against the wound. He could see her lips moving – her eyes open yet unblinking. Their depths were aglow with magic, her skin lightly shimmering. Beads of sweat formed as her shoulders and body trembled with effort.

Nem's eyes were wide and unblinking, their depths losing light as they stared into the grey sky.

Arii had told him that magic was borrowed from the world around them. With the dampening of magic in the cemetery, could she draw enough to claw Nem back from death? He did not know much about magic, but he was sure that this task would bring Arii to breaking point – even close to death herself.

It seemed impossible on her own.

But perhaps she could borrow from someone else.

"What are you doing?" barked Krepth as Elijah spun, dropping to his knees at Arii's side.

"I have no idea," he growled in answer, tearing off a glove to place his hand atop Arii's. Her skin was cool, almost deathly so.

Slowly her gaze lifted to his, and he saw tears in her eyes.

"I'm not… I'm not strong enough. She…" her voice was barely a whisper, "she is slipping away."

"Borrow from me." Elijah said, his fingers caging hers, gripping tight. "Take what you need."

She did not argue. With naught another moment wasted, she nodded.

Their gazes remained locked as a feeling of pinching began in the middle of his chest.

It was gentle at first – a tugging as if he had sprinted too fast.

And then the feeling intensified.

His breath ripped from his lungs as weight fell upon his back, as if a deluge of snow had just fallen upon his head. It was a strange feeling, an acute and sudden drawing from his pool of magic, bringing sweat quickly to his own brow. He squeezed her hand as the slaughter around them dulled and faded.

And all that existed in that moment was the two of them.

All the while, he kept his eyes locked with hers.

And within their deep purple depths he saw stars.

ARIIAYA

Power, she could feel it rippling just beneath the surface.

As she dived forward and drew from the depths, she knew this was only a shimmer on the lake which resided within him. The sacred land they knelt upon had brought down a barrier, only allowing a trickle.

She hoped it would be enough.

Clasping the borrowed magic, Arii returned to Nem, whose eyes were wide and swimming with tears.

She was still with them, but only just.

Upon her best friend's lips, she saw a word – barely formed.

No.

Nem knew what they were about to attempt could destroy all three of them. Magic such as this was to tamper with fate – divert a destiny forming. It went against everything they had been taught. Many Furies would accept death, accept it with open arms like greeting a long-lost friend, passing into the hands of the gods to fulfil a higher purpose in the afterlife.

"The gods cannot have you yet," Arii whispered in answer.

With that, Arii clutched Elijah's hand and slammed it against Nem's chest.

Magic erupted around them, a chaotic whirlwind of cosmic energy that tore at their clothes and threw the snow and leaves into a flurrying tornado around them.

Her skin was fire, her breath a rasp, her heart warring in her chest.

Thrum.

Something pulled from deep inside her chest.

Thrum.

Again, it tugged violently – causing her body to convulse.

Thrum.

Nem's scream split the air as her back arched off the forest floor, her mouth agape as a golden cord of magic erupted from her chest.

Thrum.

Arii threw her head back as another violent beat bowed her and the magic overtook all she knew. Golden threads burst forth, spiralling around and around, weaving in every direction – hundreds, perhaps thousands – a labyrinth of strings. They caressed her hands, toyed with her hair and stroked her skin, as gold and bright as the sun.

Across her mind's eye images flashed and the strings twirled.

Elijah as a child, his face round, his hair obscuring his eyes – those deep, complex, attentive eyes.

Nem's bright, rare smile, eyes crinkled at the edges as they laughed together.

Her mother's gentle touch as she dashed a brush through Arii's hair.

Her father's wise face as he pointed to something in a book, little Arii perched on his knee.

Her friends, the old and the new.

Then, the strings showed her faces unknown to her – perfect strangers. Fates entwined with her own. So many faces, a spiderweb of lives. Individually they flashed before her eyes.

And then she was there in a cloud of violent darkness.

The wraith.

Claws tore into the edges of her mind, murky and desperate as the unknown woman wrestled with the images, warping them into a calamity.

Before her eyes, her friends began to die.

One… by… one.

'You cannot alter their fate. They… will… die.'

No.

No.

No no no.

Who are you? What do you want with me? Arii threw the thought into the darkness desperately as she fought a battle of wills.

'I am what they made me. You and I are the same, split from different steel yet moulded within the same forge.'

What did that even mean?

She cried out as pain tore through her skull – violent and unbearable. Who the hell was this wraith? What did she want?

Arii did not have time to figure it out.

She tasted sweetness. She tasted blood. She tasted… life.

She tasted him.

Elijah.

He was solid beside her, bringing back her focus, their laced fingers a tether that kept her from fracturing completely. As her head inched up to look at him through the haze, she saw his eyes were squeezed shut, mouth pulled to a line, brow beaded with sweat as his hair danced in slow motion. The strings whirled around him as well, silver and gold. She recalled his fevered kisses by the fireplace, his hands upon her skin – the way he touched her like she was something precious to him. The way he looked at her, the harsh silver of his eyes softening. How that strange, invisible cord in her chest always brought her to him – even in the beginning. Despite her attempts to distance herself, she was quickly realising that distance between them was not possible. The golden threads spiralled and twined between them – brighter than the others – connecting them.

Distance between them was not possible. Never possible – for their fates were eternally entwined.

The cord from Nem's chest wavered, its end flickering and fraying, as if it were trying to find its way.

She turned her attention to it, gritting her teeth in a grimace of defiance.

'No!' screeched the voice. Arii slammed up her defences, blocking the wraith from her mind as she grabbed hold of the wayward cord, snapping a bond into place.

ELIJAH

Elijah knew the moment Arii had successfully saved her best friend.

Up until that moment he felt a steady tugging at his magic as she drew from him. An unseen force began pooling in his chest, steadily blooming through his arm, warming where their fingers twined. It was a peculiar feeling – siphoning magic. It felt as if something from deep within him was being drawn out through his fingertips, draining his energy, causing cold to seep from the top of his head to his toes.

He had stared at her beautiful face until the cold numbed his fingers and the feeling became so intense that he had to squeeze his eyes shut, fighting overwhelming vertigo. He knew he could not allow their link to break, no matter what.

The feeling seemed to only last for a few minutes, but suddenly a snap of magic stole his breath with a violent crack that tore their hands apart. White light encased both Nem and Arii as Elijah lifted a hand to shield his eyes.

As the illumination faded, he sighed in relief as he saw the two women in a fierce embrace.

Then Nem pulled back before cocking her arm and punching Arii square in the stomach, doubling her over as Nem screamed, "Are you fucking MAD?!"

"I love you too, Nem," croaked Arii breathlessly, coughing out a laboured laugh.

The silver-haired fury clasped her throat, now completely healed save for a faint scar. Her canines flashed as she continued to shriek, "I've always known you were crazy, Ariiaya – but now I know you are irrevocably insane!"

Krepth paused by Nem's side, touching blood-stained fingers to her bicep, as he eyed Arii. "You… you performed a life bond? I have to agree, little Fury – you are indeed insane. You could have died." He paused, nodding at Elijah before adding, "All of you."

"I couldn't let you go, Nem." Arii's voice was gentle as she took her friend's hand in an uncharacteristic display of affection. "Not yet – I need you."

Nem's exasperated expression eased slowly, "You've just made things a whole lot more complicated, Arii. I'm still angry at you."

"I know, I can feel it–"

"–but I'm thankful," Nem finished, standing with help from Krepth.

Elijah moved to his feet also, his eyes swiftly tracking the war zone around them.

He breathed yet another sigh of relief.

Around them were countless bodies of the undead, the wolves finishing off any which still moved. But the fight was over.

They had survived, this time.

Soon after the wolves appeared, a backup contingency of guards had followed, and the last of the small army of reanimated bodies were quickly finished off.

Elijah winced, now noticing some scratches and grazes that he had sustained during the fight.

"No sign of Klotho," said Krepth, wiping a split lip as he stepped over a body. "I've always had my suspicions with that one, and I'm not sure if I'm happy to be proven right."

"What would one of the Sisters of Fate hope to gain by allying with Valdis Kruel?" said Jero nearby, surveying the carnage as he stroked the muzzle of a particularly large, silver-coated wolf. "It could not be just to gain more assassins. There must be more to this story."

Arii straightened, dusting her pants and pulling her sweat drenched hair back into a swift braid. "Now we know who was helping Valdis power the Nexus Crystals."

"That deceitful, conniving bitch." Quinn sighed as he let a nearby wolf smell his hand, before scratching the beast behind its ear. The wolf's tongue lolled from its massive jaws as it seemingly leaned into the scratch. Quinn grinned, oblivious to Tikkani's sorrowful glance behind him. The look was fleeting as the girl moved to check her brother and Luc for any injuries.

From what Elijah could see, none were life threatening.

Thank the gods for that small mercy.

"We have much to discuss – come, let's get back to the castle," sighed Thogan.

ARIIAYA

As the group began to move, Elijah came up beside Arii, surveying her closely. "Are you alright?"

She had the audacity to try a smirk. "All in a day's work," she said, but felt her heart was not truly in it.

"Arii…"

"I'm fine – truly."

"What you did for Nem…"

"Was insane – that part is true. By all rights we should really be dead. To tamper with fate like that… I have not heard of anyone surviving the attempt. But we aren't dead and that is because of you."

Elijah moved to block her path, and she halted nimbly, looking up at him. A strange feeling had been manifesting in her chest ever since their fingers broke apart. Perhaps it was the newly made bond with Nem, or perhaps a side effect of their momentarily-shared link. She remembered the dazzling gold and silver cords linking them together earlier.

"You cannot do that again," he said.

"You can't ask that of me, Elijah."

He frowned, arms crossing his chest and she was reminded of the stoic bodyguard he once was. Gods, her time in the castle felt so long ago.

"I can, and I will."

"Ohh, finally playing the King card?" She grinned wickedly.

His brows drew as he growled one word, "Arii."

"You don't need to worry, Elijah. It is not possible to have more than one life bond, anyway." She patted his arm as she slipped past him. "The only way to sever it now is to transfer it using magic… or death."

Elijah mulled over her words for a time, before speaking again. "You thought it was Lorch."

Arii froze, twisting back to him as the group continued on behind her. "What?"

Elijah's voice was gruff, but his gaze did not waver. "In the cemetery. You thought he was going to be there."

Argh, had he seen something before, during their connection? Had he found out about the letter she sent, somehow?

"I…" She swallowed audibly, figuring it best not to bother denying it. "Yes… yes, I had hoped it was him."

Elijah sighed, letting his arms fall, "As did I."

For a moment they stood in heavy silence – no sound but that of blood red leaves scattering on a gentle breeze around their feet.

His hand gently grasped hers as he whispered, "He's alive, I… I can feel it."

"I hope that's true…" Shivers danced up her arm as his thumb stroked her wrist. In that moment though, those shivers were different – cool and timid. "Gods, to the depths of my heart – I do," she added, not disguising the anguish in her words.

Her words dropped away as the last remnants of adrenaline seeped from her body, and she stepped into his arms. There was the briefest breath of hesitation, before she felt his arms curl around her, holding her close as she rested her cheek against his chest.

Normally, when she was this close to him, there would be flames and sparks, and everything would be thrumming with sexual tension. Now though, in this moment, she felt naught but a warm, familiar flicker in her chest as she brought her arms up to circle his waist, sighing long and hard as she whispered, "Things are revealing themselves to be truly fucked up, far greater than I ever imagined."

His chest rumbled as he spoke, the feeling blooming warmth in her stomach. His laugh was tired, too. "Something tells me this is but the tip of the dagger, and there is a whole lot more we have left to discover."

"Yippee…" Arii drawled, before swallowing. "Thank you, Elijah. If not for your magic – I would not have been able to save Nem."

He smiled, resting his chin on the top of her head as he simply replied, "Don't mention it."

ETROPOS, LAKHESIS
& KLOTHO

CHAPTER TWENTY-FOUR

THE WRAITH

A woman knelt on the cold stone floor, head bowed, eyes shut, unmoving save for the subtle rise and fall of her chest. Stars winked in the midnight sky beyond the window of her tiny room, and the sound of waves crashing against the bluffs echoed a chorus against the damp stone walls.

"Now is the time. Send her," came a voice from beyond the heavily locked door that kept her a prisoner. She focused on it, listening in.

"Perhaps the distance is thinning her abilities. Or else we would have them by now," Klotho paced the dais with a scowl, moonlight filtering over the Tapestry of Life behind her. "Eliverus seems to have a natural guard in place which is making penetration near impossible – or so *she* claims."

In the cell, the woman's brows creased.

"She is not ready," said Lakhesis, watching her sister pace with unblinking eyes.

"Of course she is ready! This is exactly what she was made for – a back-up to retrieve what is ours, should any of our students… *stray*." Klotho spat the word as if it tasted foul on her tongue. "Her magic is powerful – limited in its execution – but powerful none the less. Time is no longer on our side, sisters."

Lakhesis continued to look unsure as she glanced at Etropos, who stood and made her way to the Tapestry. "Can we trust she will stay the course? She is still… mildly unhinged – unpredictable even at the best of times."

"I'm sure she is dying for fresh air, and not the kind laced with salt.

Send her, *use* her – it is what we created her for."

"Do we know where the Violet Assassin is now?" said Lakhesis, perched upon her seat, taking a dainty bite of a blood red apple as her golden eyes skipped to her sisters.

Beside her, Etropos twirled a dull string from the tapestry around her finger, watching Klotho as she paced up and down the dais, "Perhaps Klotho can enlighten us?" Her voice was light but it held a tinge of bitterness.

Klotho paused, her skirts swishing upon the old marble as she threw her arms wide, "I told you, sister – you are best to remain here with the Tapestry. Besides, my little trip was a failure. Ariiaya is lost to us – a shame really. So many years of training, wasted."

Etropos lifted her shoulders in a shrug of agreeance as Lakhesis stood and said, "Fine, send her. We haven't many options left. Sister, seek answers from the gods – see if they have anything to say." As Lakhesis spoke, Etropos knelt before the Tapestry and traced a finger along the bottom, searching for a wayward thread. After a strange silence, her voice lifted, and it wavered with uncertainty as she said, "Sisters, look."

Slowly the sisters joined one another as Etropos rose and stepped back, and as one their attention moved down. At the very bottom of the Tapestry of Life, threads were unravelling, the usual shimmering, magical material now had a dull, dark stain blooming from one corner – as if something were seeping through the strands like a curse.

Etropos whispered, "T-The Gods… they are abandoning us."

"She must go, *now*," hissed Klotho, a new sense of urgency entering her voice. "Balance must be restored. We have faltered too long."

The lips of the woman in the cell widened into a twisted smile.

NEMESIS

She was changed. Irrevocably altered, her soul the same yet different.

What Nem had seen when she hovered just beyond the white light of oblivion now flickered at the edges of her memory, just beyond reach and slowly fading. If she was asked to recall it completely now, she feared it would be near impossible. Her memory hinted at the glowing silhouette of a woman; the light behind her so bright that Nem could not distinguish her face. Who she was, Nem had not a clue – but in the hours since her near death experience she had turned over and over in her mind who the mysterious woman could have been.

A sister?

Cousin?

Mother?

Until now, Nem had no true desire to find out about her foggy past, and especially those who had been a part of it. Did she wonder if her parents were alive? Yes, but part of her had lost interest after the first few years of waiting for someone to claim her. If they still lived, surely they would have come looking for her.

Now, having been so close to the end of her life, she felt a small flame of desire to find out about her origins.

A voice dragged her from her reverie and back to the present.

"I almost lost you, you cannot do that again!" His hands were on her biceps, then cupping her cheeks as Krepth's vivid green eyes skipped along her features, critically analysing every inch of her for further injury. Blood still dotted his cheeks, dried on his thick lashes, and even on the corners of his mouth. Up close she could see a fine layer of facial hair dusting his cheeks, and against her will a thought entered her mind that she much preferred his face clean shaven. With a beard she felt the sharp lines of his cheek bones and the tiny dimple on his chin would be lost.

Dark, thick strands of hair fell over his forehead and into his eyes, and his attention was so fully upon her that he did not brush the obstruction away. So, Nem did it for him, her silver nails brushing his brows as she said, "I'll take special care not to come close to dying in the future."

"This is not the time for jokes," he simmered.

The anger, it was so unlike the spymaster to let it show. He was always so composed, so… cocky and confident. She had wondered whether anything affected him as tough times slid over him like water on a duck's back. To see him so worked up now had her feeling out of sorts.

Her natural reaction to unfamiliar feelings began to rise in her gut. Anger.

"Of course, how silly of me – next time I will ask Klotho to kindly *not* slit my throat!" she growled, slapping his hands away.

"Silver Moon–"

"Did you know?"

Krepth's eyes blinked rapidly, taken aback. "Of what?"

Nem poked a silver nail into his lean chest, her voice a low hiss as she ground out the words one by one. "Did… you… know?"

"Unlike Arii, I cannot read your mind through a life bond, Nem. I know a lot, but you're going to have to be more specific."

She leaned in, her fangs flashing. Her tone was accusatory, "Did you know that Klotho was fraternising with the enemy?"

"*That* I did not know." At her angry stare, he added, "You think I would keep such information from you all?"

"Well, it is not the first time you have kept information from us."

"The hell are you talking about–" He halted, then his lips curled, expression changing from defensive to lupin, "Ah, you speak about my history with Valerie?"

Nem spun on her heel, retreating into the centre of the medical room where they had been ushered by the Princes an hour ago, pulling a cloak tight around her shoulders.

Retreating from his tempting warmth, his tempting scent.

It angered her so much that he dredged these feelings within her.

Her silence told him all that he needed to know.

"It bothers you, my history with the pirate captain? Come now, Silver Moon."

Seeking desperately to change the subject, she whispered, "Why do you call me that?"

"Is it not obvious? Your hair, it reminds me of moonlight." His bloodstained fingers hovered withing touching distance of her straight, silky bob – hovering but not touching.

"How fitting – the moon… Something you can see yet never touch."

He was close now, their bodies so close that she felt the heat of him through the thick cloak she wore. He smelled of the forest, deep and complex – with a tiny hint of something feral that was his animal side. She hated it… she longed for it… She couldn't stand it, and worst of all she *wanted* it.

When it came to Krepth, she sympathised with Arii's plight when it came to Lorch and Elijah. He dredged up feelings wholly unfamiliar, in turn bringing with them fear. Anger became her automatic reaction to that fear.

It had been this way for many years.

Yet he still chased her, despite her cold disposition towards him. Their friendship was a peculiar dance built on tolerance and simmering, resentful attraction.

Nem turned to face him, crossing her arms as Krepth spoke.

"Perhaps – like the moon – it is instinct that keeps drawing me back to you. Wolves worship the moon, we sing to it, we long for it yet it is always just out of reach." His fingers grazed her chin, and she did not look away as his deep eyes lifted to hers, their depths swirling. "All I wish to do is worship you, Nem."

Gods, she shivered at the touch, and was not at all surprised by the heat that the motion stoked within her.

Never had she allowed anyone close enough to worship her.

For she had never been touched that way.

Never.

No one knew about her virginity, not even Arii. She had never disclosed such personal information, never feeling the need to. Sure, she played along when jokes were said, but never had she lain with anyone – never allowed someone close enough.

Perhaps it was self-preservation, perhaps it was inexperience.

It was though, very much to do with fear.

Fear of the unknown, fear of giving up control and allowing someone to see her vulnerability. Fear of trusting someone enough to grow close, only to have that trust broken and the good feelings stripped away like the memories of her past.

She believed in her heart that if she were to allow someone to see her that way, they would have to earn it. Earn her vulnerability. Earn her love. Earn her trust.

And keep it beyond that one night.

She wanted to *love* the person she was to lay with. A strange and perhaps outdated point of view, she would admit. But one she would forever stick by. She was also aware that she was not meant to have such thoughts, and thus kept them pressed deep down. Krepth had never hurt her, never stepped over the line she drew – although he danced incredibly close, as far as she let him. But never had he hurt her.

Actually, he would perhaps be a good match for her, bringing a spark of light to her dull life. His cocky grin and sultry confidence had her heating inside.

Her fear was that he may not feel for her as she could feel for him. Would he flutter off to the next beautiful face once he had what he wanted from her?

She knew it was rough to be angry at him for what he did with others behind closed doors. They weren't *together*.

She had made sure of that.

Perhaps that was her true fear, to be forgotten.

Just like her memories.

So, she kept her face impassive – her emotions hidden deep as she pressed her palm to Krepth's solid chest, the word an emotionless breath upon her pale lips as she whispered, "Never."

"You may say I do not affect you, Silver Moon, but your body – your *scent* – tells me otherwise."

"Are we really going to debate what constitutes consent right now, dog? Or shall I save you the overwhelming strain on your brain and make it clear by delivering my knee to your balls?"

"Come now–"

"I'll repeat it again for you… *never*." She drew out the word, letting her fear fuelled-frustration get the best of her.

Krepth's face turned sad, but he allowed her to press him back as his arms dropped to his sides. "You can trust me."

No, she could not. She could not trust anyone.

"I won't hurt you." He tried again, and she read the sincerity in his eyes.

Could he see something on her face that hinted at her fear?

No, surely not.

"Why do you persist. Why? Why do you…" She swallowed, hard. Her anger began to simmer as she said, "Why do you want me, Krepth?"

Sensing the darkening tilt of the conversation, Krepth cleared his throat, mustering his usual slow smirk as he said, "I suppose I'm a dog just wanting that sweet, juicy bone that I am not allowed to have? The thrill of the chase maybe."

"Hmph… you're too stubborn for your own good."

"Stubborn is my middle name." He grinned, before the grin faded and his expression was serious once more. "We have known each other for a long time, Nem, and I think I have made my feelings for you abundantly clear. I understand it though – your hesitation." As her lips parted to speak, he continued, "And so I will wait. As long as you need."

"You might be waiting a long time."

"I am not mortal, thus all I have is time."

Nem sighed, running her fingers along the healing scar upon her throat with absentminded fingers. "So stubborn." Despite herself, her lips twitched with a small smile.

He took those fingers in his own, kissing the tips, eyes smoky like a forest at dusk. "Perhaps, but I am also annoyingly patient," he whispered, letting her hand fall.

Nem felt his absence through the coolness on her fingers as he padded from the room, leaving her tugging the cloak around her shoulders and steeling her façade of stone as she swiftly dressed, and darted in the direction of Arii's quarters.

As Nem sauntered into Arii's rooms a few minutes later, she felt the tremble upon the bond that she knew was a result of frustration, and watched Arii paced the room with Lorch's golden thread dangling from her clenched fist. Emotion pulsed from her best friend in waves, tremulous and wild. Nem knew that Arii's emotions were a wild thing – life bond aside. The woman wore her feelings like a beacon now.

Years of training, years of being moulded by orders of how to think and how to feel – shattered in just a few months.

"It has not entered my thoughts since we were in Viridya, but now that the thread is back, I cannot help but think who it truly belongs to," Nem said, breaking the tense silence as she perched on the end of the bed piled high with furs and blankets. "I agree, after everything that's happened, it could not belong to Lorch. It could be Valdis, but the sisters did hint that what they saw was all pointing towards someone of the highest order – a throne and a king, correct?"

Arii worried her bottom lip, before chewing on her nails. Around her fingers she said, "We don't know what could be happening in the castle as we speak, Nem. Lorch didn't seem at all the type to be tempted by what Valdis offers, but he could well be earning that thread right now."

"You know as well as I do that the thread is only pulled when its owner carries out or decides a deed worthy of judgement from the Gods. Unless you believe Lorch has done something worthy of their ire–"

"No... No, I don't believe he has..."

Nem rubbed at her throat absentmindedly, the place where

Klotho's blade had opened her throat. Arii had once questioned the sisters' motives back in the castle, just before they had discovered the reanimated corpse of Ingrid Polaris. Nem had thought her mad back then, blinded by a growing attraction for the young King. Now though, after their run in with the dark-haired sister, Nem now thought it plausible that the sisters perhaps had ulterior motives. They knew now that Klotho was corrupt – but what of the others? And what did they wish to gain? Power? Magic? Perhaps both...

"Maybe whoever it belongs to is being protected by the sisters? Perhaps they led you astray in your mission?" said Nem.

"It's beginning to seem more and more likely."

Nem felt the subtle shift in the air before Arii whispered, "Could the Tapestry also exist to keep or restore balance? Not just to punish those who deserve it when they have done something wrong."

The silver-haired Fury tilted her head. "Perhaps? I guess in a way that is what we have been doing all along – eliminating those who contribute to the tilt of the land leaning towards one side of the battle between light and dark."

Arii paused a moment, staring down at the dark wood floorboards with a look that Nem did not see her wear often.

Uncertainty.

Usually, her friend wore a careful mask of confidence that made her seem like she knew everything – even when she was unsure. Now though, her face was like an open book, emotions so clear that Nem did not even need to tap into their shared bond to read.

Purple eyes lifted as Arii sighed, and spoke her mind, "I couldn't see the end to his power. Elijah, I mean. When he lent his magic to me to save you. Is that even possible? For one person to have seemingly limitless power with no bottom to the pool they draw upon?"

Pinching her chin in thought, Nem answered, "When his magic awoke and the iron severed his connection, it's possible his awakening was interrupted and in that moment the balance of power was thrown out. That bottom of the pool that shows us our limit was obviously smashed away during his trauma."

"He shouldn't be able to have such magic?"

"All magic has a limit, Arii. Or it *should* have a limit. Elijah's kind of magic is raw and untamed. With so much power, madness will surely follow. That part of history could indeed be true."

"You mean the male Fae who were said to have gone mad from magic? You think it's true?"

"Have you seen any signs of it in Elijah so far? Madness, I mean?"

"No… No, I haven't." Arii lifted a finger to her mouth once more as Nem narrowed her eyes, following the nail of her index finger as it inched between her teeth.

"I know you have strong feelings for him."

Arii twisted on her heel, stalking to the window and speaking around a clenched jaw, "It's… complicated."

A snort, "Nothing complicated about it, Arii. You like him, and he sure as hell likes you."

"Can't see why."

"You need to stop discrediting yourself!" Arii blinked, obviously taken aback at her friend's uncharacteristic outburst as Nem barrelled on, "You're beautiful, resilient, talented with a blade and incredibly loyal to those you care about. Not to mention you risked your life to save him, and I think you challenge him in ways no other female ever has. Yes, I'll admit you are a loose cannon with your temper, and you get awfully *stabby* when you're irritated."

"Stabby?"

"Stabby," Nem repeated, to which Arii shrugged in agreeance. "But, as an outsider looking in I can see there is something undeniable between you two. You make each other… happy, when you're not butting heads of course."

Arii, for the first time in Nem's memory, looked almost abashed as she rubbed at the nape of her neck. "Thank you, Nem – truly."

Nem offered a small smile, watching the woman tilt her head back with a long, pained sigh. "I'll admit, I'm drawn to him. Not just by attraction, but I mean on a deeper level, almost like my soul calls to his. It has been so ever since we first met. Argh…" She plopped beside Nem, bunching her fists in the downy covers.

Nem tilted her head, surveying her friend's face. "Have you considered that he could be your–"

"No…"

"Mate. It's possible, Arii."

"Possible, but I don't want to think about that right now."

Nem's brows rose, "And why not?"

"Do I really need to elaborate? He is going to be a King, and I'm…" a wave of a hand over her general area, "…me."

"You don't think you're good enough for a King?" Nem pursed her lips.

"Exactly."

"You aren't who would normally be picked to help rule the land – but that doesn't mean you couldn't. Queen Ariiaya has a nice ring to it!" She barked a laugh as Arii punched her in the arm, uttering a curse that Nem noted was very un-queenly like.

Arii sobered quickly to say, "All of these *feelings* – they're causing me more pain than pleasure."

"How so?"

Arii lifted the shimmering thread between them, pinching the dangling end and pulling the string taut. A faint gold glow reflected in her eyes as she whispered, "Elijah's magic is immense, unfairly so if you think about it. Power like that really shouldn't be limited to one person. All of these feelings will ultimately lead to pain, because as you said – the tapestry was created for an ultimate purpose…"

"To restore balance. You're saying the thread…"

Pain was plain on Arii's face as she whispered, "It could belong to Elijah."

ARIIAYA

Soon after their talk, Arii tucked the thread into her bags as Nem left to check in with the others. A gentle knock sounded at her door, and Elijah entered her rooms – still dressed in his blood caked clothing. After her discussions with Nem, Arii had found it hard to make eye contact at first, but soon she felt the ice melt away as she watched Elijah recount what he had witnessed at the cemetery while she herself had been occupied.

What the two assassins suspected of the golden thread though, they would keep to themselves for now.

"What Klotho unleased upon us in the cemetery was but a fraction of the force Valdis has amassed. We *need* to get to the west, and obtain Kadec's support, quickly. Then we need to get back to Evergrave and plan what comes next." Arii knew she was voicing the obvious, but after the battle they had just faced, she felt dread settling heavy in her bones.

They were quickly running out of time.

Thankfully, none of them had received life-threatening wounds – save for Nem's near death, and for that Arii was incredibly grateful. She had also noticed that the dark, nipping presence of the wraith in her mind seemed to have fled since solidifying her life bond with Nem. Stubbornly, she thought it best to keep the woman's presence a secret from the others. They didn't need anything else to worry about.

Arii had tried her best not to watch as Elijah stripped swiftly out of his blood-soaked clothing, but she had failed miserably. He had sustained a few scrapes from jagged fingernails, and a bruise on his thigh – but the remainder of him was thankfully unmarred save for his existing scars. Her eyes coasted over his broad shoulders, admiring the glimmering tattoo bestowed upon his bicep.

"What do you think the Prince of the west will want from me?" asked Elijah, pulling on a clean, crème coloured cotton tunic.

As he turned to her, she forced her gaze to meet his.

"Kadec may be dubbed the party boy Prince, but he is fiercely intelligent. He enjoys playing games – and I don't mean the kind with statues and a chequerboard." She pulled her belt tight and slid her daggers into their scabbards as she continued, "His games are of the mind."

"Of the… mind?" echoed Elijah.

"Kadec's power comes from his charisma and his knack for persuasion. He did not become a Prince by just sitting on his arse, like some." She paused, wincing at her own words.

"He did not ascend the throne by birthright?"

"Oh, he did, but far sooner than what would be deemed 'normal' by royal standards. Kadec talked his father and his advisers into allowing him to ascend early – when he was *nine*."

Elijah's brows rose almost to his hairline. "You're kidding."

"No. His father happily agreed – and to this day serves as his main advisor."

"That is impressive."

She grinned, "Absolutely."

Elijah tightened his sword belt. "You think his challenge will involve mind games?"

"You'll need to prove yourself to him in some form or another. What he will put you through is anyone's guess. I don't think you'll be able to get out of it using steel or your fists like last time."

"Fantastic…"

Arii patted her hand against his bicep. "Whatever he throws at you, you'll pull through. Unless it's a glittering ball where you need to scrub up and dance the tango."

His lips quirked in a lopsided smile, "It takes two to tango, and I know who I'd choose as my partner."

"Then we will both surely fail."

With a shared smile, they headed to meet with the others.

It was time to head north through The Wastes.

CHAPTER TWENTY-FIVE

ARIIAYA

The sense of foreboding over their next destination left Arii in a sombre mood, and what little words graced her usually quick mouth were as sour as a ripe lemon. Krepth practically dragged her into the township as the sky faded to the periwinkle and orange of late afternoon, claiming a distraction was needed. They followed the thick cobblestone roads to busy alleyways, mingling amongst the gruff townspeople in markets and shops. In every structure, every stone, every weaved piece of fabric, Arii saw the blood, sweat and tears of hard work.

This place was so different to Viridya. The architecture was weathered from cold, yet robust with a rugged beauty in its grey stone, whereas the Viridya township was all carefully kept archways and painted walls accentuated with gold. Erstonia was a place of labour, every day a battle against mother nature, where Viridya sunned itself under mostly mild, blue skied days.

The harshness of the southern continent showed in the people here, too. The residents in themselves were gruff, hard and standoffish, but Arii saw the way they interacted with one another – here and during her time in the town inn. Southern people were all about loyalty, bravery and fierce friendships. Trust was hard to earn, but ferociously kept. She found she had come to enjoy their few words, their strong liquor and their hearty, thundering tavern songs. Those who accepted her coin in the market were wary yet respectful, too.

It did not take them long to fill their canvas bags with supplies.

Krepth's distraction worked, and she thanked her friend as they headed back to the castle with bags full of bread, cheese and dried meats. Krepth's only reply was a smile, but in that smile she saw heavy, unspoken words. Nem's near death had done something to Krepth. He was still his sly, cocky, witty self, but there was something different about him that she could not quite place, a delicate wariness in his forest green eyes that was not there before. This had been a distraction for him too.

He hid it well, for none of the others seemed to notice.

Prince Jero and Thogan promised Arii and her party as many supplies as they could carry and made good on that promise as the group armed themselves in the dawning light of the eighth and final day of residing in Erstonia. They even gave up two southern Fjord horses, claiming they would carry most of their provisions and speed up their trek to The Wastes.

The air about the group was positive and light as they prepared their farewells at the gates they had entered through seven days before, clasping arms and exchanging brief embraces with those they had come to call friends.

Elijah clapped hands with the Princes, his face creased with genuine gratitude as Arii watched on nearby, leaning against a stone wall accompanied by Nem. Despite the buzz of nervous excitement to be moving on, Arii could not shake a heavy pit of dread in the depths of her stomach. The Wastes were akin to a nightmare, and the words of the wraith still plagued her mind – even though the woman's claws of telepathy seemed to have been removed, for now.

'They will all die.'

The words of the wraith echoed in her memory, chilling her bones. She did not want to agree with the words of foreboding, but she had to admit that the odds were heavily against them at this time.

"You have the face of a slapped arse, little Fury."

Arii's attention was snatched to Krepth, his head tilted, and eyes narrowed in suspicion. She pursed her lips and muttered at him, "That's a strange expression."

"Oh yeah! I see it!" chuckled Tikkani as Krepth passed and flicked

Arii's nose, heading to join the others. His face hinted at humour – but his eyes promised they would speak later.

She could not hide anything from him, *nosey bastard.*

After lengthy farewells to the Princes and their guide, Aaron, the crew began their descent from the snow peaked mountains, down into the slowly flattening plains of ivory white. By the time the stone city faded at their backs, the sun had drifted behind the mountains, and Arii found her trepidation growing with each step forward, her anxiety a darkening cloud that remained right behind her eyes as a slowly growing headache.

After a few days trek, they approached the outskirts of The Wastes. Snowy peaks thinned to hilly fields and red tinged dirt with drying grass crunched beneath their boots. The change was swift, as if stepping through a doorway to a completely different land. Rolling fields of green teeming with livestock were now reduced to an inhabitable wasteland. The ground shimmered underfoot, as if tiny specks of fire littered the dust, giving it a crimson tinge. During the day the distance glittered like embers, and as mid-afternoon fell, the dipping sun reflected upon the earth like tiny fiery stars. A barren wasteland of red with the curtain cloud of an oncoming storm upon the horizon. Only that cloud did not advance upon them, it stayed where it was, a barrier housing horror within.

Some would call it beautiful – but Arii knew the cause of this particular beauty was death.

Arii signalled the group to pause upon a small hillock not far from a colossal wall of mist. The mist was a thick blanket, a curtain as high as the eye could see as. It swam like oil on the top of a tainted lake – a haunted kaleidoscope of drab colours that pulsed as if it were alive. Beyond the curtain, thunder rumbled ominously.

"We cannot take the horses beyond this point. Relieve them of their bridles and set them free – they will know the way home," said Elijah, his grey eyes surveying the wall.

"Is it true what they say about this place, Arii?" whispered Tikkani, rubbing at her arms as if she felt a chill, her throat working. "That it's haunted by those who fell here in the great battle?"

Many sets of eyes turned her way as she pulled the saddle from her horse and rested it upon the discarded pile. "That, and much worse…"

"And we have to go… through it? Can we not go *around* it?" voiced Quinn as he stood by Tikkani's side.

Arii noticed their hands meet, their fingers lacing together and squeezing.

Finally.

The two had been noticeably harbouring a mutual attraction for some time, and it warmed her heart that they had finally admitted their feelings to one another. But, it also added to her growing disquiet.

"Should have stayed on the boat…" murmured Gunner, to which Lyda nodded in acquiescence. The pirates had been uncharacteristically quiet during the journey from Erstonia, and Arii could spy their discomfort from being so far from the sea.

"Going around will add days to our journey. If we go through, it will cut it down to just two days." Krepth said, moving ahead of their crew. "Every day that passes allows Valdis another day to gather bodies into his army. We must get to Ayrith, and we must get there are as quickly as possible."

Arii nodded, swallowing audibly as her gaze danced over them all. "I wish it were not so."

Elijah spoke from beside her, dark hair dancing on a breeze that did not shift the mist wall beyond them, "It isn't too late to turn back. You do not need to come too. You can all go around and make your way to Colkirk. When I have Kadec's support I will send word."

"We can't leave you." voiced Nem, arms crossed.

Arii shifted on her feet as she lifted her chin in agreeance, "Elijah is right, you should all go to Colkirk, we will–"

"Everyone – that includes you, Ariiaya."

Elijah's tone brokered no negotiation, and the group fell silent as tension crackled upon the dry air in the wake of his words.

Arii's voice was the snap of a whip as she snarled. "What?"

Each member of their party chose that moment to find something else to do.

Elijah crossed his arms, planting his feet in preparation for their argument, knowing exactly how this order would be received. Like a crossbow bolt to the head, it would not end well.

"You cannot pass through The Wastes on your own, Elijah."

"What could possibly stop me but a few ghosts?"

Arii blinked incredulously, so dumbstruck at his words that for a moment she forgot her anger. "Do you have any idea how *idiotic* you sound right now? You do not know what is in there! Hardly anyone does."

His brows drew at her condescending tone and his jaw slid forward in a stubborn look she knew all too well. "I have my magic."

"Magic which you are still learning to control."

"I will be fine."

"You will be *dead*, Elijah."

They stared each other down, both harbouring stubborn sets of jaw and narrowed eyes.

Elijah moved first, taking her hand in his. He was silent for a time, and she let the contact of their skin – the familiarity of it – anchor her and chase away her anger. His hand lifted to her cheek, brushing a honey-tipped strand behind her delicately pointed ear. "You've always had the most faith in me, Arii. Do not let that fade now."

Her gaze surveyed the blanket of pulsing, shuddering mist over his shoulder, her throat feeling dry as she forced a swallow. "I can't let you go in there alone. You're powerful, Elijah, but even *you* cannot face *that* alone."

When her eyes met his once more, her fingers drifted up and twined with his upon her cheek. She pressed a kiss to his callused palm, a rare display of affection, and her eyes were unblinking as she whispered fiercely, "Where you go, I go also."

Elijah's lips parted, a tiny hint of his canines flashing with his resigned smile. "I should know better than to tell you what to do."

Her answering smirk held a promise only to him.

"And where Arii goes, we go too," came Tikkani's voice from

behind, and Arii turned to see the group now standing with chins raised and fire in their eyes.

"We have come too far to part ways now," added Emerson, his voice holding a slight tremor despite his bold expression.

"We are like a rancid smell – no matter how many times you wash and spank your clothes against the rocks, we will remain!" threw in Valerie helpfully, her smirk widening from ear to ear.

Krepth chuckled, "Valerie is right, you cannot get rid of us that easily, little Fury."

Hands remaining firmly in grip with Elijah, not caring that the affection was on display for their group to see, Arii turned to them all and nodded. "Together then."

Lifting her chin and inhaling a deep breath, Arii turned towards the wall of mist, hoisting her pack and straightening her spine as she took a step forward.

And was swallowed by a cloud of murky white.

ELIJAH

It was as if they had stepped foot into another world.

Soft, loamy moss squelched underfoot, the complete opposite to the dry dirt they had just left. Fog lingered just before their noses, making visibility incredibly difficult as the group hesitantly made their way deeper into the abyss.

"Tread slowly," came Arii's voice from the head of their party, her eyes narrowed as she lifted a hand to swat ahead – tendrils of thick, inky mist dancing around her fingers. Above, the last rays of sun attempted to break through from the world outside, yet the dying amber light offered no help to their hindered vision.

This place – it was unlike anything Elijah had ever seen before.

From behind there was a splash and a curse, and everyone turned back to see Tikkani kicking a sodden boot. Using Quinn's shoulder, she pulled off her shoe, tipping it upside down to rid it of the water from the deep puddle she had just stepped in.

Everyone gasped, and Elijah heard a few very unsavoury words utter from Lyda's lips – words he hoped Tikkani had not heard.

The water was red.

Blood red.

"What the f–"

"Tikkani, get away from the water's edge!" Arii warned.

As their eyes adjusted to the sight, the mist upon the water's edge danced apart, revealing a shallow pool. Slowly, more pools began to emerge – fog lapping across the crimson marshes as if in a caress.

Tikkani squealed and pushed upon Quinn, who stumbled as his arms flew around the girl. Tikkani pointed at the pool as if it had uttered a curse upon her entire family. "Is that... is that *blood*?!"

Elijah had heard legends of the marshes within the mist of The Wastes – legends that the plains of grass had festered into marshes of dank pools, formed where bodies had fallen. Those legends, though, had never mentioned that they were filled with *blood*, instead of bog water.

As Arii nodded in confirmation, unable to voice the words, Tikkani's hand flew to her mouth as she gagged. Elijah felt not far from mirroring the girl's disgust, his gaze trailing over the scattered pools of red that the mist revealed.

"Blood, why does it *always* have to be blood?"

"Blood trees, blood marshes... what is next, blood *rain*?" whispered Quinn, stroking Tikkani's hair as Emerson leaned over to carefully survey the rippling red pool.

"Don't speak too soon," he said to Quinn, watching the thick pool ripple, "Bad things come in threes after all."

"You really believe tha'?" said Gunner, wiping his brow with his sleeve, the material coming away damp with perspiration. "Gods, is it just me or is it hot in 'ere?" The man was not wrong – the air was warming the further they ventured, as if the mist retained the heat from the day outside. Elijah had no doubt if the day was warm, the nights would be freezing.

Tikkani's disgust echoed about them as they continued on, picking their footfalls with care. The air was acrid, thick with the stench of death and decay that only became worse the further they travelled. Elijah stole a quick glance over their crew, before resting his eyes upon Arii at the head. As they travelled further into the mist, he had noticed she had begun to bite her nails and pick the skin around the cuticles – a nervous habit he had never seen her display before.

As time slithered on, the others began to show small signs of anxiety too. Luc scratched at his arms, Nem wiped her hands down her thighs as if her palms sweated, Tikkani wrung her hair around her palm and tugged at the ends, and Valerie swatted around her head as if invisible flies assaulted her ears. Emerson rubbed at his neck nervously, Krepth scratched at his scalp as if he had fleas, Lyda kept glancing over her shoulder as if something were tailing them and Gunner wiped the sweat from his brow over and over, the skin reddening with the beginnings of a rash. Each member had a small twitch that had the hairs rising on Elijah's arms.

Everyone seemed affected, except for him.

As the world around them began to darken, Arii gave the signal to stop for the night.

"Light a fire, we will rest here."

They all looked exhausted and uneasy.

After gathering as much damp kindling as possible from the mossy banks, Nem knelt by the gathered wood and lit the fire with a snap of magic, hooded eyes reflecting the flames as they engulfed the tinder. As the group settled down for the night, the mist seemed to come alive – tendrils of darkness dancing and skimming the surfaces of the pools like invisible fireflies.

Dank grey turned to black, and the pools began to emit an eerie red glow from within, as if dull fires simmered below the surface. Had they not been surrounded by astringent fog and lagoons of curdling blood, Elijah would have thought the sight eerily beautiful.

Words had become scarce among the group, and even Quinn, prone to word vomit, was uncharacteristically silent. Their eyes watched the flames, skin waxen in the firelight from the strange humidity of the day. As time passed, the air cooled, and everyone moved closer to the fire for warmth.

After what felt like an hour of pure silence, Gunner was the first to break the group's reverie with a loud, obnoxious sneeze. "Sorry…" he muttered, passing a hand over his mouth before wiping at his nose. "Canno' say my nose agrees with the sudden change in temperature."

Krepth handed the man a clean rag as he said, "Get some rest, all of you."

Elijah could not agree more. Fatigue weighed heavily on his own bones, and he could see that each member of their crew felt the same way. Even without looking at her, he knew Arii was staring unblinking into the flames, ghosts of memory dancing in the depths of her glazed eyes. They all needed to rest and take shelter in sleep where the abnormality of their surrounds could not follow.

"I'll stand guard first," he said, keeping his voice low. Arii shifted in protest, as he knew she would, and he raised her hand in his. The motion had her words clearly dying in her throat as he brought her attention to her chewed nails, the skin around her cuticles, ripped and already scabbing. "Allow me to watch over you this time. You have been ripping at your nails since we crossed into The Wastes and it does not take a magician to see the mist is affecting you. You are exhausted – and so are they." He motioned his chin to the wary group.

Arii's tired violet eyes assessed their weary companions. They had travelled distances far greater than this, but there was something about this place that sapped everything far quicker than before. Swallowing, she nodded before sighing. "We'll take turns," she said firmly, and he knew there was no use arguing, so he nodded back.

They settled as comfortably as they could on the muddy floor for the night, and Elijah assumed a slightly raised position to keep a better check on their comrades. He watched over them all until gentle snores filled the air. Elijah allowed the eerie sound of crickets to mingle with sounds of sleep, ushering in a gentle sense of amity.

Despite the peace, Elijah felt the hairs on the back of his neck would not ease. Thunder rolled in the distance, the sound causing little prickles of unease to caress his skin. To distract himself, he watched Arii's shoulder rise and fall, her back to him as she slept a few feet away. Even this couldn't take away the sense of impending doom as the distant rumbles sounded like a death knell on the stagnant air.

Tikkani's ear-piercing shriek split the air.

Elijah was on his feet instantly, as the girl knelt on the soggy ground, hands clutching at the dirt, wailing, "Emerson? NO, NO, NO! You can't possibly be dead. It can't be!"

Before Elijah could question the empty space in front of Tikkani, her brother writhed on the ground nearby, clutching at his throat and heaving as if he could not draw in a breath.

Drowning... he appeared to be drowning.

More screams filled the air, and Elijah spun around to see Nem, Krepth, and Luc – all clutching their skulls and writhing in the dirt, alongside Valerie, Gunner, and Lyda.

Elijah whirled, eyes widening as his gaze lifted to the mist beyond them, the air backlit by lightning strikes in the gloom.

Thrum.

The storm beyond the mist seemed closer now, the cloud pulsing and shuddering. Elijah blinked, his boots fixed to the spot as his heart crashed against his ribs, uttering a low curse as shadows moved in blood-tinged light.

Thrum.

Silhouettes danced in the dust, the outlines of people, limbs flailing as they clashed. Men's cries accompanied the crashing of swords and shields, and the stench of blood assaulted his senses, dragging haunting memories to the surface. Memories of times he would much rather forget.

He concentrated instead on conjuring a plan, his attention darting back to his friends.

One was absent, though.

As he searched for her, Elijah whirled, his glowing pewter eyes darting across the moss and dirt, his heart pounding like a war drum within his chest.

Ariiaya. Where was Ariiaya?

He did not have to look long.

She appeared out of nowhere, like a wraith of hell from the swirling mist, her eyes twin orbs of violent red, all trace of amethyst gone.

Blood red like the pools around them.

Her lips revealed a sinister crescent moon as she smirked.

And plunged a dagger into his stomach.

Her aim was incredible. The blade slid between the armour of his leathers, lodging firmly in the side of his abdomen. Elijah cried out in shock. Mist eked from Arii's mouth as if she were a moment away from breathing fire, a malevolent laugh rolling from her tongue.

Mist. It was the *godsdamned mist.*

He did not have time to ponder what calamity had befallen his friends. Arii's second dagger speared towards his chest – his heart – and he barely avoided it before it snapped past his cheek, searing a line of blood as skin broke.

Her movements were uncanny, abnormally quick, like a snake's strikes.

This was Arii unbound. This was Arii with the intent to *kill.*

Elijah reacted quickly, slamming a hand against her arm as it flew down in an arch towards his chest once more.

"Arii!" he barked – but his voice fell upon deaf ears.

Her actions were a blur, a whirlwind of steel with no holds barred. With each dodge, each parry, he went on the defensive, barely avoiding her attacks as she sliced and speared her dagger through the misty air around them.

To the chorus of tormented screams from their friends, he repeatedly yelled her name. Over and over, determined to get through to her some way, somehow.

"Arii! It is the mist – fight it!"

His only response was an angry scream. She was obsessed, murderous – bursting at the seams with untapped rage, blinded by the mist's influence. Her eyes flashed like crimson jewels as she inhaled the thick mist. Elijah yanked his sword from its scabbard to deflect her downward arc once more, the loud clang of metal clashing as sparks flew. His sword halted her attack and she clutched the hilt of the dagger with both hands, pushing.

"Monster. I'm a monster, and I didn't have a choice. They called it justice, but I recognised it for what it was: *murder*." Arii's voice resonated as their weapons shook, his muscles bunching as she continued to push her blade down towards his face. His gaze snapped from the tip of the dagger to the twist of her beautiful, violent features she spoke. "Never think... never feel... never have a *choice*," she continued; teeth clenched so tight he was afraid they would shatter in her mouth. "Bottle it up inside and press it down deep. That was what was expected of us."

"Arii, you know that is not what you truly are! You care! You care deeply, and that is what makes you strong. That is what makes you worthy of the love of those who know you, the *true* you."

In answer to his words, Arii let out a pained cry, splaying her fingers out around her weapon and grasping her magic so quickly, so effortlessly, that he did not have time to brace. Elijah's head snapped back as a phantom punch hammered into his chin and sent him careening, narrowly avoiding a collision with Nem as he angled his body to skid along the moss. Arii stalked after him, twisting her blade and rolling her neck as though in pain, all the while speaking in a low, rushed monotone. "I wasn't strong enough back then... wasn't strong enough to save her. Weak, weak, weakweakwea–"

Her?

The mist was bringing forth their deepest insecurities, and demons of the past. Arii was rambling now, her words becoming swift and incoherent.

Stars flashed before his eyes and pain sizzled along his jaw, and Elijah did not have long to ponder her words. He jumped to his feet as Arii rushed to meet him. He drew an orb of magic from his pool of power and punched it into his palms. With a cry, he threw it at Arii – who deflected the attack as if swatting away a fly.

She truly had been holding back this entire time.

But so had he.

The earth shuddered beneath their feet, and Elijah resisted as the mist slid across his skin and prodded at his lips. He breathed it in but refused to let it take hold as he reached deep within himself.

And grasped chaos.

Arii stumbled in pursuit as fissures split the ground around them, slowing her advance. Elijah braced himself for the nausea that followed this particular use of his magic, letting the chaos envelope him completely. He vanished and reappeared directly before her in the blink of an eye, static crackling in his wake as he wrenched the remaining dagger from her grip, planted his hands either side of her head, and drew her lips to his in a brutal, forceful kiss. Her enraged screech was muffled by his mouth as her hands scrabbled at his biceps, chest, and neck, and when he didn't back down, her fists began pummelling into his guts.

Elijah took the blows, felt the pain, and focused solely on her, dedicated to bringing her back to him by any means necessary. He could not think of any other way.

There was foul death magic within the mist – magic that entered the mind and played tricks behind their eyes. For whatever reason it did not affect him, an absolute blessing he would question later.

"Come back to me," he said against her lips as a breeze blew around them, tearing at the dust. The mist resisted, clinging to their skin and clothes as the unnatural, sudden wind spread to their companions.

"Please, come back to me," he begged again, his eyes squeezing shut as her punches to his stomach continued. Her hand curled around the hilt of the dagger, which was still firmly lodged in his side, twisting it. Blinding pain seared his blood, and he groaned into her mouth in agony.

Still, he did not let go.

He wouldn't. He… couldn't.

Her protests lessened slightly as the wind chased away the mist. He chanced one tentative hand to her cheek, the other to her waist as he drew her closer, tears burning behind his eyes as he whispered, "Return to me, love."

A low, heartbreaking sob broke from her.

She shivered, and he felt her arms drop from her attack on his body and rise to cup his face, fingers slipping into his hair as her stubborn lips softened. She sucked a sharp breath into her lungs, free of the haunting mist, and made a sound of agony and soul-tearing remorse. "I… I tried to *kill* you. Elijah, I am *so* sorry."

Their friends began to shake themselves free of the dark magic around them, inhaling air cleaned by the strange breeze, and slowly rising to their feet.

Before Elijah could speak, a wail sounded from behind them, and they both turned to see Lyda, hovering over Gunner with her hands covering her mouth.

Those hands were covered in blood as a knife protruded from the man's still chest.

ARIIAYA

"Gunner! Oh, Gunner, no! No, No, No. I… I didn't know what I was doing. I-I thought he was someone else. The mist! It showed me nightmares! Oh gods!" Lyda's voice grew more frantic with each word, her eyes wild as she clutched the dead man's blood-splattered tunic.

Shock punched at Arii's stomach at the sight.

Shaking himself off quicker than the others, Krepth dove for the woman as she began to wail, her cries echoing about the foggy clearing as he pulled her into an embrace while Valerie knelt beside her fallen comrade. The captain passed a hand over Gunner's open, lifeless eyes to shut them as she swallowed back her own grief. "Go now, my friend. Pass through the veil of midnight and onto the endless seas of the Beyond. May you find peace amongst the sea of stars."

Slowly, the others joined them. Tikkani wiped at her eyes and pressed her face into Quinn's chest, while Emerson and Luc linked hands in sorrow.

Anguish heavied Arii's shoulders.

This was no-one's fault but her own.

"You should probably tend to your wounds, Elijah," said Nem from beside her, bringing Arii's attention back as Elijah stumbled to his knees with a pained groan.

Panic flared alongside immense anguish at what she had done, and Arii fell to her knees before him, eager to right the wrong. "Let me heal you."

He did not protest as she helped him remove his leathers and tunic, stealing a swift glance at Nem as the silver haired Fury said, "I'll continue your spell to keep the mist away, Elijah. Save your strength now."

Arii had not even realised he was keeping the mist away until Nem pointed it out. There was a good few lengths of space between them and the thick mist now, the air thinner and easier to take in.

Saving her words, Arii swallowed back a bright and colourful curse at her dagger protruding from the lower quadrant of Elijah's stomach. Blood oozed, and she cursed again internally at the further pain she was about to cause him.

"Just do it," he growled through gritted teeth, and so she yanked the dagger from his body without further delay. She set to work quickly, staunch the flow of blood with her hands as she brought forth healing magic, all the while fighting an inappropriate grin at his very impressive string of uttered curses, ones she had never heard him use before.

She was such a bad influence.

Once Elijah was healed, she cleaned his skin and opened her mouth to apologise again, but his hand grasped hers. "Apologise one more time and I will have to kick your arse."

"Is that the *good* kind of arse kicking, Wolfe? Because if that's the case, then let me remain on my knees."

"That is wildly inappropriate for our current situation," he coughed, as Nem subtly shifted away to give them space.

"Hmm, suppose you're right," she sighed, sobering swiftly as they moved to their feet – but not before she saw his small smile. She wanted to apologise, again and again for her actions, even though she knew she had been out of her mind from the mist.

Valerie wiped tears away with her hand before rising from her position alongside Gunner. His body had been wrapped in his cloak and fastened with what little rope they had. The captain had insisted they not leave him there to become another grave pool – to which everyone had agreed. She did not blame Lyda for the accident, none of them did.

But Lyda was overcome with grief and guilt, staying close to her friend's body; ghostly silent, save for her quiet murmurs and tears. Tikkani whispered gentle words of comfort beside her.

"We must keep going," said Krepth, "Nem can keep the mist away for now but the deeper we go, the more insistent the cursed magic will become."

Arii nodded, knowing the Shifter was right, and looked at Elijah. "You have not slept yet, can you carry on until we can rest again?"

"I don't think anyone got any rest. I will be fine, besides, you gifted me with energy as well as healing. I did not know such a thing was possible," he said.

"You've got a lot to learn, Elijah." This time, Arii's smile was not mocking. "Magic has the potential to do so much *good*."

Elijah didn't respond right away, instead shifting his gaze to their travel companion's wrapped body. His voice was so low that she almost missed his words. "And so much evil."

They didn't have time to debate the merits of magic. She only hoped that over time Elijah would realise that it wasn't magic itself that was good or evil, but rather the wielder. In terms of the marshes around them, those who had died here must have done so with anger in their hearts – resulting in the curse of the mist.

The group moved as quickly as they could. Fear remained acrid in the air and the ghosts of what they had seen in the mist danced behind their glassy eyes like secrets. No one spoke about what they had each seen in their realities of pain, and they all agreed that if any of them wanted to talk about it later, they would be welcome to do so.

So far, no one had, and silence had descended. Arii noticed a subtle shift in the group's demeanour – a sense of division forming that would become detrimental. Gunner's death was an accident – they all knew it – and she knew how much it affected each of them.

But she was curious as to why the mist didn't affect Elijah like it did everyone else. She was aware of his powerful magic, but did this provide him with immunity to the curse? When she asked if he saw anything during the incident, he said he saw shadows of a battle inside the mist – as if the curse was lingering just outside his consciousness, but couldn't get in.

"Elijah may have much to learn about magic, but we have much to learn about *him*, it seems," said Nem, and Arii nodded agreement as they trod through the soft, muddy marshland. The world around them began to lighten, and hazy sunlight filtered through the foggy canopy above. As the pools of red lessened and the land hardened beneath their feet, Arii could feel the mood begin to lighten.

When they pressed through the last curtain of thick fog, they felt the tendrils of cursed magic clawing at their skin, as if the mist was reluctant to let them go.

"Thank *fuck* for that!" gasped Tikkani, falling to her knees and breathing deeply of the clear air. "What an absolutely miserable place!"

Every member of the group nodded as they gulped down mist-free air. Arii cast her gaze over the fields, spying the tips of the Dragon's Teeth mountains in the far distance.

They were in the north now, and closer to Viridya than she liked to be in the current climate.

"Let's keep going. Colkirk is a few hours' trek from here, we can make it before nightfall and rest there."

"What about Gunner?" said Lyda, her eyes remaining forlorn as she gazed back towards Krepth and Nem – who had offered to carry him the remainder of the way.

"We cannot enter the town with a body in tow – it will frighten the locals," Arii paused and gazed to the captain. "Valerie?"

The woman sighed, swiping off her hat and pressing it against her chest. "Gunner belongs at sea. Let us cremate him here as quietly as possible so that we can keep his ashes safe. He deserves a pirate's send-off, cannons and all, once we return to our ship. We will travel the western winds – out to the Boundless Sea and scatter him there. It's what he would have wanted."

Arii had no doubt. Sending the man's spirit out to sea to continue his ventures in unknown lands beyond seemed like the perfect send-off to her. The thought crossed her mind of what she would like, when her time came.

An image of one of Valdis' undead corpses flashed before her eyes unbidden, and she suddenly decided that she too would prefer to have her remains charred and scattered to the wind, somewhere in the east, she decided. Over a grassy field at sunset – one where she had watched the stars as a child with Krepth, or a starlit pool where they had once skipped rocks near Evergrave. Those options sounded perfect.

"Once we have his ashes, I think it is best Lyda and I send a crow to our crew, and return to our ship." She gave a small smile. The group was silent, shock at the sudden decision thickening the air. Valerie glanced to Lyda, who nodded sombrely.

"You're leaving?" said Arii, her voice sounding thin to her own ears.

"As much as we wish to continue on with you all, I think I speak for both of us when I say that we are best used elsewhere." Valerie turned to Elijah, her hazel eyes clear as her back straightened. "We have witnessed enough now to spread word about your quest, Eliverus. The people of this land need to know what you're doing, and what it means for *them* should you succeed."

The woman lifted a palm, to which Elijah grasped firmly. She continued, "Send us to every port in Fythnar. Let us spark embers in the bellies of all the poor souls who *need* your hope." A pause. "It is what Gunner would want, too."

Arii clasped hands with Lyda, then Valerie, noting their sad smiles. Behind the sorrow, though, she could see determination. "Thank you, for your company, and for your wisdom. It won't be the same without you – all of you."

"Don't worry, little Fury," Valerie smiled, "Something tells me we will meet again soon."

After a few more parting words, Arii joined the others as they prepared Gunner's body.

Saying farewell to their friend was a sombre and swift affair, using magic to screen their funeral pyre from unwanted eyes. The group circled the pyre, each whispering their own eulogy in remembrance of the man.

Valerie and Lyda shared their fondest memories, stories that had the group sharing soft laughter. He was a character of a man, one who Arii knew would be sorely missed.

As soon as it was done, Valerie secured a neatly folded square of cloth into her pack as Krepth spoke with her quietly. The group didn't dally long with goodbyes, for the pirates promised they would see them all again. Valerie and Lyda headed towards the sea, and as Arii watched their backs, she said, "Right, let's get going."

KREPTH & NEMESIS

CHAPTER TWENTY-SIX

ARIIAYA

The trip to Colkirk felt quick in comparison to the terrible trudge through The Wastes, and the group moved swiftly with the promise of hot food and beds to rest their weary bones. The sadness of their departed friends lingered in the air, but each member knew it was for the best. When the town tavern came into sight, Quinn groaned with anticipation as they made their way down the cobblestone street. "Gods I hope the kitchen isn't closed." His stomach gurgled loudly, as if to emphasise his words.

"I hope they have beds free. My feet feel like they're about to drop off," added Tikkani.

Sharing their exhaustion, Arii rubbed the heels of her hands against her eyes as they entered the dim light of the tavern. The last rays of the day filtered through the small, clouded windows, and the smell of roasting meat and mead hung heavy in the air.

Thankfully the space was not crammed full, and there was plenty of tables and chairs to spare. The inn matron waved them to a table. A good innkeeper could sense hunger and thirst before an order had even been placed, and Arii knew as the woman hurried to the kitchen that soon they would be greeted with hot food.

"The Inn is unusually quiet," murmured Krepth, nodding gratefully as the innkeeper placed bowls of bread on the table.

Hearing him, the matron said, "That's because many of the townsfolk are sick. Didn't ye' hear?"

Arii paused, a chunk of bread hovering. "Sick?"

The innkeeper mopped at a spill on the table. "Mhmm, some say it be the plague, some say a curse… but I know it to be Dragon Fever. Me cousin had it, and the symptoms match what he had. Took him at the dead of midnight some five nights ago."

Arii's hand dropped.

Luc murmured, "I'm so sorry," earning him a small, grateful nod as the woman continued. "There is a potion apparently – the elves in the east created it. It is not a cure, but it helps prevent the disease, even lessen the symptoms." The woman frowned, mopping a blot of spilled drink as she added, "But many are hesitant to take it, you see."

Krepth swiped a hand through his hair with a growl. "Fear of the preventative is outweighing the good that it does. It is proven to work, yet many still fear taking it because of misguided, illogical misinformation. Many have in their heads that it will cause more harm than good, and they spread this misinformation to others like rats in a sewer," he sighed, his green eyes lifting to the others. "The potion is said to be imbued with magic, and we all know what most think about magic around here. Thank you for this information, Innkeeper. Keep the change." Krepth handed the matron a small pouch of coins, to which she took with thanks.

The hunger that had tormented Arii's insides had vanished like dust on a breeze.

"Dragon Fever?" echoed Tikkani, her expression one of confusion as she surveyed Arii's obvious shift in mood.

Grief welled in the Fury's heart like a storm.

Her mother had been a victim to Dragon Fever. Arii knew of the preventative potion that had been created – Freya had created it herself a short while after her mother's death. At first many had been hesitant to take the amber liquid, fearing it had been created too quickly as outbreaks of the disease began to spread. But soon all of the people in the east had taken the dose, and the fever slowly began to dissipate, becoming a rarity.

Freya had offered the solution to the other courts, even the north – despite the rift between them. The south and west had taken it with thanks, educating the populace on the disease and its preventative.

The north – with the fear of magic still strong – had not taken as kindly to the help. Some of the people took it having lost family members and witnessed their suffering.

Others – even watching people die – still refused.

Their reluctance had now resulted in the sickness spreading like wildfire over the region. Until now though, Arii had not realised how bad it had truly gotten. When her mother was first diagnosed, not much was known, nor were there many others with the same affliction. Now though, it seemed it had become far more contagious.

Nem placed a gentle hand on Arii's back, her face dark with concern. The others shifted around the table, and the mood pitched further into desolation.

Elijah watched it all with a withdrawn expression.

Krepth answered, seeing Arii's building distress. "A terrible disease that ravages the lungs," he explained, rubbing his jaw as he said, "I did not think it was this far west."

Suddenly the doors to the inn flew open, and a man and woman barged in, causing everyone – even Elijah – to jump in their seat. The man had his arm around the woman's shoulders as he cried, "Please, please help us. It's our son… he has it – the curse!"

A bundle of blankets was clutched in the woman's arms, her eyes red and swollen with tears. From where she sat, Arii could hear the labour of the boy's tiny lungs as his body fought a battle it could not win.

"P-Please, he can't breathe," the woman wailed.

A feeble cry emanated from the bundle.

Her heart, her stupid *weak* heart withered at the sound.

She could not bear it.

Krepth's voice overtook the woman's sobs as he called, "Come, bring him here. The best we can do is try to make him comfortable."

Arii stood, her chair scooting back with a screech as she twisted towards their rooms.

No.

No.

Her vision swam, tears welling swiftly in her eyes as hopelessness threatened to swallow her whole. Her breath came in short bursts as she clutched at her emotions, failing to mould them into the neat little ball that could be stashed away. She was not a coward… but this… she couldn't do this, watch an innocent little baby succumb to the horrible sickness that robbed her of her mother.

A shadow blocked out the firelight as someone moved in front of her. Strong hands gently clasped her shoulders as Elijah's deep, smooth voice broke through her rising panic. "Arii, are you alright?"

No, she was not alright.

Even he could not soothe the blinding agony in her heart at the memory of her loss. In all the years since her mother's death, Arii had rarely allowed herself to think about that fateful night. However, now that her feelings were slowly surfacing after being suppressed for so long, she discovered that the ironclad control she once had was crumbling to splinters.

All she could manage was, "Let me go, Elijah."

"Let's not do this here, Arii." His voice was gentle yet edged with unyielding steel.

Over her shoulder she heard the commotion of bowls and mugs being brushed aside. Another weak wail sounded, and Arii closed her eyes at the sound. "My… My mother died of Dragon Fever, Elijah. There is nothing we can do for the child."

If seeing her distress fazed him, Elijah did not let it show. Instead, he glanced over his shoulder, before turning back to her and whispering, "Can we not use magic to save him?"

Her eyes fluttered open, and were greeted with grey orbs so resolute that she had to tread lightly for fear of snuffing out the hope she saw there. "That will only slow it down – if it has not fully ravaged his body beyond repair. Magic will not save him, nothing will."

Elijah's jaw slid forward at her defeated tone. "We have to try."

"It is futile to even attempt–"

"You convinced me to give in to my magic after more than twenty years of fear, you can do *anything*," he interrupted, his voice low and fierce.

Her gaze inched over his shoulder once more to the table where they had placed the child, his little forehead glistening with fever. Magic had not saved her mother… but perhaps she had lived too long with the disease in her body – the sickness ingrained into the very fibres of her being.

The child though…

"My magic is not strong enough, but *yours* could be."

Elijah shifted; expression turning guarded. She could see in his eyes that he still doubted himself, even after all they had been through. Over his broad shoulder she saw more townspeople begin to filter through the tavern doors, all tired, all hopeless and scared.

"I… What if I try and the child dies?"

"If you try and the child dies, then it was his fate."

Elijah's mouth dropped open, but she barrelled on. "The people of this land have not had hope in many years, Elijah. What they need now is to know that you exist, and you are on their side, and you will do *anything* to help them – show them that you are *trying*," she said, stepping closer. In the dim candlelight she could see his expression changing, apprehension slowly being replaced with a flicker of determination.

"I'll be by your side, every step of the way." Her hand lifted to cup his cheek. "Always."

He nodded, touching her hand before returning to the table. Arii was quick to follow, pausing as the father of the child said, "It is true, then? You're… him? The prince who was lost?"

Elijah's shoulders tensed before the small sea of eyes, some wide with awe, most with suspicion. After a moment's hesitation, he rolled his shoulders, straightened his spine and swept his hair back, revealing the delicately pointed ears that showed his true heritage.

"It's true – all of it."

As people in the crowd began to whisper and gasp – a few even dashing from the tavern to alert others, Elijah stepped forward, his eyes like quicksilver as he said, "And I'm going to do everything within my power to save your son's life."

ELIJAH

The entire town awoke as Elijah carried the bundle of blankets containing the child to the town square, and almost everyone save those too ill to leave their houses formed a congregation.

The sky was a rich mauve blanket studded with winking stars, the moon surrounded with a deep ring of orange. He'd have believed the moon was wearing a crown if he wasn't simmering with mounting desire to treat the now-gasping child.

Time was running out.

Cloak fluttering behind him, his friends kept close in tow as he motioned towards the large, vacant space where market stalls would normally be. Now though, the square was empty, nothing but some empty crates and barrels shoved aside.

"I'm not sure what is going to happen when I attempt the healing. Place as many blankets as possible in the centre and stay back," he said. They rushed to create a bed of blankets and coats where he had indicated, and he fought back a shiver of foreboding as the child's eyelids fluttered, revealing his irises. They were a shocking, unnatural blue rimmed with red.

Before heading to the makeshift bed, he turned and met the glassy, terrified eyes of the boy's parents. Elijah swallowed before saying to them, "In case this doesn't work…" The woman stepped forward, her hands clasping his arm as she kissed the boy's little forehead. Uttering a quick prayer, she squeezed and whispered, "You are a miracle, Eliverus. Anything more is a blessing from the gods. Try your best to save our boy."

She stepped back, shaking hands disappearing into her cloak.

Elijah glanced at his friends and saw fierce determination on each of their faces.

They believed in him.

Now he needed to believe in himself.

No more words were needed. A wind picked up as he knelt and gently nestled the child in the pile of blankets. Arii was swiftly beside him, silent as a wraith as he shrugged off his cloak.

"The most powerful magic is ultimately contained in your blood." She placed a dagger on the stones in front of him, its metal clatter ringing in the air. He glanced at her hands as they placed two roughly cut crystals beside the weapon. At his drawn brows she said, "Nexus Crystals."

"Aren't they–"

"Illegal? Yes – for the time being." A smirk. "A stupid law you will scrap when you become king."

"Where in the world did you get them?"

"Nem has a small stash. They are empty, but you can use them as containers for magic." He had no time to argue as she pointed to the blade. "Slice your palms and use the crystals – they should help aim your magic."

He swallowed thickly. "Right. Blood magic." He knew next to nothing about the practice, but what he *did* know was that it was extremely dangerous.

As doubt began to creep up his spine, the child started to cry.

The sound steeled his heart, and he heaved his mind into focus. The Dragon Fever was a disease that attacked the lungs, so he should start there. He shifted on his knees as Arii slid back, allowing him space. Gently he moved the blankets, revealing the boy's chest to the cool air.

"Forgive me, little one. It's going to be cold for a little while, but it will not last long."

The stone was cold and damp through the cloth of his pants as he curled his fingers around the dagger's hilt. A whisper left his lips as he slid the blade across his palm, welcoming the painful sting. He hovered his hand over the child's chest, closed his eyes, sucked in a breath…

And dipped into his pool of magic.

It rose from within like ice, spreading from his chest and through his limbs like starlight. His fingertips sizzled with static as he clasped the Nexus Crystal with his free hand and willed the magic forth tentatively. So far all he had achieved with his magic was destruction, and fear of what could happen to the tiny human had his heart thundering so hard that he could barely hear his racing thoughts.

His blood dripped upon the child's pale skin like rubies, and the babe began to wail as blue light drenched his little form, sparks snapping dangerously close to his skin.

Elijah faltered as thunder boomed overhead.

"Elijah, focus!" Arii said to him, just over his shoulder. "You can do this."

His arms trembled as he grasped the crystal tighter, and it mirrored a riot of flickering, flurrying power within. The magic sparked through him, chaotic and molten. Suddenly the light filtered to pale gold and where slithers of static had cracked seconds before, sparkles of healing light replaced them. A different kind of magic… one he had never tapped into before.

Beneath them the earth began to shake.

Elijah's eyes drifted closed, and he rolled his shoulders, before leaning further forward. His fingers rested upon the infant's chest, feeling the swift fluttering of his terrified heart as his magic seeped into skin and bone, searching flesh and blood.

There.

In the centre he saw an inky ball of darkness, directly in the centre of the child's torso. Webs of black curled and twisted, sunk deep into the child's system.

Suddenly the child's wails turned into coughs. Tiny, breathless little coughs.

No.

The child began to choke, his eyes wide and afraid – uncomprehending what was happening.

No.

He began to jerk, convulse, white froth foaming at the corners of his mouth.

"No!" Elijah bellowed. Teeth clenched and sweat running down his neck, he jerked forward in desperation as he pushed the magic further – but he was met with resistance. The dark mass of the disease writhed, sensing something coming for it, and its tendrils shot deeper into the boy's body.

He was running out of ideas as panic took over.

Frantic, Elijah did the last thing he could think of.

He sent his magic into the boy's chest, magical fingers digging in to grasp the inky mass. Then he pulled.

With a violent snap, Elijah wrenched the darkness from the child's little body.

The darkness fought him with tooth and nail. Roots clung to the child, sickly wisps of ink that wriggled and pulsed as if alive, and Elijah could see that it had no desire to leave its host.

From behind, he heard gasps and uttered curses from the townspeople.

Elijah's brow beaded with sweat as he lifted his hand, pulling the mass further from the boy's now limp form. It thrummed and wriggled in his grip, pulling back towards the ground but Elijah was determined to sever its connection. His magic pulsed, and a wave of nausea swept through him so violently that he had to swallow back bile.

A buzzing rose in his ears like a swarm of flies, and within that sound he heard a faint cackle of laughter – low, maniacal and vile, and somehow familiar, yet unfamiliar too. Pain stabbed at his temples, and he wavered, feeling sick as realisation hit him.

The laughter he could hear was his own.

It was his own voice, strange and twisted, emanating from somewhere far away, where Elijah knew no-one but he could hear.

Eyes widening and heart hammering, he wrenched his attention from his inner madness and back to the chaos before him. The darkness still writhed, and all around him he could hear the shouts of townspeople as they took cover.

As he knelt on the stone, he realised that what he had dragged out from the child was not a disease after all. The thing chanted a distorted mantra, a cacophony of voices melded into one. The words were foreign, archaic, and beyond his recognition – but he felt they were a song once hissed through angry teeth.

This was not a disease, it was a curse.

Who and where it had originated from was anyone's guess, and Elijah was not wholly sure how he knew – he just did. The dark spot roiled with resentment and anger, ancient and cold.

"Arii," he yelled, not breaking his gaze from the thing suspended in invisible shackles before him, "How do you break a curse?"

"A curse?" she yelled back, inching towards him against the pulses of magic. "They can be removed with earth, water and a banishing ritual…" As she spoke, her voice took on steel as she realised what Elijah meant.

Swiftly she called the recruits to find fresh water and soil from the nearest healthy crop.

"We haven't time for a ritual though," she called.

Elijah blinked sweat from his eyes as he continued to keep the curse from the boy's body. "Then we will need to improvise." He wasn't sure if the idea that was spinning through his mind would work, but he had to try. He recalled a piece of jewellery that his mother Colleen always wore, a simple gold pendant set with a tiny vial of shimmering, pearlescent liquid. He had asked her about it once, to which she replied, *"It contains pure starlight, meant to keep curses away."*

He *had* to try.

Arii arrived beside him, her hair a wild tempest around her face as she placed the items at his knees – a waterskin and a lidless jar of dirt.

"I need to create a bracelet," he said.

Without question, Arii began to help – uncorking the waterskin and clutching the jar of dirt. As Elijah held out his bloody palm, she piled a small amount of soil on his hand along with a small splash of water. He hissed at the pain but willed his magic forth, without any real knowledge of what he was doing. He asked, and his magic delivered, moulding earth, water and blood into a bracelet.

The metal shimmered silver, and between the delicate links hung clear crystal beads – just as he had envisioned.

Finally, it seemed his magic was on his side.

Now, he just needed starlight.

With a quick prayer to the gods for this to work, Elijah shot to his feet to hold the bracelet aloft, reaching for the stars. Clouds parted as magic exploded from him and into the sky as he reached with everything he had.

The stars twinkled brightly as he murmured. "Please, help me. Help me so that I can help him – help them *all*. I, Eliverus Herington, banish the curse and swear its intent fulfilled."

His arm began to tremble, and exhaustion forced his knees to wobble as his eyesight darkened at the edges, but he did not falter as the stars above began to shine – seemingly heeding his call. The bracelet in his palm began to glow as the spheres filled with starlight.

As the light began to fade, Elijah slid to his knees, and as he did so the darkness – the *curse* – suspended above the little boy's body began to scream and writhe, harder than before. Elijah stole a swift glance down at the bracelet, then to the curse as its terrified, distorted wails lifted in pitch, raising the hairs on his arms.

It was working. With a spark of hope Elijah set his jaw forward.

It was time to end this.

He pressed forward, latching the little chain link around the boy's tiny wrist.

And the world around them snapped.

The darkness spun before imploding in on itself with a *crack*.

Becoming no more.

ARHAYA

The change in the air was instantaneous. Townspeople slowly

emerged from cover, and the night air warmed as the blanket of stars above them began to clear from the receding clouds.

Arii moved back towards Elijah, eyes wide with awe as he slowly stood and turned to the oncoming crowd. Light gurgles sounded from the bundle he held, and as her eyes lifted from the little flailing arms and up to Elijah's face, her heart squeezed almost painfully.

He was smiling, and despite the sheen of sweat on his brow and overall look of exhaustion, she could see pure relief on his face.

The bracelet glinted on the boy's arm, his skin now a healthy shade of pink.

His parents rushed forward, and Elijah passed the bundle to the mother, tears streaming down her cheeks as she clutched the boy to her chest. The father placed a hand on Elijah's shoulder, whispering, "You saved him. You saved our boy. Thank you, how can we ever repay you for this immeasurable debt?"

Elijah shook his head. "There is no debt."

"The Prince who was lost, Eliverus Herington, he is back from the dead!" One man began, turning to the crowd and splaying his arms wide. "It's true, the rumours were true!"

A townswoman murmured, "Magic made at midnight, under a cloak of starlight."

"We finally have hope!" said another.

"Please, help my husband, he is sick too!"

"And my brother!" another person called.

The townspeople began to cheer and speak, and Arii could see the very subtle stiffening of his shoulders at the attention. She stepped forward and lifted her hands. "Eliverus needs to recover after healing the baby but when he does," she looked back at the man, who nodded, "He will create a charm for each of your loved ones."

"We will help him," called Tikkani.

"We *all* will," said Quinn as the group stood beside Elijah, a united entity.

Elijah swiped his brow and he whispered, "We have a lot of work to do."

SYBELL

CHAPTER TWENTY-SEVEN

SYBELL

"We must go back for him, Hawke. Please!" Lynnera pressed once again, the grime upon her cheeks stained with tracks from the tears that had dried a few hours after their escape from Viridya. They had not had time to wash, only sparing fleeting stops to regain their strength and tend to their horses. Her mother had pleaded that they go back, that they attempt to take Lorch with them, and as much as Sybell wanted to do that, she knew that to return now would be a huge risk.

Valdis was sure to know of their escape by now.

Sybell grunted and twisted her long, dirty blonde hair into a swift knot atop her head as she growled, "I will return for him, mother, I promise. But for now we need to find Ariiaya and Eliverus."

Her mother pressed her cheek against Hawke's strong back, letting her eyes drift shut. "Gods, I hope they are still alive."

"As do I," agreed Hawke, his voice raspy from lack of use. They had been traveling now for a solid two hours. "We must stop soon to tend to the horses."

"The School of Fate is close, right father?" Sybell did not need his confirmation, wrinkling her nose at the faint smell of sea and sulphur on the breeze as it drifted their way.

"If Arii and Eliverus were dead, I believe we would know. There is no way that Valdis would allow that kind of information to be kept secret." He tugged on the reins before adding, "Eliverus' existence threatens Lorch's seat on the throne, and Valdis' power by association."

"I still can't believe what is happening in our home," sniffed

Lynnera.

Sybell glanced over her shoulder at her mother and father, her chin high – a princess still. "And you never suspected my fath… Valdis was concocting something as heinous as necromancy? He is not right, we all knew that – but you were closest to him, mother."

Lynnera stiffened, straightening as she glanced around Hawke's shoulder. "You blame me for what he has done?"

"Why didn't you tell me?"

"Sybell," warned Hawke, sensing the rising tension.

"I wanted to see the good in him, Bell. I truly did, so badly that I turned a blind eye to the atrocities he was committing right under my nose. I am not proud of it." Lynnera rubbed the heel of her hands against her eyes before lifting her chin – almost a mirror of her daughter. "He gave me your brother. No matter how I feel about him, I cannot hate him for that. How could someone so good come of someone with such a dark and stained soul?"

"That is because of you, Lyn." Hawke said, glancing over his shoulder at her as his hand clasped the one she held around his waist. "Lorch may be tempted by the darkness that his father offers but it is because of you that he still remains in the light."

"For now," Sybell added with a scowl, earning her a side eye from Hawke. She sighed, passing her attention back ahead as she clenched her jaw. "I do not blame you, mother. I'm sorry. I'm just exhausted, as we all are."

Lynnera was silent, but Sybell could feel her mother's tension easing as she rested her cheek against her love's back once more.

It had been some time since Sybell had left the castle grounds. As Princess, she was limited to where she could travel, something she had always hated. She wanted to see the world beyond the golden castle walls, see the sights of what could be beyond the sea or past the mountains shaped like dragons' teeth. This newfound freedom had her shifting in her seat, tingles of exhilaration making her fingers curl around the reins.

She would see the sights, but only once she ticked a few things off her list first. Find Ariiaya and Eliverus, learn to defend herself, and she would return with those skills to save her brother.

Then, lastly, sate her hunger for *revenge* by killing the man who had been her father.

A snap of a twig nearby was the only warning they received.

Dark masses were suddenly upon them, cloaks and daggers a flurry as their horses reared back in panic. Red hair flew around the face of a pale-skinned woman, her teeth flashing with a wide smile as her blade pointed directly at Sybell's chest.

Fury assassins.

"Your venture stops here," announced the woman, her golden eyes flashing like gems in the afternoon light.

"Apologies, Miss Devine, we were not able to send a request to the sisters before departing, but they are the most gracious of hosts and I am sure the information we possess will be of use to them. Please, allow us an audience," began Hawke, to which Devina tipped her head in a look of mock curiosity.

"What could the Fates possibly do with a washed up commander, an old councilwoman, and a stuck up princess?" she mused, eyeing them sceptically.

"We are looking for Ariiaya–"

"You will not find her here," Devina growled.

"I thought assassins were meant to be stealthy," Sybell sneered, keeping her head high. Like wolves, these women would be upon them at the slightest hint of vulnerability, so Sybell kept her eyes steely and her face harsh.

If her comment caused any ruffle in Devina's feathers, the woman did not let it show. She scrutinized their dishevelled little party again with a wrinkled nose, like a stench proceeded them.

To be honest, it was very likely that they did smell. It had been *days* since they had washed.

"The Fates know all of what has come to pass, and all of what is to happen in your crumbling empire. You are no longer commander of the Red Guard, Hawke, and as such you do not have any authority here."

Sybell saw her father's body shift as she slid from her horse, her bare feet hitting the muck of the unkempt road. Years of training had her spine remaining straight, her posture impeccable even now. "And what about the Princess? My title has not changed."

Devina's lips rippled, gaze coasting from her bare feet up to her golden hairline, "Ahh Princess Sybell! I did not recognise you underneath all that filth."

"Beneath this *filth*, I am still your Princess. Take us to the sisters, *now*."

"Royals… you think you are above simple manners," Devina drawled, and Sybell could see her fingers twitching around her blade. Itching to stab, probably.

With a cock of her brow, Sybell retorted. "Would manners change anything?"

The Fury's grin was wicked. "Afraid not."

So, Sybell inhaled and said, "I invoke the law of the Fates."

All the Furies, including Devina, turned deathly still.

"The… what?" whispered Lynnera, just as Hawke croaked, "No!"

"For fuck sakes!" spat Devina, twirling on her heel and sheathing her blade. The assassins around her did the same, and none looked at all happy to be doing so.

Hawke subtly placed a trembling hand over Lynnera's and her next question died in her throat. A little piece of Sybell died, too.

The law was something rarely uttered, rarely called upon these days. It was akin to the execution of one's future and placing one's life in the palms of fate. This law meant that she demanded to be taken into the service of the Sisters of Fate as a Fury, forfeiting all titles, all family, all she was before. There she would remain until she passed their tests and became an assassin, or lost her life in the process.

A clean slate, or a death sentence.

Her search for Arii would have to wait for now.

Devina pulled up her hood, her scowl never faltering as they began walking towards the sounds of the ocean and she asked, "How do you know of that law?"

Instead of re-mounting, Sybell trudged the dirt road beside the woman, leading her horse along. "Many may not believe it, but I do take my job as Princess seriously, and with that my lessons of court laws. My brother may find it all boring, but I believe one should have a thorough knowledge of the ins and outs of all laws, no matter how much dust they may have accumulated over the years."

She glanced sidelong at Devina. "How else would anyone find little bits of leverage such as this?"

"You're either incredibly smart, or incredibly stupid, girl. My vote is on the latter." Devina's look was one of scrutiny as she added, "Soon, you'll see why no one utters that law anymore. No one chooses this life, and you will quickly learn the many reasons why."

Lips curled to something feline, and Sybell could not help feeling a dip of dread in her stomach as Devina said, "Gods watch over you, girl."

ARIIAYA

It had taken Elijah the remainder of the night to create a decent bag full of beads containing starlight, and as the sun rose from its slumber behind the mountains, Arii insisted he stop and get some rest. He had been reluctant, but the dark smudges under his eyes and the droop of his broad shoulders proved his exhaustion.

Soon after he had retired, Arii and Krepth headed to the town forge to give instructions to the blacksmith. Elijah was sure that all they needed to do was have a blacksmith place each sphere onto a piece of jewellery, which would then be evenly distributed amongst the people of the town.

The charm, along with the tinctures of medicine from the east, would hopefully chase away the curse if the person was not past saving.

Only time would tell, but it was more hope than the people had had in a very long time.

As Elijah slept in the room upstairs, Arii, Krepth and Nem sat at their usual spot at the back of the tavern as the remainder of the group rested in the rooms provided. A strange sense of familiarity came over Arii, and she sighed for simpler times when she and her two friends would meet like this in taverns.

"Do you really think the charms will work?" Krepth said around a mouthful of venison.

"Only time will tell. But paired with the potion created by Freya, the curse should leave their bodies. Not as dramatically as Elijah's display last night, but a slower healing process," answered Arii, sighing and skimming a hand through her hair. The knots in her ombre tresses were beyond wild, perhaps beyond the help of a mortal brush.

"A curse, who would have known." Nem sipped her ale, a line of froth blotting her top lip as she set the mug down and ran her tongue across her lips. The origins of said curse where yet to be discovered, and if they were to survive the coming weeks, Arii made a mental note to put energy into finding out. She continued in her feeble attempts to brush the tangles from her hair when she noted Krepth's eyes, following Nem's tongue. A flicker of something passing through his clear green eyes before they were once again upon Arii and he hedged, "Surprised you aren't up there with Eliverus, little Fury."

Arii tugged on a knot and paused, lips curling back. "What?" Her reaction had Krepth chuckling around his breakfast.

"Come now, we can all see what is going on between you two." He paused, brows waggling, "and for some, we can *smell* what is happening too."

Arii recoiled, "Argh, gods! Are you serious?"

Nem sighed, placing her boots on the table as she leaned back on her chair, "When is he ever serious?"

Arii groaned and leaned her cheek against the table, lacking the energy to engage with the Shifter. She found his words hypocritical considering how he and Nem had been acting lately. Luckily the majority of their traveling party had been human and oblivious to the battle of hormones in the air around them. She would be sure to rip him a new one later, once she found the strength.

"Can't help but notice the way *he* is with you too, Arii." The serious note in her friend's voice had her sitting up straight. Krepth's gaze was fixed on her, and despite Nem's words, his expression was serious. "He may just be worthy of you, little Fury. *Just*."

Her heart squeezed at the word.

Worthy.

Of course he was worthy of her, he was going to be their *King*. Their saviour, and their hope. She knew he was attracted to her, but she was sure there was nothing beyond that.

Right?

Arii pressed the anxious thoughts away as she leaned forward, eyes narrowing as she rested her chin on her palm and whispered, "So are you two going to continue to tip toe around each other like nervous, hormonal youths or do you need me to call attention to what I can also *smell*?"

Nem stiffened and Krepth coughed.

Arii's smile was feline as she stretched her arms. "It's all well and good to call out what you supposedly see happening in *my* love life – Krepth. But what about *yours*?" The Shifter stiffened as Arii's attention skipped to Nem and she continued, "It may not be obvious to the others, but I know you two better than I know myself." She straightened in her chair and crossed her arms and legs, watching them expectantly. "Now, tell me."

Arii felt a stirring along the thread of her bond as Nem's bright eyes flared and her mouth opened to speak just as Krepth's voice rose, their words mingling in perfect unison as they both barked, "Nothing."

Despite their deflection, the tension in the air was palpable and what Arii could feel through the bond told no lies.

They yearned for each other, terribly.

What was stopping them?

She paused as she thought about how she would prefer others to keep their noses out of her relationship with Elijah. She leaned forward and placed her hands over theirs, earning startled reactions from her friends. Her voice was low as she said, "Fine, I'll drop it for now. But just know that I'm here for you both, always."

With that she stood and headed for the stairs to allow them space. They shared a glance.

In her wake she heard Nem's gentle whisper, "As are we, Arii."

ELIJAH

He was laughing, the sound bounding against invisible walls. By the reverberation and echo, Elijah assumed they were made of stone, although he could not see what surrounded him. His vison was a tunnel, the dreamscape nothing but blur.

His laugh was not a light-hearted chuckle, nor a swift bark at a humorous situation. No, the sound drew from deep within his chest, rumbling forth with vigour – low and tinged with unfamiliarity.

The sound… it was not his own. It was not him.

But it was coming from him, from his own lips as his gaze shifted down, dropping towards a figure kneeling before him.

Upon his brow he felt the solid weight of metal, smooth and cool.

A crown.

In his fist he felt steel, the weapon heavy and balanced, hinting at wealth.

A sword.

He laughed again as the person – the man – lifted his head.

Twin orbs of blue stared wide, his hair a mop of roughly swept copper. His skin was leeched of a healthy glow, his lips cracked and bleeding. Hands were bound behind his back, and the man gasped for air. A scar marred his cheek.

Valdis.

The weapon made Elijah's palm itch, even more so when the man whispered, "Your family – your *race* – were a scourge upon this land." The man shifted, spittle mingling with blood on his mouth as he spoke, "They were falling into madness, where *you* will soon follow."

Pain ate at his heart, grief rose like a violent tidal wave. Elijah's laughter ceased for a short moment, long enough for him to say, "You slaughtered so many, including children... innocent children. You deserve far more than death. You deserve chaos." His voice was not entirely his own, yet the words he muttered were.

Stepping forward, Elijah drove his sword into the man's chest straight through to his spine. There was a wet, sickening crack as steel met bone, yet Elijah did not so much as flinch as he knelt on one knee and bared his teeth.

Valdis' face shuttered, the scar upon his cheek smoothing to unmarred skin, and then Elijah was staring down at the face of his best friend.

Lorch.

Still, Elijah laughed, the sound dripping with madness as he leaned forward, driving the blade farther. Blood welled in the corner of Lorch's lips as he spluttered, "M-My father is right. Madness will come for you, brother."

Elijah hesitated for a breath.

No.

No no no.

He wanted to draw back, to heal the wound and save his friend. Yet his body would not heed him. It was as if his body were under the spell of another, as his mind watched on helplessly.

As Lorch's body fell lifeless to the floor, Elijah screamed, the sound warring with his laughter as mist drifted across the floor.

"Elijah."

He fought against the invisible bonds, desperate to be back in control.

"Elijah."

Lorch's blood pooled across the floor and Elijah grappled with renewed grief, anger warring with the sickening feeling of dread and accomplishment.

Could he be a new curse upon the land if he were to take up the throne with the magic he possessed?

He felt fingers clawing at his skin, clutching his arms, his torso, his face, pulling him back. Nails raked his flesh, stinging, making him bleed.

He deserved to bleed.

"ELIJAH!"

With a shuddering gasp he was ripped from the dream like a thundercrack. Elijah shot up in bed, gulping air, desperate for breath as his eyes darted around the dimly lit room.

Arii's fingers touched his arm tentatively, and he saw her wince when he shied away from her for the briefest of moments. He didn't mean to, but his skin felt too raw… too hot.

But his movements were his own once more.

With a swallow and a quick pass of his fingers through his hair, Elijah willed his heartrate to ease as the woman shifted upon the covers beside him.

"You were having a nightmare." Arii's voice was gentle, a caress in the candlelit room they shared.

He gazed at her, resplendent in the dim light cast from a candle on the nightstand. She wore a simple white sleeping shift, the material painted gold in the light, her hair loose in cascading waves. Plain, quiet, far from the harshness he usually saw in her. It dashed away the haze of his nightmare like a cool cloth.

The air in the room was crisp, the windowpanes hazed from the cold. In that moment he was thankful, for the cool air helped abate the temperature of his scorched skin.

"It was not like the others," he whispered after a stretch of silence, his voice wavering.

Her stare was unblinking, her expression assessing. "No, it wasn't." She cocked her chin as her eyes glanced at his cheek. That was when he felt a lingering sting on his skin. "I don't normally need to resort to violence to bring you back, but unfortunately this time you were a bit harder to wake."

His hand covered the sting. "You *hit* me?"

She winced, shoulders rising and falling in a shrug, "Sorry."

He blew out a huff, "Thank you."

It was becoming far too often now that they woke each other from sleep with their nightmares. Since their heated night in Erstonia just before the trial, they had begun to share a bed together – not just because they always somehow ended up there, breathless and heated, lost in exploration of one another, but because they found that they both had demons that visited at night.

When he drifted to sleep beside Arii, her soft yet lean body fitted perhaps a bit too well against his own, and it made him feel... peaceful. More peaceful than he had in a very long time.

When the nightmares began, they were there to help one another. They did not always discuss what they had seen in those dreams, Arii was still careful with the information that she shared about herself, even now, but she never pressed for more about his own nightmares, either. In this moment he was thankful for that. He did not wish to voice what he was slowly beginning to fear about himself.

"Do you want to talk about it?" she offered, hair sliding over her shoulder.

"No, not yet," he breathed, watching concern smoulder in her dark eyes. She did not press him further.

Instead, she brushed the hair from his face, her fingers lingering at the angle of his stubbled jaw. He leaned into her touch, hearing her soft inhale of breath. She often did that, just a tiny hitch in her breathing, but he heard it as if it were a shout. It roused his beast, the part of him that he wrangled with almost constantly when they were together. It flared heat in parts of him long dormant, parts of him that threatened to take over.

Heat clawed to his stomach, spreading lower, all from one simple touch. He knew what her elegant fingers could do, though – elicit pleasure and spread fire along every nerve ending of his body, along with delivering swift and beautiful death.

Everything about her sang a song of allure to his deepest desires.

So far he remained firm on his inner wish to be a gentleman but gods she made it so *difficult*.

He shifted his mind from pleasure to pain, singling in on his smarting cheek. The hurt reminded him that he was present in the moment, even as the shadow memories of his nightmare lingered. He was still *himself*.

The silence that proceeded them stretched, but it was not uncomfortable. What began as a heavy, charged feeling between them had slowly morphed to this – something companionable. Well, when they weren't both consumed by *fire*.

She shivered.

Elijah grabbed the fallen blanket to drape over them as they nestled back into the covers, her back to his chest so that his nose brushed the crown of her head. He couldn't help it, he inhaled her scent, letting it calm his restless storm.

Arii sighed too, and as they let sleep claim them once again, Elijah knew that his demons would not visit again this night. If they did, he knew she would chase them away.

ROARKE

CHAPTER TWENTY-EIGHT

ARIIAYA

It was strange, but Arii longed for the day that they would remain in one place. She never imagined she would miss the sense of familiarity that came with being in a location known as home, let alone having that sense of desire in the first place. Despite how she ended up there, and her history at The School of Fate, Arii could not deny that it had been the closest thing to 'home', a familiar place to return to when the day was done. Sure, it had reeked of sea salt and sulphur, but the rhythmic crash of the waves upon the bluff had soothed her to sleep more nights than she could count.

The departure from Colkirk had been one that their group would never forget. As they made their way through town, they were greeted by emerging townsfolk who, despite the late hour, were all eager to thank them for what they had done, and for the hope which Elijah had ignited in their hearts.

As the sky darkened and the world faded to night, little glowing lanterns rose into the sky, fuelled by candles nestled inside their paper walls. The townspeople said they signified their wishes for a better future, and to help light their way as Arii and the group headed north.

She had not missed the moisture in the eyes of her friends, and the dark determination flickering in Elijah's eyes as they trudged on foot, soon leaving the town in the distance.

Traveling in such proximity to The School of Fate had everyone on edge, causing the sense of lingering peace created by the show of lanterns in Colkirk to dissipate. They only lit small fires, just enough to keep warm as they found shelter out of sight of the one twisted road towards the shoreline. The castle perched upon the bluffs shadowed them like a towering monolith in the dark sky. The sisters *had* to know they were near, somehow. But as the school shifted to a weight in their wake, Arii found herself convinced that they had been allowed to pass by seemingly undetected. Either that, or the sisters were distracted.

She thanked their lucky stars when the little town that was their destination came into view, gulls hovering over the slowly lightening township as dawn broke. There wasn't much to the crossing town, a dock with small boats moored, a smaller than usual inn and a smattering of shops and homes. In the distance loomed a hazy stretch of land, just visible beyond a short stretch of sea.

As their group embarked on a ferry in Border Town, Arii's attention shifted to Emerson, his cheeks flushed and uptilted eyes glassy. Luc placed a hand over his, the contrast of their skin striking as their fingers twined. "Don't worry," Luc whispered, lifting Emerson's hand to his lips to press a comforting kiss to his palm. "This ferry is far gentler than the *Murderous Lust*. We will be on land again in no time."

It had been several years since her last visit to the court in the west, and as the shoreline of the vibrant island housing the main city came into view, Arii felt her fingers tingle with trepidation. The reputation that proceeded Kadec and his court was mostly positive, with many seeing the people there as facetious and fanciful, and all about a sparkling party. People did not visit to discuss dire affairs, rather using the court for a place to escape their dull and dreary lives. Arii knew though that under a façade of fun and vibrance lay a complicated court of intrigue and manipulation.

As the ferry skirted a calm shoreline covered with lush greenery and littered with little white flowers, she felt the mood of the group becoming lighter. The grey clouds of the land left behind parted to reveal blue sky, and as they entered a wineglass-shaped bay with white sand, she found herself removing her cloak. The others did too.

"Now this is more like it," mused Tikkani, shucking out of her warm clothing and rolling up the sleeves of her crème blouse. "Arii, you never told us how stunning this place was."

Hopping from the ferry on to the sand, Arii replied, "You haven't seen anything yet, but keep your wits about you." She clicked her tongue and glanced over the green shoreline. "Not all is as it seems in the Court of Beauty."

Once a few gold coins were nestled in the ferryman's palm, they trekked from the beach up stone steps flanked with thick bushes of multicoloured flowers. The path was meticulously maintained, even featuring a steel handrail that they all began to appreciate as their path steeply inclined.

Arriving on a flat expanse, they were greeted by a well-dressed man with his hands folded behind his back.

"Welcome, Eliverus Herington, we have been expecting you."

Though his words were polite, his expression was not. Brows narrowed over eyes the colour of a lake at dusk, a deep burnished gold that studied them without missing a beat, giving Arii the impression they were being judged. It was obvious he was a high-ranking officer, with a more elaborate uniform than the two men flanking him. A sword rested on his hip, the sheath decorated with intricate detailing that looked to Arii like vines and thorny roses. His dress was immaculate, not a thread out of place as he scrutinised their frazzled party.

"I am Commander Roarke Serling, and I will be accompanying you to Ayrith castle."

Elijah nodded, responding with, "Well met, Commander Serling."

The court in the west was known by many names, but Arii knew it best by *The Court of Spring*. The reason for that was becoming more apparent to the group as Roarke led them up a slight incline framed by stone arches, the path overtaken on both sides by white and yellow roses. Plants filled the area, a rich array of colours and species revealing themselves the closer they drew to the castle.

Arii heard Tikkani's gentle gasp of awe as they sighted the old, beautiful palace stretching before them as they stepped upon an expansive rise.

Protruding from an impressive garden, thick green ivy crept up white-washed stone walls. The roof thatches and window frames were painted silver, the unusual paint shimmering in the sunshine. Tulips, daffodils, hyacinth and forget-me-nots were just a few of the plants Arii could identify in the luscious garden, arranged in rainbow bursts of colour. If spring had a scent, this air was it – sweet, delicate floral tinged with the slightest hint of sea salt.

"This place is… incredibly beautiful," said Tikkani, glancing at Quinn as the he plucked a white flower and placed it behind her ear, a small smile lightening her freckled features.

"I'll admit I'm not normally one for flowers but I agree, it's spectacular," said Quinn.

Roarke ignored their awe, spinning on the spot to address Elijah.

"Before you are to have an audience with Prince Brolikian, you will all need to be made… acceptable," the man said, with a quick, scrutinising look. "Rooms have been prepared. You will all be escorted by a personal attendant who has been assigned to care for you during your stay." As Roarke spoke, a handful of people dressed in crisp white servant garb appeared.

Arii felt an attendant was unnecessary but decided it best to keep her opinion to herself. To refuse the help would surely be seen as an insult.

They allowed themselves to be led up polished marble steps, through tall, grand front doors and into an expansive foyer. The floor beneath their dirty boots was the same grainy textured marble as the steps, the space opening up to a grand staircase twined around the thick trunk of an ancient, white tree. The newel posts, handrails and even the balustrades were carved of marble and gilded with silver, the detailing so exquisite that Arii could see that even Elijah's expression – which had up until now been impassive – mirrored awe.

The arms of the tree just tickled the ceiling, twisting to frame the foyer with thick leaves in varying shades of green that not only sprouted from the limbs, but crawled up parts of the base like smatterings of dragon scales. Those leaves whispered against balconies with handrails woven with hanging vines and flowers of crisp white.

Everywhere Arii looked, she saw lush greenery and petals.

It was just as she remembered.

Her eyes danced to Elijah and their gazes met for a moment. She didn't know what challenges they were yet to face, but that was not what had her stomach knotting, for she knew they were about to be separated. Of course, it would not be a good look if they were to share a room, and the logical part of her mind thought it best to avoid any unnecessary drama before their meeting with the prince.

Her illogical part though, wailed with sadness.

"Miss, I will be escorting you to your rooms now," said a gentle voice, drawing Arii's attention to a young maid of around twenty standing nearby. She curtsied, her servant garb swishing around her curves. "My name is Cressa Serling, and I will be attending to you for the duration of your stay. Please, follow me."

Arii had once thought the lodgings in Viridya as the loveliest she had ever seen, but as she stepped into her room, she immediately changed her mind. This was far larger, the furnishings far more elaborate, and filled with perfect floral arrangements. An enormous four poster bed took pride of place, draped with fabrics so crisp and white she was afraid she would dirty them by just breathing nearby. Sunlight streamed through the windows, painting the room in gold.

Far too nice for an assassin.

"I'll run you a bath, miss," said Cressa as she left a perplexed Arii in the middle of the room.

"Wait," Arii squeaked, but the maid was already in the adjoining bathroom. Sighing, she allowed her weathered pack to fall, thudding on the plush green rug under her feet. Soon the maid returned, clutching a bundle of silk the colour of washed-out roses.

Arii paled.

"I'm not wearing *that*."

Cressa paused, holding up the dress. "It's a perfectly good dress, miss, and far more presentable than the soiled garments you are currently wearing."

"Please, call me Arii…" At the woman's pointed stare, she added, "Ahem, you haven't anything else that is not quite so… pink? I really don't like pink."

Cressa's head tilted, her expression deadpan. Before she could speak, a realisation hit Arii. "Wait, you said your last name was Serling – any relation to the guard who escorted us here?" Arii looked at her closely. Same colour hair and skin, slightly shorter than Roarke. She was pretty, with round features and healthy, sun-kissed skin, her ash blonde hair twisted up into a messy bun, little wisps framing her face.

The change in the woman's demeanour was almost instant at her words, and she smiled.

"Roarke is my brother."

She closed the distance between them, lifting her chin as the two women stood eye to eye. A spark danced in the russet depths of Cressa's eyes, a look of challenge that Arii was not used to seeing from a servant. Unlike her brother, Cressa seemed to have a gentler disposition overall – a friendliness that made her approachable, but Arii could see the same flame in their eyes. One that screamed that they would not stand to be walked on, or questioned, no matter their position in the palace hierarchy.

"Pink will do nicely," Cressa said, no negotiation in her tone.

Well then.

As much as it itched her palms to grab a weapon in retaliation, or bare her fangs, she did not, deciding diplomacy was necessary this time.

"Fine," Arii sighed, heading towards the bathroom without further complaint, earning her a huff of laughter from Cressa. The woman followed in her wake as they prepared to meet the Prince.

†

A short time later, the group found themselves in an open parlour, the dazzling window shades pulled wide to allow beaming sunlight to light the room. A large oak table sat to the side, covered with finger foods that looked too good to be real. The interior was opulent, a far cry from the rustic, wild feel of the rooms they had left behind in Erstonia.

They awaited the Prince surrounded by stoic guardsmen.

Arii smoothed her palms down the pink silk once more – feeling utterly ridiculous in the shade – before lifting her fingers on a path to her mouth, only to be intercepted by a hand.

"Stop biting your nails, or you'll soon have nothing between your teeth and your bones," hissed Nem.

Arii shot her an acidic side eye, unable to keep the childishness from her voice as she seethed back. "Well, *you* don't look like something that should be waiting on a sweets table." She cocked her head towards an impressive array of desserts nearby. "My dress matches those cakes."

"Hmm, delicious," mumbled Krepth from the corner of his mouth, earning him a swift jerk of Arii's elbow into his gut. She surveyed Nem, ignoring Krepth's grunt and curse. She was dressed in a simple gown of emerald green laced with silver thread. She looked resplendent, her silver hair pinned in a bun at her nape, and not a strand of silver hair was out of place.

"You look fine, Ariiaya, stop acting like a child," Nem chided.

"Easy for you to say, you don't look like a cake."

"Shhhh."

Arii's eyes skipped across their group, unused to seeing everyone looking so... polished. Quinn was dapper in a deep blue tunic and white pants, tawny brown hair swept back from his face, and beside him Tikkani had her chocolate brown tresses twisted into a plait around her head, a few curls left loose to frame her face and the smile that lit her features. It was obvious that she had enjoyed her re-acquaintance with sweet soaps and the chance to wear fine clothes.

Luc and Emerson were dressed in similar shades of green and white, their hair styled and their skin free of grime from their travels.

Arii left Elijah for last, afraid of what seeing him would do to her heart.

They had dressed him in a fine vest of dark steel-coloured silk, the fabric embossed with lustrous patterns resembling the vines creeping up the palace walls. A white tunic underneath set a striking contrast, his pants a soft cream that softened the dark palate. His hair was combed back, and his light beard neatened a touch.

He looked positively debonair.

A pulse skittered just below his jawline, and she could see that he was tense. As her examination ended at his eyes, she decided that she liked this look almost as much as she liked his rugged, scowling, sweat drenched one.

Almost.

Elijah's look slowly changed, brows rising and grey eyes widening, as if he too had just finished checking her out. He inclined his head ever so slightly towards her attire, and she fought to stamp down the impulse to stick out her tongue in response. Now *that* would be childish.

The guards around the room suddenly stiffened, alerting them to the arrival of the Prince.

Kadec Brolikian dashed into the room like a whirlwind with Roarke hot on his heels. The Prince's attire was elegant and flamboyant, a deep forest green coat dripping with gold and jewels over a white dress shirt and brown vest. Arii could not deny that the man was incredibly handsome, his skin a deep sun kissed brown with eyes the colour of rich moss. His coffee-coloured hair was pulled into a tail behind his head, a few wisps left loose on his forehead to curtain bright eyes creased with laugh lines.

The Prince headed straight for Elijah, his face lit with a wide toothed smile. "Eliverus Herington! My gods, a true miracle to have you standing here before us. Holy scatter cats, you look like your father in the prime of his days." The man lifted his arms, waving a hand to them all. "Please, be at ease! You are all beyond welcome here in my court."

As Kadec grasped Elijah's shoulders and pulled him into a fierce embrace, Arii exhaled a breath as Kadec said, "Now, let's talk royal business, shall we?"

ELIJAH

It was a fleeting memory, but Elijah was sure that he had met this Prince once before. The man's friendly smile brought the memory from the depths of his mind, the same flash of teeth that had greeted him when the Brolikian family had visited his home many years ago. The memory was murky, but he remembered the boy – the same age as him – and nothing he could recall suggested there had been any animosity between them.

Much had happened since then, though, and Elijah was not the same. So far, from what he could see, none of the royals of the neighbouring courts held any ill will towards him, and that was despite the fact that Elijah had served their greatest enemy for the better part of almost two decades. He was not normally quick to trust, and even though he had been shown nothing but respect during his visits, he was not wholly convinced that everything was as it seemed. Having lived as a bodyguard, being suspicious of everyone and everything was ingrained into the marrow of his bones. But he fought the instinct and complied.

Now, as Kadec led him on a tour of the castle, he felt a strange unease tickle at the back of his mind – like there was something he was missing but could not quite pinpoint. They had left the others behind at Kadec's request, the Prince insisting he show off some of the wings of his palace that were off limits to regular folk. Elijah had felt a protest rise but stopped it from breaking free. He needed to play the part, earn the Prince's trust and support. If sauntering the castle halls and looking at artworks of old monarchs would help achieve this, then so be it.

They were now in a wing that displayed large portraits of kings and queens past. Like the rest of the castle, the grand hall was lavish in design and filled with flowers and greenery.

Kadec walked beside him with arms behind his back, his gait languid and carefree, and the same could be said about his expression as he tilted his head in the direction of a particularly impressive portrait of a man perched on a silver stallion. They paused before it and upon closer inspection, Elijah could see flowers woven into the horse's mane.

"That was my grandfather. A grand yet simple portrait, do you think? Father says that it took them three days to paint it, on account of grandfather's mount. The silly beast would not stand still long enough for the artists to paint the portrait. Three days and roughly ninety carrots later, they finally had success." Kadec chuckled, before turning to face him. "It is one of the simpler portraits, but grandfather was insistent on having his favourite horse in the picture."

Simple? In Elijah's opinion it was a highly detailed masterpiece.

"It is splendid, Your Highness, as is your entire castle and court."

Kadec waved a hand, "Off with the formalities, Eliverus. Call me Kadec."

"With all due respect, we barely know one another."

"That's true, but our family had long standing alliances, for generations, mind you. It is only right that we continue that tradition." Kadec nodded in thanks to a young woman who offered them refreshments. He handed one to Elijah, who checked the clear glass and floating slice of lemon within with a quick eye, one which Kadec may or may not have noticed, Elijah was not sure.

"As much as I appreciate the tour, Kadec, I'm sure you know of what is happening in the north." Elijah said, his tone cautious. He wasn't sure how much Kadec knew about the blights on the land, or how much isolation was caused by living on an island.

The Prince was silent for a short time as he led Elijah to a large balcony overlooking the glittering city below. Beyond the thatched rooftops and abundance of trees scattered amongst the buildings, he spied the blue of the short expanse of sea between them and the mainland. Haze filtered his view of the little town they had travelled through to get here, and Elijah absently wondered how much of the land's troubles had found their way here to this peaceful retreat.

Kadec's sigh broke his reverie, the man leaning upon a finely carved railing as he fingered the stem of his wineglass. "It is harrowing, seeing a once mighty court reduced to ruin, all because of a select few who made it their sole purpose to spread fear and discord. Your homeland was not always darkness and ruin, Eliverus. The north was once the protectors of the realm, mighty and fierce upon the backs of fearsome dragons. Tell me, how much do you know of your court's history?" He tilted his head, tendrils of hair dashing across his smooth forehead.

Elijah cleared his throat, "Well, it is not a subject they explored thoroughly in history class, and I was mostly focused on physical learning in my youth, for my strength was weaponry, rather than scouring texts about ancient history."

"Ah, I see, and honestly I am not surprised. I hear your prowess with a sword is legendary. But, let us speak of history, just a moment – we are on the same side, you and I. Your family was quite tightly aligned with my own. My family, for many generations, have been known as Gatekeepers."

"Gatekeepers…" Elijah echoed.

"Your bloodline has reigned for as long as anyone can remember, up until recently of course, and their magic was so strong that they were the only bloodline to have successfully forged bonds and kept a long-standing alliance with the dragons that you now believe extinct."

The man paused, before adding, "But they aren't extinct, of course."

Elijah only blink as Kadec continued his speech. "When your family fell, it was up to my family to ensure the beasts were able to retreat to their home realm. We Brolikians have a long history ushering the beasts between worlds. My father was the one to open the gate last time, and he was the last one to close it."

Taking a sip of water infused with lemon, Elijah rolled the liquid around his tongue as he processed the information. Gatekeepers… other worlds… home realm? He felt they were skimming the very surface of something insanely complex, something he was not sure he had the mind to grasp right now. There was still something about the dark-skinned man before him that he could not quite place a finger on, and if what he spoke of was any indication, Kadec should be in possession of magic. But after some critical – albeit secret – perusal of his features, Elijah had just assumed the man was human. Now though, he wondered if he had some magical artefacts somewhere, perhaps a secret room with items that he was sure young Emerson would love to explore. The elf had a keen interest in history and artefacts, causing Elijah to wonder if he knew anything about what Kadec spoke of. He would be sure to ask him later.

Kadec continued, "When *The Time of Darkness* began, my father rallied his closest advisors to decide on what course of action was to be taken. With violence rearing its ugly head within our own court, the Gatekeepers sent word to the north – to your grandfather – that it was time to consider a retreat. He agreed and sent his own personal dragon companion to lead the escape. Lysander, his dragon, she fought him on it, you know. She demanded they stay and fight, but your grandfather knew that the horrors on the horizon would only end in chaos. He was protecting them, and in a way, he was protecting the humans too, for despite what many say, Corvus Herington cared for the human population under his rule." Kadec sighed, "But by sending away his greatest asset, he unknowingly forfeited his best protection."

"But… didn't my grandfather's dragon die during *The Battle at Twilight*?"

"Ah, that is what many believed. A well-spun, albeit slightly untrue story fed to the masses as a cover. Only a few know the truth."

Elijah recalled fragments of what he did know as he asked, "But my grandfather was said to be…" He paused, eyes fixed on the liquid in his cup as he muttered, "Mad. Was that not true?"

The laugh that escaped Kadec was gentle, but he composed himself quickly. "No, no, he was not."

He continued. "Your family's alliance with the dragons was built over thousands of years, consisting of love, trust, respect and magic. The Fae lived in harmony with the dragons, but when the bloodshed began, we made the choice to send them away in order to save the land from complete and utter chaos. In doing so though, we doomed the Fae race." Kadec turned to him, his earlier expression wiped clean, replaced with one of determination etched with hints of eagerness, a completely different man from the one who offered his grand tour with a carefree smile moments ago. "What do you know of other realms, Eliverus? Places beyond Fythnar, beyond the Boundless Sea?"

Elijah paused at the sudden change of subject, weaving his words in his mind carefully before voicing them outright. "I cannot say I have put much thought into it."

"I guess you could blame your sheltered upbringing for that – which I know was not your choice, you knew no different. But, have you never entertained the thought that there is much more out there, beyond our existence here?" He gestured to the horizon to his right, out to the endless stretch of sea beyond the hazy shoreline. Gulls skirted the glittering waves, and Elijah's thoughts briefly wandered to the sea drakes they had encountered on their adventure. Such colossal creatures surely travelled far, and he found his thoughts mirroring Kadec's – daydreaming about what could be beyond the horizon in lands unknown. He could theorize on this for an age, it seemed, so he placed his attention on bringing their conversation back to what he truly wanted to know in this moment. Thoughts of lands beyond the sea could wait, for now.

"Can you bring them back? The dragons, I mean." The idea that they could have such a powerful force behind them in the battle to come sent tingles of restless anticipation down his spine.

"No... but *you* can."

"Me?"

"Should you pass my test, yes."

At the glimmer of hope and anticipation in Kadec's eyes, Elijah felt a weight press upon his shoulders once more. He lifted the glass to his lips, sipping at the drink in an attempt to busy his hands while his mind reeled, and that feeling of anxiety – appearing more often lately – bloomed inside his chest. What Kadec spoke of could turn the odds to their favour in the war to come, and he had to press aside his self-doubt if they had any hope to succeed. The feeling was constantly there though. He felt that such talk from the man suggested that he may just be swayed to their side in this fight. So, Elijah pressed to the point, not wishing to delay what needed to be done.

"What can I do to earn the support of your court and your armies, Kadec?"

The man smiled, as if he were waiting for that particular question, "I will be throwing a grand ball tonight. I want you to attend as my honoured guest. It will be for you, celebrating your return from the dead."

Elijah winced, and Kadec noticed. "There is far more to heading a court than preparing for wars, stocking armies and raking in finances. There is intrigue, pretty words and people to please. Without the loyalty and love of your subjects, you will find your kingdom will quickly crumble, which is what we are seeing in the north right now. Not only must you be eloquent with your sword, Eliverus, but you must be eloquent with your words. Running a kingdom not only requires strength, and bravery, but integrity and loyalty too. But above all, you must conquer your fears – and also accept them." Kadec's smile turned cunning.

Elijah squinted at the man, keeping his face natural when what he felt inside was far from still waters.

The Prince knocked back what was left in his glass before he said, "Attend my party. Prove these traits to me, rise above your fears, and my army is yours."

KADEC

CHAPTER TWENTY-NINE

ARIIAYA

"I know you despise the shade, but pink suits you."

Elijah leant against the doorframe of the library where she had found cover from the overwhelming brightness of the palace grounds they had been obliged to tour. Their tour guide, the far from sunny Roarke Serling, looked like he would rather play with a pack of rabid wolves than lead their group around the meticulously kept lavender and rose bushes. The scent of flowers had become overpowering, and on top of her worry for what trial Elijah would be put through in the next few hours, Arii found her mind in a spin that left her with the beginnings of a headache. Shortly after Roarke announced they would be attending a celebration in the form of a fancy ball, Arii had retreated.

So, she had sought respite in the only place that she knew could take those worries away – if only for a short time.

The library.

She found a medium sized tome with a deep purple cover that had caught her eye on the shelf immediately as she entered the space, drifting under the high arched ceilings depicting illustrations of swirling vines and blood red roses. Unlike the library in Viridya, this one was closed in with a few small windows. Lanterns scattered about the room lent more light, casting gold upon the spiral oak staircase in the centre. It led up to a second floor with an impressive handrail expertly forged in dark steel, following the twirl of the stairs.

Arii nestled on a plush green settee by a window overlooking the city below and began to immerse herself in an unexpectedly juicy story about a young woman who had eyes on the prince, when Elijah's deep voice had pulled her from the pages.

"Go ahead, laugh, everyone else did." Arii sighed, snapping the book shut.

He approached, casting his eyes over the neatly stocked shelves nearby. "I never though you to care for the opinions of others, Arii, especially one so immaterial." He ran his fingers over the spines, before coming to a halt a few paces from where she sat.

He was right, and she knew it. Normally she did not care for things as insignificant as the colour of her dress and what others may think of her. Really, she could not give a rats' damn what others thought, but for some reason her mind was a slowly sinking whirlpool of darkness and doubt lately.

Feeling her insides begin to churn, she groped for another train of conversation, "Your tour with Kadec went well?"

Elijah recapped his discussion with Kadec, and Arii could not help the slow widening of her eyes. "The dragons? They're not really extinct?"

"If what he says is truth, yes, but I have yet to see any proof."

"That proof may just show itself at the ball tonight."

"Wouldn't that be something – a party with a dragon," he mused.

Arii giggled but hushed the sound with the tips of her fingers.

Elijah ran his fingers over a few more old books, his expression distant. "There is something strange about the Prince that I just can't put my finger on."

"Well, if what we have seen in our adventure so far is any indication, expect the unexpected," Arii said as Elijah slid his hands into the pockets of his pants. She surveyed him, noting his drawn brows and clenched jaw. Her tone dropped a notch as she whispered, "That was a lot to take in. Are you alright?"

His eyes met hers and softened. "It was, but it's imperative that I learn as much as possible. Besides, having you to discuss it with makes me feel slightly better about it."

The closer she got to Elijah, the more fearful she was becoming. It was all on her though, for she did not think she was truly worthy of him. Seeing him now, dressed impeccably and as close to royalty as she had ever seen him, caused doubt to shiver against her inner Fae beast.

For the first time in her life she was fearful of getting hurt.

It had entered her mind shortly after their time in Colkirk and had weighed upon her like a grey cloud ever since. She had not voiced her anxiety to anyone else, and especially not Elijah. She feared his reaction… no, she feared her *own* reaction to what she had to do.

She had to put distance between them.

Whatever trial Kadec was going to put him through, Arii was sure that she could no longer be a distraction. She could see the change in Elijah as the days passed. She could see he was slowly coming around to the fact that he could make a difference in the battle ahead, and that he had the opportunity to bring about true change and a brighter future to so many lives. Upon taking back his birthright, he would unite their land once more, of that she was absolutely sure. She would not forfeit her role or the aid she could offer him, but she knew she must step back from what was emotionally forming between them – for his own sake.

Arii swallowed, steeling her nerves as she laid the book on a table nearby and stood, beads twinkling against one another on the heavy fabric of her rose pink dress as she stepped towards him.

"We… need to talk."

She could see his spine stiffen, and the thin veil of unease settle upon his face that signalled he knew he was not going to like what she had to say.

So, she cut straight to it, feeling no reason to further delay the pain that was to come.

"This – us – cannot continue. What is happening between us, I mean." She cringed internally but hardened her stance as she waved a hand between them. "If the Fates taught me one thing, it is that caring for something – or someone – can compromise a mission. Our predicament is no different. If you do not care, then no one can use that emotion as leverage against you."

"You believe Kadec would use our relationship as leverage?"

"I have *no doubt* he will use it as leverage. Courtiers and nobles thrive on gossip and scandal – this place is no different, and if I have heard correctly – it is possibly the worst."

"We could just step back while under the eyes of others, for a time. I'm sure we can do that for a few days."

"No…" She pinched the bridge of her nose in frustration. "I do not mean just now, but for the foreseeable future. You're going to be *King*, Elijah. What has happened between us up until now has been merely a bit of fun, nothing more. I care not beyond that."

"Fun?" He blinked, before his expression softened, "I know that's not true. You care, and no matter how vehemently you deny it, you care about every single person who has joined us and if they return home alive. Is this about Gunner? He knew the risks when he decided to make the journey with us, you cannot blame yourself for his death."

She blanched, because she absolutely felt responsible for the pirate's death.

Elijah continued, "I can see what you are doing, Arii. What of the moments we have shared? Do you not feel that undeniable pull, the *fire*?"

"Those moments were severe lapses in judgement," she swiped a hand through the air, her throat burning. "Lapses that *never* should have happened. I am *not good* for you."

They were inches apart now, so close she could smell his heady scent of sandalwood and pine. She had once believed it a soap he used, but now she knew it was undeniably *him*. The part of him that was irrevocably *Fae*. Even now, as they stared at one another, tension wavering thick in the air, she could not deny how much she *wanted* him… how much that primal, wild Fae side of her wanted him.

"But you are good for me. You are incredible, Ariiaya."

She shook her head, images of unseeing eyes and pools of blood from countless lives she had taken shuddering behind her eyes. Reminding her. Always reminding her. "No… No, I'm not."

Her expression had him closing the distance. "Why do you do that?" he whispered, almost painfully.

She started. "Do what?"

"Put yourself down, doubt yourself, withdraw when someone gives you a compliment."

Arii swallowed, throat working. "Because I am undeserving of anyone's kind words or praise."

"Why do you think that?"

"Because a few good deeds does not erase *years* of being a shit person."

"Your past is the past, what you do now and in the future is what matters, Arii." A pause. "And you are not a *shit person.*"

She closed the last slither of distance between them, face twisting as she said, "How many of the people I killed in the name of the gods could have been innocent? How many deserved a chance at retribution for their actions, had I just set them on the right path instead? Petty crimes… one bad choice… I didn't give any of them a chance!"

"You were doing your duty–"

"Duty? I and countless others killed innocents amongst those who were evil, all under the guise of *duty.*"

She signalled quotation marks over her head with the word duty. "When truly it was all a manipulation."

"Be that as it may, you were only doing what you believed was right at the time. You knew no different."

She could not help but wonder if his words not only spread over her past, but his as well. For many years he had served the family that had killed his own, but had known no different. What unspeakable things had he done in the name of duty?

As if he read her thoughts, Elijah said, "You speak as though it is only *your* hands that are stained with blood. The past thrust upon you was out of your control, Arii. As was mine. Nothing can change that now." He gently took her hand, running his thumb over her flickering pulse. She felt gooseflesh rise along her arms, and soon enough, those little butterflies in her stomach took flight. When he spoke again it was soft, his eyes on their linked hands. "Your world has been tipped on its axis, just like mine has. We find ourselves in uncertain times, with an uncertain future. But the one thing that has kept me on a steady path is *you*."

She felt her stomach dip painfully as she inhaled the air they shared. Elijah's eyes lifted, and she could not look away as his free hand moved to caress her cheek. Her breath held as his thumb dashed across the bow of her lips, and she watched as his steel eyes darkened.

"You need to stay away from me…" she managed in a rasp.

"What if I don't *want* to stay away," he murmured, lips inches from her own. "What if I *cannot* stay away." Heat snapped between them, a brush of his lips against hers, and she could not help the small sound that escaped her as his hand splayed on the small of her back, pressing her closer. Against his solid, now wholly familiar, muscled form. Her hands gripped the soft material of his tunic as Elijah rasped, "You fill my veins with fire, in which I will gladly *burn*."

As tears burned the back of her eyes, she inhaled sharply and whispered the only thing she could think of in that moment. Forcing herself from his hold, she stepped back.

"I don't want to be with you, Elijah."

Each word burned her throat and tore at her heart as they passed her lips, earning her a feeling she had never felt before.

Heartbreak.

His arms fell to his sides, and she glanced away before she could see the flicker of agony in his eyes. "Arii," he began.

"I will see you at the ball…" A shuddered breath stung her dry throat, but her voice was devoid of emotion as she whispered, "Goodnight."

She spun, escaping the room before he could protest further.

Before he could see the tears that she finally allowed to fall.

ELIJAH

The large room was awash with the haze of sweet incense, thick heady scents of herbs, food and perfume. Castle Ayrith employees slid about, serving guests as they quickly filled the ballroom. A woman sat to one side, fingers dancing over an ornately carved wooden harp, the sound beautiful and beguiling. Accompanying her was a man playing softly on violin while she sang a low, haunting tune.

Wine glasses clinked, music danced in the filmy air over the hushed voices and breathy laughs of the crowd. The walls and table settings burst with spring flowers and lush greenery, against a kaleidoscope of colours worn by the guests.

There were so many flickering candles that Elijah was surprised a fire had not broken out. Silver and gold woven candelabras adorned the tables and walls while three large chandeliers filled with candles cast a spectacle of light over the glittering room. Courtiers helped themselves to cigarillos and pipes, adding to the sweet haze lingering above their heads.

There was a feeling of intimacy in the room despite its grand size, the cadence of the violin rising in the air. People danced and touched, standing close and speaking excitedly. He saw many similarities to parties he had overseen countless times before. Wealth dripped from the attendees, and Kadec had spared no expense on everything on offer to them.

Part of him felt anger at the flaunting of such riches when just across the border, people in the north were starving. Kadec was not to blame for that though, he reminded himself.

Standing atop the dais with Kadec and a couple of his royal advisors, Elijah viewed the rapidly-filling ballroom. Like every other area he had seen in the castle, this room showed that Kadec was indeed well endowed in the finance department.

Lining the walls were long tables, covered in expensive white cloth and strewn with platters of roasted meats, fruits, vegetables and greens. A particularly large pig lay upon a silver platter, an apple in its roasted maw, haloed by beds of salads and exotic fruits. Carved wooden stands displayed delicate baked goods and sweets. He spied some strange little purple fruits chopped in half, packed with black seeds in gloopy yellow juice.

"Passionfruit, have you not seen them before?" said Kadec, noting Elijah's interest.

He had not, but that wasn't what caught his attention.

Their colour reminded him of a certain female with hypnotic purple eyes. Elijah shook his head, keeping his face relatively expressionless save for a small tilt of his lips.

As tempting as the food was, he could not seem to drum up an appetite since his talk with Arii. She was distancing herself, claiming she was not *right* for him. But he knew what her true motives were. She did not want to hold him back when it came to his ascension of the throne.

They had known each other for a few months now, and during that time he had come to know the subtle signs of her tells – when she was happy or sad, anxious or angry. There was a look in her eyes, like twin windows into her soul, that gave her away, and when she claimed she did not want to be with him, he saw the lie. He saw it in her eyes, heard it in the tiny waver in her voice, smelled it upon her skin.

Her words were untrue, he felt it in his heart – in his soul. He had been ready to go to war for her, for he knew it would not simply be a battle; but she had fled the library while shock still rattled through his bones.

For the remainder of the evening, he had fought against the overwhelming need to stalk to her rooms and show her just how much he wanted her, thrones and kings be damned.

But he hadn't. He had seen the look in her eyes just before she fled his touch, and it spoke volumes.

So, he gave her space, even though it tormented him inside. Tormented the beast howling in the confines of his chest.

Elijah had lived in a royal setting for his entire life, and he knew the protocol and social expectations when it came to unions in a royal family – in particular a king. It would be demanded quickly of him to marry and sire heirs, and to strengthen the Herington line once more. He really did not wish to think right now about that particular burden of being a king, and pushed it into the darkest part of his mind.

His attention shifted back to Kadec, who did not seem to notice his guest's wavering attention.

"A particularly skilled grape grower in the lower town had a bizarre thought one day to mix the juices of a passionfruit with his already popular dry wine. Now, passion wine is the signature drop of the west! Here, you must try some."

Elijah accepted the glass thrust into his hands, but the enthusiasm radiating from the Prince did not change his sombre mood. The man's flawless brown skin dimpled with his wide smile, yet Elijah could see a glint of cunning in his green eyes. Every move Elijah made, every word he uttered, every person he was to speak to tonight would be watched and analysed, and that thought set him on edge.

He had been dressed to impress in a fine tunic of deep blue silk, covered with a black vest and coat embroidered with silver thread. Upon reflection in the mirror before he had headed down to the party, he swore the design resembled a dragon, open jaws and spread wings meticulously hidden amongst weaving vines and roses. He felt strange in such fine, polished attire, so used to the weight of armour and leather. He had refused to be without a weapon though, and thankfully Kadec had agreed. Who knew who could be lurking in the shadows, even at a party such as this?

The sword nestled at his hip, pommel just peeking from beneath his coat. Even now, he found old habits rise as his palm hovered within easy, subtle reach of the weapon. Standing upon the dais, overlooking the ball, Elijah felt a sad sense of déjà vu. Countless times had he stood back, watching from the shadows as Lorch entertained guests. He would have put his life on the line without a thought to protect him, and even now Elijah was sure he still would. There was a void in his gut that churned every time he thought of his friend... his brother.

The difference now was that the guests' eyes sought him out, assessed him, gazed upon him with awe, curiosity – and mild distrust. He could see it as plain as day on each courtier who looked his way, chatting to others in swift whispers while hardly breaking their stares.

The crystal flute tingled against his fingertips, and he sucked in a swift breath in an attempt to subdue the magic sizzling along his nerve endings. Seemingly unbeknownst to his discomfort, Kadec clinked his glass against Elijah's before moving to the middle of the dais. Steeling his spine and breathing deeply again, Elijah joined him.

As he did, he saw *her*.

Ariiaya.

She stepped into the room alongside Nemesis and Krepth, her chin high, her strides elegant. Her hair was swept up on one side, pinned with a glittering silver hairpiece, the remainder loose and draped over her shoulder, honey tipped ends styled into perfect, lightly curled waves. Her bright purple eyes were lined with kohl and a hint of dark powder on her eyelids. The dessert-hued dress she had worn earlier was gone, replaced with a gown the colour of deep amethyst, hugging her curves and falling to the floor like liquid. The sleeveless bodice hugged her tight, complementing the light olive of her skin. As she moved, he saw the material shimmer, as if the night sky had been pulled into making the enchanting fabric. It wasn't until his eyes lifted from her gown and back to her beautiful face that Elijah realised he had been holding his breath.

Their gazes met briefly, and she was first to break away, turning to join her friends who had gathered nearby.

But not before he saw a flash of longing and pain cross her face.

When Elijah's attention returned to the prince, Kadec's eyes were on him, brows raised ever so slightly.

Elijah internally kicked himself at his slip. To cover it up, he lifted his glass in a small salute, which thankfully Kadec took as a sign to begin their introductions. The Prince's smile was wide as he threw his hands out, gesturing to the full room below. The music eased and conversation paused as the Prince addressed his audience.

"My esteemed guests! Welcome to Ayrith! Please join me in a warm welcome to a very special guest tonight, for I have no doubt you have all heard the rumours. Yes, Eliverus Herington – the Prince who was lost – is lost no more." Kadec moved into a sweeping bow, which was mirrored by all of the people below. "Please drink, eat and converse, for our long-lost ally has much to catch up on. Make him welcome. Tonight, my home is yours!"

No sooner had he finished his speech, the music began anew, slightly more upbeat than before. Elijah couldn't deny the tingle of nerves he felt along his skin, his senses high in preparation for whatever Kadec was going to test him on, and his gut feeling was that it was going to be far more complicated than just talking to a few councilmen and pretty courtiers. There was a gleam in the Prince's eyes that hinted at power, and Elijah had to ensure he had his wits about him.

So, he nursed the wine for the time being, smiling with as much friendliness as he could muster as a small group of courtiers approached him. The women batted their eyelashes and the men sized him up, their eyes taking in every little detail from his hair to his shoes. He knew they were seeking out signs of weakness, or any titbit of gossip that they could take away from this night.

Kadec tilted his head towards a small sea of colourful dresses, the wearers fidgeting and eager faces bright. "Time to mingle, Your Highness."

Elijah swallowed, forced a small smile and followed Kadec's lead.

ARIIAYA

"Arii, Nem! You both look absolutely incredible!" breathed Tikkani, fingering the soft silk of Nem's midnight dress. "Gods, it looks like you're draped in the night sky!"

Quinn bumped his hip against Tikkani's. "You look just as beautiful, Tikk," he said with a smile, causing the young woman to sigh and lace her fingers with his.

Arii's eyes skipped across each of her friends. Nem was dressed in a gown the colour of raven's wings with tiny beads glittering in the fabric, and indeed it looked like a night sky full of stars. Tikkani was in silver, her brown hair pulled into an elaborate bun accentuating her high cheekbones and uptilted, golden eyes. Her skin was clean of the grime of travel, cheeks tinged with pink. She looked the happiest that Arii had seen her in weeks. Quinn was polished in a dark grey suit, silver embroidered sleeves. He held out his arm to Tikkani, bowing slightly as he said, "Care to dance, m'lady?"

Tikkani practically swooned, throwing Arii a grin over her shoulder as they headed to the dancefloor.

Arii couldn't help a smile in response.

"Ah young love," sighed Krepth, watching in their wake. Arii leaned her hip against the heavy table, popping a grape in her mouth as she eyed her oldest friend. He wore a suit of deep, dark green, stitched with a shiny green thread. His hair had even been brushed, the inky strands clean and shiny. Deliberately loosening her limbs, Arii plastered on a fake smile to hide the turmoil of pain she felt inside after seeing Elijah atop the dais, looking like pure royalty.

"Speaking of *love*…" purred the Shifter.

Krepth's words had her halting a second grape between her teeth.

"Are we truly to start this again? Right now?" She could not mask the bite in her words. Trust Krepth to rouse her short-leashed temper.

Nem shifted in her peripheral vision, "I have to take Arii's side on this one, Krepth. Shut your trap."

"Are we all going to ignore the way he looked at her just moments ago? Even *I* felt the temperature of the room rise a few degrees."

Arii glared. "Do you have a fucking death wish tonight? I don't think Kadec would take kindly to a murder on his dancefloor."

"Krepth…" Nem warned.

"Hah, calm down, little Fury. Lighten up, make small talk and drink wine. I'm going to go keep an eye on our Prince and see what kind of dirt I can dish up. I do *love* a good party." His smile was lupine as he threw Nem a wink, before disappearing into the crowd.

Arii exhaled, swiping a glass of wine from a passing server and throwing it back with far too much enthusiasm. When she stifled a cough with the back of her hand, Nem said gently, "Will you be alright tonight?"

Shortly after Arii had fled the library, she ran into Nem, who – to Arii's embarrassment – had seen the tears as they flowed down her cheeks and blotted her ghastly pink gown. She had attempted to hide them with swift swipes of her hands and fingers, but that was no use, with the bond they shared. Before Arii could protest, the silver-haired Fae had led her back to Arii's rooms, where Arii repeated what she had said to Elijah.

As she had a few hours ago, Nem repeated the words now, her intense, unblinking gaze never wavering, "You're wrong, you know."

"Nem, please…"

"It pains me, and your friends, to see you torment yourself like this when we can all plainly see what has been growing between you two over the last few weeks."

Arii kept her eyes on the flurry of dancing bodies on the polished marble dancefloor. "I'm doing what is best for him… for us both."

"You're stronger together than you are apart." Nem threw back.

Arii rounded on her friend, voice hushed and laced with anguish. "And when this is all over, when he ascends the throne and becomes King, what then? He cannot be with an assassin, there is no future with someone born of dregs and not of noble birth. You know royal protocols. I'm saving us *both* a whole lot of future hurt."

Nem met her stare with one of her own, unflinching and calm. "I feel Elijah would bend all the rules to be with you. You yourself advocate for him to bring about change, and I'm sure that could also translate into being with the one who makes you happy above any royal protocol."

Arii huffed, crossing her arms and casting her eye over Luc and Emerson, who danced nearby. Their faces were lit with happiness, their affection on full display without a care for who could be watching. Arii had never been one to wish for a relationship like that in the past, but she was finding a shift in perspective on many things since allowing her emotions to take hold.

"Be that as it may, I cannot imagine myself as Queen. I'm not cut out for the duties it entails."

"A Queen acts with the land's best interests in mind. Is that not what you have been doing this entire time?" Nem pointed out, her eyes finally breaking away to search amongst the crowd. "Personally, I think you would make an astounding Queen."

Pinching the bridge of her nose, Arii murmured, "Gods help me, is no one on my side? I'm going to get another drink." Slipping away from the table, she slid along the outskirts of the party.

Her eyes, of their own accord, sought the floor for Elijah. She would keep her word and maintain a distance, but that did not mean she would let her guard fall. She would be naive to think that danger could not touch them here. Not everyone in this glittering throne room could be happy about the return of the true King of the north.

Elijah stood a few paces down from the dais, conversing with two immaculately dressed courtiers, a young woman and a man. Judging by the jewels draped around their necks and rings glinting on their fingers, Arii assumed them to be nobles, no doubt. The woman, much younger than the man, smiled and swept her gaze low as he gestured towards her. The woman fluttered her lashes, and it was then that Arii realised what was happening.

The man was introducing his daughter in hopes of sparking a union.

She knew that this was going to happen. Now with the return of the King, she had to expect that noblemen would be offering up their daughters in the hope they might catch his eye and seal their future with the prospect of marriage.

The thought of Elijah marrying someone else had a sick feeling welling in her stomach, and the feeling turned to nausea when he offered the girl a tentative smile and the crook of his arm.

As if sensing her attention, Elijah's eyes lifted and locked with hers.

She couldn't look away.

Suddenly an arm looped with hers, and she was pulled onto the dance floor as the music rose in tempo.

"Come, dance!" said a voice, lost upon the sudden beat of drums mixed with violins.

The room spun, faces blurring until all she saw was *him*. It was like the world around her did not wish to be in focus, cruelly drawing all her attention onto the one person she was determined to stay away from. The entire time his eyes were on her, grey and shuttered with storm clouds.

Finally her dance partner caught her attention and she seized the moment of reprieve. She wordlessly thanked her unknown saviour with a squeeze of her fingers but she could not remain amongst the rabble of bodies any longer. It was too hot and too many people around her. She took a breath, but it wasn't enough.

The air was too thick, suffocating her.

Unable to stand it anymore, Arii turned and broke from the floor, slipping between partygoers on the sidelines and dashing towards a balcony and the cool evening air. Flustered and not as agile as normal, she dodged a woman in a spinning frock of yellow, causing her to thump right into a solid chest.

"Sorry," she murmured, making to move around the man. A hand found her bicep, fingers warm as they halted her retreat.

"Finding some air? Allow me to join you."

Her eyes darted to the long, strong fingers, pale as moonlight, then up to the face of the man who had pulled her on to the dancefloor. Any other time she would be rudely declining the offer from the stranger, but his strange, foreign accent had her pausing. It had a strange lilt, musical and clear that gave Arii the impression of high education – and birth in a land far from their own. It was not unpleasant... charming, actually.

She studied his equally foreign attire with narrowed eyes. Dressed in black, his suit was tailored in a way she had never seen before. The coat hugged his lean frame, dipping in at his waist before lightly flaring into what she thought resembled a swallow's tail. The material was smooth, the stitching clean and crisp, silver buttons trailing a neat line down his tunic, and pinned on his breast was a house crest, one Arii did not recognise. It was a serpent, curled into a figure eight as it consumed its own tail. It was simple and far plainer than the other suits dancing around the room, but it was elegant and masculine.

When her eyes met his, she was greeted with crooked smile on a devastatingly handsome face. Eyes the colour of a clear blue sky, framed by thick lashes, slightly full lips tinged with pink, skin so flawless he probably spent no time in the sun. His hair was dark, short, with a small blonde streak through his fringe.

Strange, strange indeed.

She had a feeling this man had broken many hearts in his short lifetime.

The stranger took her hesitation as an invitation, nimbly passing her to open a nearby door. "After you," he said with a flourish.

She needed a distraction, so she took it. Passing by him, Arii headed into the slightly cooler evening air, inhaling a long breath.

The beautiful stranger sidled up beside her, leaning casually on the balustrade and casting his attention over the sprawling city below. Then, he looked at her, his voice smooth as silk, that peculiar accent gracing every syllable of his eloquent speech. "I must admit, the overpowering smell of sage and cigarillo smoke would wear upon the dullest of senses, but upon that of a Fae? It must be torture."

She eyed him suspiciously, "What makes you think I am a Fae? I could be of elf heritage."

The man tilted his head, striking eyes assessing. It was then she noticed that they were not the same shade. The right featured a slither of green in the iris, like a little island in a lake. There was a strange air about him, one that should have set her on edge but only piqued her curiosity.

He shrugged. "I suppose so, but you have an air about you that screams that you could defeat me in a fight in seconds flat. That's the impression I get from most Fae females."

Hedging, she said, "Your accent is… peculiar. You are not from

Fythnar."

"Is it that obvious?"

"Absolutely." She paused, turning to press her back against the stone, fingers twirling one of the soft green leaves that draped the railing as part of the floral decorations. She had to admit, this man was providing her whirlwind mind a brief reprieve, for which she was grateful. Her chin lifted as she said, "Where are you from? And perhaps slightly more important, who are you?"

"Do you truly care as to who I am or where I'm from, or do your attentions lie with the future King of the realm?"

She felt her lips quiver with the start of a snarl, but before she could spit acid at the stranger's attractive face, he chuckled, "I'm Nocturne. But my friends and family call me Noct."

"Well, *Nocturne*." She drew out the name as if it tasted like soil on her tongue, "I would refrain from speaking on things you know nothing about."

"I seem to have hit a nerve. Forgive me." Noct's words seemed sincere, yet that annoyingly sinful, half notched smirk remained. His flirtatious and carefree demeanour reminded her of Krepth, as did his dark hair and bright eyes. Perhaps he was a long-lost cousin from another land.

"I should honestly have learned from the last time I pissed off a Fae," Noct added, piquing her interest though she did not let it show.

Arii tilted her head and let her eyes shut against a pleasant breeze. "The fact you are still breathing says you did not try hard enough."

He chuckled, and the sound was a curious caress across her senses.

"You're such strong folk, but I've got to say – when it comes to matters of the heart, you can be wildly unpredictable. Well, that is what Kadec thinks, at least."

Arii stiffened. "Excuse me?"

Noct sipped from his wine glass, stretching the silence between them to the point that she began to feel pain. "He believes your Herington Prince to be a slave to his emotions, thus perhaps making him unfit to rule."

The way this man spoke, it was as if he knew Kadec like a close friend. She assumed he was human, judging by his rounded ears, yet there was still something bizarre about him that she could not quite put her finger on. His gaze was cool, calculating, assessing – hinting at high intelligence. He was insanely attractive, but his earlier words rang true – a little fact she would most certainly not disclose to him, lest his ego inflate further than it already seemed to be. He smelled of rosewood – spicy with a mixture of floral notes and woody facets with inflections of cedar wood. She could not help but feel like a mouse under the hungry eyes of a cat as those calculating eyes slipped down to her lips.

She rolled her shoulders and feigned calm, straightening and casting her eye back over the perfect stranger. "Thank you for the company, but I should be returning." A feeling of anxious dread fluttered down her spine, a feeling that told her that the trial was just about to begin. No matter where they stood in their relationship, Arii swore she would still support Elijah through whatever was thrown at him. Noct's eyes glittered as he straightened from his lean, and she saw he was the same height as Elijah.

She had to find him, and quickly.

Noct moved to subtly stop her retreat. "I'm afraid where he resides now is somewhere you cannot follow, Violet Assassin. He must do this alone."

She had not mentioned a hint of her intentions, leading her to suspect Noct was a spy for Kadec.

The man's move was not subtle enough, for she had noticed.

She moved swiftly, dipping and retrieving the dagger strapped to her thigh. She struck, aiming her weapon at his stomach. As quick as the movement was, it was not quick enough. Noct jerked with a swiftness that belied his smooth appearance, twisting to catch her arm in a trained hold. Arii snarled, spearing her free hand towards his face with a second piece of steel clasped in her fist. He dodged, and she sliced at empty air. She swept out a foot to take him down, but the man moved like a dancer – casting himself backwards into a flip.

Cursing, she shot forward, daggers flying.

All it earned her was a wide smile that caused irrational irritation to flare.

"Were you sent out here by Kadec to preoccupy me?" she yelled, narrowly missing his cheek. "Stop fucking moving so I can kill you."

Noct barked a laugh. "Could it not have been because I was a little bored, and was simply curious about you?" He ducked another narrow slash. "The party was lacking… excitement. This is much better!"

"You're excited right now?"

"And mildly aroused, yes."

She made a sound of disgust at his grin, as if he took her death threat as a sign of endearment. She dropped her dagger and jerked forward, throwing a palm out and summoning her magic. It flew to her call, coalescing as purple fire and flickering between her fingers. Had they been in a normal situation, she may have just found this man appealing and maybe she could have even liked him enough to engage in the banter. But they were not in a normal situation.

Before she could throw her magic straight in his face, Noct made a complicated sign with his fingers just over her shoulder, whispering, "Apologies, Princess."

All she saw was a flash of blue light, illuminating his handsome face, his hair thrown back as a violent gust of wind picked up from behind her. Before she could turn to see the cause, she felt something pulling her back.

Then she was falling.

CHAPTER THIRTY

ELIJAH

"Thank you for your precious time, your grace. It was an honour to make your acquaintance," said the woman with a note of unhappiness, slipping into a bow after Elijah gently repeated that he had someone else he needed to speak to. In all honesty he did not, and he hated the lie as it left his lips, seeing the glint of hurt in the young courtier's hopeful eyes. But the room was becoming stifling with the dancing of bodies moving to the rising tempo of the violin.

Before he could find a corner to retreat to, a hand came down on his shoulder. Had he not heard Kadec's footsteps approaching prior, he might have jumped. The man sidled close as he said, "You speak well, and you know just how to rebuff the attentions of overly eager suitors. I think you absorbed more from the people you guarded in Viridya than you care to admit. I cannot help but notice, though, you seem distracted. More wine?"

So Kadec had noticed his wandering attention throughout the night. He internally kicked himself, thinking he had kept his glances at Arii subtle and fleeting.

Elijah took another sip of the wine he had been nursing, surprised to find it was pleasant and still cold. He rolled the golden liquid around his tongue, tasting the tang that he presumed was the passionfruit, and the bitterness of the alcohol. Masked amongst the flavours was something else, too. Something he felt was familiar, but he could not quite put his finger on it. He took a healthier gulp, earning him a grin from Kadec.

Kadec proceeded to re-fill his glass. "Manners and social etiquette come naturally to you it seems, but I would like to see how you would handle a more stressful situation." As he spoke, courtiers who had been dancing on the floor before them began to part, the music fading to a hushed drone as the candles about the room dimmed.

Elijah blinked rapidly, glancing down at the glass in his hand as Kadec slid behind him, moving to his opposite side.

"Wars are not just won with weapons of steel, but with weapons of words. And not all combat is constrained to a battlefield. It is easy to swing a sword and end lives but how will you handle strife within your own court, silent as assassins and sometimes with familiar faces?"

Bodies shifted, faded, shuddered. If Elijah had been paying closer attention, he would have seen ten hooded figures wading through them like snakes through water, converging on his location.

But his attention was a quickly fraying ball of yarn.

As Kadec spoke, the crowd appeared to disperse to either side of the dancefloor as a scene was revealed to him, just as he pinpointed the familiar taste swirling on the back of his tongue.

Magic.

"Elijah!"

His eyes swiftly lifted to see Arii, holding a knife to the throat of a wide-eyed Lorch. She was dressed in assassin's leathers, kohl lining her eyes so thickly that it looked like warpaint. There was a curl to her lips that he knew well, and a glimmer in her purple eyes that haunted his dreams when he were not suspended in a nightmare. Elijah blanched, hesitation warring with instinct to leap down the dais and save his friend. But Arii… she was his friend too. More, she was so much more. Confusion as to why they were on the dancefloor had him spinning back to find Kadec before his throne, a strange breeze toying with the prince's clothing and hair. Pointed canines glinted within the crescent moon of his widening grin.

With a flourish of his hands, Kadec dropped a glamour, revealing what Elijah had begun to suspect only moments ago. He spied delicately pointed ears where seconds ago the man had the rounded ones of a human.

Kadec was a Fae.

Elijah supposed he should not be surprised that even more male Fae existed, and just like the twin leaders of the South, they were hiding in plain sight under simple glamour. Part of him was thrilled with the revelation that he was not alone, but now was not the time to celebrate, not as the castle ceiling above faded away to a sky of red, dark grey clouds rolling overhead. The walls fell away soon after, leaving no one but himself, Kadec, Arii and Lorch in the middle of a dry and desolate wasteland.

His shoes crunched upon gravel, drawing his attention to his feet.

Not gravel.

Dry, old bones. The land was littered with them, leached to bright ivory and cracked with time, and it did not take Elijah long to realise human bones were in amongst those of animals of all shapes and sizes. The dirt that danced in flurries was as red as blood, dried and ancient.

Elijah's head back to Kadec who stood a few feet ahead of him. "This isn't real, you're using magic! You're a Fae!"

The world around them was a ruin, yet Kadec's expression shone with excitement. "I did wish to tell you outright, Eliverus, but one cannot be too careful when our kind have been hunted to near extinction. Humans are easy to fool, it is true, but I knew you would figure it out quickly, especially once you tasted the wine. Your mind is a well-built fortress, so you will have to forgive me for resorting to the use of magic-infused liquor in order to communicate like this, but in the mind, there is nothing to hide."

Elijah gestured at the apocalyptic world around them, tossing the wine glass to the ground as thunder rolled in the distance.

He growled. "Is this an illusion?"

"Of a sort, yes. But it is best to name it as foresight. This–" he spun and thrust his hand out at the desolate land and dark mountain peaks in the distance, "–is the fate of our land if you should fail. If we all should fail. I have seen this vison many times, as have my forefathers." Speckled embers drifted in the acrid air, and Kadec's face faltered, dark brows drawing into an expression of sudden seriousness that he rarely seemed to show. "We have been waiting so long for you, but you must prove you are the glue to bind us all back together. You must prove you have what it takes to rule the kingdom, and to bring them back, thus restoring balance."

"Them?"

"The dragons."

Red lightning snapped in the distance at his words and Elijah swallowed past a lump in his throat. Did he truly have what it took to bring the legendary, majestic beasts back from their home realm? But having that kind of support in the battle to come would be invaluable.

He glanced back at Arii and Lorch, voice coming out stronger than what he felt inside. "I don't understand."

"Fear comes in many different shades, Eliverus. Light shades, like fear of speaking in public or fear of spiders, to darker shades like fear of being rejected, fear of loss, death, what we cannot control, fear of betrayal."

He was trying to gauge what Elijah feared the most. Kadec's trial was not only exposing those fears to the Prince of the west, but to himself too. What did he fear the most? Was it the responsibility of ruling a kingdom? Was it the horrors manifesting in the north, or was it indeed fear that those he trusted the most would betray him?

"You think I fear my friends betraying me?"

"I think everyone fears such things, and as King you will find people change when they think they can get what they want from you."

"Arii wouldn't betray me," he said firmly. "None of them would."

Kadec's eyes flashed. "You truly believe so?"

"I know so," Elijah bit out, even though the image of her pushing him away flashed to mind. He shook it off. "Tell me what I need to do, what you need from me."

"I need you to show that you can do what must be done in order to rise up and save our land." Kadec gestured back to where Arii stood, blade still pressed to Lorch's neck.

Elijah swallowed again, throat bobbing, eyes narrowing as the man approached him, and his dark hand hovered over Elijah's chest – right above his thundering heart. "We Fae draw the most strength from our emotions, and power like that cannot truly be tamed into submission." Kadec's eyes roved over Elijah's broad shoulder. The Prince continued, his voice low. "But with such powerful emotion comes unpredictability, for hearts are fickle things that can throw all rationality and reason from the mind. But where they can weaken us, they can also give us strength. To bring back what will be your greatest asset – aside from your own raw power – you must find focus and display balance. But above all, you must sacrifice."

Arii and the friends he had made in the last few weeks had given him direction and reason for being. Before he met Arii, he was content to pace through life without true purpose, other than to protect his best friend. He supposed his priorities had not changed, they now extended to more than a handful of people.

Now it extended to the entire land.

But Kadec's words confused him. Who or what was he to sacrifice, and why?

"Tell me, Eliverus, do you fear death? Or do you fear what death can take from you?"

Elijah swallowed, his eyes seeking Arii's and meeting emotionless amethyst. The illusion, Kadec's words, none of it was making sense. The Prince wanted him to conquer fear, but despite what he said, Elijah couldn't help but think Kadec was trying to tell him something else.

After a long pause, Elijah whispered, "I would greet death as a friend knowing everyone I care about is far from its clutches, if only for a time before they too greet it with open arms."

A tiny quirk of Kadec's lips was the only indication that he took his words on board, for the rest of him was stark. He lifted his arm, and Elijah gripped the pommel of his sword on instinct. He could see a flicker within the man's eyes, something that hinted to him that the Prince was not yet wholly convinced. He eyed Elijah's movement as he said, "It is not me that you will be fighting, Eliverus. But yourself."

Suddenly Kadec's palm flared magic and he thrust forward, slamming it to Elijah's chest.

And then Elijah was falling.

His back hit the bed of a shallow pool, water splashing and shocking the breath from his lungs. He gasped at the sudden chill, rolling over to thrust himself back on his feet. Gazing up, he saw a dark and endless sky of stars, mirrored upon a boundless still pool that reached off into the horizon. Around him the world was dark as pitch, the void above a twinkling galaxy of suspended diamonds.

A thick mist slithered around his feet.

Arii stood just a few paces away, still wearing the assassin's garb, but Lorch was nowhere to be seen. She was different, so different to the woman he had come to know. Her eyes were desolate, skin paler, lips tinged red with blood. The honey tips of her hair were stained red, and he noticed more droplets of blood speckled upon her neck and jawline.

Then she changed.

Her face and body warped, morphing into to a familiar face that wore a malicious smirk, a drawling laugh leaking from the lips of his new foe.

The face was suddenly his own.

Kadec's voice hovered in the air around them, "The magic you possess is beyond powerful, it is catastrophic. One day it will consume you, unless you do something about it."

Elijah watched in disbelief as his doppelganger lifted his arms, and the water behind him bubbled violently as something emerged. Water fell away as a draconic creature clawed from the earth, emerging with an earth-shattering roar.

A Kryvern?

No… not a Kryvern.

The beast's neck was longer, arching from a barrel chest covered in thick, glittering scales. Its body was muscled, spines flowing down the centre of its back to the tip of its long tail. The horns protruding from its skull were longer, the proud head featuring a thick jaw and severe brow ridges, housing glowing gold eyes. Powerful wings lifted and flared, tipped with claws; wings that looked entirely strong enough to lift the beast from the earth with just a few strokes and a push of its powerful hind legs. Its scales glittered crimson, golden eyes narrowing into slits. The beast moved, lips rippling over dozens of jagged teeth as a menacing orange glow flared in the throat behind them, a terrible growl rumbling from within its chest as flames escaped between its teeth.

A dragon.

Magic flared up Elijah's arms, snapping into his palms as he blinked water from his eyes.

This was not real, it was a trick – a test, set by Kadec to prove his heart could be without fear.

But he was not without fear.

It stole his breath, quaked his limbs and numbed his fingers, threatening to drop his sword. He could not deny that he feared the immense power within him, unending and seemingly limitless. He feared the price of such power. He feared he had the potential to go mad.

No-one was truly without fear, no matter how much training they endured, how much they steeled their mind and honed their body. Fear was engrained into the fibres of all beings, it was unavoidable.

What really mattered was how he overcame his fear, how he dealt with it right now.

Elijah recalled Kadec as he spoke of his family history and the way his eyes shimmered and his tone hinted at incredible respect for the creatures his family had spent lifetimes protecting. As one of those magnificent, colossal creatures moved before him now with flames licking between parted teeth, he knew he had mere moments to decide his next course of action, and that action would greatly influence his fate, and that of everyone he knew and cared about.

Elijah had always prided himself on his outward composure and knew many believed him to be fearless. He had been the King's shadow – his bodyguard – a man who was one with darkness, living by and one day presumably dying by the sword.

But he had never been without fear.

He understood why Kadec's trial was being carried out this way. There was no way to hide his true thoughts, his true feelings, when connected directly mind to mind. If this were taking place in the real world, he would rush in and face the threat head on without much thought. When Arii had spoken about the possibility of Kadec putting him through 'mind games', this was not exactly the first thing to come to mind.

Had Arii known of the Prince's hidden Fae heritage? Surely she would have told him if she had known.

Kadec's earlier words about betrayal wearing a familiar face briefly entered his mind, but Elijah was swift to strike it down.

Now though, he was at war with his emotions, which had him pausing and thinking. Perhaps that part of the illusion was a test to see how he reacted to facing the dragon. The beast was formidable, and he had to admit that he did feel a spark of apprehension curl in his stomach. Kadec surely did not wish for him to kill the creature, one whom his family had helped protect for generations, not to mention a being of which he believed would be their land's saving grace. Its appearance here now suggested that Elijah had a deep, perhaps unexplored fear of those beasts, or it was an object of symbolism. There was much of his family history to explore, and part of him feared the rumours that had been fed to him while growing up – those about madness in amongst the immensely powerful magic.

He made a choice then.

The dragon shifted, neck arching as its eyes narrowed into slits.

Elijah steeled himself, lifted his weapon and pointed it forward.

Then he opened his palm and let the sword fall.

ARIIAYA

The world passed her falling body so quickly that all she could see was a whirl of stars. There was no clarity, nothing to indicate where she was, or when her body was to collide with solid ground. She screamed, limbs flailing as her body jerked with shock.

When contact with solidarity did not happen immediately, Arii realised this was an act of magic; and this kind of magic was nothing she had ever experienced before. It pressed upon her skin with weight, and what she tasted was not of this world – it was deep and decadent like dark chocolate, tinged with a foreign spice she did not know, almost choking her.

Ancient, frenzied, endless and absolutely terrifying.

She could still see the fading sphere of light through which Nocturne had pushed her, now but a speck in a cosmic race through space. It had felt like ages had passed, but she sensed it had in fact been mere seconds.

Evergreen decorated walls suddenly snapped into focus around her as the sounds of voices and music rushed into her ears, giving her a second to brace for impact.

But impact never came.

Arms enveloped her, one behind her head and the other snaking around her waist as her saviour used the momentum of her fall to dip her into an elegant move that could have been mistaken for the conclusion to a dance, the tips of her hair just brushing the polished marble floor. Light flickered about them, highlighting the small, inconspicuous space in the castle that she had been thrown into. A quick sweep of her gaze told her it was the end of a hallway.

Her breath broke free with a gasp that she could not control, head spinning and stomach churning as she lifted her head to meet bi-coloured eyes and a wide, languid smile.

Nocturne.

The light around them winked out with a snap, as the warped hole of magic she had fallen through shut.

Anger flared back to life quickly as they straightened, and she threw her hands up to shove him away, just as a second wave of terrible nausea swept over her before she could throw a curse. Instead, she threw herself to the side, clutching the rim of a nearby pot plant and hurling what little she had in her stomach into it.

"Ah, I remember my first time. The nausea passes once you have voidwalked a few hundred times."

Arii spat into the flowerpot, wiping her mouth with the back of her hand as she groaned, "I'm going to kill you."

Noct's grin only widened, eyes glittering, "Oh Arii, please refrain from further threatening my life, because all it will do is turn me on… unless that is your intention?"

"The hell is wrong with you?"

"Many, where I come from, wonder the same thing."

Figures rounded the corner, and Arii felt who was approaching before she saw them. Nem dashed down the hall towards them, glittering obsidian and silver and closely flanked by Krepth.

"Arii? What happened to you? You disappeared!"

Arii pointed an accusatory finger at the dark, tall man across from her, spitting. "He pushed me through a… hole? Through a… cosmic split in time and space… what even in the gods-bloody-hell was that?!"

Noct brushed at his lapels, looking almost bored. "It was a Void, and I would have given you prior warning but honestly, I normally kiss then tell."

Nem drew her dagger, a snarl curling her lips as she spoke to Arii while keeping her eyes on Noct.

"You dropped from our bond, Arii. I thought you had been killed!" Her aquamarine eyes were slightly glazed in the dim light and Arii saw the last remnants of fear leaving their depths. Nem pointed the weapon at Noct, whose lopsided grin never faltered.

Krepth placed a hand on Nem's arm, his expression one of carefully compressed fury. His voice was even though, as he said, "He –

whoever he is – will have to explain later. Something is happening in the throne room."

Elijah.

Krepth's words diverted the tension, and they hurried towards the throne room.

Saving her rage for now, Arii ran ahead, silently cursing her form-fitting dress as she pushed her legs to move faster underneath the heavy fabric. Her body was protesting, still recovering from her fall through time and space, but she ignored it with the promise she would seek retribution by mutilating Nocturne's perfect face – later.

Music continued to play, and guests still milled about, piling food on silver plates, sipping wine from crystal glasses and conversing in perhaps slightly more hushed tones than before – but all appeared unchanged from when she had left to get some air.

"I'll find the others and cover your backs," whispered Krepth, shooting a quick glare at Nocturne before slipping away.

"Something feels... off," said Nem as they pushed through the crowd, aiming towards the dais.

Arii scanned the room, letting her senses flare open.

Of course, her friend was right.

The candles were dimmer than before, the walls draped in shadows. The music seemed quieter, too, yet people still danced as if nothing were amiss. The scent of food and incense still hung in the air but there was something else lingering, twisting along her senses as she inhaled deep.

"Magic," sighed Nem, her shoulders tensing, just as they came within a few feet of the dais.

There was no mistaking the sweetness that coated the back of her tongue, or the shiver that skittered across her skin, causing the hairs on her arms to stand on end. She searched for the source, her gaze flying along the elaborately carved chairs on the dais to rest on Kadec. To the untrained eye, it looked as if he were simply standing with arms crossed, a smile upon his face as he oversaw the people dancing before him. But to Arii, she could see the dim flame in the depths of his green eyes and the ripples of power emanating from his skin that told her he was using magic. It was not the kind that she and Nem used; a show of light and flame and sparks. It was the kind that was contained behind the eyes and within the mind.

As they neared, the guests parted to reveal Elijah standing like a statue. He held a glass of amber wine, and his free hand hovered an inch from the pommel of his sword as his eyes stared into the distance – gaze fixed on something far away. Sweat beaded his brow, and a tiny twitch was visible on the corner of one hazy grey eye. Within those eyes, shadows danced.

Spellbound, he was undoubtably spellbound.

Arii jerked towards him, just as the cool blade of a weapon pressed to her neck.

"Move, and I'll open your throat in front of all of these fancy partygoers," hissed a familiar voice.

"Hello, Devina." Arii hissed.

Just as she wondered how on earth Devina had got into the castle, her attention flew to a tussle nearby. A cloaked figure shoved Nem violently to her knees, red rivulets of blood trickling from her nose as her head was jerked back by her hair, a blade pressed to her throat too.

More cloaked figures brought her other friends to the floor.

Collectively the assailants pulled back their hoods, and each face was familiar.

Furies.

Shit.

An older man approached Kadec's side, his skin the same deep brown, his eyes the same striking shade of green. His eyes were winged with wrinkles, the same creasing his mouth. "What is the meaning of this intrusion?" he thundered.

Kadec's glance shifted to them as his arms dropped, but his eyes still flickered with magic.

"Fury assassins crashing my party?" He clucked his tongue. "Well, this is a first."

"We are here on behalf of the King's Hand, Lord Valdis Kruel.

Hand over the traitors to us and no one will be hurt this night."

Arii's eyes dashed to Elijah in desperation, and yet he still stood as if he were a statue.

Why had Kadec not released him from the spell yet?

"Does Lord Kruel forget the existence of messenger birds? It would have saved you and your troupe the effort of making your way here, Miss Divine. I'm afraid I must decline your request and ask you to leave," Kadec fired back.

The blade pressed tighter to Arii's windpipe, and she felt the flame-haired Fury tense behind her. "What part of a blade to your guest's throat do you not understand, Prince? My question was merely a formality and honestly I am being generous, for I want nothing more than to slice Ariiaya's pretty little traitorous throat and spill her blood!"

"I missed you too, Devina." Arii choked.

"Shut the fuck up!" she bellowed, cheeks rosy with frustration. Arii wondered what Valdis had offered the Sisters of Fate for the services of their assassins... or what he had threatened. It was becoming clearer now that the women she thought she knew, the women she thought existed to keep order and balance in their land were turning out to be as acidic as a pit of vipers. She should have known, should have not been so naïve and blind. Arii supposed she should be open to an explanation on their part, but with a dagger presently at her throat and the prospect of death seconds away, she was not feeling very impartial at the minute.

Arii's eyes darted to Elijah again as she called, "We need you, Elijah. Fight it!"

Devina made a sound of disgust.

Kadec sighed, sweeping his hands out at his sides. "I'm afraid my answer is still no."

The muscles in Devina's arm tensed, and Arii heard the woman's satisfied intake of breath – a whisper against her ear. She heard the smile in her voice as she said, "Blood it is then."

So, this was how she would die. Not swinging her weapons upon a gore-covered battlefield as she fought for a better future – but as a lamb for slaughter.

Regret stabbed at her heart.

Wishing she had the chance to tell him – to tell them all – that she was sorry, and she had been wrong.

CHAPTER THIRTY-ONE

ELIJAH

As the sword fell, Elijah's gaze lifted to the beast before him. His eyes widened and his heart leaped as the dragon's jaws parted wide, the back of its throat glowing red hot. He hardly had a moment to brace as golden flames bellowed from the dragon's jaws in a raging torrent.

He threw his arms up to shield his face, squeezing his eyes shut and choking back a cry as the flames slammed into him. He expected fiery pain before total annihilation, but when that did not happen and all he felt was warmth, he opened his eyes a crack and saw that he was standing within a vortex of fire.

The flames evaporated soon after they had erupted, and Elijah suddenly found himself in the centre of Viridya's throne room.

His breath left him in a rush.

The normally golden walls and immaculately polished marble floors were a ruin of blood and gore, furniture upturned, floor riddled with broken glass. It was so real, so gruesome that he could smell the tang of fear mixed with the copper of blood. Beyond the room, he could hear the sounds of the castle bells, droning in a lumbering death knell.

Bodies littered the floor, common garb as well as castle servants and Red Guard uniforms, and as Elijah slowly walked towards the golden throne on atop the dais, he heard a voice whisper just over his shoulder.

"There is no kingdom without sacrifice."

Elijah spun, clutching at his hip for his weapon, but he cursed when he realised that he had not retrieved it. Drawing upon his magic, blue fire ignited on his palm as he faced the voice's owner, only to find it was his own face staring back at him once more.

The man was dressed in cloak and hood and the bodyguard armour which he had worn for many years. The hood shadowed his face, but Elijah could see a hint of his own strong chin and mouth. That mouth was pulled into a smile; a smile showing pointed teeth as his image began to laugh. The man removed his hood, slowly resting it on his shoulders. His hair was wild, matted with blood, as were his cheeks, his neck, his brow.

It was then that Elijah spied blood on his armour too, so dark that he had not noticed it before.

Had… had he killed all of these people?

"What will you sacrifice for your kingdom come, Prince who was lost?" The man who wore his face swept a hand over the bodies. "With war comes collateral damage." Piercing grey eyes met his own. "And I think you fear not what Valdis and his army will do to the innocent lives of those around you if you fail – but what *you* will do to them when you win back your throne."

"No! Why are you showing me this?" Elijah bellowed into the air, searching for Kadec. Perspiration drenched his back, his heart beating faster as a shiver of dread coursed his spine.

The blood-soaked version of him chuckled. Elijah hated the sound, yet he knew – deep down – it was his own.

"You and I both know that fact is untrue. You are seeing me – seeing yourself – here now because you fear what is inside you more than anything else. More than betrayal, more than death itself."

"That is ridiculous–"

"But true," his twin interrupted. "I can see it in your eyes, Eliverus – you fear the part of yourself that you know lies deep within, the part of you that craves more *power*."

"No." Elijah snapped, fisting his hands at his sides. "You're wrong!"

"You cannot lie to yourself, no matter how hard you try. You have felt the dark whisper of madness lingering like a shadow in your mind since you began to embrace your magic. You are the very thing that you were raised to fear. Power such as yours comes at a price. Are you willing to pay it?"

Elijah felt sick. Every time he used his magic, every time he reached into the dazzling, endless pool of power, he felt more alive than he ever had before. He felt indestructible.

Would he use too much and burn out? Would he lose control and hurt someone innocent?

He was not at all surprised that such power would come at a price, on his own sanity. He was not as naïve to think he could not do anything he wanted with such power – he could. He could not deny the pull he felt when touching the magic.

Mostly the magic aided him, understood him, accepted his whole being, no matter his past.

But there was a dark stain lingering far beneath the silver surface – a dark stain that was slowly beginning to spread.

Magic sizzled along his skin now, without his prompting. His mirror image barked a laugh as a figure rose from the marble floor at his feet as if emerging from a pool of still water – taking form as his best friend.

Lorch knelt on the floor, obediently lifting his gaze and tilting his head back as Elijah's illusion twin placed a blade to his throat.

"How could you do this, Elijah? You were my brother," Lorch sighed, his voice heavy with emotion.

Elijah's breath caught and he took a step forward as Lorch's striking blue eyes found him.

"That is not me, Lorch, that will *never* be me. I will never hurt you."

If this illusion was to suggest he sacrifice his best friend, he would never accept it. He would rather die.

His scattered, frantic thoughts magnetised together, now pointed towards one thing, and Elijah shook with the dawning realisation.

Sacrifice.

Arii's golden thread meant for Lorch flashed inside his mind.

No, not for Lorch…

"What road can I take that won't end in the world falling apart?" he choked, wincing at a sudden itch igniting on the tips of his fingers. Elijah lifted his hands, turning them over to gaze at his palms as black ink began to seep across his skin, starting at his fingertips and slowly making its way down his hands.

The image across from him said, "Death is a part of war, Eliverus, we know this. You cannot save everyone, and as hard as you try you cannot stop the darkness within you from spreading. It has happened within your bloodline before – long, long ago. The sacrifice you will make for such a heavy burden of magic is your own sanity."

"Make it stop," Elijah rasped. The darkness continued to spread, itching at his elbows now. "Stop!"

The man tilted his head, eyes unblinking. "The only way to stop this, to stop *all* of it, is for you to die, Eliverus."

Disbelief warred with truth like a clashing of thunderclouds inside his soul.

"The only one who can stop the coming apocalypse is you. But not without *sacrifice*."

Sacrifice.

"Magic such as yours should not exist and cannot exist without eventually causing calamity. Tell me, Prince who was lost… Will you do what is wrong, to make things right?"

Elijah's eyes darted between his fingers, and it was then he noticed that the other version of him had blackness trailing up his arms too. Words from his adopted mother passed through his memory as he recalled a time when he had been afraid, before his first battle as a young Red Guard soldier, and Colleen had soothed him.

There is no courage without fear, Elijah, and wars are not won without sacrifice. Trust your gut and lead your heart.

He swallowed, her absence piercing his chest like a knife.

Slowly Lorch's face warped, as if slugs floundered beneath his skin, and suddenly another took his place, light olive skin and wide purple eyes set in a face so beautiful it stole his breath.

Ariiaya knelt in her stunning purple dress, knife held to her neck by his mirror image, her hair coming undone from the silver hairpiece as she growled, "Do it, Elijah. You know what must be done. Accept the fear, face it, *defeat* it. We need you. Fight!"

Her voice resonated across the sleek floor, strong and fearless, and there was a strange quality to the tone, as if she was speaking through an invisible barrier between them.

As if her words were not just within Kadec's projection, but beyond it.

Her voice tugged at a familiar feeling deep inside his chest. Longing bayed to her from deep within his soul.

Face to face with the devil that was him, Eliverus Herington suddenly realised he was not afraid.

Back in the throne room, back by Arii's side and with his friends was where he should be.

Anger bubbled in the back of his throat, burning hot and white. In that moment he did not care if he earned Kadec's support. His heart suddenly yearned for home, for a past lost and for a future promised.

Never had Elijah truly accepted himself, but over the last few weeks, he had come closer to inner completion. With the whisper of madness threatening his future, he knew what he had to do – and knew that when he entered the battlefield against Valdis, neither of them would return.

It was his burden to shoulder, but for now, he focused on his own face as the man smirked, and Elijah summoned his magic to form a crystal dagger in his palm.

Arii moved to the side just a fraction, and it was enough.

His twin's eyes widened as Elijah shot forward to sink his blade through flesh and bone.

Straight into the man's heart... his *own* heart.

"I will sacrifice what I must – including my own life – to free this land from despair. I would rather die fighting on my feet than live on my knees," Elijah hissed.

His image's mouth opened in shock as Viridya's throne room

fell away. Spilling away like water, the illusion of his own face disappeared, replaced by a woman in black, her red hair passing over pale, freckled cheeks.

She fell, and Elijah caught her, his crystal dagger protruding from Devina Devine's chest, her last breath rattling from her lips as she died.

He knew the path ahead would not be without sacrifice.

Will you do what is wrong, to make things right?

With tears in his eyes he whispered, "Forgive me…"

ARIIAYA

The blade disappeared from Arii's throat in a rush, leaving a shallow line of fire as many things happened at once.

A blur of black streaked by as a huge black wolf took out the Fury holding Nem hostage, jaws sinking into flesh as Krepth tore the assassin's hand from her wrist in one violent strike. Nem shot to her feet, blood dotting the side of her face as she rushed at the two assassins holding Emerson and Luc, just as Tikkani slammed the back of her skull into the nose of the black-haired Fury behind her.

Arii twisted nimbly in time to see Elijah catch Devina as she fell, a crystal dagger deep in her chest. She knew instantly the woman was dead, her body lifeless like a rag doll as Elijah gently lay her on the floor. She heard his whispered apology, the pain in those few words causing her chest to ache for him.

He knelt by Devina's side, passing his fingers over the eyes of the dead Fury as he uttered a parting vow.

Kadec threw up his arms, eyes glowing with magic, a hum shuddering in the air as the remaining assassins fell to their knees and grasped their skulls with silent screams. Arii was not sure what he was showing them, but assumed it was not pleasant.

Arii's eyes met stormy grey as Elijah moved to her side, silent as a wraith and as gentle as a breeze. His warm hands moved to her waist. She did not need the assistance but welcomed his touch in that moment. He was silent, but his eyes told her what words could not.

I've got you, whether you like it or not.

"Take what I have shown you as a message of warning to the Sisters of Fate. I hope they re-evaluate their stance on this war, and choose their next actions wisely," called Kadec, his expression severe as the magic faded from his eyes. The assassins slowly recovered from Kadec's hold on their minds. He added, "Take the bodies of your fallen sisters and leave – before I change my mind."

Nocturne stepped forward, his hands moving in a swift gesture. There was a crackling sound as a rippling, magic-laced void, like the one which had swallowed Arii, opened up behind the assassins. The women stared at the rippling image of the School of Fate atop the bluff. Calm grey skies backgrounded the familiar scene, dotted with cawing gulls, and the gentle crash of waves against the rocks. Seeing the place she once called home wrung conflicting feelings within her. After her talk with Elijah hours ago, she had made a promise to herself that everyone deserved a chance to explain themselves before facing their fate. She would have extended this to Devina, too. Her mind then skipped to the death of her archrival. She hated Devina, their rivalry spanning many years and their animosity had dashed far beyond simple contest, warping into something toxic and violent. She would have tried to help her see reason, though, despite their past. Arii was not completely unreasonable, it seemed. She also hoped to hear the remaining sisters' side of the story, and perhaps convince them to choose more wisely in the war to come. Despite their harsh upbringing, she was sure there was good in them too, somewhere deep down.

She heard swift intakes of breath from her friends at the strange new magic, which elicited a small bubble of nausea, a ghost of memory from her fall through the void. She *really* did not want to do that again.

She was surprised the assassins did not object, but instead gathered Devina and their fallen comrade and disappeared through the portal.

Shortly after, it winked shut with a snap of dust and sparks, as if it had never existed. She heard Tikkani murmur, "Where was this guy when we began the hard slog from the south? We could have saved *so* much time."

The others were too stunned to reply.

Her gaze swept over the ballroom as the music stepped up from dull background noise and guests continued to party as if a death had never occurred on their dance floor. She wondered how much had been visible to them, or had Kadec used his magic to ensnare their minds, oblivious to the danger?

She noticed then that guards were once again stationed around the room. In the heat of the moment she had not noticed their absence. Anger begin to bubble, as she put pieces of a puzzle together in her mind and glared at the Prince.

"Your guards disappeared just before the assassins arrived. You *let* the Furies in, didn't you?" She felt Elijah stiffen beside her as she barely kept the rage from her voice.

Kadec's warm brown skin had a light sheen of sweat which he dabbed away with a white linen cloth. "You have keen eyes, Miss Trillia, not to mention a voice that can pierce the nether world. I knew Prince Eliverus would prevail – even with the unexpected visit from your estranged sisters."

Arii suppressed the urge to glance sidelong at Elijah with Kadec's mention of a nether world, telling her curiosity that she would learn of his experience soon enough. After her trip through Nocturne's warped void, the notion that other worlds could exist did not surprise her now.

As the adrenaline dissipated, Arii felt the brush of Elijah's sleeve against her bare arm, and shivered. Swallowing, she stepped away from him, stubbornly taking up her earlier stance of putting space between them.

She did not look at him.

Their friends converged around them, a united front as they gazed up at the Prince of the west. Nocturne stood nearby, dusting the lapels of his suit, a wicked gleam in his eyes. He nodded to Kadec, a silent look of approval that seemed curious coming from the stranger as the Prince sought a similar look from his father nearby, before turning his attention to them once more.

"Love, loyalty, sacrifice, fearlessness and respect. I have seen all of these traits displayed here tonight amongst your people, Eliverus." Kadec glanced at each of them, before resting on Elijah. "Yours is a court of hope, for these people beside you now are the foundation of your reign. You have proven not only your strength, but your integrity too. Heavy is the head that wears the crown, but with help, the burden will be far lighter to bear. What you faced today was but a trial in preparation for the true battle to come."

Arii stole a glance at her friends, feeling a release of tension in each of them as Kadec descended the dais and halted in front of Elijah. Behind him, every member of Kadec's court, including the mysterious Nocturne, swept into respectful bows. The entire party followed, their outfits creating a wave of colour.

Prince Kadec fell to one knee, head bowing and hand upon his heart as he announced, "I will aid you, Eliverus Herington, brother who was lost. You and your court have my full and unfaltering support."

ELIJAH

All eyes were on Elijah as Kadec's father approached him, holding a small box of pure gold. Arii and the others moved aside to give the Princes space on the dais. The heaviness that had pressed upon his shoulders at the beginning of the evening had not eased, although he had a feeling that the night was nowhere near over. What he had learned hovered upon his mind like a wraith of shadow. Kadec had addressed his future as King, but he was aware that there would be no future for him until he found a way to overcome his fate.

Adrenaline lingered in his muscles, his magic waiting just beneath his skin – a comfort and a curse to him now.

The music dimmed to a hum, the people watching in awe as the gilded box was handed to Kadec, who flicked the lock and lifted the lid. Inside, nestled on a bed of red velvet, was a midnight blue, perfectly shaped oval stone. Its exterior was polished to perfection, as if made of glass, and Elijah could see a hint of pattern that looked like scales just beneath the surface. Beyond that, a faint illumination flickering at its core, speckled with shimmering stars as if the night sky were encased within. He wondered if perhaps it resembled a dragon's egg.

He felt an ancient power radiating from the stone, and he was unable to deny the pull he felt towards it.

"This is a Void Stone – an object of power that will act as a beacon to call your greatest allies home. It has been in our family's care for over twenty years, awaiting the return of its rightful owner. I bestow it upon you, Prince Eliverus Herington. Keep it close, keep it safe. When you are ready, and when *it* is ready, only then will it open for you."

Kadec closed the lid and placed the box in Elijah's hands. The courtiers began to clap, which soon turned into cheering. The Prince of the West smiled wide.

Elijah placed the box under his arm, allowing himself to sweep into a low bow, free hand on his heart. "Thank you. Your trust will not be placed in vain."

Captain Roarke approached, his face a little less hostile than before. He bowed quickly, placing a hand to his heart also as he said, "Allow me to place the stone in your chambers, Your Highness. It will be safe there until the celebrations are over."

Once the adrenaline wore off, Elijah was not sure he would be able to remain standing, let alone continue to dance and speak. The room was still abuzz with excitement and there was no sign of the party ending anytime soon. He gazed up at the windows, seeing a hint of an orange sunset. It had only been a few hours, it seemed.

So much had happened in just a few hours.

"Thank you, Roarke."

With a nod, the soldier took the box and headed for the doors, flanked by two other guards.

Releasing a long sigh, Elijah's gaze travelled back to Kadec. Now that his glamour was gone, Elijah could see quite obviously that he was Fae. He glided with supernatural elegance, his acute eyes missing nothing. It raised many questions as Kadec's hands fluttered, summoning two glass goblets of wine. He handed one to Elijah. "You have questions. We are allies now, whatever questions you ask – I will answer."

Elijah accepted the wine and found himself analysing the man's profile. "Were we not always allies?"

Kadec barked a good-natured laugh, glancing at him from the corner of his eye. "Yes, that is true. But, when the safety of your realm rests upon one decision, one moment where you must make a choice that could alter the course of the future – you do find yourself placing up some barriers of protection."

Elijah couldn't help his smile. "It is what I would have done."

"Then you will make a good ruler, Eliverus."

Kadec's words were light-hearted but there was heaviness behind his eyes that was not lost on Elijah.

Things were going to get far more difficult than Elijah could have ever imagined. For now though, he would focus on one thing at a time.

Sipping the wine, Elijah's gaze roved the room, and soon his eyes found the one he had been seeking.

Ariiaya stood with Nem, Krepth and the others just off the dancefloor, within arms' reach of a table stacked with food. Krepth had his hands on her shoulders, his face stern yet gentle, checking her for injuries. Arii batted him away as a new face approached the group.

Elijah had seen him earlier, atop the dais, the one who summoned the strange void. He was tall and immaculately dressed in an unusual suit, with tailoring he had never seen before. The man, his dark hair featuring a streak of blonde, swept into a shallow bow, which earned him a half-hearted scowl from Ariiaya. Her shoulders shrugged in a sigh, and the language of her body changed from stand-off to reluctant acceptance as they spoke. He had seen the same look directed at him once upon a time, and now it dredged up strange feelings inside.

He felt his beast rise from slumber, the Fae part of him that was unpredictable and wild, a growl rumbling deep as if it had some sort of claim over her. Elijah attempted to stamp it down, telling himself that she was not *his*, and she could be with whomever she wanted. She had made her feelings perfectly clear last night, though the message had clearly not gotten through to the overbearing creature inside him. This feeling was unfamiliar, but he realised quickly what it was.

Jealousy.

Who was the stranger?

Instead of voicing *that* question, Elijah said, "Are there more surviving Fae than we were led to believe?"

Kadec's voice lowered, "Many more. You are not the last male Fae, there are many of us, hiding in plain sight."

The admission had Elijah's attention darting back to the Prince. "How?"

"Exactly as you saw it here before your own eyes. Magic. It was our downfall, yet also our saving grace."

"You mean there could be more Fae living in secret in the north? Despite what happened there?"

"You will find we are stubborn creatures, Elijah, harder to kill than the humans like to believe, and many love the north with their hearts and souls. It will forever be their home, even if they risk their lives to remain."

This information pierced like an arrow to his chest. More Fae living in secret, risking death every day just to remain in their homes, a secret society waiting to be liberated. He wondered what Valdis would give for this information.

How many he would kill if he obtained it.

Elijah felt the gravity of how many innocent lives were relying on him, and that weight doubled now knowing there was a population of Fae who would have to meld back into a society that had been conditioned to fear them for a very long time.

"Who is he? And what was that magic he used?" Elijah finally asked, inclining his chin at Nocturne.

Kadec swallowed his wine audibly before answering. "Nocturne Tempest. He harnesses magic ancient and not of this realm. It doesn't exist here, and it is highly coveted where he is from. Noct risks much to be here, and he is highly valuable as my advisor of realms."

So he had to learn about the magic of other realms, as well as that of his own? It was almost too much for his exhausted mind to comprehend.

He put it aside to investigate later, nodding in response to Kadec's explanation. "The existence of other realms is powerful information."

"And it must remain here and here alone, Eliverus. To fall into the wrong hands would surely spell further destruction to our world."

"I will keep it secret, you have my word."

Elijah watched Arii and Noct's further interactions with a forced look of nonchalance, his goblet hovering at his lips as he said, "You saw everything that took place in the trial, did you not?"

Kadec's tone was careful, but light. "Yes."

"Is it true?"

Without need for elaboration as to which part of the trial Elijah meant, the Prince sighed and nodded. "I'm afraid so. I know you are familiarising yourself with the laws of magic, Eliverus, but power such as yours throws off the tenuous balance of things."

"Is there no way around it… a loophole?" Elijah refused to let the gnawing in his stomach grow worse at the prospect of his eventual demise.

Kadec's brows pulled as he paused mid-sip from his glass, "I do not wish to offer you false hope, but there is something – whether or not it will aid you, I do not know, but it is a start. Seek out the Ouroboros, it may give you the answers you seek."

"The Ouroboros," Elijah echoed.

"It is something of immense symbolism and power in the world where Noct comes from, but rumour has it that it can be found here, too."

"Thank you, Kadec." Elijah said to him, meaning it. He tucked that knowledge away to investigate intensely later.

As of yet, he had not decided if he was to tell his friends of the revelation he uncovered in Kadec's trial – he was not sure how they would react. He was not sure how *Arii* would react, most of all.

Kadec tapped his fingers against Elijah's bicep. "Being a ruler is a challenge, one that no-one can do perfectly and no-one can do on their own. Choose your court wisely, confide only in people you can trust but also guard your secrets, for those who are most likely to betray you will wear a face you know."

That turned Elijah's attention squarely on Kadec, "You speak from experience?"

"No, I speak from learned history. Valdis Kruel was your father's most trusted advisor, and the King's Hand." He paused as weight hovered with the truth between them. Elijah's heartbeat elevated as the words sank in, and Kadec's eyes took on a harsh edge as he whispered. "He was also the one wielding the knife that killed him."

NOCTURNE

CHAPTER THIRTY-TWO

ARIIAYA

The party ended past midnight, the revellers thanking their host and bowing low to Elijah as they retired, bleary-eyed with exhaustion from the excitement, and perhaps a tad too much wine. Many of the people she spied seemed different since the Fury attack, and Arii realised that some of the courtiers were in fact Fae. It was as if a glamour has lifted, and she saw pointed ears, and sharp canines as they conversed and laughed as they moved gracefully.

One woman – supported by another – wobbled and giggled as she slurred, "Ah, hope has come in the form of a tall, dark and handsome lost prince. What I wouldn't give to be *his* princess." She was quickly ushered from the room before she could fall face first onto the marble floors. *She* had been human.

Arii stiffened but tried to ignore it.

The room was almost empty, and all that remained was herself, her friends, Kadec and a few last advisors, Elijah and Nocturne.

Noct poked her with his elbow, his accent having thickened over the course of the night. "You're more tightly wound than a bow, princess."

Arii sighed and rolled her shoulders – he was not wrong. She had not fully forgiven him for his attempt at distraction in the form of a world-jumping void, but she had decided to extend an olive branch in response to his apology after the trial had ended. Her friends had quickly warmed to the rogue stranger, their curiosity over his dress, his accent, and most of all the magic he wielded becoming the topic of conversation for the remainder of the night.

Which gave Arii opportunities to spy on Elijah, who had been deep in conversation with Kadec for most of the night. His expression was guarded, the space between his brows creased, his eyes as harsh as steel. Only once had his eyes met hers, and when they did it was only brief, for she was the one to glance quickly away.

It broke her heart.

"Care for another drink? Or perhaps a walk? Doesn't have to be here, it could be anywhere." Noct continued, earning him a scrunched face from Arii.

"I'd rather lick the inner rim of a chamber pot than go anywhere with you."

Noct snorted a laugh as she continued, "And I'd rather not relive the feeling of my insides being warped to a point where I lose my lunch and liquor again. No, thank you."

"It gets better the more you do it, trust me." He grinned roguishly, leading her to believe he was not speaking just about walking through voids.

Arii regarded him with speculation. "Perhaps it will remain a rubbish experience no matter how many times you do it."

Noct chuckled, leaning close, "Only one way to find out."

She met his sparkling eyes with a sly smirk, "Not even if we were the last two beings left in the realm."

Despite her words, she momentarily considered the prospect of taking him to bed, in the hope that a rebound would help the pain that she felt. But she had learned a lot about herself over the last few weeks. A rebound with him would not help heal her heart at all.

"Can you jump through time as well? Or just space?" said Emerson, arm and arm with Luc. Arii winced, hoping he had not heard Noct's attempted propositioning.

Noct turned his heavy gaze from her to her friends. "Unfortunately, no, only space and realms."

"Realms?" piped Tikkani nearby as Quinn draped his coat over her shoulders.

Luc rubbed at his temple. "I think talk of realms and other worlds can wait till morning. I don't think my brain can take it after all the food and drink. Besides, we have exciting news." He straightened, and Emerson's lips pulled into a smile as Luc announced, "We are getting married!"

A spark of energy rippled through them all as Tikkani squealed, "He said yes?! Finally!"

Emerson laughed, nodding in confirmation as Tikkani flew into her brother's arms.

Krepth locked hands with Luc, thumping him on the arm as he grinned widely. "Congratulations, your persistence paid off." Beside them, Quinn threw his arms around Emerson's waist and lifted him into the air, twirling him around.

Nem embraced the two of them in a rare show of affection, stepping back quickly with a small smile.

Pure happiness welled in Arii's heart as she embraced Luc, then Emerson, holding the recruit at arm's length as she whispered, "I am so happy for you both. Truly."

Emerson's cheeks were scarlet, but his golden eyes were the clearest she had seen in a long time. "Thank you, Arii." He nodded at everyone, "Thank you all."

"A wedding? How fantastic!" shouted Kadec, joining them. Elijah was not far behind, offering the newly engaged couple a broad smile and words of congratulations. It made Arii's heart hurt anew.

Emerson and Luc both grinned, taking turns to bow. Their shows of respect brought a tinge of pink to Elijah's cheeks. He whispered, "Hardly necessary, you two."

"I suspect you are all worn out from this very exciting night, so please feel free to retire. Tomorrow night I will hold a dinner in celebration of the engagement of Emerson and Luc. It will be my treat." Kadec announced, smiling at Elijah's awkwardness.

They bowed again, Emerson's face now flaming red. "That's extremely generous of you, Your Highness."

Kadec grinned, motioning to his remaining advisors to wrap up the night as court employees dashed about, tidying up.

Arii found herself lingering, one of the last to leave. Her muscles still hummed with energy, though her chest felt tight. She was conflicted, feeling happiness for her friends, yet restless from the events of the evening. Not to mention pent up frustration at the awkward situation she had put herself in with Elijah.

As they entered the beautiful foyer with the large, candlelit willow tree, Arii felt his presence behind her.

She always felt his presence, no matter where he was in the room. It had been so since the moment they met, that feeling of weight upon her shoulders and the shiver that caressed her spine. That feeling drew her to him – even now.

She fought it with all her might, told herself not to look his way, lest their gazes lock and she once again fell into the soft storm clouds of his eyes.

Murmuring a soft goodnight, she dipped into a bow before spinning on her heel and fleeing towards her rooms.

Leaving Elijah and Nocturne side by side in her wake.

ELIJAH

"Well, I don't need to be Fae to feel the mountain of tension between you two. My gods, she is remarkale, isn't she? Dangerous, untameable, irresistible, a beacon drawing moths like me to her flame." Noct said.

Elijah kept his features stoic, although what he felt inside was a roiling storm. She had hardly locked eyes with him all night, yet he had felt her gaze on him when he hadn't been looking her way.

The turmoil of emotions was causing him a raging headache.

And now this stranger, this tall and lean man who had his eyes on Arii all night was now alone with him in the foyer, and Elijah felt the Fae beast inside moving with the restlessness of a caged wolf. His inhibitions left him at the eagerness he sensed in the man, as if he craved the challenge that Arii offered.

She is not yours, Elijah.

Before he could stop them, the words left his lips in a low, dangerous hiss. "Stay away from her."

Noct glanced at him with raised brows. "Pardon?"

"You heard me," he whispered, turning to the man. He was but an inch taller, and he used that inch as his eyes narrowed to slits.

All it earned him was a grin as Noct rocked back on his heels and buried his hands in his pockets.

"Your Highness, you have nothing to worry about."

Elijah felt his spine relax ever so slightly, until Noct sent him a covert look as he left, eyes dark and full of secrets. "For she will come to *me*."

ARIIAYA

Orbs like chipped ice hovered above her, darkness obscuring all but his eyes and sadistic smile as iron sliced her skin and burned acid through her veins. Her back bowed, jaw clenched so hard that she was surprised her teeth did not shatter. The pain was excruciating, pushing and pulling her between consciousness and darkness in a cruel tug of war. She wished so desperately for sweet oblivion to take her, so she did not have to endure the torture any longer.

Turn it off.

Make it stop.

Please…

Cold stone pressed against her back, her fingernails clawing as wetness greeted her skin. She knew it was blood – her own – overflowing and seemingly endless as Valdis's voice hissed from above.

"We will have you to thank, Ariiaya."

She screamed behind closed lips.

"For you have helped unlock what was needed to bring about the land's destruction."

No.

No no no.

"No!" Arii shot up in bed with the word riding her lips. Panting, she wiped at her sweaty brow, leaning forward to place her head between her knees.

Deep breaths… one, two, three.

She inhaled through her nose, and out through her mouth in an attempt to calm her raging heart. Against her will, her eyes slid to the empty space beside her, pillow untouched, sheets hardly rumpled. The sight had her heart squeezing with slithers of regret.

She had done the right thing… She repeated the thought over and over, for she wanted to do just that, to redeem herself just a bit from the darkness of her past.

Attempting redemption, though, did not heal her broken heart, nor did it stop the nightmare from resurfacing, haunting her nightly.

She pressed the tips of her fingers to her temples, circling the throbbing hurt there.

Moonlight stroked glossy fingers over the polished hardwood floors of her bedchamber, preceding a sudden flicker of light. Thunder rumbled outside, lightning snapping past her open window with a crack, causing Arii to leap out of bed.

Storms like this were an extreme rarity in the west, so when another boom shuddered the glass windows in their frames, Arii knew immediately that *this* storm was not natural in occurrence.

Her bare feet hit the floorboards, and she dashed towards the door. Static snapped at her skin as she clutched the handle, yanking the door wide.

Her breath caught.

Elijah stood in the doorway, his hair dishevelled, crème sleeping tunic unbuttoned to reveal his heaving chest. His hands were fisted by his sides, and she swore she could see them shaking. Had he been fighting a war within himself just inches from her door? As her slow assessment returned to his face, she spied a familiar twitch on his jaw – the one which appeared when he was holding himself back.

Her eyes met his, and what she saw within their silver depths had her whispering his name, unable to mask the pain that had been slowly coalescing inside her. That one word held all of the pent-up frustration and emotion from the night before.

"Elijah…"

His eyes darted to the room behind her, as if checking she was alone. Suddenly he snapped and rushed forward.

She did not stop him as he roughly pulled her to him. Her hands flew to his face, bringing his lips to hers.

Damn it all to the depths.

She kissed him then, kissed him as if she were starving, and he met her desperation with his own. Absentmindedly, she heard the bedroom door slam shut behind him as she pressed backward, but she was drowning with need and desire so powerful that she could hardly fill her lungs with breath. The entire night of stolen glances, near touches of sizzling fire and forced distance had affected him just as much as it did her.

She knew he had been checking she had not taken someone else to bed. He need not worry, though. Arii knew she was permanently altered after meeting Elijah, and no other would feel *right* in the space she had designated for him and him only. She knew this would probably end with her alone, wallowing in a misery that may just heal after a few hundred years or more.

These emotions… they were a ruthless master and she, their pliable slave.

"Tell me to stop… tell me to leave," he whispered against her lips, his voice breathless and heavy with anguish.

She pulled him towards the bed as lightning flashed, illuminating the room in silver. Her nails dug into the soft skin of his nape, gliding to his tense shoulders. His body quaked in time with the rolling thunder as he held her closer, a sigh escaping her at the contact when he added, "Because if you don't, I'm afraid I won't be able to stop."

A thrill rocketed down her spine.

"I know you are trying to force distance between us because you fear you are not good enough for a King." He cupped her cheek, bringing her gaze to his. "But what you are yet to realise is that it is *I* who must prove to be worthy of a *Queen*."

Her mouth opened in protest, but he continued. "And I will spend the rest of my life proving that you are worthy, if that is what it takes, Ariiaya. Whatever is happening between us, it is worth fighting for, because you captivate me, Arii. You bewitch me, mind, body and soul, and not only do you set my insides on fire with a desire I've never felt before, you calm the storms raging inside me, and you also test me beyond limits I never knew I had. You beguile not only my eyes, but the beast inside me too. Us… this?" he squeezed her shoulders, "It's chaos, but it's filled with threads of *possibility*. That is worth fighting for, and never letting go. Fate, destiny, society, gods be damned."

He paused before inhaling a shaky breath, "But if you wish for me to leave, to stay away, I will do it. Not because I want to – that is far from the truth – but because I respect you and your wishes, Arii."

Arii was rarely left speechless. A long pause stretched as he studied her face, his thumb caressing her cheek tenderly. Her throat worked on a harsh swallow as she found she was once again burning his face – his strong, incredible face – to memory.

She couldn't do this to herself anymore. There was far too much pain in her past. She wanted happiness, the kind she saw between Emerson and Luc, unfaltering, pure. She knew her relationship with Elijah was different, though. They came together like fire and ice, chaos and passion melding, and over time she had realised that what they shared was beyond lust.

They were fated to love one another. She knew it in her heart.

So, she decided on allowing herself some happiness, even if it were just for one night, and shoved away thoughts of the future for another day. Wallowing in the past and fearing the future was only causing her strife, and she was sick of sitting in the middle of the scales as they teetered from side to side.

So, she promised herself something different.

No longer would she allow misery to be her only company. The future was still uncertain, and if she were to die on a battlefield in the coming days, she would have no regrets over a little moment of happiness.

"I don't want you to go," she finally whispered, "and staying apart from you was never what I truly wanted. I'm just… afraid. Afraid that we may not have a future together. It's not something I've ever thought about, my future, but now it seems *all* I can think about." She winced at the confession, yet felt it was time to be truthful to the person who had been bearing the brunt of her ill temper, yet still wished to make her *happy*. Wanted her to realise that she had some good in her heart.

Up until this point she had not been truly living, but merely existing. With him, she felt she was finally *alive*.

She grazed her fingers over the scars on his chest. "I'm so sorry, Elijah. For everything."

His lips grazed her forehead, "You have *nothing* to apologise for. You were protecting yourself. But you don't need to do that with me anymore, Arii. The future is uncertain, but I know *my* future is with you."

Her heart squeezed, and she looked up into his intense gaze. "Show me a night where the future doesn't matter, Elijah," her voice wavered, "because I can't be apart from you any longer."

A sound she had never heard him make before sighed through his parted lips as his mouth met hers once more, and her heart – which had been slowly shrivelling to blackness – swelled with emotions so sweet that her defences blew apart and she allowed her thoughts and fears to scatter upon a boom of thunder.

Flash.

A blaze of lightning dazzled the room, illuminating his broad chest as his shirt fell to the floor. Magic aided them in ridding each other of their clothing, until they were naked in silverlight. She worshipped his scars, kissing the little ridges on his chest as they moved to the bed, fingers clutching, exploring his lightning-lit skin.

Flash.

He whispered promises dipped in honey that had her toes curling. Heat radiated from his chest as he pressed against her back, sweeping the thick mass of her hair from her neck, fingers brushing over her stomach as he pressed long, slow kisses along the curve of her neck. A strong arm curved around the lower of her ribcage, and when his exploring fingers dipped lower, finding her heat, her knees quaked. He held her though, keeping her on her feet as fissures of pleasure shot down to her toes. His hardness pressing against her lower back had her tipping in a spiral.

Flash.

She spun to face him, a blur of motion as she clamped a hand on his, pulling him to the bed. They landed on the blankets as another lightning bolt flashed by the window. A crack of thunder shook the panes of glass as he clutched her thigh with one hand and cupped her breast with the other, his teeth skimming the hard peak. Arii groaned, arching her back in pleasure.

Flash.

They did not speak, for their actions showed what words could not. His body was familiar now, and no matter how much she saw, heard and felt, Arii knew she would always be completely infatuated by every little thing about him. The gentle yet firm dancing of his fingers as he played her like a violin, the way his silver eyes lit from within, the subtle sounds he made when she touched him just right.

It was a melody she wanted to hear for all eternity.

It took everything inside her not to resort to begging him to take her then and there in a streak of moonlight, every nerve ending tingling and teetering on the cusp of her freefall towards release. She remembered his wish to wait until they were not in the borrowed rooms of another kingdom and knew that vow still applied. His shoulders shivered, and she could feel a hum beneath his skin. He was holding back, reigning in the beast inside, as was she. This did not hold them back from wringing as much pleasure from each other's bodies as they could.

Flash.

She came undone with the last thunderclap, riding the pleasure wave as it peaked and dropped, the friction of his fingers causing blissful mayhem as she undulated her hips against him, tearing a gradual, thundering release. She rocked against him for a few precious moments, limbs and bones as languid as sweet jelly before letting herself float to serene waters.

Breathing deeply and bodies damp with a light sheen of sweat they parted to catch their breath, Arii fell beside him, palm against her forehead.

"Gods," she sighed.

Elijah's callused hands skimmed her stomach, and she sighed, kissing his shoulder, revelling in the feeling of just *being* with him, exploring him, breathing in his scent and tasting his skin. She rested her head on the crook between his shoulder and neck, marvelling as her body slipped perfectly against his side. Her fingers walked over the ridges of his stomach towards his navel, but his hand stopped her.

"It's your turn," she purred.

His voice held a smile, "Not if I hope to remain a gentleman."

"Then don't be. Be a *Fae*."

The silence was not strained, nor was it uncomfortable – nothing but the sounds of their breath and the gentle gusts of wind outside. The storm had subsided, and as she watched the steady rise and fall of Elijah's chest, she knew that the storm had been his.

"Something tells me that if I were to do that, then we could be here for days. When I finally make love to you, I don't think I'll be able to let you out of my sight, nor out of my arms until you are thoroughly... mine."

She quivered with delight at the thought. Even the way he described their imminent coupling as 'make love' had her insides warming like freshly baked bread.

"And I cannot promise it'll be only making love... It'll be far more than that, for one thing I can promise is that you will not be able to walk when I'm done with you."

Pure, animalistic, carnal Fae. She liked this unexplored, utterly *promising* side of him.

"Spoken like a true Fae male," she chuckled, the sound coming through a little more breathless than she had intended. They did not have days to waste though.

She felt his beard skim the top of her head as he said, "I'll remain a gentleman then. For now."

Between her legs throbbed at the dark, sensual note to his deep voice. Oh goddess, she had to change the subject before she decided to try everything within her power to make him *wreak* that vow. So, she said; "You were having a nightmare before you came to my rooms, weren't you?"

His voice remained dropped as he replied, "There is hardly a night where the demons of my past don't visit me in my dreams." He shifted slightly, resting his cheek against her forehead.

"Me too."

"I know," he sighed. "I could… feel your distress." He laughed, but the sound was devoid of humour, "How can that be possible? Another perk of being Fae? It's boggling my mind."

Arii was silent for a time, feeling her body tense up against her will. He had mentioned small things like this before, intuition to her feelings that he really should not be able to feel. At first she believed he had the qualities of an empath, but soon realised that he did not display those abilities with anyone but her.

Nem's words echoed in her mind. *"He could be your mate, Arii."*

"Is everything alright?" he whispered, tracing his fingers along her arm in a feather-light caress. She was not ready to explore that possibility yet.

Despite his declaration earlier, she could not shackle him with that knowledge.

So she twisted to rest her chin on her hand, smiling down into his curious, stormy eyes. "Never better."

His smile was gentle, yet his eyes encased flames. He drew her face to his, kissing her so deeply that her toes curled, before breaking away and moving from the bed. Arii watched as he stood, drinking in the hard, defined ridges and shadows of his body with appreciation, even the long, macabre scars down his back. There was nothing she did not love about him, she realised.

Her gaze swept further down. She had seen him plenty tonight, but the sight of him now had her breath stealing away. Everything within her came to life once more.

"I'll back in a moment." He threw a small smile over his shoulder and headed to the adjoining bathroom.

Just as he disappeared, and she considered following to pounce on him like a pesky alley cat, a gentle knock sounded at the door.

"I'm still sleeping," Arii called, pulling the sheet over her head, suppressing a groan.

Roarke's voice came through the door, drily. "I'm hearing your voice, so I'll cut right to the chase. A letter has come for Prince Herington, but he was not in his rooms. Do you know where he is?"

Pulling the sheet back and gnawing on her bottom lip, her eyes drifted to the bathroom as silence stretched. Strange, who would be writing to Elijah? Her first thought was Freya, and then perhaps the princes of the south. Surely it could wait just a little longer? She didn't want their morning to end, tingles still remaining on her swollen lips and elsewhere from his kisses. "He is… a little preoccupied right now, could you leave it at the door?"

Roarke spoke again, and the strange tone of his voice had her sitting up straight in bed, sheets falling around her.

"I don't think this can, nor should it wait, My Lady."

Elijah returned, wearing a towel around his hips, beads of water glistening on his neck and forehead. His brows were furrowed, wariness on his expression. Arii swiftly dressed before he approached the door, opening it wide.

Roarke stood in his full guard regalia; his expression black as he thrust out a small, neatly folded piece of parchment. His gaze swept over Elijah's shoulder to Arii, who decided it best to remain stoic by the window lest her face give away her curiosity.

Elijah flipped the letter, inspecting the wax seal on the back.

His shoulders stiffened.

Roarke bowed low. "Should you need me, I will be by your rooms, Your Highness."

Elijah nodded absently as he gently closed the door, his eyes never breaking way from the letter as he turned, and Arii could feel the change in the air. Magic skittered along his fingers, and she spied his throat working.

Carefully she asked, "Elijah, who is it from?" as she took a step towards him.

His gaze lifted to her, but it took a few moments for him to speak. She could see conflict, anger, grief, even heartbreaking hope, all churning in his expressive eyes. She approached, fingers gently gliding along his hands as he released the letter to her.

She inspected the glittering gold seal stamped on the paper as Elijah spoke low. "The seal is unique, one that looks simple, yet we used this symbol to communicate between one another when I was away on missions for the crown."

She felt his next words hit her square in the chest as he said, "It is from Lorch."

CRESSA

CHAPTER THIRTY-THREE

ARIIAYA

Anticipation warred with apprehension in her stomach as she handed the letter back to Elijah, waiting with bated breath as he gently broke the seal and opened the letter.

Unable to contain her nerves as Elijah's eyes skimmed the neat handwriting, Arii began to pace, shoving a fingernail between her teeth. The letter was for him, and she needed to allow him time to process it before she demanded answers.

His voice was careful as he said, "He wants to meet, in two days' time. Alone."

"Absolutely-fucking-not! It will be a trap!" She exploded.

Elijah's expression showed he knew that this would be her reaction. He read the letter again. "It may not be…"

Anger rose like a viper, her voice a hiss as she swept out a hand. "Don't be naive, Elijah!"

His face snapped up, "This is the first true communication we have had in weeks. I can't just ignore it."

"Of course you can, it's too big a risk!"

She inhaled, a rush of possible scenarios quickening in her mind. Valdis using iron to cage him, torturing him within the confines of a stone dungeon. An army of undead ambushing Elijah, tearing him apart before he could retaliate. It was ridiculous, really. She knew he would not be taken down so easily but her mind was reeling back to Bonemire, to the pain and all she had seen there. The memories almost overpowered her and reduced her to a curled-up ball. Her voice was hardly recognisable as her own as she said, "You *can't* go.

I cannot let you go. Please."

As if he could sense the fire flaring inside her, Elijah's face softened and he placed the letter on the bedside, before taking her hands and skimming thumbs over her palms. "Breathe, Arii."

She inhaled.

Then released.

Repeating a few more times, she looked up at him. His eyes were gentle. Staring at his face slowly calmed her insides, yet her anxiety still remained. "Could you not send a letter back? Meet at more neutral ground where you can take protection with you?"

"I will confide in Kadec and get his opinion on the matter." He cupped her cheek, and she found herself leaning into his touch. "This was not how I envisioned our morning ending…" he whispered.

"It doesn't have to end," she pointed out, but then sighed. "But it must. We have to speak with Kadec."

He nodded, dressing quickly. He looked semiformal, yet slightly unhinged as he passed a hand through his hair and draped his jacket over his shoulder. He turned to her, a crooked smile lighting his rugged features as she tried to untangle the wild knots in her hair with her fingers.

She gave up as someone else knocked. She rose on her toes as his arms enveloped her, curled her fingers in his hair as he pressed his lips to her collarbone. The touch sent a delicious shiver down her spine.

"Miss Trillia? I'm here to help you get ready for breakfast," came Cressa's voice through the wood.

Destined to be interrupted…

"See you at breakfast," Elijah sighed against her lips as they broke apart from a kiss that she wished would never end. He moved for the door, opening it and offering a small bow to Cressa as he passed.

The maid stood stunned, blinking rapidly before coming to her senses and hoisting the clothes in her arms. Then her face changed, a wide smile of wicked delight lighting up her features. "A Prince, well then."

"I would ask that you keep this quiet for now," said Arii, to stop any more chatter as she headed for the nightstand and mirror. She took a seat on the green velvet chair, surveying the perfumes and glittering hair trinkets laid neatly on the dark wood surface.

Cressa picked up a hairbrush and Arii worried her bottom lip between her teeth as the maid tugged at the knots in her hair and smiled. "Don't worry, your secret is safe with me."

Arii glanced at the woman in the reflection of the mirror, eyebrows raising. "Really?"

Cressa placed the hairbrush upon her brow in a mock salute, "Really. Not that I think it makes any difference, Prince Herington can be with whomever he wants until his coronation."

"Until his coronation…" Arii tested.

The woman continued to work, expertly ridding her hair of the tangles until it shone. "Once coronated, he will be required to begin his search for someone of noble birth to marry." As she spoke, Cressa's eyes adopted a faraway look as she stroked the brush down to the tips of Arii's hair. Then she whispered, "Unfortunately."

Arii suddenly recalled the woman's long, sad glances at Kadec as he peacocked in front of the throne last night. Something told her that they were no longer speaking just about Elijah. She was careful, choosing her words with caution as she said, "Prince Kadec… you're in love with him." It was not a question but a keen-eyed assessment.

Cressa dropped the brush as she came out of her reverie. "What?"

Arii turned in her seat, "You're in love with Prince Kadec."

The woman sighed long and hard, "It's that obvious, is it?" Her burnished gold eyes shadowed with sadness. So, they had something in common, it seemed. "It's been years, *so* many years, yet I cannot stop. It began when we were children. He was – still is – my brother's best friend, and through that bond he met me. We grew up together. My father is one of his longest standing advisors, but my mother was a kitchen maid. I know there is no future for us, and there is nothing I can do about it."

"Does he feel the same way?"

"Yes," her eyes were sad, and she continued brushing, "But he has a long, strong Fae bloodline to uphold, one which *I* would surely weaken. I'm not Fae. All I can offer him is my talents with a needle and thread, and perhaps bad jokes to lighten the mood after a dark day."

Arii rounded on the woman with a scowl, "If you love one another, then *that* should be all that matters–" she snapped her lips shut as her own words dawned on her, and the fact that they also could apply to her situation with Elijah. Clearing her throat, she continued with: "Can Kadec not… bend some rules?"

"Perhaps, but there are much more important things going on at the moment. With the darkness blooming in the north and return of Prince Herington, Kadec must focus on ensuring we all survive the coming storm." She smiled ruefully, placing the brush down beside Arii's clenched fists. "Perhaps we can think about our future when that future is a little more certain."

She was right.

"I'll draw you a bath, and once you're done, I will have some clean gowns for you to choose from. Don't worry, I brought everything but the colour pink." Cressa tipped her head with a smile, but it did not meet her eyes as she left Arii alone with the chaos of her thoughts.

ELIJAH

Her skin was like silk, her lips made of satin as they explored his body, her touch confident in bringing him pleasure. He did not remember his mind ever being so quiet, yet so chaotic at the same time. He had wanted to take her, then and there, and gods he had been seconds from breaking his own stupid vow. But against the rampage of his beast he was relentless, telling himself over and over that this woman – this stunning, fierce, incredible woman – her heart forged of steel and her tongue of silver, deserved to be shown just how special she was to him.

To Elijah, who rarely opened his heart let alone shared his bed, this meant that when they finally took that final step, it would be somewhere where he could fully let go. The beast inside – the Fae side of him – was like a pacing wolf inside a cage, desperate to be let free. It was a feeling that he found hard to explain, and for a strange reason he was reluctant to discuss it with Arii, for he only felt that way around her and no other.

Every time they were alone, he feared the very fine tether binding him with his control would snap, and what could be unleased would be devastating. He was not sure what would transpire if he allowed that to happen, so he was trying incredibly hard to pick a time and a place where there would be no… casualties.

Surely it was not normal, this feeling bordering on obsession. He understood why she had attempted to put distance between them before, and one of the reasons was surely because of the distraction she caused him. There was still so much for him to learn about himself and the Fae. The fact that there was a secret society of his kind hiding, surviving until they could finally emerge once more, solidified the urgency for him to focus on the events at hand.

Conflict raged inside him. He wanted to spend as much time with Arii as he could, for these moments could be their last. Then there was the significance of his training, the trials and his growing magic.

And the shadow of madness that would one day bring him undone.

Every day that passed, the stronger his magic was becoming, and Arii's words early on in their journey rang in his head; *"Magic is like a muscle, the more you use it, the stronger it will become."*

He recalled her expression after he had read the note from Lorch. Her violet eyes encased flames, and the hard set of her jaw brooked no argument. So, he agreed – not only to appease her, but to toss the pros and cons over in his own mind.

Now, alone in his rooms, he opened the letter again and sat on his bed, staring at the neat and achingly familiar script.

Elijah,

We were brothers once, and because of this I will allow you the chance to explain your side of the story. Meet me just beyond Border Town in two days' time.

Alone.

Your brother,
Lorch.

His eyes tore from the letter to the open, velvet lined box beside him. To the oval stone within. He hovered a hand over the Void Stone, watching the little galaxy of stars flare to life at the mere nearness of his touch. A bead of water dripped from his still-wet hair, falling onto the glass surface, and he stared as the orb flashed briefly with light, and he swore he could see thunder clouds rolling inside, little flashes of lightning sparking wildly. He blinked as the bead of water was absorbed into the stone.

What in the hell...

A knock sounded at his door, and Elijah placed the letter inside the box before closing the lid. "Enter," he said as he stood, buttoning up his tunic.

Roarke came in, his demeanour all business. "I am to accompany you to dinner, Your Highness."

Elijah shrugged on a royal blue vest over his white shirt, folding the cuffs with deft fingers, "Not necessary, Roarke, but appreciated."

The two men walked down the hallway, afternoon sun dappling the walls with orange and gold. He could hear excited voices up ahead speaking over one another. As he entered the room, riotous laughter assaulted his ears, and he could not help a smile.

A large table was piled high with an array of food set upon polished silverware. Three whole turkeys basted with herbs sat on a bed of leafy greens, ringed with roasted potatoes in a thick, fragrant white sauce. Bowls of vibrant green salad sat to one side with sliced tomatoes and purple onions sprinkled with a crumbly white cheese. Dishes of thinly sliced venison and freshly baked bread rolls twisted into golden knots accompanied trays of lightly charred vegetables. An abundance of fruits and delicate pastries showered with icing sugar completed the offering, amongst beautiful flower arrangements.

Elijah found his stomach gurgling in anticipation as he joined his friends.

Tikkani threw back glasses of wine as Luc and Quinn cheered her on, laughing. Emerson pinched the bridge of his nose, but Elijah could see a smile behind his hand as the elf shook his head. Krepth and Nem sat nearby, deep in conversation, the Shifter animatedly using his hands to explain a story, while Nem nodded, allowing a tiny smile.

Elijah's eyes found Arii, in a light, silky dress the colour of a robin's egg, a dusty shade of blue that complemented her olive skin tone. The bodice hugged her tightly, before flaring lightly at the hips, a veil of tulle draping like mist to the floor.

Her eyes soon found his too, and he could see her cheeks becoming rosy under his gaze. She looked feminine, beautiful, radiant... absolutely enchanting. Her hair cascaded down in honey-tipped waves, a delicate piece of sparkling, layered jewellery woven into her hair and across her forehead. She turned, leaving Kadec and Nocturne by a table of wine, to walk towards him. Her confident swagger and the look on her face had him blinking as words failed to climb his throat.

She threw up a finger before he could speak. "Before you say anything, I was given a choice between this–" She swept her hand down the front of her, "–or something akin to a frilly nightmare the colour of baby vomit." She glared quickly in Nem's direction, longingly sliding her eyes over the woman's attire. "I miss pants."

"It has only been a few days."

She ignored that. "There is a positive though." She grinned, her canines glinting as her hands disappeared into the fabric at her sides, before she swished the dress. "It has pockets!"

Elijah chuckled, watching the smile that such a simple yet unexpected feature brought to her face. Gods, he was finding that he was beginning to live for that rare smile. "Let's be honest, Nem may have threatened death upon her maid if she was to be made to wear a dress again."

Arii snorted a laugh, "You know her well."

"And I know *you*, Arii. You aren't completely wretched about wearing a dress." He accepted a glass of wine from a server, smiling in thanks before bringing the amber liquid to his lips.

Arii tsked and accepted a glass also, unable to mask the humour in her eyes. "Ah, you have uncovered my deepest, darkest secret. I must admit, I *do* feel beautiful."

Elijah gazed at her over the rim of his glass, his eyes darkening, "As much as I love the dress on you, I do prefer you *without* it."

Her cheeks flared a deeper shade of pink, and he felt a hum of satisfaction from his beast.

"Behave, Your Highness," she chided, but the smile never left her face.

There was a loud, unanimous cheer. Luc punched the air as Tikkani swigged the last glass in the row before her, throwing her hands up in triumph.

Elijah's brows rose as he took a seat.

Arii sat beside him, enjoying watching the commotion.

"No liquor from the north nor the west can bring me down," announced Tikkani, throwing up a hand into a slightly intoxicated salute.

The feeling in the room was light, a reprieve from the burdens they all carried. Elijah knew it would be short-lived, returning with sore heads tomorrow.

Kadec soon joined them, followed by Nocturne.

Elijah kept his gaze from the dark-haired man, for he did not trust himself not to show his dislike. Jealousy was foreign to him, and he was not familiar with preventing it. It was easier to ignore Noct for now.

The maid, Cressa, entered the room and approached Roarke, who stood guard nearby. Similar guards in plain uniform were stationed about the room in silent watchfulness. The curvy, pretty woman handed Roarke a bread roll with melted cheese on top. Roarke tried to refuse, but the woman pressed the snack into his palm. Elijah heard her say, "Eat, brother! Honestly, mother would be turning in her grave if she knew how frequently you skipped meals."

Roarke blushed as he whispered, "Thank you, Cressa."

The maid nodded, spinning on her heel to head back towards the doors, but not before her eyes halted on Kadec, and Elijah saw the moment that passed between them.

It was sadness and regret tinged with longing.

The Prince recovered as the maid retreated, to say, "There was the strangest storm last night. A peculiar riot of rain that very nearly damaged my rose bushes in the castle gardens." Kadec speared venison into his mouth, eyes skipping to Elijah as he chewed and swallowed, before continuing, "Did you happen to bring some bad weather with you, Eliverus?"

Tikkani pointed her fork from Elijah to Arii as she said around a mouthful, "Oh, that has happened a few times, that's because they were close to fucki–" Emerson slapped a hand over Tikkani's mouth just in time.

Kadec bellowed a laugh in response as Arii melted like gravy into her chair. Elijah cleared his throat awkwardly, taking a bite of a cinnamon-dusted sugar bun and looking anywhere but at his friends.

How embarrassing.

Elijah pressed his mind to wander, keeping his features indifferent as he thought about how he had adopted a sweet tooth since their arrival here. Then his mind shot back to the conversation at hand like a thunderclap.

Close? How could they possibly know they had been *close* to…
Arii.

His head tilted in her direction, and he spoke through the corner of his mouth – his voice low so that only she could hear, "And I thought Tikkani was the one without a filter between her brain and her mouth… but you? I'm surprised."

She huffed defensively, "I cannot control what Nem feels through the bond, let alone what she says to Krepth–" her voice rose slowly and steadily as she sat up in her chair and leaned forward, eyeballing the wolf Shifter across the table, "–who then cannot keep his *big fucking mouth* shut!"

Krepth's face lit with a devilish grin and he leaned back in his chair. That only seemed to stoke Arii's flame as she motioned to her eyes, then pointed at her oldest friend with a very dramatic finger. "Sleep with one eye open, dog!"

Elijah loosed a sigh as insults began to fly over the table, turning from the embarrassing scene to converse with Kadec. He confided in him about the letter, to which Kadec advised it best to send a messenger in his stead. His keen Fae hearing picked up the accented lilt of Nocturne's voice as the man chuckled and said, "Now, this is entertaining, and it's worth returning to if you all survive the impending storm."

His words had Elijah's mind drifting to dark places, images of the bleak wasteland that Kadec had shown him during the trials levitating behind his eyes. The mood of the room remained light, conversation shifting from their love life to the topic of weddings. Luc described a large wedding in Evergrave, surrounded by friends, family, the entire population of the town, and extending the invitation to the other courts too. Emerson argued a smaller, more intimate affair. Nonetheless, Elijah felt a dark cloud form and linger on his back.

As the dinner concluded and their party shifted to plush lounges in a nook nearby, Elijah tried to keep up a mask of interest to cover the slowly building determination flaring inside his chest. Roarke stood nearby, and he motioned for the guard to accompany him. The man obliged, slipping beside him. "Your Highness?"

"Ready a horse and order a ferry to depart before dawn, Captain. Discreetly."

The man nodded, not a flicker of a pause as he accepted the undertone of an order in Elijah's deep voice. For that, he was grateful. He did not need questions being raised, and in that moment, he required unfaltering compliance. The man was a loyal soldier, and Elijah noted to thank him should he return tomorrow.

The night came to an end with the group bidding each other goodnight and heading in the direction of their rooms. Emerson propped up his happily intoxicated fiancé, grinning as the young man said loudly, "I can't wait to marry you, Emmy," before placing a wet kiss on his cheek, which earned him a soft giggle.

"Did you touch your wine at all?" Arii observed, silently sliding beside Elijah as they headed towards their quarters. He hadn't even heard her approach, and he cursed his momentary slip in alertness and hoped she had not heard his conversation with Roarke.

"Though I enjoy a glass or two, old soldier habits die hard. I prefer to remain alert but I don't mind being your designated arm to guide your wobbly steps, though."

"My steps aren't–" she muffled a curse as she tilted, clutching his arm for support. She sighed and pressed her cheek to his bicep, "Fiine…"

He let the warmth of her touch seep through to his skin, but unlike times previously, he found it didn't quite touch his guilty heart. They walked in silence back to his rooms, the gentle swishing of Arii's dress like a metronome to the chaos in his mind.

Later, as the stars emerged and the silence of night took hold, Elijah watched as silver light from the rising moon slowly made its way across the dip of her waist and shoulders as they rose and fell in sleep. He made a choice then that he knew would require him to seek her mercy later and do whatever he could to earn that trust back. He had to accept Lorch's invitation of a meeting. He had to try, or he would spend his days wondering if he had missed an opportunity to prevent bloodshed.

Perhaps prevent a *war*.

If he could end this war before it was to begin – peacefully – then it was a risk he was willing to take.

CHAPTER THIRTY-FOUR

ARIIAYA

Her hand glided over the cool sheets beside her as she emerged from sleep, the surprise of finding them empty pulling her quickly to consciousness. "Elijah?" she called around a yawn, sitting up and stretching. Her mind wandered to the night just passed, the gentle kisses they had shared just before drifting to sleep wrapped up in each other. For the first time in her life, Arii had felt content… as if she were truly *home*. At first, she had thought home to be a place or a building, but she soon realised it didn't have to just be a place, it could be a *someone* too.

Thanks to her swift Fae healing, she seemed to have escaped an alcohol-induced headache, thank the gods. Instead, her heart began to increase its tempo. When no answer came to her call, she looked around, eyes narrowing as she noticed his clothing – which had been draped neatly over the back of the nearby settee when they had retired for the night – were gone.

"Guard," she called, and a soldier opened the door and poked his head into the room.

"Miss?"

"Where is Prince Herington?"

"He exited your rooms a little while ago, Miss Trillia. Said he'd be back but it's been an hour or two now."

"Has he called a meeting with Prince Brolikian?"

"Negative, Miss. The prince is still retired."

Dread began to pool heavily as her eyes drifted to the dark world outside her window. There was the faintest trace of light over the gardens below, hinting that the rising sun was not far away.

"Send word to ready a ferry and two horses, urgently," Arii barked, and the man nodded before disappearing.

Could he have slipped away to meet with Lorch, despite her expressing that it was an extremely bad idea?

Arii swiftly dressed, and as she pulled her tunic over her head, Nem blew into her room – dressed and ready with steel at her hips. "He's gone, hasn't he?" her best friend said simply.

Lips pressed into a hard line, Arii did not need to respond as the woman continued. "I can feel your distress, your anger, Ariiaya. If we are swift, we may just prevent a war from starting right at the border."

Arii had confided in Nem last night and told her all about the letter. Krepth had been near, so she had told him, too. They had taken the same stance as she – agreeing it was definitely a trap.

Shit.

She didn't dawdle, hoisting pack and weapons over her shoulder as they moved quickly down the dark hall. Krepth soon joined them, lifting his hood as he appeared, from the room which she swore had been assigned to Nem. Their link told Arii all she needed to know about their relationship, and she knew that they had been harbouring feelings for some time. Nem and Krepth, like herself and Elijah, butted heads frequently, but she knew they adored each other fiercely, and she also knew, like herself and Elijah, they felt that undeniable pull to one another – like moths to flame.

Arii's fear reached a crescendo, bringing with it a knee-jerk response of anger. "I should have known he was contemplating meeting him. He was distracted last night. Goddess, how could I have been so blind?"

"How long ago did he leave?" said Krepth, keeping pace as castle servants passed them in the halls.

"Not long," Nem checked the straps of her weapon belt as they went, "But we need to hurry. Valdis may have him already. Gods know that Lorch would not be meeting Elijah alone and would have brought a force with him."

Arii's chest tightened further with fear for him, making her breaths short and sharp. Would they execute him right on the outskirts of Border Town? Or would the take him back to Viridya and make an example of him? Knowing Valdis' taste for theatrics, Arii assumed the latter.

She pressed her way out into the crisp morning air, sucking in small, measured breaths as they headed for the harbor. She did not have time to hyperventilate, they needed to get to Elijah as quickly as possible.

As they alighted the steps that lead to the docks where they had arrived days before, she was thankful to see a small barge with horses safely tethered to sturdy poles, ready to transport them. As the ferryman signalled from the shore that he was about to sail, they hopped aboard, drawing up their cloaks.

"As quickly as you can, please," urged Nem to the man, and he nodded as she pressed silver coins into his wrinkled palm.

The short trip over the waves seemed to drag as Arii leaned over the side of the ferry, hair flying in ripples behind her as she urged it on.

Once on the barnacled docks on the mainland, Krepth's hand gripped at her sleeve. "Arii, we cannot just barge in, we need to scope out their forces first."

All rational thought faded from her head as visions of what they could be doing to Elijah flashed before her eyes, and with those thoughts in mind, she turned on her friend with a snarl on her face. Before she could say anything, Krepth grabbed her hand and held her fingers tight. "We need to approach with caution, little Fury. Nem will remain in town, and if all goes to shit, she will know because of her connection to you. She can begin an evacuation of the people there if need be."

Gods, she had not even thought of the innocent townspeople, who would be caught in the crossfire should a battle begin. She cursed her single-minded focus in that moment as she nodded to Krepth, offering a quick, appreciative smile.

Then she chewed her lip as her gaze darted from her friend to the road leading out of the town.

"Let's hope it won't come to that. Quickly, we need to hurry."

ELIJAH

He looked like the Lorch he remembered, yet he also did not.

The man sat astride Caviar, the black stallion Elijah once claimed as his own, and he sat with a rigid back. Lorch's eyes were hard as ice – their depths filled with the shadows of inescapable horrors that he had no doubt seen, and shiny with betrayal. His copper hair lacked its usual healthy shine, and his cheeks were sallow – the bones protruding sharply beneath eyes bruised with emotional exhaustion.

Flanked by a severe looking man with closely cropped blonde hair – no doubt Elijah's replacement – and a contingent of undead, who swayed in wait of their orders. Within the mass stood a Kryvern, a large tear on its chest where a Nexus Crystal replaced its heart.

Elijah met them in a morning mist, a lone figure of one against dozens.

He had retained hope that Lorch would meet him alone, peacefully, but now he realised it was but the hope of a fool. He would not attend this meeting alone. Surprisingly, Elijah noted that Valdis was nowhere to be seen.

Perhaps he would have a chance to sway Lorch after all.

Lorch pulled the reins of his mount as the beast stomped its hooves in agitation, the light of dawn glinting off his gold crown as Elijah stepped from the brush, hands raised as the King's forces shifted. Glowing blue eyes snapped his way – yet the animated corpse soldiers did not move to attack.

Lorch's eyes swept the empty space around his old friend, lip twitching as he spoke, "You were always one to follow orders to a fault, Elijah, I see that has not changed."

"What has changed is your lack of integrity, Lorch." He nodded towards the soldiers, "You said you would meet me alone."

"And leave myself defenceless to Fae scum? Unlikely."

"Those are not your words, Lorch, but those of someone else who has been blinded by hate and blood." His meaning was not missed on Lorch, who shifted in his saddle, brows narrowing.

"She is not with you," the King whispered.

Elijah knew who he referred to. It was not a question, so he did not answer, instead waving a hand towards the bodies surrounding Lorch. "Come down from your mount, brother, let us speak on level ground. I will not hurt you, you have my word."

Lorch passed his eye over the man at his flank, the commander, who replied wordlessly with a shake of his head. When the King's gaze fell on Elijah once more, his face was further devoid of emotion. "No, I do not trust you like I once did, Elijah. You paraded by my side under the guise of a human man, but unbeknownst to me you were in fact the very thing we have been working to eradicate."

"Eradicate? Lorch, listen to me, the Fae are not a threat." He suddenly thought better of his next words, changing his mind as to not give away those hiding away in secret. "There are no males left."

"Until *you.*"

"I had no knowledge of what I truly was. No memories of my past to figure that out."

Lorch's hand cut through the air, and he bellowed, "*Liar*! You are a fucking liar! It is so obvious now. The hood, the hiding of your face. Gods, how could I have been so blind!"

Elijah held his head high – even though the words punched against his heart as if it were a straw dummy in a training ring.

"You knew you were different, and you never once confided in me. You were my brother in every sense but blood!" Lorch continued, spittle flying from his lips as anger overtook him.

"And how do you think that would have gone down with your father?" Elijah shot back, anger bubbling within him too. Anger and hurt, not only for what he had put his best friend through – but for the secret he had been unknowingly harbouring for so long. "Once we figured out who I was, he would have killed me, Lorch."

"I would not have allowed it!"

"Yet you allow him to desecrate innocent lives and bring them back with the magic we feared for so long, all to fill the ranks of his army. *His* army, Lorch, not yours!"

"He is protecting us–"

"From what?" Elijah bellowed, stepping forward, "From an uprising of evil? Lorch – he *is* the uprising of evil that you all fear, and his is going to *destroy* this land and all we hold dear."

Lorch's hands pressed to his temples, as if the words physically inflicted pain.

Elijah swallowed, hating seeing his friend so tormented. Taking a step forward, he lifted a hand, pleading. "You can help us end the darkness before it consumes us all. Come with me, Lorch. Magic is wild and wonderous, not at all what I once thought. Not only can it heal mortal wounds, but it can make life *better*. Let me show you what I have learned. Please." He did not mention the possibility of madness with the amount he possessed, but that would be a subject to broach *if* he could calm Lorch's building storm.

Elijah summoned his power with his hand outstretched, generating a sparkling crystal ball of light on his palm. The ball gradually transformed into the image of a stag, rearing on its hind legs as sparkles glistened around its antlers. "See?"

Lorch was silent for a few moments, watching the display as the soldiers shifted around him. Then his eyes lifted to meet Elijah's. What Elijah saw within them was haunting. A flash of desperate pleading mixed with the slightest spark of surprise.

He was still in there somewhere, he had to be.

Lorch shifted, squaring his shoulders as he whispered, "It is too late." The words were so soft that had it not been for Elijah's heightened hearing, he would not have caught them.

"Guards, seize the traitor at once."

The magic dissipated and Elijah's hands fell to his sides. The few men who were not mindless shells converged towards him with weapons drawn.

"Over my dead, stinking corpse."

She stepped from the forest behind, daggers already drawn and eyes alight with purple fire.

Ariiaya.

She shifted to stand in front of him, and Elijah saw Lorch's eyes narrow at the sight of his old flame. Tongue darting across his lips, Lorch's hands tightened on the reins as he leaned forward. "*That* can be arranged. Hello, my dear saviour."

His eyes shifted again and Elijah tilted his head to see Krepth appear beside him. The Shifter met his eyes briefly, his gaze telling Elijah everything he already knew. *You couldn't expect her to stay back.*

Arii hitched her chin, no fear and all determination as she stared down the small army before them like they were *nothing*, her body language screaming what words need not.

If you want to hurt him, you'll need to go through me.

"Lorch, listen to him. You know your family has no true right to be on the throne. Your father orchestrated the slaughter of Elij... Eliverus' family – the *rightful* rulers of the north." Arii's voice carried across the short clearing as she stepped forward. "Please, allow him to take up his place upon the throne and bring back balance to Fythnar."

Elijah was surprised she had allowed this brief time to negotiate. But he did not need to see her face to know that emotions were raging through her at the sight of the King. She cared for him, deeply.

"Please, Lorch, let's talk about this."

There was a pregnant pause as Lorch frowned, his throat working on the words. Elijah could see that he was fighting a war within.

Finally, the golden King said, "You didn't kill me, even though that was your reason for being in my castle in the first place. Why?"

"Why?" Arii didn't mask the pain in her voice, letting it coat her words. "Because I grew to care for you, Lorch. And I learned quickly that you weren't deserving of your fate." A pause, before she swallowed audibly. "I *still* care for you. I never meant for things to go the way they did, I never meant to hurt you–"

"But you did!" bellowed Lorch, causing the bodies behind him to twitch with phantom agitation. "You broke me, you tore my heart apart."

Arii's head shook. "I'm so sorry."

Elijah stepped forward, his fingers lacing with Arii's as he moved to her side, a united front, always. "This does not need to end in bloodshed, Lorch. Stand down your army."

Lorch's gaze dropped to their clasped hands, a quiver on his lip. When Elijah followed his gaze, he felt dread knot in the pit of his stomach as Lorch muttered, "This was *always* going to end in bloodshed, Elijah."

Elijah realised his mistake.

Lorch had been waiting for confirmation of his relationship with Arii, and he had just given it to him. The simple gesture of their twined fingers spoke volumes. Elijah should have known that Lorch's infatuation with Arii would cloud his normally clear judgement.

It was about her, and always had been.

"Lorch," Elijah warned, feeling a shift in the air as the King nudged his mount, twisting to his commander.

"Seize him! Seize them *both*, bring them to me alive!"

The soldiers and undead charged, just as a crow cried and took flight overhead.

Krepth shifted with a flash of light, maw agape with a ripped snarl, hackles flying up as Arii and Elijah armed themselves.

The undead were upon them first, their eagerness at being unleashed making them frenzied. Dressed in armour and armed with swords, they moved with wicked swiftness and chilling screams.

Arii flew forward first, a blur to Elijah's eyes as she used her blades to slam the first man's sword aside. The thing faltered with a cry and before he could recover, her blades were crossed at his neck. With one swift jerk, the daggers severed its head from its neck, showering her leathers in black blood. Arii booted the soldier in the chest, a feral snarl tearing from her bared teeth.

Once he would have blanched at the ferocity he saw in her. Now…
now he saw her as she was.

A fucking goddess of war.

Elijah summoned his power, the snap of sparks alighting on the
blade of his withdrawn sword as he met two human soldiers, a black
blur showering him in dust as Krepth flew at another undead man.
The two humans he struck swords with were wide-eyed behind their
helmets, the reflection of blue highlighting their fear.

As he angled his sword to block their unified blow, Elijah pleaded,
"Stand down and you will not be harmed. You are only following
orders – I am trying to prevent what has befallen your comrades!"

"We can't," is all one of them said, his voice familiar as they
reformed their assault.

Sykes.

They targeted his flank as a third moved in to circle him. A clink
of metal drew Elijah's attention, a pair of heavy manacles glinting in
the morning light.

Iron.

Abandoning thoughts of reasoning with them, Elijah snapped into
offensive mode. He could feel the shackles near, as if the air around
them were being absorbed into them like a sponge. He could not
allow them anywhere near him, or Arii.

He hurled himself at the men, connecting the pommel of his sword
with the guts of one, watching him crumple like a sack of bones before
he stuck out at Sykes with a punch of magic. Sykes flew backwards
through the air, landing heavily at Lorch's feet.

The soldier with the shackles stood rooted to the spot, knees
quaking like a newborn foal.

Before Elijah could act, twin blades thumped through the man
from behind, their tips peeking through slowly blooming flowers of
blood on his heaving chest. The man jerked and crumpled, revealing
a heavily breathing Arii behind.

The man hadn't even been armoured properly, he realised with a
start.

The undead soldiers though wore glimmering plate armour splattered with gore where they lay headless. It was bleakly obvious to Elijah then that Valdis valued his already dead men over those who used up his precious resources.

"It seems you will not come willingly – so I will offer you a deal." Lorch cried.

Elijah prepared himself for a second onslaught, or perhaps the unleashing of the Kryvern salivating in the wings of their battalion.

With a wave of Lorch's hand, two soldiers brought forth a person in chains.

Elijah's heart leaped into his throat, and it took every ounce of will to keep his face emotionless as the soldiers dragged his mother to the head of their contingent.

Colleen.

Her hair was matted and her usually immaculate maids' uniform soiled with holes and blood. She had been their prisoner, and they had not been gentle. Anger warred with sudden hatred inside him, but all that surfaced on the outside was grief.

Taking a step forward, Elijah lifted a hand, his voice gruff with emotion. "Mother?"

Colleen, despite her frail frame, shrugged against her captors, and her gentle eyes met his. Defiance was alight in their depths, depths he knew so well, which shimmered with love for the boy she had found in the forest. He was not her son by blood but she had cared for him like he was her own. She had saved and raised him without a word of complaint, watching him grow and thrive, even though she must have known he was different.

"Eli, you cannot go with them. You *must* not. Do not worry about me."

Elijah's voice shook. "Let her go!"

"If you come with us now, no harm will come to her," Lorch shifted, watching the exchange with a strange look in his eyes. A look Elijah would later register as apprehension and doubt. Lorch knew this woman like a second mother, her kindness extending beyond her adoptive son and to everyone who knew her.

He would not harm her.

Surely not.

The men shoved Colleen to her knees on the road, and one drew an axe – the sound grating down his spine like nails on stone. The Kryvern shifted nearby, nostrils flaring at the scent of acrid fear and tension on the air, flanks quivering with anticipation of blood.

Elijah shifted, so close to agreeing to Lorch's request – the words on the tip of his tongue as Arii's hand gently touched his arm. "Elijah, you can't go with him. You know that."

Swallowing back bile. He knew her words to be true.

But he had to save his mother.

"We can come to another arrangement, Lorch. No one needs to get hurt."

"No one will get hurt if you *submit*." He drew out the word in a snapped hiss.

"I cannot. You know I cannot. If I do, darkness will descend upon the north and the rest of Fythnar will follow."

"Then you leave me no choice."

Lorch's words were soft on a sigh of resignation, and without hesitation he turned to his soldiers and lifted a hand.

Colleen braced, spine rigid, wisps of hair slicking against her face, fingers clutching the dirt as her pleading eyes locked with her son's and she whispered, "Be the man you were always meant to be. Bring back magic." She jerked forward against her bonds as she yelled, "Long live the true King of the North, Eliverus Herington!"

Then she whispered, "I love you, my son."

And the axe came down.

Silence.

His mind was nothing but droning silence.

Buzzing filled his ears, drowning out all other sound as her head hit the dirt with a *thump*. He blinked, trying to comprehend what he was seeing as the world warped into slow motion.

He shouldn't have come here.

This was all his fault.

All *his* fault.

Her body slumped to the ground, blood gushing from her severed neck in rivulets, blooming a swift pool of crimson around her still-twitching form. Her head came to a stop a few feet away. Light brown hair fanned around her face, sightless eyes turned to the sky, her jaw slack in a silent scream. Never to breathe again.

No.

No.

No no no no no.

Beside him, chaos reigned as Arii's scream shuddered against the numbness seeping through his mind, through his body and into his bones like acrid mist. The buzzing intensified, and Elijah dimly registered Arii's hands grasping before she was wrenched away.

Something sprayed against his neck and the side of his face, a showering of blood that shot from a soldier's slit throat under Arii's striking dagger, but the feeling barely registered.

He just stared at her body.

At his mother's headless, lifeless body.

She was dead.

The realisation hit him deep.

And he *ruptured*.

Numbness within his chest flickered to an ember then swiftly erupted into an inferno as Elijah's glassy eyes lifted to his childhood friend. His best friend. Once his King. His brother.

Then he welcomed sheer chaos as pain – as overwhelming *rage* – took over.

His scream was inhuman as he fell to his knees and allowed the magic and the madness to take over.

Elijah's fists slammed to the dirt, his bellow bringing forth sheer oblivion as the earth trembled beneath their feet and magic rocketed out in a raging blanket of blue fire.

The Kryvern and the soldiers that rushed them vanished into quivering mist, as if they had never existed, nothing but fine bloody dust on the soil, taking out half of Lorch's force in the blink of an eye.

The King's mount reared with a cry, and Lorch held on as the ranks of his soldiers blew into disarray. Fissures snaked out from where Elijah knelt in the soil, tearing open, swallowing numerous undead soldiers into the earth.

The King's eyes flew over the chaos, seeing his forces diminishing with each passing second.

"My King!" yelled the commander. "We must retreat!"

Lorch seemed to retain enough sense to realise the man was right.

"Fall back!" He grasped the amulet from under his tunic and lifted it into the air. The stone within flared with light as he commanded, "Back to the castle, now."

His gaze found Elijah once more, and even with the distance and the pandemonium lashing the air, Elijah heard his words as if spoken by his ear. "Let this prove my worth to you, father."

With a cry, Lorch spun his horse, sending the mount barrelling in retreat.

Sheer agony warred with blinding anger to leave him numb on all fours, images flashing before his eyes as he dragged himself towards his mother.

Colleen tending to his wounds after taking him in, placing cool cloths against his skin as his little body battled against the trauma of his ravaged skin.

The blinding pain of too much magic seared his veins, tore at his lungs and nerve endings as white dotted his vision, yet he forced his arms to work, to bring him closer to where she lay.

Colleen brushing his mop of hair over his ears and dusting dirt from his knees. "You are different, Elijah, and being different is not such a bad thing."

He drew near, tears pricking, dirt mixing with blood on his hands as he stared down.

"They will not pick on you forever, my little Prince. Never let others allow you to feel any less than what you are, and that – my son – is someone bound for the extraordinary."

His hands began to shake, vision blurry with burning hot tears.

"Death is a part of life, Elijah. One day I will no longer be here in body – but I will always remain with you here." She pressed a hand to his teenage chest, on a day he had felt incredibly alone.

Pain had his breath coming in shuddering gasps as he brushed Colleen's hair from her sightless eyes.

She grasped his hand and held it tight, her eyes like granite as she pressed a hand to his chest. "Steel your heart and trust what is inside you, Elijah."

How could he trust his heart when it was now surely and irrevocably broken?

He could feel the agony tearing through his steel defences; defences he had only ever let slip for a handful of people.

Now, he no longer cared to guard himself.

Tears cascaded down his cheeks as Elijah whispered his fingertips over his mother's eyelids, leaning into the mud to press his forehead to hers. As his sob broke the silence of the clearing, a woman stepped into his vision, blocking a ray of the midday sun.

At first he thought it was Arii, coming to help ease his agony after the army's retreat.

But something did not *feel* right.

His eyes trailed from the woman's immaculately polished boots up the pitch-black assassin's garb to stop upon her face.

It stole the breath from his lungs.

For the face he saw was that of his long dead sister.

"Ghila?"

His sister's lips curled in a sardonic smile as she stepped forward. Her hands clasped his face, nails digging into his skin as she said "Hello, brother."

His pain peaked to something beyond agony, beyond this realm, turning his mind to shadowed dust.

She forced her way passed his sundered defences and into his mind, sinking her talons deep as darkness took hold of all he knew. Everything he was. Everything around him. Shock allowed her into his mind as easily as stepping through an open door. She was a black tidal wave of darkness, her mind a force of acidic madness as his vision clouded at the edges.

He began to scream.

The last thing Elijah saw was his sister's wide, steel grey eyes – so much like his own – as a blackness claimed him.

Taking him away.

ARIIAYA

Before his retreat, Ari swore she saw regret in his expression as Lorch kicked his heels into his mount and the remnants of his battalion turned to flee. That small, fleeting look spoke volumes, and told Arii that there was still a slither of the man she knew. If only she had the chance to speak with him, but amongst the pandemonium, that was not possible.

This had not gone the way she thought it would, at all. She had expected a trap, but not the murder of his mother and then Elijah's complete combustion that turned half Lorch's contingent into bloody mist. No, absolutely not.

Elijah's yell rose high in the clearing. Arii wrenched her blades from the chest of a fallen solider, wiping the weapon on her blood-stained pants as she twisted and broke into a run to find him.

There, on the road beside his mother's headless body, a woman leaned over his shaking form, her hands clasping his face as tendrils of darkness slithered around her like black ink.

Confusion quickly overtook Arii's panic as the woman spoke to Elijah. "Rise."

That voice, she knew it – still heard it like a ghost in her nightmares. A long-nailed caress that broke skin and left blood in its wake. The wraith. This was the wraith who had plagued her mind, who whispered doubts and promises of death.

Elijah began to stand at her command, head bowed, static sizzling along his bloodstained leathers as he turned to her.

Slowly.

Painfully slowly.

Arii saw the wicked smile that afflicted the woman's beautiful face as she shifted behind him, her features but a flash as Arii's focus honed solely on the face she knew so well.

On the eyes that saw through to her soul.

They had changed. Flat, devoid of the glitter of life that usually pierced the grey storm. Now nothing but clouds, pupils disappearing behind hazy mist set in low-lidded orbs. Soulless, like granite.

His eyes were not his eyes at all.

"Elijah?" Arii whispered.

His face – his face was not the same either. As a slow smirk curved the corners of his lips in a look she had never seen before, she felt something tear apart in the depths of her soul, to leave nothing but a feeble thread behind.

A blanket of frost shuddered over her heart as Elijah blinked, nothing but a promise of cold death in his eyes.

He smiled in a way that was wholly unfamiliar.

This man was not Elijah.

The man she knew, the man she loved was *gone*.

CELADINE

EPILOGUE

CELADINE

The small room was hot – almost stiflingly so – as a woman tossed and turned upon a tiny bed. The scent of herbs was thick in the air as the woman flopped onto her side, brows scrunched, her thick, brown hair a wild tangle of curls stuck to her sweaty forehead.

Normally the medicinal plants that overflowed from the shop out the front and into her room would offer her a comfort from the dreams that sometimes plagued her overactive sleep, but tonight they were of no help.

It had been an unusually busy day, which had prevented her from fixing her usual sleeping draught. Today, unlike other days where she was but a helper in the background, she was called upon to deliver a pain draught directly to the King. That small interaction alone had taken the most out of her. She had never seen the man up close before, having only spied glimpses whenever her services were called to the castle. But today, when she had lain eyes upon their ruler, she knew he was becoming a ghost of himself. She did not know Lorch Kruel well, but even she could tell that his shoulders had become plagued by a heaviness that had not there before.

When she arrived home late, her bones laced with fatigue, she had foolishly sprawled upon her bed, thinking she would rest her eyes for but a moment.

Sleep had claimed her as soon as her head hit the lumpy pillow.

And then the dream – no, the *nightmare* – began soon after.

There was blood and fire and chaos, and no matter where she looked, she saw bodies, countless bodies sprawled across the rubble of the destroyed castle courtyard. Her gaze flew across them, her heart thumping in time with the drums that thundered upon the golden walls above. Screams filled the air, pleading voices mixed with inhuman sounds that she knew would follow her beyond this dream.

She broke into a run, passing more bodies as her bare feet slapped the cobblestones. Her eyes lifted, desperate to avoid seeing the faces of women, children and men – broken, bleeding and desperate – and instead she focused on the path ahead.

She knew not where she was going, knew not her destination as she streaked past the town square and the temporary gallows, an empty noose swinging on a breeze.

She gasped for air as she dashed towards the open front gates, the massive doors blown off their hinges, barely holding on.

She wailed as she passed the threshold, for what she saw before her had her heart stuttering in her chest.

The town – her *home* – connected to Viridya castle was in utter, chaotic ruin. Fires consumed buildings as people fled, smoke polluting the air. Guts splattered the stone streets and blood coated the walls of homes and shops, shattered glass glittering like crystals on the roads. Bodies were littered here too, so many lives ripped from existence by unimaginable violence, as sparks and ash drifted in the air.

All the devastation she saw could not prepare her for what was next.

As tears streaked down her cheeks, Celadine, a mere city apothecary, dropped to her knees, her eyes taking in the vermillion sky. Something dark began to form above the city, a colossal black hole rimmed with energy as it slowly grew bigger and bigger. A low, droning sound preceded the anomaly, lightning snapping from the depths of the gaping void.

Then, from within the depths of the black hole, gargantuan fingers appeared, black and charred and tipped with claws, curling on the outer rim as something large – something terrible – began to emerge.

The herbalist wept, clutching herself as a resonating boom of thunder shook the earth. Her fingers pressed against her chest as she began to rock back and forth.

Wake up.

This was no longer a nightmare. It was a premonition of a future to come.

Wake up.

Everything she had done, everything she fought for was for naught. It would all end in death.

"Cela! Wake up!"

She woke with a gasp, eyes snapping open as she shot up in bed. Strong hands grasped her arms as she sucked in hasty breaths – swift and shallow breaths that burned like fire in her parched throat. Without words she spun to her bedside chest, fumbling for her sketchpad and charcoal as her father rasped, "Cela, speak to me, what did you see?"

At the foot of her bed, a little girl clutched a severely loved teddy bear, her eyes wide and cheeks pink with worry. Normally Cela would downplay an event such as this as to not worry her daughter, but this was not a normal nightmare.

Cela's fingers moved furiously, desperate to get what she had seen onto the paper before her shock could erase some of the memory. It was all chaos in the forefront of her mind, but one particular symbol burned behind her eyes. It had been inked with blood upon the walls she had dashed by and stained with residual magic on the stones of the courtyard where her dream had begun.

Silence thickened the air as the woman inhaled a shuddered breath, slowly placing the paper on the covers between them.

A serpent curled into a figure eight, jaws swallowing its own tail.

The symbol of the Ouroboros.

Cela's eye drifted closed, words tasting like smoke as she said, "All will end in fire, fury and chaos. And I fear there is nothing we can do to stop it..."

MelissaJKincaid

Acknowledgements

I want to go straight into thanking *you*, my dear reader, for sticking with the story of Arii, Elijah, Lorch and the gang. I had an absolute blast writing this book, and even though it's a stepping stone towards the third and final book, I feel there has been lots of growth – not only for the story's characters, but for me as an author too!

I have lots more people to thank, so I'll hop right to it.

To my husband, Greg, thank you for being my pillar of strength, my personal accountant and my biggest although quietest fan. You put up with my ranting and raving when I thought I was writing too slowly, or when a scene wasn't working and although you'd have no idea what I was talking about, you would listen anyway. I know you'll read my books someday, although I know you're waiting for them to become audio books. When that time comes, I hope you enjoy them.

To my son, Elijah Gregory. The Elijah in this book was conceived long before you were, but the name has held a special place in my heart for a very long time which is why I bestowed it upon you. I hope one day, when you're older, you will enjoy reading and creating things just as much as I do, and I hope you are as proud of your mum as I am of you.

To my parents, Lynne, Allan and Carolyn – you all helped shape my love of reading from an early age, and most of all you have shaped me to be the person I am today. Without your encouragement I never would have taken this leap to publish something that is truly my own, nor had the courage to continue to a second book. You have been so incredibly supportive, and I know you are my biggest fans. I love you all immeasurably.

To my family and friends, thanks for being my endless cheer squad, and for showing so much excitement during the process of writing this book. I really hope you enjoy it.

To Kate, thank you for always being so excited to read my work, and for being the first to return a manuscript full of sticky notes. Your feedback and suggestions have helped the story immensely. You are invaluable to me.

To Alisha, who is always in my corner, cheering me on, telling me how much my marketing is improving, flinging ideas my way and helping me with my author photos. It's obvious how invested you are in these characters, and I know you'll remain invested no matter what. I appreciate you beyond words.

To my editor, Carolyn Gilpin, thank you for agreeing to work your magic on my second book, and for all your positivity and encouragement. I appreciate you taking the time to offer constructive feedback on my story, which has helped me immensely in my writing journey. I owe so much to you.

To Kalynne (Kalynne_art on Instagram), thank you for the incredible illustrations of Arii, Elijah, Lorch, Krepth and Nem. You absolutely nailed them like always, giving these incredibly special characters life so that others can envision them as I do. Your enthusiasm and encouragement, not to mention excitement to continue illustrating for me, has been the absolute best.

To my BETA readers, Sandra, Keirra, Lauren and Dee, I could never thank you all enough for taking time from your busy lives to read and lend your honest feedback to this book. Your enthusiasm, positivity and critique has helped polish this stone into a gem, and I will be eternally grateful. I hope you love this final version as much as I do!

To James and the Team at Dymocks Knox, because of your willingness to support independent authors like me, I was able to see my book on the shelf of a real bookstore - which was an absolute dream come true. The fact that *Love, Blood and Fury* was your third highest selling book in the fantasy genre for 2022 is a testament to your support of my dream. I look forward to delivering you the next one.

And lastly, to all the incredible people on social media who reach out to me by taking photos, creating videos, posting recommendations of my book and sending messages to say how much they enjoyed my work - you make my day and fill me with so much joy. I cannot thank you all enough.

I truly hope you enjoyed this instalment, and I also hope you'll stick around for the next one, because it's going to be chaos, and I know how much we all love a bit of chaos!

See you in book three!

Melissa J. L. Kincaid is a fantasy author from Melbourne, Australia, who has a passion for creating worlds filled with magic, adventure, and heart. Known for her rich world-building and strong female leads, her stories often weave together forbidden love, powerful magic, and epic battles, a blend that draws in fans of both fantasy and romance.

Melissa took the plunge into self-publishing in 2021 with her debut novel, *Love, Blood & Fury*. She went on to release *Magic, Midnight & Starlight*, before bringing the trilogy to a breathtaking close in 2024 with *Fire, Fury & Chaos*. Not yet ready to leave the world behind, she returned in 2025 with *After the Fury*, a spin-off that invites readers back into the realm they had come to love.

With a background in graphic design, Melissa brings her creativity full circle by designing her own covers and book interiors, ensuring every detail matches the vision of her stories.

When she isn't writing, illustrating or curled up with a fantasy book, Melissa enjoys exploring the outdoors with her husband, Greg, and their son, Elijah Gregory, often camping under the stars.

www.**lotsoflovecreations**.com.au

 /melissa.j.kincaid

 #melissa.j.kincaid.author

 @melissa.j.kincaid.author

Melissa J Kincaid

ROMANTIC **FANTASY** AUTHOR

WWW.LOTSOFLOVECREATIONS.COM.AU

Available in Paperback, Hardback and eBook.

Did you enjoy the story?

PLEASE LEAVE
a Review!

KALYNNE ART

goodreads   fable   THE STORYGRAPH

Reviews help independent authors like me reach more readers. Every review means a lot!

Scan the code to go to Goodreads.